Praise for David Wishart:

'[I]t is evident that Wishart is a fine scholar and perfectly at home in the period.' *Sunday Times*

'Witty, engrossing and ribald ... [*Sejanus*] misses nothing in its evocation of a bygone time and place.' *Independent on Sunday*

'The Lydian Baker, a fabulous, solid gold, four-and-a-half foot statue gifted to the Delphic Oracle by King Croesus is hot stuff, and when Roman amateur sleuth Marcus Corvinus is commissioned to find it, he soon get his fingers burned. But at least he doesn't get his head bashed in or his throat cut as happens to others who come into contact with the statue. A classical crime caper out of the top drawer.' Steve Craggs, *Northern Echo*

'Tales of treachery, betrayal and murder always make good reading, but Carnoustie author David Wishart's novels have an extra dimension – they are set in ancient Rome ... David takes real people and weaves his novels around them ... For while the dramatis personae have Roman names and live in Roman times, they speak in modern English which is both familiar and natural.' *Dundee Courier & Advertiser*

The Horse Coin

David Wishart

FLAME
Hodder & Stoughton

First published in Great Britain in 1999
by Hodder and Stoughton Ltd
First published in paperback in 2000
by Hodder and Stoughton Ltd
A division of Hodder Headline

A Flame Paperback

10 9 8 7 6 5 4 3 2 1

A CIP catalogue record for this title is available
from the British Library.

ISBN 0 340 71531 6

Printed and bound in Great Britain by
Caledonian International Book Manufacturing Ltd

Hodder and Stoughton
A division of Hodder Headline
338 Euston Road
London NW1 3BH

To Terry, Elli and Richard, and to their horses

LIST OF CHARACTERS

Only characters who appear at more than one point in the book are given. Historical characters' names are in upper case.

ROMANS

AGRICOLA, Gnaeus Julius: born at Forum Iulii (Fréjus) in AD40. Senatorial tribune, currently on Paullinus's staff. He later (AD77) returned to Britain as governor and mounted a major campaign in what is now Scotland. He was the historian Tacitus's father-in-law (see Author's Note)

Albilla, Arrenia: Severinus's fiancée

Aper, Titus Julius: Severinus's father

Bellicia, Sulia: Albilla's mother

CATUS, Decianus: the provincial procurator. Following the revolt he fled to Gaul, and his later fate is unknown

CLASSICIANUS, Julius Alpinus: Catus's successor (see Author's Note)

Clemens, Publius: Severinus's predecessor as commander of the Foxes

Homullus, Pompeius: Catus's deputy in Icenia

Modianus, Juventius: the Foxes' senior centurion

Montanus, Quintus Adaucius: the procurator's agent at the Colony

PAULLINUS, Gaius Suetonius: governor of Britain (see Author's Note)

Severinus, Marcus Julius: Only son of Aper and Ursina. Born AD38 at Augusta Treverorum (Trèves) in Belgian Gaul

Sulicena: Aper's cook

Tirintius: a cavalry veteran

Trinnus: Aper's house-slave

Uricalus, Publius Arrenius: a merchant, head of the Colony's council and Albilla's father

Ursina: Severinus's mother

•

Vegisonius, Quintus: a merchant

BRITISH

Ahteha: Brocomaglos's younger daughter

BOUDICA: widow of Prasutagos and queen of the Iceni. After the final battle, she committed suicide. Her daughters' names, Segoriga and Belisamovala, are inventions

Brocomaglos: chief of the Trinovantes; Senovara's father

CARATACOS: one of Cunobelinos's sons. He successfully resisted the Romans for several years in what is now Wales but was eventually defeated and captured

CARTIMANDUA: over-queen of the Brigantes and a long-standing supporter of Rome

COGIDUBNUS, Tiberius Claudius: Romanophile king of the tribes south of the Thames, based at Calleva (Silchester). He probably owed his kingship (and certainly the large extent of his kingdom, which extended from Kent to the Severn) to his unswerving loyalty to Rome

CUNOBELINOS: king of the Catuvellauni who, in the period before the Roman invasion, conquered the Trinovantes and established a small empire in what is now southern England. His death and the subsequent struggle for power precipitated the invasion. He is the original of Shakespeare's Cymbeline

Dumnocoveros: a Druid

Ecenomolios: Boudica's war leader and adviser

Eisu: tenant of a jewellery shop outside the south gate

Inam: a Trinovantian; one of the rebels

Matugena: Brocomaglos's wife

PRASUTAGOS: king of the Iceni, Boudica's husband, now dead

Senovara: Brocomaglos's elder daughter

Tigirseno: Brocomaglos's son

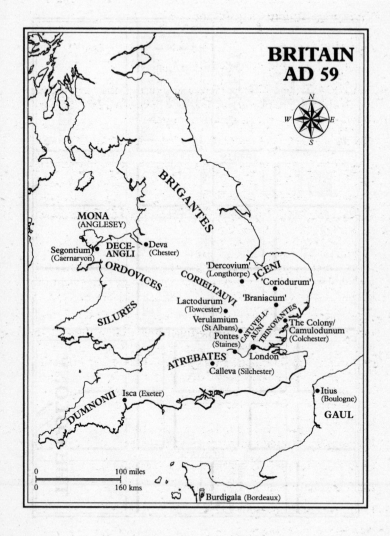

**BRITAIN
AD 59**

N
W   E
S

BRIGANTES

MONA
(ANGLESEY)

Segontium
(Caernarvon)

DECE-
ANGLI

●Deva
(Chester)

ORDOVICES

'Dercovium'
(Longthorpe)

ICENI

CORIELTAUVI

'Coriodurum'

'Braniacum'

SILURES

Lactodurum
(Towcester)

Verulamium
(St Albans)

Pontes
(Staines)

CATUVELL-
AUNI

TRINOVANTES

The Colony/
Camulodunum
(Colchester)

London

ATREBATES

Calleva (Silchester)

Isca (Exeter)

DUMNONII

Itius
(Boulogne)

GAUL

0   100 miles
0   160 kms

Burdigala (Bordeaux)

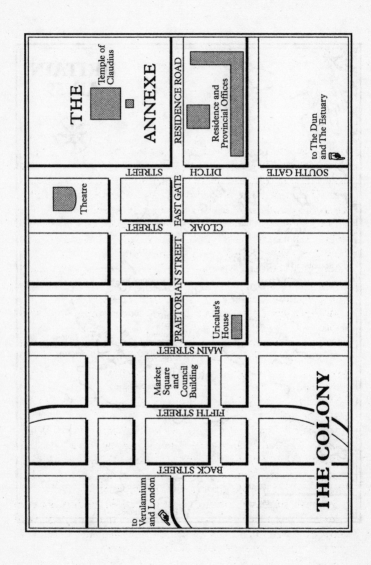

THE ANNEXE

Temple of Claudius

RESIDENCE ROAD

Residence and Provincial Offices

to The Dun and The Estuary

EAST GATE STREET

DITCH

SOUTH GATE

Theatre

CLOAK STREET

PRAETORIAN STREET

Uricalus's House

MAIN STREET

Market Square and Council Building

FIFTH STREET

THE COLONY

BACK STREET

to Verulamium and London

I

Marcus Severinus crouched low against Tanet's mane, hugging his shield close against the wind. It was cold waiting for the signal; dankly cold, as mid-December afternoons in the Colony most often were. The mist blowing up from the estuary drifted across the parade ground, turning the riders of the second team a hundred yards to his left to ghosts, bringing with it the eerie piping of the marsh birds. Annwn voices, the British called them: the voices of the dead beyond the firelight.

Tanet shifted beneath him and he reached down to fondle her ears, quieting her. He glanced towards the distant platform where his father stood with the new governor.

Mothers, he prayed, don't let me fumble! Grant me a good Knot!

'Happy birthday, Nero bloody Caesar!' Behind his shoulder the veteran Tirintius leaned over and spat into the half-frozen mud. 'Sweet Mothers alive! For a horse lover the overbred bastard chose a damn silly month to be born in!'

Severinus's lips twisted in a grin. 'It's too cold for treason,' he said.

'Treason be damned.' Tirintius edged his horse forward until its muzzle rested against Tanet's flank. 'Riding the Knot's hard enough at the best of times, and with this mist it's murder.'

'We'll manage.' Severinus's grin widened and the strap of his cavalry helmet rubbed against the underside of his jaw.

'Will we so, boy?' Tirintius's teeth flashed behind his own helmet. 'There'll be spears adrift today, you mark me, and with a governor watching that's not good.' He spat again. 'Mind you, give it ten more minutes and the bugger won't see a thing.'

Beside the platform the low sun had caught on bronze as the signaller raised his trumpet.

'Here we go,' Severinus said.

Tirintius grunted and pulled his horse back. 'Thank bloody Jupiter! Hey! Try not to fall off, all right?'

The trumpet sounded. Severinus steadied himself as the line of horsemen behind him shifted with a rattle of shield on shield as their ranks closed. His left hand dropped to the holster that lay against Tanet's flank, pulling out one of the javelins, transferring it to his right and checking that the others would not snag. The mare began to fidget, and he pulled her in sharply.

Two heartbeats to go; one . . .

The trumpet blared again. Heart pounding, he crouched low in the saddle and dug in his heels. Tanet sprang away from the line, reaching for the gallop. Gripping her sides with his knees, he glanced over his left shoulder. The chaser from the other team was fifty strides behind and closing, his javelin raised; too far yet for a cast, but like Tirintius Pontius had been one of his father's best, and when he did throw he wouldn't miss. Severinus slackened his left rein, freeing his shield-arm.

Pontius rose, his body moving back then forward. The javelin came straight and hard. Severinus twisted round to meet it, raising his shield, and the blunted point thudded against the boss, jarring every bone in his arm from wrist to shoulder.

One down. The next would be more difficult.

The turn was only a few strides ahead. He crouched even lower, his chest hard against the horns of the saddle, right knee poised to drive into Tanet's ribs, both eyes on the chaser. Two strides from the mark he saw Pontius lift. The javelin struck as he hit the turn, his knee jammed against the mare's flank, bringing her round. Its six-foot shaft caught the shield-rim's leading edge with a screaming slither of wood on metal as it shot past his exposed neck . . .

Close! Far too close! Severinus was sweating as he pulled hard on Tanet's left rein, his knee still pressed against her side. He threw himself backwards and the mare's hindquarters dropped. She twisted round, her hooves scattering clods of earth. Digging both heels in, he gave her her head and sent her flying towards where the first of the targets sat his horse, waiting.

Two strides to wipe the sweat from his eyes; another three, to bring him into range . . .

Matching his movements with Tanet's and bracing his thighs

against the saddle-horns, he rose and threw. The first javelin struck the target's shield-boss square, the second, two breaths behind it, a hand-span within the rim. Then he was past. Two hits, both clean: not bad, not good. Tirintius would score three at least. He might even . . .

Something flickered at the edge of his vision.

Mothers! Fool!

He whipped round and raised his shield a heartbeat before the second chaser's javelin slammed into it. The force of the blow knocked him sideways and he caught at the saddle-horn to steady himself, his knees locking against the mare's ribs.

Careless! Careless and stupid!

At least Tanet had not broken stride. Raising his hand, he wiped the sweat away and glanced ahead. The second target was almost in range: old Verus, his shield already raised. Severinus shook his head to clear it and reached into the holster, touching the shafts in their dividing pockets. Four more, but there would only be time for two; three if the Mothers were kind . . .

He pulled the first clear, rose and threw, already reaching for the second, then a third. One and two hit clean a hand-span from the boss, three was snatched, but Verus shifted into its path and it clipped the edge of the shield-rim to count for a third. Then he was past, breathing hard, tugging on the right rein. His knees and his heels slackened their grip, allowing Tanet to slow, and he brought her in a long arc round the platform to the right to take up his final position at the Knot's end.

He was shaking. Well, he hadn't disgraced himself at least: five hits. Five!

While his breathing slowed, Severinus watched the others of the troop, strung out behind him, complete their own runs. Some managed six hits, but the mist was closing in. Most of the tail-enders – and there were good riders among them – managed only four. Five javelins on the mark was the best run he'd ever made. His father would be impressed.

More important, so might Paullinus.

2

The mist had changed to hail, sweeping in from the north beyond
the river in rattling gusts that numbed Severinus's face and hands
as he guided Tanet through the Colony's south gate towards the
newly built provincial offices. It was a pig of a night, and getting
worse by the hour. Ditch Street was deserted, its shops closed
and shuttered, the Annexe – the huge building site dominated
by the scaffolded Temple of Claudius which would be the new
city centre – a sea of blackness with not a single light showing
from the caretakers' huts. Severinus turned along its edge into
Residence Road and the residence itself. That, at least, was lit.
Pitch-pine torches, shielded from the wet, burned in the cressets
set along its front, and despite the cold the door was open,
spilling lamplight across the courtyard. He dismounted and
handed Tanet's rein to the waiting slave. Tirintius and the
others would be settled in a wineshop and halfway down the
first jug by now. It wouldn't be too late. He could simply . . .
  'Is there something wrong, sir?' The slave was looking at
him.
  Swallowing his nervousness, Severinus shook his head and
went up the steps.
  He had never been inside the residence, not even the cramped
old building near the market square that had been the Twentieth's
headquarters before the original fortress was decommissioned. This
newer version was purpose-built, a showpiece like Claudius's
temple. The lobby was floored in coloured marble, and in the
embrasure to his right was a fresco of grapes and Damascus
plums, so real he could almost taste them. Framing it, two
massive candelabra held lamps burning scented oil. The lobby
smelled of Rome. Only the cold and damp that blew in through
the open doorway were British.
  'Your cloak, sir?' The door-slave held out a hand. Severinus

undid the fastening and passed it over. 'The party's in the main reception-room. If you'll follow me, please.'

The room was full: a men-only gathering of the Colony's brightest and best. As he crossed the threshold another slave came forward with a tray of steaming cups. He took one gratefully, wrapping his hands round the metal to thaw them.

Someone tugged at his sleeve and he turned, almost spilling the wine. Arrenius Uricalus was beaming up at him.

'A splendid show, Marcus. My heartiest congratulations.'

'I'm glad you enjoyed it, sir.' Severinus kept his voice neutral.

'It was first rate.' Uricalus's wired gold tooth gleamed in the lamplight. 'Simply first rate. Bellicia was most impressed. And Albilla, of course. She told me to pass on her congratulations especially.'

'That's kind of her.' Severinus sipped his mulled wine. It was Burdigalan, and heavily spiced: the governor was obviously not a man to do things by halves. 'Give her my regards, and my best wishes for the Festival.'

'I'll do that. She'll be pleased.' Uricalus hesitated. 'Apropos of which, Bellicia and I were wondering if you and your parents might care to . . .'

'Marcus! Over here!'

Severinus looked up in relief. His father was halfway down the room by one of the braziers, close enough to touch the flames, talking to a man in a broad-striped mantle.

'Marcus!' Aper was beckoning. 'Come and be introduced!'

'Excuse me, Uricalus.' Severinus's throat was suddenly tight. 'I have to go. We'll talk later, if we may.'

'Most certainly.' The little Gaul's smile broadened, and he moved aside. 'Doesn't do to keep a governor waiting, my boy.'

Severinus pushed his way through the crowd. His father's single eye closed in a wink before he turned back to Paullinus.

'My son Marcus,' he said.

It was the first time Severinus had seen Paullinus close to. The governor's face had a fixity of expression more suited to a bronze or marble statue than to flesh, but his scent was pure aristocratic Rome: a mixture of leather and expensive talc.

'You did well this afternoon, young man,' he said. 'Very well indeed. An excellent bit of riding.'

'Thank you, sir.'

'Oh, Marcus cut his first tooth in the saddle.' Aper was flushed with pride and spiced wine. 'A family tradition. And he's been riding the Knot since he was twelve.'

'Indeed?' Paullinus's thin lips, incongruous in that broad face, twisted briefly. 'What's your mount, Severinus? Libyan, wasn't she?'

'Almost, sir.' Severinus cleared his throat. 'Tanet's Spanish-bred. Numidian, from a Libyan sire.'

'They're the best horses in the world, the Spanish. You can keep your Parthians.' Paullinus had been holding an empty wine cup. Now he signalled to a slave and, without looking at the man, set it on the tray and took a full one. 'Quite handy with the shield and javelin too, aren't you?'

'Not half handy enough,' Aper growled. 'The lad should be ashamed of himself. That second shot of Pontius's had him cold.'

Severinus felt his nervousness evaporate. It wasn't a serious criticism, he knew: his father would've cut his own tongue out before he criticised his son to the governor. He grinned.

'You noticed?'

'Jupiter! I couldn't help but notice!' Aper was still scowling. 'A hand-span to the right or a moment sooner and he'd've nailed you. Watch your back, boy. If I've told you once I've told you a hundred times.'

Paullinus smiled: a cold smile, ice-brittle. 'Come, now, Commander,' he said. 'You're being a little hard, surely. The other man chose his moment well.'

'That's no excuse, Governor. Next time the javelin may have a proper head to it. A British head.'

'The chaser was one of our own veterans. A professional.' The smile had disappeared. 'Fortunately for us, the British haven't the advantage of Roman training, or indeed the mental capacity to appreciate its value.'

Severinus glanced at his father. This time Aper's frown was genuine.

'I wouldn't go quite as far as that, sir,' he said. 'They may not be quite in our league but they're dangerous all the same. And they're superb horsemen.'

'Discipline comes with civilisation, Commander. And as far as civilisation is concerned the British have a long way to go. That's why we beat them. Why we'll always beat them.'

'Aye, perhaps so, but—'

Someone coughed. Paullinus turned, his face bland.

'Ah,' he said. 'Uricalus, isn't it? Join us, please.'

'Thank you, Governor.' The little merchant's lips spread themselves. 'Good evening, Aper. A fine ride, as I was just telling young Marcus here.'

'And my congratulations to you, Senator,' Paullinus said. 'The emperor will be delighted to know his birthday was celebrated in such admirable style.'

Severinus winced at the tone, but Uricalus did not seem to notice the sarcasm in the governor's voice. His smile broadened and he smoothed the fold of his lambswool mantle.

'It's good of you to say so, sir,' he said. 'Very good indeed. But as I told my colleagues, celebrating the emperor's birthday's a privilege, not a duty.'

'Quite. Indeed. Absolutely.' Paullinus's eyes had fixed on a point beyond Uricalus's shoulder. 'Forgive me.' He raised his voice. 'Gnaeus! A moment, please.'

A young man came forward, dressed in the uniform of a senior tribune. Paullinus laid a hand on his shoulder.

'Gnaeus Julius Agricola. Of the Second Augustans, and currently on my staff. Gnaeus, this is Titus Julius Aper, former commander of the First Thracian Wing and his son Marcus Severinus. Severinus led the Knot this afternoon.'

'We share a name, Tribune.' Aper was smiling. 'Are you a Spaniard, by any chance?'

'No.' There was no answering smile. 'My father's a senator.' He glanced at Uricalus. 'A *real* senator. I was brought up in Forum Iulii.'

'Then it's a pleasure to meet a fellow countryman.' Uricalus beamed. 'I'm Burdigalan myself.'

'You'll forgive me, sir, but that's hardly the same thing, is it?'

Severinus looked at Paullinus. The governor was nodding. He and Agricola, it seemed, were well matched.

'True, true.' Uricalus's smile had set; pompous or not, the man was no fool. 'You've been in the province long?'

'Two years. I came with Veranius.'

'Ah.' Uricalus turned to Paullinus. 'A fine man, your predecessor, Governor. A fine soldier, and a credit to Rome. It was a shame he died. Although of course had he not it would have deprived us of your own presence.'

'Indeed.' Paullinus's voice was dry. 'Let's hope that his work won't go to waste.'

'Oh, I'm certain it won't.' Uricalus chuckled. For a horrified moment Severinus thought he meant to dig his elbow into the governor's ribs. 'You've had experience of dealing with mountain tribes yourself, sir, I understand? Mauretania, was it not?' Paullinus nodded stiffly. 'Then I've no doubt our home-grown variety will give you less trouble than spitting. If you'll forgive the expression.'

'I'm flattered by your confidence. I'd be grateful if between now and the spring you could persuade the Deceangli to share it.'

Uricalus leaned back on the built-up heels of his sandals.

'Hit them hard, sir,' he said. 'Hit them very hard. It's all these fellows understand.'

'Thank you. I'll bear your advice in mind.' Paullinus turned away. 'And now if you'll excuse us I have things to discuss with the commander here.'

Uricalus blinked. 'Of course,' he said. 'Certainly.'

He bowed and moved across the room to join Paternius and Vegisonius, two of the Colony's principal shopkeepers. Before he was properly out of earshot, Paullinus had turned back to Aper.

'Bloody merchants,' he grunted. 'Give them half a chance and they'd run the world for you.'

'Governor, forgive me, but now it's you who're being hard.' Aper was looking over towards Uricalus, who was carefully ignoring them. 'If we're to build a province then we need merchants as well as soldiers.'

'So Procurator Catus keeps telling me.' Paullinus smiled. 'I tell him that the fellows are his concern, not mine. That's why the good gods created procurators and cursed us with London.'

'But surely you must assume some responsibility for them?'

'Ultimate responsibility, of course, but in practical terms my sphere and the imperial procurator's are quite separate. Which suits me perfectly. As the senator has so kindly just pointed out, my prime duty is to finish what my predecessor started and settle the hash of these hooligans on my western borders.' He turned to Agricola. 'Am I right, Gnaeus?'

'Yes, sir. Totally.'

Aper pulled at his ear. 'I'm sorry, Governor,' he said, 'but I don't agree. You're right as far as the mountain tribes are concerned, of course. But what about the tribes who're already beaten? Our own Trinovantes, for example, or Prasutagos's Iceni?'

'Commander Aper, please!' Paullinus was not smiling now. 'I know the theory as well as you do. Shave their moustaches, put them in mantles, give them a bath and the result's civilisation. Do you genuinely believe that?'

'It worked in Gaul.'

'True. And given time it'll work here, I'm sure. But you've answered your own question. *When they're beaten*, you said. The British will never be properly beaten until we control the whole island. That'll be a long, hard struggle. Perhaps Gnaeus and your son here will complete it, but I certainly won't, although I intend to do what I can. Which reminds me.' He turned to Severinus. 'I understand that the present commander of the First Aquitanians is overdue for promotion. I make no promises, but it seems that there's already a family connection.'

Severinus's brain went numb. He opened his mouth, but no sound came.

Paullinus was looking at Aper. 'I'm right, am I not?'

Aper smiled. 'Aye. I had them myself as a first command twenty years ago. Marcus'll look after them, won't you, lad?'

Holy Mothers! The Foxes!

'Marcus?' His father elbowed him in the ribs. 'Marcus!'

'I'm sorry. Thank you, sir.'

'No need for that.' Paullinus caught the eye of a passing slave and put his half-empty cup down on the man's tray. 'Good officers are rare, and from what your father tells me I think you'll make an excellent one. Leave it with me for the present. And now I'm afraid I really must go and write up some reports. For the moment, then.' He turned to Agricola. 'Gnaeus, you're in charge down here. Circulate. See that your long-haired compatriots don't auction off the spoons.'

'Yes, sir.' Agricola gave a smile that was younger brother to Paullinus's. 'Commander, we'll meet again soon, I'm sure. Severinus, a pleasure. And my sincere congratulations.'

He moved off to join a group that included the port commander Licinius Castor. Aper watched him go, frowning.

'A good man, that,' he said, 'although a little close between the eyes.'

'You knew, didn't you, Dad?' Severinus said. 'About the Foxes?'

Aper chuckled and patted his son's arm. 'Aye, of course I did. Before Paullinus himself, in fact. Now, have you had enough? Or should we go and unruffle Uricalus's feathers?'

Severinus grinned. 'No,' he said. 'Let's go home.'

3

The hail had turned to sleet when they left the residence, and their cloaks were heavy with freezing water long before they had ridden the four miles to the villa and made out the glow of the torch that Trinnus the house-slave had set beside the door. The wind died as they walked the horses through the outlying garden into the shelter of the yard.

Severinus slid from Tanet's back. The villa door was already open, and Trinnus was running to meet them, his short, stubby body completely hidden beneath a hooded cloak.

'You get inside, sirs,' he said. 'I'll see to the horses.'

'Bless you, Trinnus.' Aper dismounted and shook himself like a dog, scattering slush from the folds of his cloak. 'Jupiter! What an awful bloody night! You've the furnace lit?'

Severinus smiled. The furnace that fed the hypocaust beneath the dining-room floor was Aper's pride and joy. Having it installed by the Twentieth's chief engineer when he had built the villa ten years before had cost five jars of Burdigalan and one of Damascus figs in honey. Apart from the governor's own it was still the only one in the Colony.

'Aye.' Trinnus took a firm grip of the reins: Tanet and Pollux were already moving towards the stable. 'The mistress told me to fire it up when you left. We've burned half a forest today already.'

'Good.' Aper blew on his fingers. He was shivering. 'Mothers, I'll have the bone-ache for this tomorrow.'

Severinus grinned. 'Get inside and dry off, then,' he said. 'I'll give Trinnus a hand with the horses.'

'Right you are, boy. A hot mash and new bedding for both of them, Trinnus. They've deserved it. Oh.' He paused beneath the porch roof. 'And we'll have the other half of the forest while you're at it, please.'

*   *   *

The dining-room was hot as an oven: Trinnus had brought in an extra brazier, and a jug of wine simmering on its edge added a layer of aromatic steam to the scents from the kitchen. Severinus's mother Ursina lifted her plain square face to be kissed.

'Your father's told me about the Foxes,' she said.

Severinus moved to the brazier and warmed his hands at the coals before pouring out a cup of the spiced wine. 'It wasn't a definite promise, Mother.'

'Nonsense, boy.' Aper, comfortable now in an old tunic and slippers and red as a boiled lobster, sipped his own wine. 'The governor wouldn't've spoken otherwise. Besides, he's right: Clemens is overdue for promotion. He's a good man, cavalry to the bone, and he's had the Foxes five years now.'

Sulicena, the family's only other slave, appeared from the kitchen with a casserole. She set it down and lifted the lid, filling the room with the scent of pork stew and sage. Severinus brought his cup to the table and lay down, tugging the old woman's pigtail in passing.

'So it went well, sir,' she said to Aper. 'The meeting with the governor.'

'Aye.' Aper held up his plate. 'Very well indeed. We'll have another wing in the family yet, Sulicena. And that was a good Knot today, Marcus. The lads can be proud of themselves.'

'They'll be drunker than Silenus's donkey tonight, then.' Ursina was smiling: post-games celebrations came as no news to the daughter of a legion's First Spear and the wife of a cavalry commander.

'And good luck to them. Who's buying, Marcus, did you hear?'

'Dannicus.' Severinus moved out of the way of Sulicena's ladle.

'No surprises there, then.' Aper chuckled: traditionally, the least successful rider in the troop bought the night's beer and wine. 'Dannicus'd be my choice, too. He deserved it, the silly beggar.'

'His horse stumbled at the cast. Or so he claimed.'

'Is that so, now?' Aper licked a splash of gravy from his thumb and spooned up a dumpling. 'It may've happened once, but twice is stretching things. He'd two clear misses on the run and a third so close to old Pegasus's stifle it shaved the hairs. That's not bad luck, it's sheer bloody carelessness, and he won't live it down in a hurry. Mind you, I'd've expected a better excuse than a stumble from a prime con-artist like Dannicus. When I think of the times I had the devious beggar up on a charge and he wriggled out . . .'

'You were too soft.' Ursina took the bowl of vetch from Sulicena. 'You were always too soft.'

Aper sighed. 'Bear-cub, rules are made to be stretched. You know that yourself. Dannicus was a good trooper, and he did well enough when it mattered.'

'Maybe.' She was smiling as she served the vetch. 'So, then. How does our new governor measure up?'

Aper broke a piece of bread from the loaf.

'Well, now,' he said, 'I think I might let the young commander here answer that. If he's going to start assessing men he'll need the practice. Come on, boy, let's have it; answer your mother. How would you rate Paullinus on a scale of ten? Foxes aside, mind.'

Severinus knew he was being tested and that he was expected to pass: soft or not, father or not, Julius Aper took his duties seriously. And before the Icenian knife had taken out his eye at Alodunum and sent him into retirement he had been one of the best commanders of cavalry west of the Rhine.

'As a soldier or a governor?' he said.

'Good lad.' His father nodded in approval. 'We'll have both, please.'

'All right.' Severinus paused, marshalling his thoughts. 'He's an experienced soldier. Successful, too. That's a matter of record. He knows his own mind, he has the courage of his convictions and he isn't afraid to put them into practice. As a general he'd be hard, thorough and fair.'

His father grunted. 'Very well. Marks out of ten?'

'Eight.'

Aper's eyes widened and he leaned back.

'Only eight, eh?'

'He thinks in too straight lines. And he believes he has the answer to everything.'

'Good boy.' Aper was nodding. 'You wouldn't trust him to make an important decision, then?'

'No, not altogether, not if it meant taking several factors into account.'

'Aye. I agree.'

'On the other hand he'd base any decision he took on hard facts, or at least the facts as he saw them, and once he'd taken it he'd push it through whatever the odds. So the end result might be the same.'

'You think so?' Aper frowned. 'Well. Maybe. We'll let it pass. Not bad, Marcus. Not bad at all. Now as governor, please.'

'The same applies. He'll govern the way he commands. No discussion and no argument.'

'Is that so bad?' Ursina put in. 'We're a frontier province. We need a strong governor.'

'Marcus?'

Severinus hesitated. 'I agree up to a point. He can be trusted with the military side of things, certainly. On the civilian side I'm not so sure.'

'Good lad. You'll have your wing yet. Now your reasons.'

'You saw how he treated Uricalus, Dad; that wasn't necessary, or wise. Nor is the hands-off agreement with the procurator. Whether Paullinus likes it or not the merchants are important, and he can't afford to ignore them, let alone put their backs up. He looks set to do both.'

'Aye.' Aper shifted. 'Again I agree. Now, boy, what about the British?'

'The mountain tribes? I told you, I've no quarrel with Paullinus there. Like he said himself, we have to beat them before the province is secure, and the sooner the better.'

'I don't mean the mountain tribes, lad. Paullinus was right about them, they're too dangerous to leave. I mean the others.'

'The others aren't a factor, surely. Or not an important one. Even the Brigantes . . .'

'The Brigantes are federated. They're not part of the province. I'm talking about the tribes inside our borders.'

'You mean like the Catuvellauni and the Trinovantes?' Severinus set down his spoon. 'They've been settled for years. Even in the Icenian revolt they gave us no trouble.'

Aper sighed. 'Marcus, lad, if losing an eye taught me one thing it's not to ignore native feelings. If Governor Scapula had paid more heed eleven years back to that bastard Subidastos's grumblings over his disarmament order—'

'*Titus!*' Ursina snapped.

'I'm sorry, Bear-cub.' Aper leaned over and kissed her cheek. ' "Beggar", then.'

'That's better.'

'If Scapula had paid more attention to that beggar, Marcus, then there wouldn't have been a revolt and I'd still have my eye and my career. That's a lesson I won't forget in a hurry. You take my point?'

Severinus shook his head. 'Dad, I'm sorry, but the situation's different now. We've a firm grip on the province and the tribes know it. They're disarmed and peaceful. There may be grumbles, but the British are born grumblers.'

'Maybe so. But then they have something to grumble about. We've conquered them, after all.'

'That's the way the world works. And it's for their own good in the long run, you know it is.'

'Certainly. Only it's a question of convincing them of it. And we won't do that by treating them as beaten enemies.'

'What more can they expect?' Severinus felt his temper begin to slip. 'The citizenship? Colonists' privilege? Paullinus was right about that, at least. As a province Britain's four years younger than I am. You can't move from barbarism to civilisation in sixteen years.'

'True. But then again we'll never turn the British into good Romans by grinding their noses in the dirt, which is what we're doing. Take the Trinovantes, for example.'

'Jupiter, Dad! Forget the bloody Trinovantes! They haven't—'

'Marcus.' Ursina put down the piece of bread she was holding. 'That's enough. Change the subject, please.'

Aper laid a quiet hand on her arm. He was still looking at Severinus.

'No, Bear-cub,' he said. 'This is important. Marcus, you know yourself what Brocomaglos's folk think of us, and why. We've taken a sizeable chunk of their best land to set up our Colony, we tax them to pay for the building and when they can't pay the taxes we force them to accept loans from us at a rate of interest that's little short of crippling. Now the emperor's strapped for cash these loans are being called in. When the poor beggars default, which they invariably do, we take more land in forfeit and feelings run even higher. Now can't you see that a policy like that's idiotic?'

Severinus shook his head. 'Every province in the empire pays taxes. The British're no more hard done by than anyone else. And like I said it's for their ultimate good. In time Britain'll be as rich as Gaul and the whole population will benefit, not just a few nobles, the way things were before we came.'

'Their ultimate good, aye. I agree.' Aper pushed his plate away. 'And yes, the Conquest was the best thing that ever happened to them, whether they appreciate it or not. I'm not stupid, Marcus. I know you can't build a province out of nothing. But if we carry on the way we're going it could lead to trouble. Serious trouble.'

'That's what the army's for. I'm sorry, Dad, but I think you're making too much of this.'

'I agree,' Ursina said calmly. 'This is a family meal, not an operations tent.'

'Jupiter alive, Bear-cub!'

'Leave Jupiter out of it, Titus. Discussions I don't mind, but at arguments I draw the line.'

Aper took a deep breath. 'My apologies,' he said. 'Better?'

Ursina's lips twisted in a half smile. 'Better. Keep it like that, please. Both of you.'

Aper turned back to Severinus. 'Marcus, listen to me. In three months' time there won't be an army. When Paullinus launches his campaign he'll take most of it with him.'

'Paullinus isn't a fool, Dad. He won't strip the province altogether.'

'Oh, I'll grant you that. The man knows his business. But with the tribes on edge already it wouldn't take much to push them over, even our Trinovantes, and with three-quarters of the province's garrison tied up half a month's march away that's worrying.' He paused. 'You've heard about the Druid?'

'No.' Severinus had picked up his wine cup. Now he set it down slowly. 'What Druid?'

'There's a rumour one's been seen in the area. Unconfirmed, but the British all believe it. The news has gone round the Annexe work gangs like wildfire.'

'Mothers!' Severinus was staring at him. 'Does the governor know?'

'Aye. He told me himself. You see my point now?'

Severinus did. Druids were poison. The sect had been suppressed within the province since the Conquest, but its influence beyond the borders was as strong as ever, and capturing its base on Mona was the main objective of Paullinus's spring campaign. If the Druids were trying to stir up the provincial tribes against Rome in the governor's absence then his father's fears were well founded.

'What does Paullinus intend doing?' he said.

Aper's face was expressionless. 'He wants to send Eagles in to search the Dun.'

'That's insane!' Ursina set down her spoon.

Aper looked at her. 'Aye. I know.'

'You advised him against it?' Severinus said. The man had to be caught, that was certain, but to send legionaries to search the British settlement without warning would lead to trouble. Especially with the Trinovantes in their present mood over the loans.

'I persuaded him to wait, at least. The Trinovantes aren't all hotheads, and they aren't fools, either. I suggested he let me go up to the Dun tomorrow and have a word with Brocomaglos myself.'

'You think he can get them to hand him over?'

'I hope so. If the rumour's true, and he can set hands on the beggar. Brocomaglos is a reasonable man. And he knows the alternative.'

'It's still too much of a risk. Paullinus can't afford to let a Druid go, whatever the cost.'

'Of course. But we don't know for certain that he's on the Dun at all. And, lad, I'm afraid you're making the same mistake as Paullinus: you're treating the British as irresponsible children.'

'Isn't that what they are? Harbouring a Druid's illegal. And, yes, irresponsible, because when he's caught the whole tribe'll suffer. If the Dunsmen can't see that for themselves then they must take the consequences.'

Aper sighed. 'Well, perhaps that's so. Maybe your mother's right, and I'm too soft.'

Ursina stretched her hand out and without a word touched his wrist.

Severinus got up and went over to the brazier. The coals were dying now, but the jug of wine was still hot. He carried it over to the table and filled his father's cup.

'You think Brocomaglos will agree to help?' he said.

'I hope so, for everyone's sake,' Aper said. 'But I won't know until I ask him. It's not something I look forward to.'

'Then you'll need company. If only for the ride.'

Aper raised the cup and sipped.

'Aye,' he said. 'Thank you, Marcus. Company would be welcome.'

4

It was Severinus's first sight of the Dun: Colonists were not welcome in the native settlement, and in any case there was no reason for them to make the effort. It lay two miles to the south-west of the Colony itself, behind a curving screen of earthworks that had formed, with the river, its original defences; not a town, not even a village, but sprawl of farmsteads linked by tracks that the December rain had already turned to mud. In the sparse fields on either side of the road leading up from the gates half-starved cattle watched with dull eyes. The air was filled with the acrid smell of dung, human and animal, and Severinus tried to breathe in as little of it as possible as he guided Tanet between the potholes that made riding at any more than a gentle walk impossible.

Camulodunum, Fortress of the War God, he thought. Mothers alive! How can people live like this?

'Nice place, isn't it?' his father said.

Severinus grinned in answer. It was difficult to believe that the Dun was the largest native settlement in Britain; capital of the island's wealthiest and most powerful king, Cunobelinos, whose death seventeen years before had plunged his kingdom into the futile bickering and bloody little tribal wars that had made the Conquest possible. If Rome ever had to justify her empire and how she managed it, Severinus thought, then the War God's fortress was all the proof she needed.

The road bent to the right, and he saw his first Dunsmen – the first, at least, on their own ground. Most watched them go by in silence much as the cattle had done. Only one, an old man pulling the feathers from a dead chicken by the roadside, reacted in any way, spitting beneath Pollux's hooves as they passed. The man's left ear was missing and the scalp above it was a mess of puckered flesh. Severinus glanced at his father, but Aper's single eye was fixed on the track ahead.

'Keep going, Marcus', he said. 'Don't react. And whatever you do, don't get angry.'

Tanet was beginning to fidget, and Severinus calmed her, doing his best to ignore the closed, expressionless faces on either side. He could feel the hostility pressing in all around him, and the hairs rose on his neck.

'How much further?' he said.

'Not far now, lad.' Aper pointed ahead. 'The gate's over there.'

Severinus looked. There was little to distinguish the Trinovantian chief's farmstead from any of the others: a stretch of rough grass behind a shallow ditch lined with hurdles, with the hut itself at the far end. As they passed through the gap in the ditch a dog leaped forward to the end of its chain and stood barking. A pre-pubescent girl sitting in the mud in front of the hut clutching a piglet scrambled to her feet and ran inside. The piglet followed.

Aper dismounted.

'Leave the talking to me,' he said.

Severinus nodded: it was an order, superior officer to junior, and he accepted it as such. He was beginning to regret, now, that he had come at all. Swallowing, he slid down from Tanet's back and waited, closing his nostrils to the midden stench that surrounded them.

His father winked, but did not smile. They tied the horses to the tethering-post. The hut door opened.

Severinus had seen Brocomaglos before, but not face to face. The Trinovantian chief matched his name; he was thick set and muscular, with a badger's broad neck and shoulders and large, spadelike hands. Although he could be no older than Aper, his hair and moustaches were already streaked with white.

'Be quiet, Durnos!' he growled. The dog stopped barking and stood beating the air with its tail.

'Greetings to you, Brocomaglos,' Aper said in Celtic.

'Ah, so it's yourself, is it, Commander?' Brocomaglos changed to slow, careful Latin. His eyes shifted to Severinus. 'And your son the horseman.'

'Durnos? "Fist." A small name for such a big dog.' Severinus spoke in Celtic as his father had done.

'So.' Brocomaglos's shaggy eyebrows rose. 'The commander's son has a British tongue in his head?' His own Celtic was liquid, flowing. Severinus said nothing. 'Aye, Fist it is. Even big dogs start small, and he's always been a fighter.' He stepped aside. 'Come inside, the both of you, and welcome.'

The hut's main room was large and dark, but far cleaner and sweeter smelling than Severinus had expected, with fresh rushes on the floor and a log fire burning in the hearth. There were three chairs set round a low table, and against one wall a storage chest and dresser.

Brocomaglos pointed to two of the chairs. 'Sit down. Rest yourselves. You've breakfasted?'

'Aye.' Aper sat, and Severinus did the same.

'Wait, then.'

Brocomaglos disappeared through a second doorway curtained with a blanket woven in broad stripes. From beyond it came the sound of voices. A moment later, the curtain shifted and the girl they had seen before put out her head. Severinus winked at her and she stared back with liquid eyes.

'Stop your gawping, Ahteha.' Brocomaglos had reappeared. He touched her neatly braided hair with his huge hand in passing. 'Go and help your mother mull the wine.'

The girl gave them a last stare and withdrew. Brocomaglos eased himself into the third chair. 'So,' he said. 'Be comfortable before we talk.'

Perhaps it was no more than politeness – no native would think of asking a guest to state his business before the formalities of welcome were observed – but Brocomaglos's eyes were guarded. Severinus wondered if the chief already knew why they had come. He looked across at his father.

Aper ignored him. 'Your family's well, Brocomaglos?' he said.

'Well enough. And I needn't ask about yours, my friend. Not about this one at least.' The massive head turned. 'You are welcome, Marcus Severinus, not least for the pleasure you gave me yesterday.'

'You were there?' Severinus was surprised: natives, unless they were servants or slaves, rarely came within the Colony bounds. It was a Roman town, for citizens only.

'How not? We're not prisoners here on the Dun, or penned beasts. Your father's son is a fine rider. And it's always good to find a Celtic tongue in a Roman mouth.'

'There are Romans and Romans,' Aper said. 'I'm half a Celt myself, as you know, and no less Roman for it. Marcus is the same. He was born at Augusta. The Belgic Gauls are cousins to the British, and their tongue's the same, or near enough.'

'Cousins. Aye, well, perhaps they are, but their Gallic blood's grown thin since they sat at Rome's fireside.' Brocomaglos's eyes twinkled. 'I'm told, Commander, that in the Colony the Gallic merchants even take baths instead of washing themselves like civilised men. Would that be true, now?'

'Why not?' Aper laughed. 'There's nothing wrong with a bath on a winter's morning.'

'Aye, maybe.' Brocomaglos tugged at his ear. 'For Romans, I agree. You're salamanders, you need heat. We are different. Heat dries the marrow in our bones and makes women of us. What's good for one nation may not be for another.'

'That's nonsense. Two peoples can learn from each other, surely.'

'Aye, to be sure they can, when both profit equally. Our Gallic cousins taught you Romans to ride, and what do they have in return? You shave their sons' moustaches and teach them to sell olives. That is not learning, Commander.'

Aper laughed. 'There's more to Rome, Brocomaglos, than smooth mouths and olive sellers.'

'So you keep telling us.'

'Are we liars, then?'

'No.' Brocomaglos smiled, but his voice was serious. 'You are not liars. You Romans are a great people, and this civilisation of yours is a great thing. And even if it were not there is still one reason why we should accept it willingly.'

'And what would that be?'

'Because it's all you've left us.' Brocomaglos turned as the curtain was drawn aside and a woman came out with a tray of hot wine and cakes. 'Enough. Your bellies will think your throats are cut. My apologies for this lazy wife of mine.'

'Lazy, is it?' The woman laughed as she set the tray down. 'Honey cakes don't make themselves, and your guests would have been served more quickly if you'd been more sparing with the last batch.'

'The apology's mine, Matugena.' Aper smiled at her. 'We're disturbing you.'

'Oh, for me it doesn't matter.' She lifted the wine jug and poured. 'And this one never minds visitors, whatever the hour. Especially if it gets him a cake or two over the odds.'

Severinus picked up his cup and sipped.

'It's good, Matugena,' he said. 'What is it?'

'Elderberry juice, fermented with herbs and honey. You've never tasted elder wine before?' Severinus shook his head. 'Aye, well, perhaps our Old Lady can teach your Roman gods a thing or two after all. The cakes are at your hand, Brocomaglos. See you leave a crumb or two for our guests.'

She left chuckling.

Brocamaglos took a mouthful of his own wine. 'So,' he said. 'You're warm and you've seen me scolded. Now tell me what brings the Boar and his son so far and so early from their own fireside.'

Severinus was aware of a tenseness in his voice. He knew then – and was sure his father also knew – that Brocomaglos had not needed to ask the question. Remembering what Aper had said, he sat back cradling his wine cup and said nothing.

Aper took a cake. 'There are rumours of a Druid in the area.'

'Druids are forbidden the province by your Roman law. And what would one be doing so far from the mountains?'

'That I can't say, Brocomaglos.' Aper blew on his wine. 'The rumours may be false, but if they are not, well, my friend, you've said it yourself. The sect is outlawed and Paullinus will have to act.'

'Meaning?'

'To begin with, a search of the Dun.'

Brocomaglos set down his cup. 'That would be foolish,' he said quietly.

'Aye.' Aper was looking straight at him. 'I agree. Completely.'

'There's no Druid here. For that you have my word. The new governor would be stirring up trouble for no reason.'

'I know that. So does he. Paullinus is no fool. But he'll have no choice, Brocomaglos, unless you can also give me your word that the rumour has no truth to it.' The other man said nothing. 'You see? He exists, and he must be caught, wherever he is. No one wants trouble.'

'As the wolf said to the rabbit.'

'Brocomaglos.' Aper set down his own cup. 'Listen to me. I don't make the rules. And whatever the rights and wrongs of it the rabbit is still a rabbit.'

'And the wolf a wolf.' Brocomaglos looked, Severinus thought, suddenly old and very tired. 'So. You expect this particular rabbit to do the wolf's work for him?'

'If there is a Druid among the Trinovantes then Paullinus can't ignore the fact. The Dun is his obvious starting point. He will send soldiers to search and ask questions, and being soldiers they will not be gentle. Eventually someone will talk, they will find the man, wherever he is, and kill him; but before then a great deal of damage will have been done on both sides. Perhaps irreparable damage. Neither of us wants that.' Aper paused. 'In this business, Brocomaglos, there can be no winners. Do you understand me?'

Brocomaglos held his gaze for a long time. 'Aye, aye, I understand you,' he said at last. 'Even so we see things differently, you and I, and that cannot be discounted.'

'Brocomaglos, I am sorry, bitterly sorry, but these are facts, and neither you nor I can change them. However we look at things.'

'However we look at things.' Brocomaglos's fingers tapped the arm of his chair. 'Well enough. Good facts they may be. Still, Roman eyes are different from ours.'

'Eyes are eyes. And facts are facts.'

Instead of answering, Brocomaglos stood up. He walked over to the storage chest that stood against the wall, opened it and took out an object wrapped in a cloth.

'If that is so,' he said, 'then look here, my friend, and tell me what you see.'

He undid the wrappings and held the object up. The thing was a human head, brown as a nut, its smoke-tanned skin stretched tight over the bones of the skull. The flaking lips were drawn back from the teeth in a parody of a grin, and the blue shell eyes glared out from their shrunken sockets. What little hair was left on the scalp had been combed and neatly braided.

'Sweet Jupiter!' Aper whispered.

'What's wrong, Commander?' Brocomaglos set the head on the table next to the plate of honey cakes and laid his hand on the braids as gently as he had touched his daughter's. 'You are honoured. This is my greatest treasure. My great-great-grandfather killed him in battle. His name was Eppillicus, and he was a prince of the Catuvellauni, a famous warrior in his day. Will you not greet him?'

He lifted the head, kissed the dry lips and held it out towards them. Severinus felt his stomach crawl.

'Put it back,' Aper murmured. 'For the Mothers' sake, Brocomaglos, put it back.'

Brocomaglos did not move. 'At least touch him,' he said. 'He will not bite; he is a friend.'

'A *friend*! Sweet holy Mothers!'

'What else? He is held in honour, with his name remembered. His spirit is happy and brings the family luck. Will I ask little Ahteha to come and show you how we rub him with bear-grease to keep him supple? She would consider it a privilege.'

'No.' Aper's mouth was a hard line. 'You've made your point, Brocomaglos. Put the thing away.'

'"Thing".' Brocomaglos kissed the head again, bundled it up carefully and replaced it in the chest. 'Aye, well. "Thing" let him be. My apologies. I would not for the world have insulted a guest beneath my roof, but *you* had to understand this. We are not Romans, nor will we ever be. To you the Druids are criminals; to us, even if we live now under Roman laws, they are still very special. Remember that, when you ask us to betray them. These are *my* facts, and those of my tribe. And they are as sound in their way as yours.'

There was a long silence.

'So you refuse to help?' Aper said at last.

'If I did I would be as much a fool as your Paullinus. I will do what I can. For the sake of both our people. More I can't promise you. Now go. Go in friendship.'

'Sweet Jupiter!' Severinus could still feel his hands shaking as he guided Tanet through the gate of the Dun and down the track towards the main road. 'The man's a savage!'

'No.' Aper was looking far older than his fifty years. 'Brocomaglos is no savage. Each of us was asking for something that in the other's terms was too much. The only difference was that rabbits must always give way to wolves. That's a fact in both our worlds.'

They rode home in silence.

5

Five miles to the south, at the edge of a broad shallow pool on the island at the mouth of the river, Brocomaglos's son Tigirseno crouched behind a screen of reeds, his eye fixed on the sloping patch of hoof-churned mud and his right hand gripping the shaft of his hunting spear. A drop of rainwater from the branch of the ash tree above him splashed against his cheek. Tigirseno felt it run down the line of his jaw and slip beneath the edge of his cloak. On any other morning he would have wiped it away, but not today.

Today the gods were watching him.

A shadow moved within the shelter of the facing alders. Tigirseno stiffened as the hind stepped into the sunlight. She lifted her muzzle to sniff the air and stopped.

Tigirseno forced himself to stay absolutely motionless. *Horned One*, he prayed, *lay Your hand on her nostrils and on her eyes. Let her neither smell nor see me. Give her to me, if that is Your will.*

Something flickered at the edge of his vision, and it took all of Tigirseno's training not to turn his head. A wren had darted from the trees beyond the deer and was perched on a reed-leaf no more than a hand's breadth from his shoulder, watching him. The hairs crawled on Tigirseno's neck.

The wren was Taranis's bird. It would seem that not only the Horned One had heard him.

The hind's muzzle drooped. She moved forward and lowered her head. As her lips touched the water Tigirseno rose and threw. He caught a glimpse of startled brown eyes as she straightened. Then the spear struck, its blade sliding in above the breast-bone and piercing the heart. The hind, dead on her feet, stood for an instant then crumpled, forelegs first, as if kneeling to him. Tigirseno sprang forward and drew his knife, but there was no need: the eyes were already fixed and staring, and the light had gone out of them.

Quickly, he gutted her and washed her clean of blood. Then he lifted the carcass over his shoulder and set off for the grove.

The wren went with him.

He stopped at the edge of the trees, his fist pressed hard against his brow, waiting for the man who sat with his back to him to acknowledge his presence. The wren was perched on a dry yarrow stalk to one side. It was still watching him, its eye a tiny speck of black fire.

'Father?' he said. The word stuck in his throat. He swallowed, and tried again. 'Father, I've brought you food.'

The Druid turned. He showed no sign of surprise, but Tigirseno had expected none.

'A deer, Father. I killed you a deer.' Tigirseno's mouth was dry as sand.

'So?' The man smiled. He was younger than Tigirseno had expected, no more than thirty, his short plaited beard and the hair on his partly shaven head red as a fox's pelt. The cloak he wore was black and grey, speckled like a starling's coat and heavily stained with mud. 'My thanks. Set it down.'

Tigirseno did as he was told, trying to control the awe he felt in the other man's presence. In his sixteen years of life he had never seen a Druid, let alone talked with one. The hairs crawled on his scalp.

'Enter. Be welcome.' The Druid was still smiling. He was a good hand-span shorter than Tigirseno, sturdily built with thick muscular arms and a broad face that could have belonged to any farmer on the Dun, but appearances meant nothing. Tigirseno moistened his dry lips with his tongue. Despite the invitation, it was taking him all his courage just to stand his ground. With a Druid, you did not take liberties.

The man had not moved. 'There's nothing to fear,' he said. 'I don't bite. Come and sit a while.'

Carefully, as if he were walking barefoot through thorns, Tigirseno stepped into the clearing.

'Your name?'

Tigirseno's head went up. 'Tigirseno. Son of Brocomaglos,

son of Dercovicos, of the line of Imanuentios, chief of the Trinovantes.'

'So. So.' The Druid did not offer his own name, and Tigirseno did not ask. 'A good name. A warrior's name. My thanks for your gift, Tigirseno. Fresh meat is always welcome. How did you know I was here?'

'The whole of the Dun knows. By tomorrow my whole tribe will know.'

'Indeed. And the Wolves?'

'No, Father. And they will not, either.'

'You're sure?' The eyes were watching him with what Tigirseno suspected was amusement. He felt his cheeks redden, and hoped the Druid had not noticed.

'Who would betray a Holy One?' he said.

'Aye. Just so.' The corner of the Druid's mouth lifted. 'I hope you're right. I like my privacy.'

Tigirseno frowned. He had not expected a Druid to make jokes, and the man's accent was strange, difficult to understand, the words flatter-sounding and more drawn-out than was common in the south. Even Druids had tribes, although they were not bound by tribal loyalties. Perhaps he was a Brigantian, or from somewhere beyond the mountains; from Mona itself, even.

He gathered his courage to ask the first of his questions.

'The marshes are cold in winter, Father,' he said. 'Will you not come back with me to the Dun? My tribe would be—'

'No.'

Just that; a single syllable, spoken quietly but with complete finality. Tigirseno tried to keep the disappointment from his face. He had imagined, all the way to the island, bringing the Druid home. Even his father could not refuse a Holy One the protection of the tribe.

The Druid was waiting patiently. Tigirseno swallowed, and asked his second question.

'Is it true, Father, that the Wolves are planning to attack Mona?'

'Aye, it's true.'

'The Holy Island?' Tigirseno felt his eyes widen. 'And the gods would allow it?'

'Perhaps. Perhaps not. Perhaps they want only to test the people's faith.'

Tigirseno hesitated. 'Father, forgive me, but if they wanted to test the faith of the tribes then would they choose that way? You know how strong the Wolves are. Surely . . . ?'

'Tigirseno, are you questioning the wisdom of the gods?'

Tigirseno felt the fear rise from his stomach like vomit.

'No,' he said. 'No, of course not.'

'We have warriors of our own, and the Wolves are not a mountain people. The mountains will break them, as they did before.'

'What warriors, Father? They say the Silures are beaten, and the Ordovices and Deceangli are no more than broken reeds. The new chief of the Wolves is a better mountain fighter than even the last one was. How can you . . . ?'

Without warning, the Druid reached out and laid a finger across Tigirseno's lips. Tigirseno felt his tongue freeze, stiff as a block of wood, and he gagged.

Slowly, the Druid lowered his hand. He was not smiling now, and his eyes were chips of stone.

'So,' he said. 'The stories are true after all. The tribes of the east and south are become women.' Tigirseno reddened and tried to speak, but the spell held him fast. 'Perhaps I came too late, and there are no warriors left between the mountains and the sea. Perhaps the gods have thrown you lowlanders to the Wolves, and you are no longer worthy to be called their sons, or when you die to take you place beyond the River. Is that, then, Tigirseno, how you would have it, you and your folk?'

Tigirseno felt his eyes bulging as he choked with the effort to speak. He knew what the Druid was threatening. For him – for any Briton – it was the worst fate of all: to be cast out from the family of the tribes and live on cursed, set apart from men and gods alike, and after death to wander cold and alone on the near side of the River with no hope of rebirth. He sank to his knees and pressed his forehead to the earth.

Strong hands gripped his shoulders. He felt himself lifted and stubby fingers force themselves between his teeth, prising his jaws apart. He choked, coughing on his own spittle as the bands around his throat slackened and life returned to his tongue.

The Druid watched in silence until the racking spasms eased. Tigirseno bit hard on his lip and wiped his streaming eyes.

'Father,' he said, 'I am sorry. Tell me what to do.'

'That is better.' The man was smiling again. 'And spoken like a warrior. The gods have not abandoned you, or your tribe. Taranis has already shown me. Now let him show you, and through you the Trinovantes.' The Druid stepped back. 'Come. His messenger is waiting.'

Tigirseno looked up and round.

The wren had been sitting patiently, watching them. As the Druid moved, it flew across the clearing towards one of the trees at its edge.

'Go where he leads, Tigirseno. Don't be afraid. There is no danger.'

The bird did not stir as Tigirseno walked towards it. At the base of the tree where it sat was a thick pile of rotting oak leaves.

'Look closer.'

Tigirseno looked, and the breath caught in his throat. Lying half buried among the leaves was the skeleton of a wolf, picked almost clean of flesh. The skull with its yellowed fangs and empty eye sockets pointed towards the mainland.

The hairs on Tigirseno's scalp rose.

'Father, there are no wolves on this island,' he whispered. 'I've hunted here often and I would have seen them.'

'Aye.' The Druid had not moved, and his voice was as soft as Tigirseno's own. 'Yet he's here all the same, dead beneath Taranis's tree. Do you still doubt the gods?'

Tigirseno shook his head. He felt, suddenly, a great surge of joy.

'That's good. Go, then. Tell your people. Tell them to be ready.'

Tigirseno picked up the spear that he had dropped and backed away, his fist pressed against his forehead; then, heart thudding, he turned and ran from the grove.

This time Taranis's bird did not follow.

Brocomaglos sat staring into the fire for a long time after his guests had gone. He felt old and beaten, thin as a threadbare cloak.

Aper was a good man, he knew; but he was still a Roman. For him there would never be the agony of having to compromise even when the act of compromising brought with it nothing but contempt; self-contempt most of all. That, in this new world which the man-god Claudius had brought, was a chief's role. On the one hand lay complete submission and the death of the tribe's spirit; on the other, revolt, rebellion and the death of the tribe itself. And rebellion would mean death, physical or the slow death of a slave: that Brocomaglos knew as well as he knew that the other way was equally bad, and equally inevitable.

A log shifted in the grate and fell in a shower of sparks. Rising, Brocomaglos went over to the chest and took out Eppillicus's head. He unwrapped it and laid it on the table, wedging it upright on its spiked pedestal. Then, moistening his fingers with wine from his half-empty cup, he touched them to the open lips.

Time passed that was no time.

'Brother,' he murmured at last, when he had Eppillicus's leave to begin, 'I need your advice.'

The blue shell eyes stared into his.

Why do you ask me, they said, *when the answer is obvious?*

'It is not obvious. The Wolf commander is right. They will take and kill the Holy One whether I help or not. But if I refuse that help, then the tribe will suffer.'

You are being foolish. A Druid is a Druid. And perhaps it is good for the tribe to suffer.

'I don't understand.'

Do you not, then? The eyes hardened. *Aye, but I think you do. You only pretend not to, to me and to yourself. Perhaps the tribe needs to suffer. It will remind them that they are men.*

'What use is that if they're powerless?'

Men are never powerless. And if they suffer enough, eventually they will take revenge.

'You're saying that is good?'

Revenge is always good. Revenge clears the soul's account, on both sides.

Brocomaglos sighed. 'Eppillicus, the world has changed since your day. For the tribe to hope for revenge where Rome is concerned is madness. Surely it's better to accept what she gives in the hopes that it will lead to better things than to lose everything by opposing her? That is the course that the Druids would have us take, and you can see where it has brought them.'

At least they are men. Men do not compromise. When a man surrenders his right to choose he ceases to be a man.

'I don't agree. To see things like a blinkered horse is not to have free will but its opposite. It's better, surely, to accept what is inevitable and then try to change it from within.'

You imagine that that is possible?

'I hope so, certainly.'

The new chief of the Romans. He would share your views?

'No. But the Romans are not all like Paullinus.'

Are they not? Have the Wolves ceased to take what land they like without asking leave? Are they paying, now, to build their own temple and keep its altar smoking? Brother, you have much to learn! You talked to the commander of the wolf and the rabbit. Since when did wolves listen to the views of rabbits?

'Men are not beasts, Eppillicus.'

And the Trinovantes, by the same reasoning, are not rabbits. You would do well to remember that. It might save you trouble later. Now put me back. The consultation is over.

The shell eyes dulled. Brocomaglos moistened the lips again with wine, kissed the head and replaced it in the chest.

6

The next day was the eve of the five-day Winter Festival. Severinus stabled Tanet at the blacksmith's by the old east gate and walked towards the city centre. He glanced up at the sky. At least the rain was holding off, although from the looks of the grey clouds massing in the direction of the river that wouldn't last for long. He had only two more presents to buy, for his mother and Sulicena. If he was lucky, and finished quickly, he could get down to the Cloak Street baths before the weather turned. Sulicena's was easy, although it would involve a long wait: Vegisonius's was the most popular shop in the Colony at this time of year. Ursina's present would be more difficult, a cloak brooch to replace the one she had lost a month before.

The luxury-goods shops along Praetorian Street were packed, and the queue outside Vegisonius's stretched almost as far as Main Street corner. At its head a woman was arguing over the price of a jar of cherries in sweet vinegar.

'Marcus, my boy! Doing your last-minute Festival shopping, I see.'

Severinus turned to find Uricalus and his daughter Albilla behind him.

'Good morning, Uricalus,' he said. 'I'm trying to, at least.'

'Well, it's only once a year. Fortunately for our purses. Were you looking for anything in particular?'

'A jar of honeyed figs for Sulicena. I buy her one every year.'

Albilla grinned up at him, her lively, pretty face flushed with the cold. 'You're lucky, Marcus. Our cook's weakness is raisin wine.'

'Is that so, now?' Severinus grinned back. He liked Albilla. They had known each other since they were children, and she was as unlike her parents as chalk from cheese.

'Albilla, behave yourself.' Uricalus touched her arm, then

turned back to Severinus. His gold tooth flashed. 'If it's a matter of a present then I can recommend the quinces in syrup. A delight, my boy, an absolute delight. Vegisonius has just had a consignment delivered, and honestly I don't think you'd find better in Rome itself.'

'Father, really.' Albilla was looking as doll-like as she always did, her oval face carefully made up beneath a hairstyle that must have taken her maid hours to arrange. 'It's none of our business. Marcus can choose his own presents.'

'Just a suggestion, my dear.' Uricalus smiled at her. 'Oh, and Marcus, speaking of presents, I've been fortunate enough myself to get hold of some very choice pieces of glassware. A direct shipment from Massilia. If you haven't thought what to give your mother yet then perhaps you'd care to call in at the shop and take a look. Tell Juventius to show you the best pieces.'

'That's kind of you, sir.' Severinus's eyes strayed back to Vegisonius's counter. The woman had finally won her argument and the queue was shifting forwards.

'In fact I'm sure that Albilla would be more than happy to help you choose. Would you not, Albilla?'

'Actually, sir, I had something in mind already. A cloak brooch.'

'Really?' Uricalus frowned. 'Well, you know best, of course. By the bye, you and your family will be free, I hope, to drop round for a small get-together on the last day? Just a few friends, nothing formal, although I do have hopes that the governor himself will favour us with his presence.' His fingers stroked the fringe of his mantle. 'In any case Bellicia and I would be honoured if you and your parents could join us.'

'I don't know if we can, sir,' Severinus said carefully. He knew that what Uricalus called a 'small get-together' would be nothing of the kind. Especially if the governor had been invited. 'I'll have to check.'

'Fine. Then we can expect you. I can promise you an excellent evening.'

'I'm sure Marcus is looking forward to it, Father,' Albilla said demurely.

Severinus stifled a grin.

'That's right.' Uricalus was already turning to go. 'Well, I won't keep you, Marcus. My best wishes for the Festival when it comes. Do remember about the quinces.'

'Yes, sir.'

'That's a good lad. We'll see you at the party, then.'

As they crossed the road, Albilla turned round.

'Come if you can, Marcus!' she shouted.

Severinus bought the figs, then carried on in the direction of the Market Square. The jewellers' shops and hucksters' stalls were full of brooches, but there was nothing, he knew, that Ursina would like, and he was more than half sorry that he had not taken Uricalus's advice, if only for the sake of Albilla's company. He stopped in at one of the fish stalls in the market to pick up a jar of oysters for the next day's stew, then retraced his steps to the old military baths near the south gate.

'You're late this morning, sir.' The bath-owner, Passerinus, handed him a towel. 'Got your presents in?'

'All but one.' Severinus handed over the jars for safe-keeping. 'I'll try again later.'

'Aye, that's always the way.' The old legionary grinned, showing his gums. 'Did you have anything in mind?'

'A cloak brooch. But I wanted something out of the ordinary.'

'Try the shops outside the gate. I picked up a nice brooch for my youngest there. Local stuff, but good-quality silver, well-made. Cheap, too.'

'I might do that. Which shop did you say?'

'Eisu's. Tell him I sent you.'

Severinus stripped off and made his way through to the hot room. Passerinus had been right: he was late, and the wooden benches round the walls were already full. One of the bathers raised his head, and Severinus recognised Tirintius.

'That you, Marcus?' he said. 'Dannicus, you awkward beggar, where's your manners? Give the lad a seat.' The big sour-faced Gaul to his left grunted and edged along the bench. Tirintius grinned. 'Don't mind him, Marcus. He's got a sulk on. What's it doing outside?'

'Blowing through rain' – Severinus squeezed into the space – 'and cold as hell.'

'We're better in than out, then,' the third member of the trio, Reburrus, said. 'You should've joined us when you'd finished hobnobbing with the governor the other night, boy. You missed a good evening.' His elbow jabbed into Dannicus's ribs. 'Free wine, too.'

'Shut it.' Dannicus was scowling. Reburrus chuckled.

'That's enough, Reburrus.' Tirintius lifted his towel to wipe the sweat from his face. 'You heard about the Druid, then, Marcus?'

'Aye. Bad news.'

'Bad's right. Rumour is the governor's sending in the Eagles to search the Dun.'

'Fat lot of good that'll do,' Dannicus grunted. 'The ironbellies couldn't find their own backsides with both hands.'

One of the bathers on the bench opposite cleared his throat. Severinus winced: the man had the broad callus of a legionary helmet beside his jawbone. Dannicus, he knew, had seen it too; but then Dannicus had always been fond of trouble.

'You watch your mouth, horseboy,' the man said.

Dannicus grinned at him. 'And who,' he said, 'is going to make me?'

The ex-legionary half rose. Tirintius closed his eyes and swore softly.

'Sorry, friend,' he said. 'No offence. Let me handle this for you, okay?' He leaned across. 'Dannicus, you bastard, cut it out.'

'Jupiter, I only . . . !'

'Cut it, I said! We're here for a bath, and I haven't the energy!' He turned to the legionary. 'Sorry again, soldier.' The man settled back with a growl. 'You hear anything yourself, Marcus?'

'About the Druid?' Severinus was wiping the sweat from his neck. 'My father had a word with Brocomaglos yesterday. It may not come to a search.'

'He was wasting his time, then. You don't mess around where Druids are concerned, boy. Nor trust to natives, neither.'

'Maybe so, but there's no point asking for trouble.'

'Trouble? From the Dunsmen? Marcus, Marcus! The day these lazy beggars show fight old Claudius's statue'll come down from its pedestal and take a swim in the river. It's them that'll get the trouble if they ask for it. And with all respect to the commander, treating them soft's a bad idea. It only leads to problems.'

'Right' The man opposite, next to Dannicus's friend, was nodding. Severinus noticed the puckered ridge of an old scar on his chin, just above where the cheek-pieces of his helmet would have met. 'Dead right. Treat them hard and they'll respect you; give them an inch and they walk all over you.' He turned to Severinus. 'Don't waste your sympathy on Dunsmen, sir. They've got it easy.'

'Word is the emperor's called in the monkeys' loans,' another man said. His Spanish accent was thick as mountain cheese. 'Would that be right, now, sir?'

'Aye,' Severinus said. 'It's right enough.'

'Then there'll be a few oxen going cheap by the ploughing season.' The old Spaniard grinned through a mouthful of broken teeth.

'Not just oxen, either.' His neighbour dug him in the ribs. 'There're some handy lasses up there on the Dun.'

'Ach' – the Spaniard cleared his throat – 'I'll settle for the oxen, me, and you can keep the women. These British bitches don't even make good whores.'

The brooch shop lay behind a farrier's yard. It was a hut rather than a booth with a slatted, rush-thatched porch running the length of its frontage, freshly lime-washed walls and a sign in well-spelled Latin over the lintel. Eisu, or whoever owned the place, evidently had pretensions. There were two native ponies tied to the hitching-posts, with a larger horse, saddled and bridled Roman-fashion, beside them. Severinus fastened Tanet's leading-rein to the remaining ring. He was raising his hand to the latch when someone inside screamed.

He thrust the door open as the man standing with his back to it spun round. Severinus's eye caught the glint of a knife. Without thinking, he lunged forward. His right shoulder slammed into the the man's chest, sending him sprawling. The knife slipped from his fist and skittered across the floor towards the far wall.

Severinus straightened. There were three other people in the

• David Wishart

room, a man and two women. One of them was Brocomaglos's wife Matugena. Her eyes were wide with shock, and one hand was still raised to her mouth.

'What happened, Matugena?' he said in Celtic.

It was the second woman who answered. The low sun, shining in through the unshuttered windows, burned on a mass of red-gold hair. She could be no older, Severinus thought, than eighteen.

'We were buying ribbons. This piece of offal came in and—'

'Senovara!' Matugena snapped.

The girl turned to her, her green eyes bright with anger. 'Is there a better word for him? He would have slit Eisu's throat for a handful of coppers.'

The man was on his feet now, one hand massaging his bruised ribs through the cloth of his patched army tunic. He was glaring at Eisu.

'I'm no thief,' he said in Latin. 'I was collecting what's owed me.'

'That's a lie.' The shopkeeper was scowling. 'I owe you nothing.'

The veteran lunged at his throat. Severinus gripped the man's arm and pulled him back.

'That's enough, soldier,' he said. 'We'll talk this through. What's your name?'

'Paternius.' The man levelled a finger at Eisu. 'And it's no lie. This monkey's on my property and he owes me rental. Two full months.'

'I paid you in kind!'

'You call that payment? One scrawny pig? I want cash, and I want it now.' He turned back to Severinus. 'That's Colony law, isn't it, sir?'

Severinus hesitated. 'Aye,' he said, 'if you're the legal owner. But . . .'

'You're taking his part?'

Brocomaglos's daughter was staring at him. She was tall, almost as tall as he was, and their eyes were on a level. He had never seen anyone so angry.

He shrugged. 'I can't do otherwise. If the rent hasn't been paid then the lease is forfeit.'

• 42

Matugena was tugging at her daughter's sleeve. 'Senovara, please! The commander's son knows what he's saying.'

'Does he, now?' Senovara pulled away. 'Then it seems to me that someone should call this fine Roman law of his for what it is. A heap of stinking dog turd.'

'*Senovara!*'

Severinus winced and turned away.

'Hey, now, lass!' Paternius's lips were twitching too. 'I'm asking for no more than my due. We've an agreement, signed, sealed and registered. I've been patient for two months, and that's a month over the odds. If the monkey can't pay his debts he's got no one to blame but himself.'

'But he paid you! He paid you with a pig!' The green eyes flashed. 'And do not you *dare* call him a monkey!'

'Jupiter!' The veteran groaned and turned to Severinus. 'Sir, tell this . . . tell her, please.'

'The shop is this man's property, Senovara,' Severinus said. 'A pig is no proper payment. And if he insists on Roman coin then that's his right.'

'You see, lass?' Paternius said. 'All above board. No harm done. Now if you'll just leave us to settle up I'll be on my way.'

Senovara ignored him. She was still glaring at Severinus. 'And is it his right to insist at knife-point?'

'No. Not even under our dog-turd Roman law. But then I think there he had the worst of the bargain. Or wouldn't you agree?'

'That's so, sir.' Paternius chuckled. For a moment Severinus thought the girl would smile in her turn, but her lips were still set. 'And you can ask your friend the m— your friend Eisu here whether I'm lying or not. Twenty silver pieces he owes me. We'll call it seventeen, allowing for the pig, and that's generous.'

'Eisu?' The girl turned to the shopkeeper.

'Aye?' The man was still scowling, but his expression was wary.

'Is he telling the truth or not?' She paused. 'Eisu! Answer me!'

'Aye, perhaps so,' he said at last. 'But I can't give what I don't have.'

Senovara nodded, once. Then she pulled back the sleeve of

her tunic, unfastened a slim gold bracelet and offered it to Paternius.

'Here,' she said.

There was a silence. Finally Paternius said quietly, 'I don't take a woman's jewellery, lass. Certainly not for another man's debt.'

'Eisu is my father's tribesman. His debt is the tribe's.'

Paternius cleared his throat. 'Put it back,' he said. 'Maybe I was hasty. I can wait a while longer.' He looked at Eisu. 'Another month, no more. Agreed?'

The shopkeeper swallowed, his eyes on Senovara. 'Agreed.'

'Fine.' He bent to pick up his knife and tucked it into his belt. 'Then we'll call the matter settled.'

He left. The door closed behind him.

Eisu turned to Severinus. 'My thanks, sir.'

'Nothing.' Severinus took out his purse. 'Now. I came for a brooch.'

'Aye.' The shopkeeper grinned. 'Of course. If you'd care to . . .'

'The price will be fair, Eisu.' Senovara was watching him, her green eyes hard. 'Is that clear?'

The grin slipped. 'Yes, lady.'

'Good.' She slipped the bracelet back on her wrist and moved towards the door. 'My thanks to you also, Marcus Severinus. Mother?'

They went out.

Severinus and the shopkeeper looked at each other.

'You know her well?' Severinus said.

'Aye. Well enough.' Eisu scratched his ear. 'From a distance, at least. And I'd be happy to keep it that way.'

'Is she always like that?'

'No.' The grin reappeared. 'We were lucky. Today was one of the good days.'

7

Titus Medullinus was worried; seriously worried. His orders were clear and exact: having crossed over to Estuary Island he and his ten-man detail were to proceed with caution through the woods in a south-easterly direction for a distance of approximately half a mile, at which point he would find the clearing where the man had made camp. Once located, he was to be arrested, or failing that killed out of hand and his body brought back.

Medullinus had been a soldier for twenty years, and a centurion for five. Orders like these needed no thinking about; they were bone of his bone and he didn't question them.

Still . . .

His jaw tightened. This was no ordinary subversive. This was a Druid. And centurion or not, professional soldier or not, the prospect of dealing with a Druid made the hairs on his effing neck crawl.

'Centurion?'

'Aye, Caudex?' He turned. His second had joined him. He, too, stared towards the south where the marshland stopped and the woods began.

'It's a bastard, isn't it?' Caudex's face had a tightness to it that Medullinus hoped was not reflected in his own.

'Aye. It is that.' Medullinus kept his voice expressionless. 'Bad country for searching if the beggar's not at home.'

Caudex looked at him sideways. 'That wasn't my meaning,' he said. 'It's the lads. They're a bit nervous, like.'

'Are they, so?' *Nervous* wasn't the word; Medullinus could smell the effing fear rising off them like sweat, and it set his own nerves jangling. 'That's good, then, because they've cause to be. If we come back empty-handed I'll have their effing guts.' He paused. 'Yours, too.'

Caudex's mouth opened, then closed. He cleared his throat. 'You ever come across one of them yourself?' he said. The tone was too casual. 'A Druid, I mean?'

Medullinus considered his answer, and decided on the truth.

'Aye,' he said. 'When I was a squaddie at the Conquest. The beggars were thick enough on the ground then. And we had plenty up north, the time of the Brigantian troubles.'

'No, but close up, like?' Caudex waited for an answer that didn't come. 'It's just they say they've got powers. That they can change their shape. Call up mists. Things like that.' Momentarily, the whites of his eyes showed.

'Do they, now?' Medullinus turned to face him, trying to ignore the touch of ice at his own neck. 'Is that so?'

'Aye.' A drop of sweat was running down Caudex's cheek. It reached his lips, and he licked it away. 'You think it's possible? I mean if we have to catch the bugger then the lads'll have to know. I mean—'

'All right!' Medullinus snapped. 'That's enough!' Whatever his own feelings might be, he knew that this had to be stopped, and quickly. 'Who've I got here? A squad of Eagles or a bunch of limp-wristed fairies?'

Caudex stiffened. 'I was just . . .'

'Screw your *just*!' Medullinus dropped his voice. 'You tell them. We're after a man, an ordinary man. One word about effing hares or effing curses from anyone and the beggar's mopping out latrines from now until his discharge. And that goes double for you.' He glared. 'Now do you *effing just* understand *that*?'

Caudex swallowed. 'Yes, Centurion.'

'Fine. Then remember it.' Medullinus straightened and took a deep breath which he hoped Caudex would not notice. If it had to be done, then the sooner it was over the better. 'And tell the lads we're moving.'

Caudex saluted and hurried back to the troop.

Half a mile away, in the grove at the centre of the island, Dumnocoveros sat watching the wren perched a scant yard from his hand. It was, he knew, the same bird that had brought the young Trinovantian warrior to him the day before.

The wren ducked its head. The sharp black eye turned in his direction, catching the sun's light and throwing it back.

'I'm listening, brother,' Dumnocoveros said quietly. 'Tell me.'

The wren's head tilted, its beak opened, and it made a hard churring sound. Suddenly it darted arrow-fast towards the oak tree where the wolf bones lay and settled among the roots.

Dumnocoveros rose and followed the bird across the clearing. He was not afraid of startling it – it was the gods' messenger, after all, and would know he meant no harm – but its every movement was significant. Besides, when the gods chose to speak to men one had to give them room. He stood waiting, his hand held across his mouth in an attitude of respectful silence.

The wren was sitting on the wolf's skull, just above the right eye socket. The tiny beak tapped against the yellowed bone, and Dumnocoveros counted: nine . . . ten . . . eleven strokes. The bird moved along the line of the jaw, perched for a moment within reach of the teeth, then hopped across to what had been the animal's right shoulder. The ruff about its neck spread and it shivered, as if shaking dust or water droplets from its feathers.

Dumnocoveros nodded, his face grave. 'Thank you, brother,' he said. 'I understand.'

Again the black eye flashed. Then, with a liquid trill of notes the bird rose into the air and flew off through the trees to the east.

Stopping only to pick up his staff and leather bag, Dumnocoveros set off down the path which the gods' messenger had shown him, away from the advancing soldiers.

Medullinus knelt beside the abandoned fire. The ash was light and powdery, but the blackened stones yielded a very faint warmth to his hand. The fire had been dead hours, at most.

'There's part of a deer carcass over here, Centurion.' One of the lads – Pertinax, the smartest of the bunch – was pointing. 'He can't be long gone or the crows would've had it.'

'Aye.' Medullinus had already noticed the neat pile of deer bones. These, too, would have attracted scavengers quickly, and yet the pile was undisturbed. The fire might have indicated a hunter's camp, but the deer bones suggested something more. And that could only mean the Druid. 'It's our boy, all right.'

'You think he's gone for good?' Caudex was at his shoulder. He sounded hopeful.

Medullinus stood up and wiped his hands on his tunic. 'Maybe. He had plenty meat, so he wouldn't be hunting. There again, he may have other business. Who knows what these bastards get up to?'

He regretted the words at once, because Caudex's eyes shifted. 'Aye,' he said. 'That's true enough.'

'Caudex!'

'Sorry, Centurion.' Caudex hesitated. 'Then again, maybe he was warned.'

'Maybe he was, at that.' Medullinus looked round the troop, then raised his voice, forcing a grin. 'You bastards made enough noise coming through them woods to warn a deaf man. Eh?'

No one smiled. They knew – as Medullinus knew – that the orders about moving quietly had been obeyed to the letter. Not so much as a crow had lifted.

If the Druid had been warned then it was no doing of theirs.

'So,' Caudex said after a silence that went on too long. 'What now?'

'We search the ruddy island until we find the beggar! What else would we do?'

'Lot of rough country out there, Centurion,' a trooper murmured: Chlorus, the windy one.

Medullinus turned on him, glaring. 'Then we'd better get moving, then, hadn't we, son?' he said. Chlorus lowered his eyes. 'Where's Salvius?'

'Here, Centurion.' A lean-jawed soldier shuffled forward.

'Right. It's all up to you now, boy. You're our best tracker, or so you're always telling us. The beggar isn't long gone, he must've left signs somewhere. You show us which way he went.'

'I'm not sure I can, Centurion. It's not like—'

'Jupiter!' Medullinus's patience snapped. *Do it, will you? Just effing do it!*

'Yes, Centurion!'

The troop waited in nervous silence as Salvius began, carefully and methodically, to work his way around the clearing's edges.

Dumnocoveros was moving north-eastwards at a steady run. He

was not afraid, least of all of dying; death meant nothing. To die in the gods' service was a holy thing. But if death was not to be feared, failure was. Dumnocoveros could not afford to die. The eastern tribes were discontented, the Wolves were pressing them hard, and if he could turn them then the new governor would be forced to think again about the spring campaign. If the gods willed it Mona could be saved.

For the holy island to fall was unthinkable. He would give his life ten times over, and willingly, if it meant that Mona survived.

First, though, he had to survive himself.

That would be difficult enough: barbarians though they were, the Wolves were clever, and they did not give up. *Taranis*, he prayed, *Wheel-lord, Sun-lord, don't let them catch me! Stretch out Your hand above Your servant and take Your light from my pursuers' eyes!*

Ahead of him a tiny bundle of feathers smaller than a child's fist rose and darted between the trees, flying then stopping, flying then stopping, matching its pace to his own. Seeing it, Dumnocoveros smiled, content. Taranis had not deserted him. He was still being led, and he had nothing to fear.

He ran on.

'He went this way, Centurion.' Salvius was kneeling by a patch of grass between two trees at the north-east edge of the clearing. 'Not long since, neither.'

'Good lad.' Medullinus nodded, satisfied, feeling his fear evaporate: a man who left traces that could be followed was something he understood. Now it was only a matter of time. 'You go on ahead. The rest of you' – he glanced round the troop – 'keep your eyes peeled and your javelins ready. You see him, you nail him. No warning, no second chances.'

There were several relieved nods. A few grins, even.

'I thought we wanted him alive, Centurion,' Caudex said.

'You heard me.' Medullinus had thought carefully before giving that order, and he knew it was the right one. 'We throw to kill. Let's see the bastard magic away a foot of iron between the ribs.' He drew his own sword. 'Right, you buggers. Let's have him.'

* * *

The woods were opening up, with oak, beech and hazel giving place to alder and willow. The marshes could not be far off now. The ground beneath Dumnocoveros's feet was changing, too, becoming softer, more yielding. Clumps of moss had begun to appear, and he could see reed tops waving in the distance. From straight ahead came the *oh-boomp* of a bittern, and a marsh harrier hung above him as if nailed to the air.

The wren was still leading the way, a steady dozen paces in front. Neither the distance nor the direction varied. The god must have a particular place in mind, a safe haven to which he was being taken. Dumnocoveros glanced behind him. There was no sign, yet, of the Wolves, but he knew that meant little. Unless they were very, very foolish they would have at least one experienced tracker with them. True, if he could reach the marshes before they saw him then his chances of escaping were far higher, but hiding in the marshes held its own dangers. Once he had chosen a place to hide, any further movement was impossible. All the more reason, then, to choose well.

Guide me, lord, he prayed, knowing that his fate lay in the god's hand, and content to have it so. *Taranis, protect Your servant!*

The boar took them by surprise, lifting suddenly from under a gorse bush, its tusks ripping into Salvius before he had time to shout. Then it was gone, running westwards, back the way they had come. None of the javelins they threw touched it.

Medullinus dropped to his knees beside the writhing, screaming soldier. The boar's tusk had laid open the length of his thigh, and blood was pumping out on to the grass in a steady stream. Pulling back his arm, the centurion drove his fist hard into the man's jaw, and the screaming stopped. He looked up and round, trying to ignore the fear that clawed at his gut.

'Fetch me a stick!' No one moved. 'Jupiter! Are you all deaf? Find me an effing stick!'

Quickly, without bothering to make sure the order had been obeyed, he undid the man's kerchief and tied it round the leg above the wound, placing a pebble against the artery on the inside of the thigh to concentrate the pressure. A pale-faced

squaddie handed him a length of broken branch and he tightened
the tourniquet until the bleeding stopped. Then he bound up the
gash as best he could with his own kerchief, sat back on his heels
and tried to collect himself before raising his eyes to meet those
of his troop.

They were gathered round, watching him, their faces expressionless. Several had their hands clenched in the sign against witchcraft and strong magic.

Medullinus spat from a dry mouth. 'It was a boar, lads,' he said
quietly, careful to keep his voice from shaking. 'Nothing else. Just
a bloody boar.' He tried a grin that didn't work. 'Salvius always
was unlucky.'

There was no answer. Some of the men shifted nervously.
Finally Lucrio, the big Sicilian with the pucker of an old knife-
scar running the length of his cheek, cleared his throat.

'I was looking, Centurion,' he said. 'One minute it wasn't
there, the other it effing was. And it made straight for Salvius.
The poor bugger didn't stand a chance.'

Medullinus swallowed back the coldness that was seeping up
from his own stomach.

'Shove it, Lucrio,' he said. 'It was an accident. Pure bad luck.
The bastard came out from under a bush and Salvius was the
first one it saw.' His voice sharpened. 'Jupiter alive, what the
hell's wrong with you all?'

'Where's it now, then, Centurion?' The young squaddie who
had brought him the stick was showing the whites of his eyes.

'Where would it be, you fool? Half an effing mile off and
still running! You saw it go yourselves!' Medullinus was aware
that he was shouting. He closed his eyes momentarily. Back in
control, he stood up and pointed at random. 'Chlorus. Senex.
Make a stretcher, javelins and cloaks. You're to take him back
while the rest of us go on.'

'Not much bloody point in that, is there?' Lucrio muttered.

Medullinus rounded on him, anger driving out the fear. 'And
just what the hell's that supposed to mean?'

The big Sicilian looked at him sideways. 'You said it yourself,
Centurion. We'd be wasting our time. The bastard's half a mile
off by now in the other direction.'

Medullinus's jaw set. He turned slowly on his heel, his eyes raking the circle. The soldiers shifted, none of them meeting his gaze.

'That's enough of that,' he said. 'Move it. And keep your eyes skinned, the lot of you, because now we're running blind.'

Dumnocoveros left the forest behind and entered the broad open stretch of boggy meadowland that was the island's northern edge. A few hundred yards more would bring him to the reed-beds that stretched out into the waters of the strait. There, with the god's continued help, he could lie hidden until dark. After that . . .

Behind him, someone shouted. Dumnocoveros glanced over his shoulder as the first of the Wolves emerged from the screen of trees barely two hundred yards away: eight men, armed with javelins. Panic caught at his throat, driving the breath from his lungs.

Taranis, he prayed. *Help me!*

Stumbling over the tussocky grass, splashing through pools fringed with bullrushes, Dumnocoveros ran for his life. He had no illusions about escaping: even if he were lucky enough to avoid a javelin in the back before he reached the shelter of the reeds he would have no time to hide, and the Wolves would not give up now they had him in sight.

Out of the corner of his eye, he saw something shoot into the air with a bubbling trill of notes. He looked up. The wren was skimming across the boggy ground to his right, weaving a course between the pools. Without pausing to think, Dumnocoveros swerved and followed. He glanced behind and saw the Wolves turn also, taking a course that would intersect with his. He increased his speed and felt his lungs burn with the effort. Ahead, a wall of reeds lifted high across his path. He burst through them . . .

And suddenly there was no ground, only water; deep, ice-cold water that closed above his head. For an instant he panicked. Then his feet found a purchase and he stood upright.

The water came no higher than his shoulder. He had fallen into a steep-sided ditch, less than a body's-length wide, that ran inland from the open strait and formed the western border of a broad stretch of mossy bogland. This was the end. Although he was screened for the moment by the reeds at his back, the protection they offered was no more than temporary. To go on, across the open bog, would be madness. He had only two choices left: to follow the line of reeds inland, or north towards their seaward edge, and with the Wolves so close behind either way would be fatal.

He was dead, and he knew it.

Inland it would have to be. Perhaps Taranis would raise a mist to hide him from the soldiers. Nothing else, now, could help him. He set his palms to the ditch's edge, pushing his body upwards and out of the water . . .

The whole bank dipped and sank beneath the surface. He lurched sideways, unbalanced for a moment, then steadied himself, unable to believe the evidence of his own eyes. As the pressure of his hand relaxed, the ground beneath the spreading fingers rose again to its former level.

He looked up. The wren was beside him, perched on a still-quivering but now sodden clump of moss. It ducked its head and spoke a hard, churring phrase.

Dumnocoveros stared. Then, as his eyes and brain cleared, he laughed.

Thank you, lord!

He had been a fool. He was safe, after all. The god had given him the perfect hiding place. This was no ditch; he was standing within the western edge of a deep inlet, a finger of the sea itself. What he had taken for solid ground was a huge floating mat of compacted moss that had grown out across it, covering its surface from one side to the other. And if he had been deceived then surely so would the Wolves be.

Quickly, he took the knife from his belt and cut one of the reeds, lopping off a section the length of his forearm. Clutching the hollow reed together with his knife, he filled his lungs and eased himself, face up, beneath the floating mat until it covered him completely. This close to its edge it was no more than a hand-span thick, and the knife went through it easily. He pushed the reed into the hole and, with the last of the air in his lungs, blew the tube clear.

The water that surrounded him was bitterly cold, but it was a coldness that could be mastered. Tucked safe beneath his spreading blanket, joined to the upper air only by the slender tube of the reed, Dumnocoveros waited.

Above his head Taranis's bird rose singing and flew off towards the woods.

8

The hut door slammed open, sending smoke from the hearth billowing around the room. Brocomaglos, intent on fixing an arrowhead to a new ash-wood shaft, glanced up. Tigirseno stood in the open doorway glaring at him, ignoring the startled faces of his mother and sisters on the women's side of the fire.

Brocomaglos forced himself to carry on with the task, slipping the iron tang into its groove and binding it in place with a length of twine. He knew what was coming; he had expected it. Carefully, he tied the final knot and pulled it tight with his teeth. Only then did he raise his eyes to meet his son's.

'Close the door, boy. There's a draught.'

Tigirseno's foot lashed out. The door thudded home against the jambs.

'The Romans have sent men to Estuary Island.'

'Aye.' Brocomaglos laid the arrow aside. 'I know.'

'You told them where to go.' The boy's face was red with fury. 'Didn't you?' Then, when there was no answer: '*Didn't you?*'

'I told them.'

'Sweet Lord Taranis!' Tigirseno's clenched fist slammed against the door post. Still Brocomaglos did not react.

'Your father had no choice, Tigirseno.' Matugena laid a hand on her younger daughter's head. The child's eyes were round as an owl's as she stared at her brother, but she did not speak. 'The Romans already knew the holy one was here. If he hadn't told them where to look the whole tribe would have suffered.'

'And would that be worse than what he's brought on us himself?' Tigirseno's finger stabbed out. 'We're cursed, Mother! If the holy one dies his blood will be on all our heads!'

'He may not die at all.' Senovara had been stitching a torn cloak. Now she picked it up again and thrust the needle through the cloth. 'He may escape.'

Tigirseno turned on her. 'And if he does that would excuse us? Senovara, our father has betrayed a Druid! There's no worse crime than that! None!'

'He came here uninvited.' The girl's voice was cool.

'Since when does a holy one need permission to travel where the gods tell him to go? His presence is honour enough for any tribe!'

Senovara said nothing, but the line of her lips stiffened.

'Tigirseno, listen to me.' Brocomaglos was still speaking quietly. 'Your mother's right. I had no choice. The Romans would have sent soldiers, taken hostages, tortured them if they had to. The secret could not be kept. When the Druid had been found and killed they would have come back, and more would have died. That is truth, and you know it.'

'Truth!' Tigirseno spat the word. 'No one would have told, Father, even under torture! As for the soldiers, we could have fought them. Not all of us are cowards. There are warriors left among the Trinovantes, even if their chief has forgotten how to fight.'

Matugena sucked in her breath, and Senovara glanced up sharply. A log on the hearth shifted, releasing a cloud of sparks.

Brocomaglos rose to his feet, his eyes on his son's, his face dark with anger. Without a word he reached up to the neck of his tunic and jerked his hand downwards. The tunic tore to the waist and gaped open, revealing the long, puckered scar that ran from collar-bone to ribs.

Father and son stared at each other.

'Has he, indeed, now?' Brocomaglos said softly. 'Tigirseno, your mouth is too big for your wits. Don't talk to me of forgetting, or of fighting Romans.'

Tigirseno lowered his eyes, but his fists were still clenched at his sides, the knuckles white. 'Father, I didn't mean . . .' he said.

'Aye, but you did, though. You know you did.' Brocomaglos covered up the scar as best he could and returned to his place. 'There are no cowards in this house, or on the Dun.'

'Perhaps not, but—'

'Perhaps nothing! Even to think of fighting the Romans is senseless, Tigirseno. We've fought them already, we and the other tribes, and for all the Druids' promises and their spells and curses we lost. Does that tell you nothing, you fool?'

Tigirseno felt the anger rise cold in his belly. He looked at his father, hating the man's hypocrisy; scar or no scar, Brocomaglos was afraid; his fear shouted itself in every word he spoke. 'What should it tell me?' he said. 'We were beaten once. That doesn't mean we will always be beaten.'

Brocomaglos's huge brows came down. 'Aye, if we'd been beaten only once, and narrowly, then I might agree with you. Or if when we fought we had lacked the courage or the skill or the leadership to win. But we've fought Rome often enough with all those things behind us, and still we've lost. That is fact, and fact it remains.'

'Prince Caratacos fought and won. He would still be fighting if the Brigantian queen hadn't betrayed him.'

Brocomaglos sighed. 'Tigirseno, Caratacos proves my point. He was the best we had, a great warrior and a great leader. But to the Romans he was only a hindrance. Now he's in Rome, kept alive for their emperor's pleasure like a dancing bear. I ask you again, does that tell you nothing, or are you too blind or stupid to understand?'

'Perhaps what it tells me is that to keep the halter round our necks Rome needs the help of her good British *friends*.'

'Holy Camulos! Are you accusing me of treachery as well as cowardice? My own son?'

'He meant no such thing.' Matugena gave Tigirseno a quick look.

'Did he not?' Brocomaglos's eyes had not left his son's face. 'Then let him say so himself!'

Tigirseno swallowed, but his expression did not relax. 'My father heard me clear enough,' he said. 'The Wolves' strength lies in our own weakness. How many are they, Father? Twenty thousand? Thirty? For each of them there are a hundred of us, more. If the tribes rose together . . .'

'Then they would be fools! And very soon they would be dead fools!'

'To be a dead fool is better than to be a live coward!'

'Holy gods, Tigirseno!' Brocomaglos's fist slammed down. 'I have seen these Romans fight!'

'And Caratacos saw them run!' Tigirseno was shouting now. 'But then, Father, Caratacos was a warrior, while you—'

'*That's enough!*' Matugena had risen to her feet. Her right hand smashed hard across Tigirseno's cheek.

Mother and son stared at each other while the silence lengthened. Then, without a word, Tigirseno turned away. Pausing only to snatch up a hunting spear from the rack against the wall, he wrenched the door open and ran outside.

He ran without thinking, blindly, past the barking Durnos and on towards the gate of the Dun. All the way, his cheek burned where Matugena had slapped it, and he felt shame for his father's cowardice and hypocrisy clutch at his throat. Coward! Coward and traitor! What was the Wolves' power measured against that of the gods? Nothing! Less than nothing!

The thought drove out the shame and filled him with the same joy he had felt when he had seen the dead wolf in the grove. When the tribes rose, as they must surely do if the gods had foreshadowed it, he would show his father that he, too, could fight.

At the entrance to the Dun he stopped, knowing that this was the moment of final choice; knowing, too, that the choice was already made. He had not looked to quarrel with his father, but a quarrel had been building for a long time and now the break had come he welcomed it. He would not be going back.

So. But if not back, then where?

Taranis, he prayed, *give me a sign!*

He waited, all his hunter's senses alert, for the space of fifty heartbeats. Nothing. Fifty more. Nothing. Another fifty. Nothing. Tigirseno was close to weeping. He would kill himself. Perhaps that was the only way . . .

In the grass to his left, something stirred. Tigirseno jerked his head round. Frightened by the movement, the shrew began to run, darting along the side of the old rampart then bearing away from it into the open field, the rippling grass marking its passage. Tigirseno watched it go, his hand pressed against his mouth in awe. Taranis had answered, of that there was no doubt, but what did the sign mean? A holy one could have interpreted it clearly enough, but he was no Druid. He could only guess.

Think! he told himself. The answer is there, if you only think!

He looked around him. The rampart. A boundary, a dividing line. And the shrew had run beyond it into the open country . . .

Perhaps the god was telling him to go north-west, beyond the Wolves' province; to join the mountain tribes and help them save the holy island.

He knew, as soon as the thought came, that it was the right one. Again he felt a surge of joy. *Taranis, lord,* he prayed, his pride a knot at his throat, *I thank you! Make me worthy!*

Gripping his spear, he began to run.

Above the gate where Tigirseno had been standing a sparrow-hawk hung motionless, watching. Below her, something moved: a stirring in the grass out of time with the wind. The hawk drifted lazily on the air currents until she was poised directly over the tussock. Time passed, but the hawk was patient. Not even her wings stirred. Finally, beneath her, a tiny nerve broke. There was a flurry of movement, a running . . .

The hawk was ready, and hungry. She folded her wings and dropped, talons spread.

The shrew died quickly. But by then Tigirseno was already far away.

'The fault wasn't yours.' Matugena touched her husband's shoulder. 'He'll be back when his head has cooled and his belly begins to rumble.'

Brocomaglos laid a hand over hers. He felt empty, his anger gone. 'Aye,' he said. 'He's a good son. And I think, perhaps, not as foolish as I made out. Less, maybe, than his father.'

'You are head of the tribe. The decision was yours to make, no one else's.'

'That does not mean it was the right one.' Brocomaglos closed his eyes. Was I wrong? he thought. My son spoke the truth: to betray a Druid is a terrible thing, whatever the reason. Who am I to think I understand the gods' purpose well enough to break their laws? 'And if I am the head of the tribe, it is only because it suits the Romans to allow it.'

'That's nonsense, Father.' Senovara had taken Ahteha on her lap and was unwinding the braids in the girl's hair. 'The tribe elected you fairly. They trust you, rightly so. Oh, they hate the Romans, but they aren't the fools my brother is. Besides, the gods are old enough to take care of themselves.'

'Senovara!' Matugena looked up.

'Well, and are they not, then, Mother? Perhaps they're following a plan of their own. And if so they must be getting very tired of hearing us tell them what they think.'

Brocomaglos found himself laughing. Senovara, his eldest child, had always been his favourite, and as she grew up it was obvious that she would also turn out the wisest. He rose and hugged her.

'Have you been eating hazelnuts or swimming with the salmon, then,' he said, 'that you know the gods' minds so well?'

'No.' Senovara picked up the comb that lay beside her. 'But I know my own. That should be enough for anyone.'

'Aye.' Brocomaglos kissed her forehead. 'Well, and perhaps it is. And what does it tell you about the Romans?'

Senovara shrugged as she drew the comb through her sister's hair. 'That they're no different from anyone else. There are bad and good. Some of them are almost civilised.'

'Indeed?' Brocomaglos's eyebrows lifted. 'My daughter the Druid is generous with her praise.'

'Almost, I said.' Senovara's mouth twitched. 'Like your friend the commander's son.'

Matugena stood up. 'Listen to the wind! It'll be cold tonight. Ahteha, when your sister has finished your hair you can help me make the soup for supper.'

No one mentioned Tigirseno as they ate, nor when Matugena had fed Durnos the remains of the barley broth and banked the fire for the night.

There was no sign of him the next day, either.

9

Trinnus brought the coach to a halt outside Uricalus's imposingly panelled front door. In Colony terms the place was a mansion, a sprawling single-storey building occupying a full half block, and tonight it was lit up like a candelabrum by a dozen torches set along its front. They hissed and sparked as they gulped down the stray flakes of sleet that blew in under the eaves.

'The beggar's pulled out all the stops, tonight, hasn't he?' Aper grunted.

Severinus grinned as he opened the carriage door and climbed down.

'Watch your feet,' he said. 'The mud's an inch thick out here.'

It was typical Festival weather. The day's rain had turned the gutters to rivers, and the water formed standing pools where the gravel lay thin over the underlying soil.

Aper joined him, pulling the drawstrings of his hood tight around his face.

'We won't stay late,' he said.

Ursina, following behind, adjusted her own hood as the wind caught it.

'Nonsense, Titus,' she said. 'Remember it's the Festival. It was very good of Uricalus to ask us.'

'Aye, maybe.' Aper's eye twinkled at her. 'Tell me that again after two hours of Bellicia.' He looked up at Trinnus. 'Be back for midnight, lad. No later, or I'll have your hide.'

'Enjoy your evening, master.' Trinnus grinned.

'Less of your bloody cheek,' Aper grunted and turned away.

The door was already open, and Justus, Uricalus's door-slave, was standing aside to let them pass.

'Compliments of the season, Commander,' he said.

'The same to you, Justus.' Aper undid his cloak and handed it over. 'We're not the first, are we?'

'Most of the other guests've arrived, sir.' The slave took the cloak along with Severinus's and Ursina's. 'They're in the main sitting-room. You know the way?'

'Aye.'

'If you'll go through then I'll take these to dry off.'

'Good lad.' As Justus left in the direction of the kitchen Aper cupped his hands round the flame of one of the dozen oil lamps that hung from the massive candelabrum next to the statue of Mercury in its wall niche. 'Mothers, it's cold!'

'Titus! Behave yourself, now!' Ursina was smiling.

'Just getting warm, Bear-cub.' Aper straightened and gathered up the obligatory armful of mantle. 'Let's join the party.'

The sitting-room was brightly lit and cheerful, its walls and ceiling hung with ribbons and spangles, and the braziers at each of its corners had been fed with chips of aromatic wood which mingled their scent with the smell of mulling wine. As they crossed the threshold Uricalus hurried forward to meet them.

'Aper!' he said. 'Delighted you could come!'

'A happy Festival to you, Uricalus.' Aper shook hands.

There were three other people in the room besides Bellicia and Albilla: the merchant Vegisonius, his wife Regulina, and the young tribune from the governor's reception. Agricola was in uniform. He looked bored and uncomfortable and was making no effort to hide the fact. Severinus raised a hand in greeting and got a sour smile in return.

Uricalus was beaming as usual. 'We're almost met,' he said. 'The governor, alas, had other commitments, but I expect the honour of the procurator's presence.'

'Catus is coming?' Aper helped himself to a cup of spiced wine from the waiting wine-slave's tray. 'I thought he was in London.'

Uricalus's smile broadened and he leaned back on his heels. 'He arrived here two days ago. Urgent business with the governor, so I understand. In any case, he was gracious enough to accept the last-minute invitation.'

That certainly made sense, Severinus thought. The governor might get away with representation by proxy – why else would Agricola be here? – but not the procurator. Uricalus controlled too many of the province's growing trading interests to be ignored. Besides, Catus was a merchant himself, or he had been. Before the emperor had given him the procuratorship he had run a trading house of his own in southern Gaul. Catus, at least, would be at home here . . .

'Marcus! Have you had a good Festival?'

He turned. Albilla was standing beside him, looking stunning in a mantle of white Coan silk. They were alone: Uricalus had led Aper off to talk with Vegisonius, while Bellicia and Regulina had claimed his mother.

'Yes, not bad, thanks,' he said. 'You?'

Her carefully made-up eyes sparkled. 'Father gave me this.' She indicated the mantle. 'He ordered it specially from Rome. Do you like it?'

'It's beautiful.' It was also expensive; not just Roman, but from one of the best shops. 'And it suits you.'

'Does it? I'm glad.' Albilla's nose wrinkled. 'There was a great clanking pair of earrings that came with it that I've left in their box. If I'd worn them I'd've had earlobes down to my shoulders. Father tries, Marcus, but sometimes his taste slips. You were right not to take him up on that glassware, it's completely hideous.'

Severinus was laughing; he liked Albilla. He liked her very much.

'Perhaps it's just as well I found Mother the brooch, then,' he said.

'Is that the one she has on tonight?' Albilla glanced round. 'It's nice. Where did you get it?'

'One of the native shops outside the south gate.' Severinus told her the full story. Albilla stared at him.

'You mean the girl actually offered to pay the man's debt with the bracelet from her own arm?' she said.

'That's right.'

'But why on earth should she do that?'

Severinus shrugged. 'She saw it as an obligation. At least that was what she said.'

Albilla laughed. 'But that's lovely! So sweet and unspoiled!'

'I wouldn't exactly describe Senovara as sweet.'

'How about unspoiled?' Albilla's eyes were mischievous.

'Perhaps. In a way. Who had you in mind as doing the spoiling?'

'Oh, us, of course! Us Romans. We spoil everything and everyone; we can't help it, it's the way we're made.' She looked over Severinus's shoulder. 'Isn't that right, Tribune?'

Severinus turned round to see Agricola standing behind him. He moved aside reluctantly.

'My apologies.' Agricola still looked bored. 'I really wasn't listening.'

'Of course you weren't.' Albilla was smiling up at him; like her father she was tiny, barely the height of Severinus's shoulder. 'But let's pretend you were. Don't you think we Romans spoil everything for the natives? I mean, wherever we go we take away the poor dears' culture and destroy their traditional way of life and so on. It's sad, wouldn't you say?'

'Not at all.' Agricola spoke stiffly. 'Barbarians are barbarians. We have a duty to civilise them.'

'Really?' Her eyes widened. 'Wouldn't you like to be a barbarian, Tribune? Just now and again?'

Agricola frowned. 'How do you mean exactly?'

'Oh, not a proper barbarian. I'm sure you're right, all those wives in common and things, it must be dreadfully messy.' Albilla smiled. 'Just a pretend one.'

Agricola's frown deepened. 'I'm not altogether sure, Arrenia Albilla, that I quite understand what . . .'

'Just for fun, of course. Barbarian costume parties are all the rage at Rome. Didn't you know? The emperor's very fond of them, so I'm told.'

'Ah.' Agricola's brow cleared. 'Actually, I really don't think . . .'

'We could have one here. You'd look simply marvellous in trousers and a stick-on moustache. And we could have a buffet with whatever barbarians eat.' She turned to Severinus. 'What *do* barbarians eat, by the way, Marcus?'

Severinus had been happily watching the flush spread upwards from Agricola's neck.

'Barley porridge,' he said. 'And pike.' Agricola stared at him, eyes bulging. He smiled back blandly.

Albilla made a face. 'Well, I'm sure our cook could work something out. It's still a marvellous idea. I'll mention it to Father. You'd come, wouldn't you, Tribune?'

A wild, trapped look had appeared in Agricola's eyes. He gave a stiff bow and without another word left to join Aper and Vegisonius in the far corner of the room.

Albilla watched him go. She was looking smug. 'I enjoyed that,' she said.

'So I noticed.' Severinus was trying very hard not to laugh.

'Well, the poor man does take himself so terribly seriously. And I wasn't altogether joking. I think the costume party's a lovely idea. You could ask your girlfriend to lend me a dress.'

'Girlfriend?'

'The one in the shop. Senovara.'

This time Severinus really did laugh. 'Albilla, she'd spit in my eye! And I don't know her at all!'

'Is that so?' Albilla smiled. 'Well, it doesn't matter.' She looked up. 'Oh, that must be Catus.'

Severinus turned round. In the doorway behind him was a small dapper man, not much taller than Uricalus and impeccably dressed in a narrow-striped lambswool mantle. The mark of rank apart, there was nothing particularly remarkable about him. Where Paullinus had stood out in the crowd, Severinus had the impression that Catus would escape notice, as much from choice as by nature; he exuded at the same time a grey anonymity and an air of self-assurance.

Money, Severinus thought. Money and power. And he knows he has both, without having to prove it to anyone.

'Marcus?'

'Hmm?'

'You're wool-gathering.' Albilla reached over and took his arm. 'Come on. Now the procurator's here we can finally eat. You're sitting beside me. I've arranged it.'

10

The dining-room was large and opulent: Uricalus had bought the furnishings through an agent in Rome at the auction of a disgraced senator's estate, and the couches and table – or so he liked to tell his guests – had once belonged to an eastern client-king. They waited for the major-domo to place them. Catus was in the place of honour, and, as Albilla had said, she and Severinus were sharing the couch nearest the door, along with Agricola.

'Well, now.' Uricalus lay down on the host's couch with Bellicia beside him. 'This is cosy, isn't it? I hope you're all hungry.' He held out his hands for the slave to wash. 'Delphidius!'

The major-domo snapped his fingers and the trays of starters began to appear. Uricalus's cook, like everything else the man owned, was the best in the Colony. Tonight he had obviously been told to impress, and he had succeeded.

'Holy Jupiter!' Severinus murmured to Albilla as the table filled. 'Are we supposed to eat all of this?'

'I'm going to have a good try, Marcus.' Albilla was already reaching for a stuffed olive. 'I've been starving myself since breakfast.'

'Albilla!' Bellicia, reclining directly opposite between Uricalus and Ursina, glared at her. 'Remember the emperor, please!'

Albilla drew her hand back quickly, and Severinus grinned. Even Albilla took notice of Bellicia. Uricalus's wife was a head taller and fifty pounds heavier than her husband, with a prizefighter's jaw, eyes like bradawls and a voice like a legionary centurion's. As the daughter of Burdigala's richest wine shipper and the wife of the Colony's most prominent private citizen she had definite opinions on etiquette.

The last of the slaves emptied his tray and the emperor's statue was brought in. While Uricalus sprinkled the pinch of incense on to its burner, Severinus glanced across at his father, lying on the third couch with Vegisonius and his equally large taciturn wife. Aper shot him a wink.

The statue was removed. Uricalus watched with satisfaction as the wine waiters carried round their jugs.

'Fine,' he said. 'This should keep us going for the moment.'

It was obviously a rehearsed remark. There was a ripple of answering laughter, but although Uricalus had had his eye on the procurator Severinus noticed that Catus did not join in. He wondered whether the man ever smiled, or reacted to anything in any way.

'Arabian truffles, eh?' Vegisonius had been inspecting the dishes with professional interest, prodding the nearest with his spoon. 'Where the hell did you pick these up, Publius? Not from me, that's certain. I've been after them for months.'

'Quintus!' His wife nudged his arm. 'Not now, please, dear!'

'Just a question, Regulina.' Vegisonius showed no embarrassment.

'From a London trader.' Uricalus was shelling a pea-hen's egg. 'A new man. Name of Barates.'

'An Armenian?' Vegisonius's eyebrows lifted in surprise. 'You don't see many of them west of Corduba.'

'Claudius Barates is from Syria.' Catus spoke quietly. His voice was as grey and anonymous as the rest of him. 'His family is originally Palmyran, so I believe, but they own an old-established trading firm in Antioch. I'm right, am I not, Uricalus?'

'Indeed, Procurator.' Uricalus turned to him eagerly. 'And quite a valuable addition to the province he is. One of the many recently. You're working miracles in attracting new blood, sir.

'I really have very little to do with it, Uricalus. Give London another twenty years and at its present rate of growth it'll be one of the largest centres of trade in the western empire.'

'Is that so, now?' Vegisonius laughed and reached for the pickled scallops. 'Maybe we should all move south, then, before it's too late.' He dug his wife in the ribs. 'Eh, Regulina?'

'I'm quite comfortable where I am, dear.' She sniffed. 'You'd agree, Bellicia?'

'Absolutely.' Bellicia's massive gold earrings caught the light as she nodded. 'The Colony's bad enough with all this new building, but London would be insufferable. All those dreadful warehouses.' She turned to Ursina. 'You'd hate it as well, wouldn't you, dear?'

His mother, Severinus noticed, had been keeping her head down. He didn't blame her: trapped between the two other women she had clearly decided to keep a low profile. She smiled and said nothing.

Catus's plate was still empty, and he had not touched his wine. 'You misunderstand me, Bellicia,' he said. 'Personally I envisage a partnership between the two centres with, for the foreseeable future at any rate, London playing the junior role. The governor, I'm sure, would concur.' He glanced towards Agricola. 'That's so, isn't it, Tribune?'

'Yes, sir.' Agricola had been looking bored. Now, with the procurator's eyes on him, he snapped to attention. 'The governor's most eager to encourage trade.'

Severinus hid a smile, noticing that Uricalus, too, had buried his face tactfully in his wine cup. Vegisonius grunted but said nothing.

'As every sensible man must be.' Catus selected a truffle and chewed with no obvious pleasure. 'Especially if he has charge of an imperial province. The emperor expects it.'

'I'm not surprised,' Albilla said. 'He must be getting through money like a gannet through a half-pound loaf.'

There was an embarrassed silence. Agricola, on the girl's other side from Severinus, made a small choking noise which was not laughter.

'*Albilla!*' Bellicia snapped.

Albilla turned wide, innocent eyes in her direction. 'But that's what Father always says!' She looked at Uricalus. 'Isn't it, Father?'

Uricalus reddened and concentrated on the pea-hen's egg he was holding.

Catus had reached for a truffle. 'Possibly not in company, my dear,' he said. 'And not in those precise terms.' He raised his eyes. 'All the same, you're right. It's no secret that the imperial finances are at a low ebb at present, which does mean to say that even a new province like ours must be largely self-financing. The new silver mines will make an appreciable contribution, of course, and calling in payment of the native debts will help to some degree, but I'm afraid that even taking our latest prospective windfall into account we're still considerably behind target and liable to remain so.'

'You're going ahead with that, then, sir?' Severinus said. 'Recalling the debt payments?'

'Naturally.' The pale grey eyes turned in his direction. 'Or, in default of payment, with the necessary sequestration.'

Aper cleared his throat.

'Without prejudice to the emperor's powers of judgment, sir,' he said, 'foreclosing on the loans has always struck me as a most misguided course of action.'

Catus half turned. 'Indeed, Commander? An interesting viewpoint.'

Aper didn't blink. 'Especially,' he went on, 'given your own very laudable desire for provincial prosperity.'

Severinus smiled: his father could be tactful, too, when he liked.

'That's a different kettle of fish entirely, Aper.' Vegisonius held up his wine cup for the slave to fill. 'The procurator was talking about us, not about the bloody natives. These beggars are out of the picture. As far as the economy's concerned they're irrelevant.'

'I disagree.' Aper was still looking at Catus. 'A discontented native population's always a threat to peace, and trade needs peace to thrive.'

'That's surely the governor's concern.' Catus gave a thin smile. 'He represents the military arm. We've invested sufficient funds in the maintenance of a garrison force for civic unrest to pose no threat. The natives can be as discontented as they please.'

'And if they're discontented enough to rebel?'

'Commander, that is most unlikely. The province has been quiet for years.'

'Aye. But now Paullinus is withdrawing troops for the spring campaign. And with Mona under threat the Druids're active again.' Aper looked at Agricola. 'You didn't catch the man, Tribune, did you?'

'No.' Agricola's face was expressionless. 'Unfortunately not. But we will.'

'I wouldn't be too sure about that, lad.' Severinus noticed that Vegisonius's hand, half hidden by the table, sketched the sign against magic. 'I heard the beggar disappeared into thin air. If he can do that once he can do it again.'

'There was no "disappearance", sir.' Agricola gave him a cold look. 'The centurion in charge of the detail was careless. He's been disciplined.'

Vegisonius shrugged and helped himself to a handful of pickled walnuts.

'One Druid is no particular matter.' Catus spoke quietly. 'Hardly enough to hang fears of a revolt on, certainly. Aper, you surprise me. I had not thought the ex-commander of a cavalry wing would be quite so . . . well, quite so negative in his views.'

Severinus saw his father's face harden. Quickly, he said, 'You mentioned a prospective windfall earlier, sir. What might that be?'

'Ah.' Catus had been lifting his wine cup to his lips. He hesitated, then continued the movement, took the barest sip and set it down. 'We – at least, the governor, and through him I – have just been informed of the death of the Icenian king Prasutagos.'

There was complete silence around the table. Only Agricola seemed unsurprised.

'Sweet holy Mothers!' Aper set down the spoon he was holding.

Catus reached for his napkin and wiped his fingers carefully. 'Naturally the political implications are considerable,' he said, 'although these are none of my concern. In fact, although I said "our" windfall – meaning the province's – my only involvement is as administrator of the emperor's private estates.'

'Prasutagos has left Icenia to the emperor?' Like Uricalus, Vegisonius was obviously keenly interested. Understandably so: if Icenia were to become part of the private imperial estates the implications for trade were huge.

'No.' Catus had pushed aside his plate. 'Prasutagos's will, I understand, names him as co-heir with his two daughters. Which means in effect, the girls being minors, that the property is held in trust by his widow Queen Boudica.' Catus folded the napkin and set it down. 'Now forgive me, Vegisonius, but that's really all I know myself at present. Perhaps we could change the subject.'

Meaning that Catus didn't want to say any more, Severinus thought. He glanced at his father. Aper's face was grim, and he could guess the reason. Prasutagos, originally ruler of only part of Icenia, had been Rome's ally since the Conquest. He had stayed loyal when the rest of the tribe had revolted eleven years before and been rewarded with the over-kingship; since when he had held the Iceni on a tight rein. If they had not been particularly open to Roman influence, like the southern tribes which Cogidubnus ruled, then they had at least caused no further trouble.

But that had been wholly Prasutagos's doing. Now he was gone, the strong hand on the reins had gone too.

Jupiter!

Severinus felt a dig in his ribs, and turned. Albilla was grinning at him.

'Marcus, I didn't bribe Delphidius to put us together just so you could make eyes at the procurator,' she said.

'Was I?'

'Soulfully.' Her lips were no more than an inch from his ear and he could smell her perfume. 'Would you do something for me?'

'Maybe.' Severinus grinned back. 'That depends what it is.'

'Pass me the pea-hen's eggs. Before my father guzzles them all.'

He laughed, and reached for the plate.

11

'It's bad news, Marcus.' Aper was staring out into the darkness beyond the carriage windows. 'Very bad. The worst I've heard for a long time.'

'Catus seemed pleased enough.' Severinus remembered the procurator's dry, satisfied tone. 'And Uricalus and Vegisonius were delighted.'

'Aye, they would be. Do you wonder? For the procurator and the merchants Prasutagos's death is a godsend. The Iceni have governed themselves up to now, and they've taken just as much from us as they want and no more. The will changes that. With the emperor as co-ruler the kingdom's wide open for the first time since the Conquest. And if I'm any judge of character Catus intends to make the most of it.'

'But it's not that simple. Even Catus must see it isn't.'

'The man's a procurator, boy. Forget common sense, they've minds like bloody abacuses. It's how they get where they are. Especially with that lout in Rome throwing money around like nuts at a wedding.'

Ursina, half dozing next to him, opened an eye. 'That is no way to talk about the emperor, Titus,' she said.

'Is it not? I'll bet my pension against a mouldy loaf the greedy little beggar's ordered Catus to milk this for all it's worth. And Catus, being the good bureaucrat he is, will do exactly as he's told.'

'Come on, Dad,' Severinus said. 'Paullinus will have a say, surely. As governor he—'

'It has nothing to do with Paullinus.' Aper shifted his back irritably against the cushions. 'Catus made that clear enough. Prasutagos made a personal bequest to the emperor, which means that under law half of Icenia becomes Nero's private property. His *private* property, Marcus, not just a part of the province. Oh, I can see the man's reasons. It's been done often enough in the past; give the emperor his share and he'll ratify the other terms of the will. Only Prasutagos was dealing with the wrong man. Hoping that Nero'll be content with half's like asking a dog not to eat the whole of a pudding.'

'Dad, Catus isn't stupid.'

'I never said he was. I said he was a bureaucrat. An Icenia under direct control would be tidier than a client-kingdom. More profitable, too, and with men like Catus that's what counts.' Aper puffed out his cheeks. 'Ach, perhaps I'm doing the beggar an injustice. How did you get on with Albilla?'

'Well enough.'

Aper grunted. 'That's what it looked like. You watch yourself there, Marcus. That girl has her eye on you.'

'Titus.' Ursina opened both eyes this time. 'Marcus doesn't need your help. Or your hindrance.'

'Is that so, now, Bear-cub? Well, if I'm to be related to Uricalus and Bellicia I'd like a little warning. If only to put my soul in order. You hear me, Marcus?'

'Aye.' Severinus was laughing. 'Don't worry, Dad.'

'Oh, I'm not worrying.' Aper looked sideways at Ursina. 'She's a good lass. I wouldn't pass her over myself, even with Bellicia for a mother-in-law.'

Ursina leaned over and kissed him. 'Then perhaps it's as well that you're married already.'

'Dad' – Severinus felt the grin pull at his mouth – 'I like Albilla, she's a good friend but that's as far as it goes. Does that satisfy you?'

'I couldn't care less about myself, boy. But don't forget you've been warned, and you can't speak for the girl. If I'm right she has other ideas. Not to mention that family of hers.'

'I think, Titus,' Ursina said carefully, 'you may be wrong, about the family at least. Bellicia was definitely casting glances at young Julius Agricola.'

'Was she indeed?' Aper chuckled. 'Then you may be off the hook, Marcus. Or if you are interested you'd better get a move on. A senatorial tribune'd be a prime catch, better than an auxiliary cohort commander, and unless I miss my guess that particular lad'll go far and fast. Bellicia knows it, too. The girl's another matter altogether, though. Again I may be wrong, but she didn't seem exactly taken with our polished young namesake.'

'She isn't.' Severinus felt a small unaccountable surge of satisfaction. 'Besides, Agricola's on the governor's staff. He'll be leaving with Paullinus when the campaign starts in the spring.'

'So you have been thinking about it?'

'Maybe.'

'Jupiter preserve us all!' Aper lay back.

Five miles away, the Druid Dumnocoveros crouched amid the encircling reeds, preparing for his journey. It had taken him three days to find the roots and herbs that he needed. Most of them did not grow on the island, and he had had to risk capture by the Wolves who, he knew, would still be searching for him despite their Winter Festival. Even so, the lateness of the season had made certain substitutions necessary. He offered up a quick prayer to the gods and placed the tiny wad beneath his tongue.

Its bitter juices filled his mouth, burning their way towards his empty belly: the rite had demanded fasting. Wrapping his rain-damp cloak tightly about his shoulders, he lay down and waited for the magic to take him.

Time passed, and slid imperceptibly into no-time . . .

He was walking along a causeway; a road of hard-packed earth laid atop a base of half-rotted wickerwork and alder logs beneath which the mud oozed. All around him the land stretched beneath a dome of blue, shield-flat and empty to the horizon. The sun, low at his back, bright and cold as a coin, shone on a sparkling maze of water, rough grass and light green moss broken by clumps of willow, ash and osiers, tall reeds and bullrushes. Overhead, legs trailing, wings slow as heartbeats, a single heron flew, the tail of a fish projecting from its bill. A brace of grebe paddled among the sedges, oblivious of his presence.

Dumnocoveros looked around him. He was in the marshes, but they were not the marshes of the estuary: there was no sea-smell, only the dark brown scent of standing fenwater. This was nowhere that he knew.

A man was coming towards him, running along the causeway

with the steady jogging trot of a hunter. As he came closer Dumnocoveros noticed that, hunter or not, he was painted for war. Across his bare chest lay a huge belt, and the cloak round his shoulders was fastened with a double brooch.

Dumnocoveros waited. As he came closer, the man slackened his pace. When they were no more than a spear's length apart he stopped, his hand raised palm outwards: the greeting of equal to equal.

'Well met, Druid.' His voice was soft and pleasant, and the three great jewels on his belt glinted in the light. Like Dumnocoveros, he cast no shadow on the road ahead. 'You're bound for the Dun?'

'Should I be, lord?' Dumnocoveros knew, now, where he was. And, more important, who the warrior was. The spittle had dried in his mouth.

'How not? The king is already dead and the wolves are sniffing at the corpse.'

'Is it far?'

The man shrugged. 'Not in days' travel, but with the wolves running no journey is short, and the safest roads are crooked ones. You should go now, if you don't wish to miss the start of the feast.'

'You're not bound there yourself, then, lord?'

'No.' The man smiled. 'But it will follow me southwards, and there'll be enough for all. Meanwhile I have my own hunting to do.'

The hairs on Dumnocoveros's neck lifted. 'I wish you success,' he said.

'Aye.' The man's steel-grey eyes looked into his. 'Success to all of us, and a clean kill at the end.' He paused. 'You understand me, Dumnocoveros?'

'Yes, lord.' Dumnocoveros nodded, feeling nothing. 'I understand you completely.'

'Completely?' The lips arced. 'A big word, and not one I'd care to use myself. But go to the Dun with my blessing. Tell the queen I'll be waiting to greet her and her folk when all is over. On the far side of the river.'

'I'll tell her.' Dumnocoveros swallowed. 'She will be honoured, lord.'

'None deserve it more. And now time is short, and we are both hurried.' The man's voice shifted. 'Bid Boudica follow the hare, Dumnocoveros!'

Something moved between his feet. Dumnocoveros glanced down at the white hare that had sprung suddenly from beneath the hem of the hunter's cloak and was already racing southwards along the line of the causeway. When he looked up, the man had again raised his hand. The cloak brooches at his shoulders and the jewels in his belt pulled light from the sun and caught fire, red, yellow and blue, spreading until the colours blotted out his body and the landscape around him. Dumnocoveros stepped back, hands raised to cover his eyes.

When the light faded he found himself alone and in darkness, no longer lying wrapped in his cloak but standing erect, looking upwards. The clouds had cleared. Above him, etched silver on black, lay the Belted Hunter, his face towards the River and with the Hare running beneath him. As Dumnocoveros watched, the star that marked the point of the Hunter's leading shoulder seemed to pulse, momentarily outshining all the rest before fading to its customary dimness: Segovica, the Woman Warrior.

His belly heaved. Crouching, racked with pain, he spat the wad of herbs from his mouth, and with it a stream of bile mixed with specks of blood. The spasm passed, leaving him empty, hollow as an old snail shell.

He scraped a shallow hole in the ground and buried the herbs, stamping the grass flat. The Wolves had no magic, but it was as well to be safe.

Then he began the journey northwards.

12

With the new year the weather grew drier and colder. Now, in mid-January, ice reached out from the banks towards the centre of the river and the reeds stood frozen in the estuary pools. It had snowed in the night, the first snow of winter, and the sweep of the Dun's rampart was softened by a white blanket that sparkled in the late-morning sunshine.

'You honestly don't mind me dragooning you like this, Marcus?' Albilla said as they rode towards the gate. 'I really am grateful. Father knows nothing about horses, and he wouldn't be seen dead out here. I had to fight like mad to get permission, and Catti's laid up with his back again.' Catti was Uricalus's groom. The cold wet weather always brought on his rheumatism.

'Why should I mind?' Severinus smiled at her. 'It's a beautiful day, even if the horse does turn out to be a worm-eaten nag.'

'Oh, nonsense. With a name like Lacta I'm sure she'll be absolutely lovely.'

'Jupiter!' He laughed. 'If that's your criterion for buying horses, Albilla, then you need all the help you can get!'

'Beast,' Albilla said. She looked very beautiful here in the snow, her cheeks flushed with the cold air, her dark hair shining against the white ermine fur of her hood.

They passed through the gate. Albilla pulled at her pony's rein, bringing Phoenix to a halt.

'We should come here more often. It looks nice in the snow, doesn't it? Even the dung heaps are pretty.'

Severinus pointed. 'If your directions are right then Mori's compound should be over there,' he said. 'Remember to let me do the talking.'

'I'll have no choice, Marcus. The poor man doesn't speak a word of Latin, my Celtic's non-existent and I'm hopeless at bargaining anyway.' Albilla's nose wrinkled. 'You'd think they'd build proper houses, wouldn't you, not these shack things. They're all very picturesque and everything, but it must be horrible actually to live in them. Do you think we'll be asked inside?'

'Probably.' Severinus urged Tanet forward along the snow-covered track. With the hard frost of the last few days, the mud had frozen solid and the going was much easier than it had been when he had come this way a month before. 'And if you do decide to buy the horse then certainly.'

'Oh, well, it'll be an experience. And I've never tasted fermented mare's milk.'

Severinus stared at her. 'What the Mothers has that to do with anything?'

'I thought that was what the natives drank. Or am I confusing them with Germans?'

'Aye, I think you probably are.' Severinus was trying hard not to smile. 'Although I'm sure they'd find some for you if you asked.'

'No thank you.' Albilla made a face. 'I'd drink it, of course, out of politeness but that doesn't mean—' From the compound ahead of them came a furious squealing and grunting. 'Juno, what on earth is that?'

They had the answer as they came through the compound gate. In the middle of the yard in front of the farm hut was a pig. Four men were hauling on the ropes that fastened its legs, while a fifth held a knife to its throat. Nearby a woman waited holding a bronze bucket.

'They're killing it!' Albilla had reined up sharply. 'How horrible!'

As they watched, the man with the knife slit the pig's throat. The squeals changed to a bubbling cough, and the men with the ropes leaned back as the animal's struggles grew more frantic. The woman held out the bucket and blood gushed into it, splashing her hands.

Albilla was watching in fascinated horror.

'Marcus,' she whispered, 'help me, please. I think I'm going to be sick.'

The pig collapsed, twitching, its legs spread wide, and the coughing changed to a wheezing gurgle. Then that, too, stopped and the pig's head lolled. Severinus glanced at Albilla. Her face was chalk-white Quickly, he dismounted and helped her down. She turned away and vomited while he held her shoulders.

The man with the knife came over.

'Is the lady all right?' he said in Celtic.

'She'll be fine,' Severinus said. 'Your name's Mori?'

'Moricamulos, aye.' He wiped the knife on a scrap of straw and tucked it into his belt. 'You'll have come for Lacta? She's in the paddock behind.' He hesitated. 'My wife'll take the lady inside. It would be better.'

'What did he say, Marcus?' Albilla had taken a napkin from beneath her cloak and was wiping her lips.

'He asked if you wanted to go in.'

Albilla's eyes went to the woman with the bucket. She was big and brawny, almost as well muscled as her husband. The pig's blood had splashed over her bare arms and mottled her face with specks of red.

Albilla shuddered. 'Tell him no thank you. Marcus, that was horrible!'

'It was only a pig-killing. You've never seen one before?'

'No.' Albilla took a gulp of air. 'You can let go of me now. I'm all right.'

'You're sure?' He dropped his arm reluctantly.

'Of course I'm sure! Marcus, stop fussing, please!' She took another deep breath and held it. She did not look at the pig, now a mound of dead flesh on the red-soaked earth. 'Is this the right place?'

'Aye. The horse is round the back.' Severinus turned to Moricamulos. 'The lady will come as well. My thanks, though, for the offer.'

'Is it the morning sickness? Lacta's quiet enough, but perhaps not the horse for a woman in cub. I've another that might suit her better, if you'd care to see it.'

'No, she's not pregnant.' Severinus stifled a grin. 'Just squeamish.'

'So.' Moricamulos nodded, satisfied. 'My sister's daughter's the same. Heaven help the man she marries. Well, come you both this way.'

He led them round the side of the hut.

The mare stood alone in the paddock, pulling at a net of hay fastened to a hurdle. She was a beauty, milk-white like her name and a full fourteen hands, almost Tanet's size and much bigger than Severinus had expected. Younger, too, no more than four years old. Judging by the sheen on her coat and the ripple of muscle at shoulder and hind she had been well fed and looked after. That, at least, he had expected: the British cared for their horses as well as they did for their children.

'She's broken to the saddle?' he asked.

'Aye.' Moricamulos had stopped a good three yards short of the hurdle; he would go no closer, Severinus knew, with the smell of blood on his hands. 'I did it myself.' He whistled, and the mare cantered over readily and stood waiting without any trace of nervousness: another good sign. 'Go you in and look, sir. Take your time.'

Severinus moved the hurdle aside. The mare watched him, but she did not move.

'You want to come too, Albilla?' he said in Latin.

'Of course.' Albilla still looked pale. 'She's lovely, isn't she?'

'Aye. And the man seems honest enough.' Severinus walked across the patchy grass, his eyes taking in the mare's points. They were all good: strong hip bones, a clean coat with no bald patches, spine straight with no bowing. He reached out and touched her head. The mare shifted and blew down her nose, bending her muzzle down to butt his chest. 'I'd say you're in luck. She's a fine animal.'

'Can I try her out? Just here in the paddock.'

'Best let me first.' He turned. 'Moricamulos!'

'Aye.'

'Have you a saddle and a set of tack we can borrow?'

'Surely.' The man disappeared in the direction of the barn.

Albilla was stroking the horse's neck while she fed her the apple she had brought. Her eyes were as bright as the mare's.

'Marcus, she's absolutely beautiful,' she said. 'And I'm sorry for being so silly earlier. It was just . . .'

'Forget it.' Severinus had squatted down and was examining the horse's hooves. They were thick and strong, with no splits. 'I didn't expect it myself. Most of the farmers have done their winter slaughtering long since.' He straightened and wiped his hands on his cloak.

'What did Mori say to you, by the way? Just before he brought us round?'

'He thought you might be pregnant.'

Albilla laughed. 'That's lovely! I hope you told him I was.'

Their eyes held for a moment. Severinus looked away.

'There's a good stretch of field here,' he said. 'I'll take her round it and if she handles well then you can have a go yourself. Then if we're both still happy with her we can get down to talking price.'

'Good.' Albilla paused. Then she said, in a different voice, 'Marcus, why don't you like me?'

'What?' He raised his eyes, startled.

'It's a simple enough question.' She was fondling the lock of hair on Lacta's forehead, not looking at him. 'You don't, do you?'

'Of course I like you!'

'No, you don't. You know what I mean. You make that quite obvious.' She turned. 'Or maybe it isn't me, or just me. Maybe it's my parents. Oh, I know they can be pains, but they're quite sweet, really, even Mother on a good day, and they try so hard.'

'Albilla, for the gods' sake! I don't dislike your parents!' Severinus found himself flushing: he had never felt comfortable with lies, even white ones.

Albilla shook her head. 'I wouldn't have mentioned it,' she said, 'but, well there's that stuffed fish Gnaeus Agricola. He's very good-looking, of course, and Mother's quite keen. I don't actually dislike him, but the thought of an engagement . . .'

The word had been said. Severinus looked away, and the silence lengthened.

'Here we are.' Moricamulos reappeared carrying a saddle, saddlecloth and harness. 'I'll have her ready for you in a moment.'

'No, give them to me.' Severinus turned away from Albilla. 'I'll do it myself.'

He saddled and bridled the mare while Moricamulos watched with critical approval. Then, still not looking at Albilla, he mounted the horse and gathered up the reins.

'I'll just take her across the field,' he said.

'Fair enough,' Moricamulos grunted.

Severinus raised his hand and swung the horse round, feeling her eagerness between his thighs, the ripple of firm muscle and taut sinew. He set her off on a light rein towards the gap leading from paddock to field, then brought his knees together and crouched low, giving her her head.

She took off like a bird and the wind caught him, cold against his exposed skin with a dusting of fresh, powdery snow. He dug his knees in harder and felt the mare respond, reaching for the gallop. A bare three strides from the broken line of the beck at the field's far side he dropped the rein and pulled her round hard in a cavalry turn, then as her hindquarters dropped drove both knees into her flanks and crouched low into her withers, sending her downstream like an arrow. At the edge of the field he turned again in a flurry of earth and snow and brought her to the gallop in a long, wide sweep towards his starting point. As he neared the hurdle where Moricamulos and Albilla were waiting, he straightened in the saddle, pulling gently on the reins. The mare slackened her pace to a walk. He pulled her up short and dismounted.

Moricamulos had been watching him closely.

'Aye,' he said. 'Good. Very good. I couldn't have done much better myself.'

'She's a fine horse.' Severinus patted the mare's flank. 'You've trained her well.'

'I've taken a bit of trouble with her.' Moricamulos grinned. 'She'll be as good as any in a year or two, a proper swallow. Mind you, I'm thinking that the lady will be somewhat less demanding.'

Severinus offered Albilla the reins. 'Your turn,' he said.

She shook her head. 'How was she?'

'Perfect. A beauty, soft as milk. You were right, she's well named.'

'Then we'll buy her.'

'You don't want to ride her first?'

'No. I'll take your word for it. Besides, in these conditions I'd probably fall off.' Albilla grinned, although the smile did not touch her eyes. 'Isn't that what Mori was saying?'

'No.' Severinus felt uncomfortable. 'Not at all. You're sure?'

'I'm sure.' Albilla kissed the mare's nose, then looked up again. 'Anyway, I don't care if I can never ride her, Marcus. She's sweet. Buy her for me?'

'If you want.'

'Yes, I do want. Very much.'

Her eyes were still on his. Severinus turned to Moricamulos. 'The lady is asking the price,' he said.

Moricamulos reached out and touched the horse's muzzle. 'It's cold out here for haggling. We'll go inside and settle matters in comfort.'

The hut was smaller than Brocomaglos's, but just as neat and clean, and the fire was bright and smokeless. At its edge, set on an iron grid, a jug steamed.

'You'll take some ale?' Moricamulos said.

'Gladly.'

The Dunsman poured two horn cups and held them out. 'Your health. Yours and the lady's.' He indicated two wicker chairs beside the hearth. 'Sit you down and warm yourselves.'

Albilla sat carefully. Severinus noticed that her lips puckered as she sipped the honey beer, but she did not set the cup aside.

'So.' Moricamulos had pulled up a stool for himself. 'Our Lacta pleased you.'

'Very much.'

'She should. Her grandmother was from the old king's stable.'

'The old king?'

'Cunobelinos.'

'Is that so, now?' It could have been a ploy – Cunobelinos's horses were already legendary – but the mare had good blood, that was obvious. 'She's big for a native-bred horse, all the same.'

'Aye.' Moricamulos blew on his beer. 'She's a cross. Her father was one of yours, a Spaniard, although I had him from the Iceni.'

'The Iceni breed from Roman stock?'

'For racing, aye.' Moricamulos laughed. 'They're mighty racers, the Iceni.

Severinus looked at Albilla. She was sitting prim as a schoolgirl, holding her cup with both hands, sipping at it like medicine. 'So. What price would you set on this princess among horses?'

Moricamulos rose and took the jug from the hearth. Carefully, he filled his own cup, then Severinus's.

'Ten gold pieces,' he said.

Severinus caught the finality in the man's voice: there would be no haggling, it seemed, after all. The price was high, but fair. He turned to Albilla and repeated it in Latin.

'Does the lady agree?' Moricamulos sipped his beer.

'Tell him yes, Marcus.' Albilla was smiling.

Severinus smiled back. 'Then you've bought yourself a horse,' he said.

They set off back towards the gate of the Dun, Albilla in front. Moricamulos had included the borrowed saddle and harness in the price and she was riding Lacta with her pony following on a short halter. Severinus was frowning as he rode. He liked the girl; of course he did, he liked her very much, he always had. Perhaps he even loved her. But she had been right all the same . . .

'You're very quiet, Marcus.' Albilla had turned round.

'Mm?' He jerked on the rein and Tanet's head came up. 'I'm sorry. I was just thinking.'

'What about?'

'That perhaps we should get engaged.'

The words were out, too late now to call back. Albilla pulled Lacta up and waited for him to draw level.

'That's not funny,' she said. 'Not even remotely so.'

'It wasn't meant to be.'

They stared at each other, knees touching. Then, very slowly and carefully, Albilla leaned over and kissed him.

'In that case, yes,' she said. 'Yes, I would like that very much.'

Severinus laughed. He leaned over and pulled Albilla towards him. The two horses shifted.

'Marcus! Be careful!' Albilla was laughing too now. 'You'll have us over!'

He slackened his grip. 'My father's going to kill me for this. You know that, don't you?'

'Not if Mother gets you first. She's invited Gnaeus Agricola to dinner tonight.'

The horses began to move apart, and they straightened in the saddle. Albilla's face was bright red. Severinus suspected that his own was, too.

'Then it's the perfect time to break the news,' he said.

13

'You're *what*?' Aper stared at him from where he lay on the dining couch.

'Engaged to Arrenia Albilla.'

'Jupiter's holy beard, boy!' The book his father had been reading rolled itself up unnoticed in his lap. 'It's not a month since you told me—'

'Titus, that's quite enough.' Ursina leaned over in her own chair and hugged her son. 'Congratulations, Marcus. From both of us.'

'It surprised me, too, Dad.' Severinus kissed his mother's cheek. 'If that's any consolation.'

'None whatsoever.' Aper wound the worn translation of Xenophon on to its spool and replaced it in the box at his side. 'You daft young bugger!'

'*Titus!*'

Severinus laughed. 'It can't be that bad, surely?'

'It's all right for you,' Aper said. 'Albilla's a good enough girl. But, oh, gods, Marcus, I could've done without Bellicia for a relative!'

'Don't be silly.' Ursina smiled and wiped her eyes on her mantle. 'Do her parents know yet, Marcus?'

'Albilla's probably telling them right this minute.' Severinus sat down and helped himself to a cup of wine from the jug on the brazier.

'Uricalus'll be cock-a-hoop, that's certain.' Aper held out his own cup for Severinus to fill. 'The old devil's been angling for this for years. Bellicia now . . . well, with that young tribune almost in the bag I reckon if we listened hard enough we could hear the screams.'

'Nonsense, Titus.' Ursina's lips twitched. 'Bellicia will be delighted, I'm sure, like the rest of us.'

'Aye, maybe. And pigs might fly.'

'When is the wedding to be, Marcus? Have you and Albilla decided?'

'Not for a while yet. At least a year. I don't break all my promises, and I've the Foxes to consider.'

'I'm delighted you remembered that, at least, boy,' Aper grunted. 'It shows you haven't lost your senses altogether.'

'I seem to recall that you were quite anxious yourself to get me in post after we were engaged, dear,' Ursina said.

'That was different, Bear-cub. You know it was.'

'Was it?'

'I was stationed at Mainz. Braniacum's the back of beyond.'

'It isn't all that far away. Just this side of the Icenian border.'

'Dad's right, Mother,' Severinus said. 'We can wait. Besides, I doubt if Albilla's in any hurry to swap the Colony for a barrack block.'

'She'll have to eventually all the same. If she's lucky and you get permission to take her in post with you.' Aper's eye rested on his son. 'You've both thought of that, I suppose?'

'Aye. We have.' Severinus tried to keep his voice light; Aper had made a valid point, and all of them knew it. Ursina had been a soldier's daughter herself and used to forts, while Albilla was from a merchant family. His father was right; there was all the difference in the world. 'She'll be fine when the time comes.'

'Of course she will,' Ursina said quickly. 'You're very lucky, both of you.'

'That you are.' Aper stood up. 'Well, I hadn't expected to be drinking Falernian tonight but events seem to demand it. We've a jar in the cellar I was keeping for a special occasion. Come and help me find it, Marcus.'

Severinus shot him a puzzled glance, but his father was already on his feet and moving off. He got up and followed.

The wine cellar lay down a half flight of steps to the rear of the kitchen. Aper picked up an oil lamp from the table, lit it at the stove and led the way in silence. At the bottom he turned. His expression, in the flickering light of the lamp, was serious.

Severinus knew trouble when he saw it. Whatever his father wanted with him, it was not help with the wine.

'Dad, I . . .' he began.

Aper waved him down. 'No, boy, it's nothing to do with your engagement. Or not directly. Albilla has her head screwed on, and she knows what she's letting herself in for. I've no quarrel with her.'

'So you don't mind?'

'Jupiter, would it matter if I did?' Aper half laughed. 'I'd have made a different choice, especially with Uricalus and Bellicia as parents-in-law, but that's neither here nor there. Don't worry. You have my blessing, as always.'

Severinus smiled. 'So what is it?'

His father set the lamp down on the stone rack that stretched the length of the cellar.

'A bit of news. While you were off gallivanting this morning I was talking to Adaucius Montanus.'

'The procurator's man?'

'Aye. It seems he's had instructions from London about Prasutagos's will. Montanus doesn't like them more than half, but there isn't anything he can do about it. He's to send assessors to the royal Dun at Coriodurum to make a complete inventory for requisition. Public and private. By force, if necessary.'

'Mothers!' Severinus stared at him. 'The Iceni'll never stand for it!'

Aper's face was grim. 'That was Montanus's first thought too. He sent word back to Catus to that effect and got his backside chewed off for his pains by return.'

'But no one's that stupid! Not even a procurator'd—'

'Montanus is of the opinion that Catus doesn't care. He wants to provoke a revolt so we can annexe the kingdom.'

'But that's criminal!'

'It's politics, boy.' Aper shrugged. 'And criminal it may be, but more to the point it's bloody dangerous. Especially now.'

'Can't he be stopped? Surely the governor would never . . .'

'I talked to Paullinus myself. That was Montanus's reason for telling me. He's a good man, but he's no soldier. He knew if I went to the governor I'd have more chance of being listened to.'

'And were you?'

'Like hell I was! I had my own backside chewed off for interfering in matters that didn't concern me. Paullinus doesn't consider the Iceni a threat, or nothing Cerialis and the Ninth can't handle if they have to.' Aper's voice was sour. 'Also, of course, Catus is acting for the emperor. Even a governor can't ignore that bastard.'

'So what's Montanus going to do?'

'Carry out the order. He has no choice. Oh, he can delay things for a month or so, maybe longer, but before the year's much older he'll have to do as he's told. Which is why we're talking down here without your mother listening. You understand me, Marcus?'

Severinus felt slightly sick. Braniacum was a border posting, at the edge of Icenian territory, less than a day's ride from the royal Dun itself; quiet enough at present, but if the Iceni did rise then the Foxes would be first in line, perhaps even before the legion at Dercovium or the other auxiliaries to the west had time to intervene.

'Jupiter!' he murmured. 'Sweet holy Jupiter!'

'Aye.' Aper picked up the lamp and examined the labelled jars carefully. 'Well, at least you're forewarned. Now we'd best find that Falernian or your mother'll think I'm explaining the facts of life to you.' He grinned. 'Don't worry, boy. You can handle it, and if you do well you'll be on your way to a Wing.'

'You think I should talk to Albilla? Postpone the engagement?'

'That's for you to decide.' Aper had found the jar. He pulled it out by its handles and blew off the dust. 'Or perhaps for her. If it were up to me I'd say no, just as I've no intention of saying anything about this to your mother. Not for the time being, at least. There's no point in worrying either of them before it's necessary.'

'You think the Iceni will rebel?'

'Maybe, maybe not.' Aper swung the jar on to his shoulder. 'Who knows? It's in the gods' hands. Paullinus could be right. When the campaign gets under way he's leaving the Ninth intact, and an Eagle on your doorstep's a big disincentive to trouble. By all accounts Boudica's no fool, and she'd think twice before breaking the peace. Now forget about it for the moment, Marcus. I'm sure you've other things on your mind today than politics.' He winked. 'Come on. Let's get the best cups out and toast your future health properly.'

14

There were four of them in a circle around her, all men, their faces a blur but their hands very real, lifting her off her feet and pulling in different directions. Albilla screamed and struggled, but her arms and legs were held as if by ropes. She lifted her head. At the edge of the circle a fifth man stood with knife in his hand. In desperation, Albilla drew her right foot back as far she could and kicked out hard . . .

Her foot crashed against the corner of the bed-frame, and the noise and the shock of the blow jerked her awake. For a long time she lay trembling, disoriented. Her sleeping tunic felt cold and clammy against her bare skin.

Finally, she drew a deep breath and shuddered.

Killing pigs! she thought. Yuch!

She untangled herself from the sweat-soaked blanket and put the dream out of her head. The day had been worth a nightmare. Oh, yes. And her parents had been pleased with the news, even Mother. Albilla smiled to herself. When she'd told the tribune at dinner that she was engaged to Marcus he'd congratulated her without a blink. Agricola was Rome at her coldest. Thank Juno she'd spoken to Marcus before her mother could take things any further. Facing Marcus had needed all the courage she possessed, but it had been worth it.

Engaged!

Light was showing round the edges of the closed window shutters. Ignoring the chill that cut through her tunic, she got up and crossed the room. Its marble floor was ice-cold beneath her feet. When she and Marcus were married she would make sure that their bedroom had a wooden floor with thick native rugs.

She opened the shutters and looked out across the red tiled roofs of the Colony. Cold air and grey light flooded the room, bringing with them the scent of snow, woodsmoke and new bread. It was barely dawn, a bright, fresh morning with hardly a cloud. The slaves in the blacksmith's shop opposite were filling the charcoal bunker and blowing the fire to a red heat. One of the bellows had a hole in it, and for a moment the breathy wheezing reminded her of the pig in Mori's yard. Only for a moment: Albilla was too happy to think of nightmares. Down the road, her father's door-slave Justus stood chatting to the carter who was making his usual morning delivery of flour to the bakery on the corner. From the direction of the market came the creak and rumble of wagons.

The Colony was waking up.

Marcus would be awake, too: she knew that in the early morning he always took Tanet out for a gallop across the open land between the marshes and the river. If she hurried she could catch him.

Albilla dressed quickly; her mother wouldn't mind her going out alone, even to meet Marcus. Not now they were engaged . . .

She hurried down to the stable. The old groom Catti was snoring among the straw: the bout of rheumatism had passed, helped by the change in the weather and the wintergreen ointment that he made himself. Albilla woke him and had him saddle Lacta.

This was the difficult part. She pulled herself up into the saddle and sat with her eyes closed, feeling her head swim and fighting down the fear that pinched her stomach. Albilla knew she was no rider. If Marcus hadn't been so obviously impressed with the new mare – and if Albilla had not wanted so very much to impress *him* – she would never have bought her.

'Are you all right, miss?' Catti was looking concerned.

'I'm fine.' She shook her head to clear it and tried to smile down at him. 'She's big, isn't she?'

'Aye, she is that.' The old man patted Lacta's flanks and the mare shifted and tossed her head. 'And lively as a barrel of eels into the bargain. I can still saddle Phoenix for you, or if you were wanting company . . .'

'I said I was fine!'

Catti shrugged and stepped back. 'Suit yourself. You just be careful, though. You've only one neck to break, and that one's capable of doing it for you.'

Before she could change her mind, Albilla wheeled the mare round and out of the yard.

The estuary road was deserted. She bit her lip and tried to control the shaking of her hands on the reins. *Look at the world through the horse's eyes*, Marcus had told her again and again. *Read it like she does, and she won't surprise you.*

All right, she thought, I'll try. She forced herself to urge Lacta into a trot. The breeze in her face freshened with a scattering of powdery snow, and she tightened her thighs against the mare's flanks. Lacta responded at once, and Albilla, moving already as fast as she was used to, fought down her panic, resisting the urge to grip the mane. She's no different from Phoenix, you idiot, she told herself. Just bigger and stronger. You can manage her. You *can*!

As the fear began to slip away Albilla raised her head. She was almost at the bridge that led over the stream halfway to the marshes, and Lacta was moving at a steady canter, as fast as Phoenix could have galloped. She grinned. She was doing well; Marcus would be proud of her.

Lacta's hooves thudded on the slats of the bridge. Beyond it to the left the woods opened out into fields and grassland, and Albilla could see almost to the estuary. In the distance was another rider.

Marcus. It had to be Marcus.

Albilla laughed, and waved. There was no response, but he would have seen her, too. Conscious of his eyes watching, she slowed Lacta, then pulled the mare's head round, digging her right knee into her flank and sending her off the road, over the ditch and across the open country towards him.

She realised that the rider was not Marcus just at the moment when Lacta's left foreleg plunged into a dip hidden by the covering snow. The horse stumbled and lurched sideways, throwing her from the saddle.

The world turned over. She stretched out her hand to ward off the ground as it rushed up to meet her. Someone shouted. Pain lanced through her left arm and shoulder and her head thudded against a stone.

Then there was nothing.

*   *   *

Senovara had stopped to watch the lark.

It had sprung from the grass almost under her pony's hooves, a small unremarkable bundle of feathers that had bored a hole in the sky above her head and poured its music into it. She listened and watched entranced as the bird climbed, higher and higher into the clouds, its song still clear when its body had long since vanished. Her mother would have said that it was singing now for Taranis, and Senovara half believed it. Larks were Taranis's poets, and there was no greater honour for a human poet at death than to be reborn from a lark's egg.

Romans, she had heard, ate their tongues.

The last notes faded, and Senovara rode on.

The shrine in the marshes was difficult to find, especially in the pre-dawn dimness, and she had never been here before. Like the groves further inland, it had no altar and no image; the place itself was what had made it holy since before the tribe's memories began. There were only the twists of ribbon and strands of women's hair tied to the reeds and bullrushes to distinguish it from a thousand other spots along the estuary's banks.

Senovara felt her skin prickle as she slipped down from the pony's back. The faint mist rising from the water was curving into spirals that broke and re-formed independently of the breeze, and she could feel eyes watching her. Aye, she thought, shuddering a little, this place is special right enough.

The pony dropped his head to drink, then lifted it again as his lips met the salt. Senovara unfastened one of her braids and pulled out nine strands of hair, counting them carefully before binding the braid up again. Then she waited patiently for the sun to rise.

He came up over the marshes, a red curve of fire fringed with purple clouds, sending streamers north, south and west. On any other morning she would have stood and watched, but now there was no time. Quickly she tied the nine hairs around one of the reeds and stepped back.

'*Keep my brother Tigirseno safe, wherever he is,*' she prayed, knuckling her brow as she spoke. '*Bring him home alive.*'

The reed shook in the dawn breeze. The strands of hair fluttered, and suddenly the eyes seemed all around her.

Senovara turned. Without looking behind her she caught up the pony's reins, remounted and rode quickly away.

She had almost reached the road that led to the Roman port when she saw the girl fall.

Albilla woke. Something was pressing against her forehead where the pain lay, something soft and cool that leaked water into her eyes. She shifted her left arm, then screamed as new pain, worse than the other, shot through it. There was a small grating sound. She could not feel her fingers.

'Rest quiet,' someone said: a woman's voice, low and firm. The pad of moss against her forehead was moved away, then replaced. She opened her eyes, blinking the water from the lashes.

She was lying on her back. Inches from her she could see Lacta's muzzle. The mare's head was drooping and her reins trailed in the grass.

'Is she all right?' she said.

The girl moved round into sight while still keeping the pad pressed to Albilla's forehead. Her eyes, green and cool against the whiteness of her skin and her thick red hair, flashed with sudden amusement.

'You break your arm and you think of a horse?' she said. 'There's hope for Romans yet. She'll do well enough. A ... twisting. That's the word? Nothing worse.'

'You speak Latin.'

'A little. Or have you Celtic?'

'No.' Albilla tried to sit up. The pain came again and she turned and vomited into the grass. 'I'm sorry.'

'About having no Celtic? Or about the sickness?' The girl laughed. 'Neither matters. I told you, rest quiet while your soul comes back.'

Albilla felt the tears begin to prick against her eyelids. She forced them away. 'I want Marcus' she said. Even to herself she sounded like a sulky child, but she was past caring.

'Your husband? Brother?'

'Fiancé.' The girl's brow furrowed as if two strong lines had been cut there with a chisel. Albilla chose an easier word. 'Betrothed.'

'Ah. He's near here? He lives near here?'

'Yes. Marcus Severinus. Julius Aper's son.' Albilla's ears had begun to buzz, and she felt as if she were speaking through soft wool with a mouth that had suddenly stopped being hers. Someone else's voice said: 'Could you fetch him for me? Please?'

The girl's lips moved, but no sound came. There was only the buzzing in Albilla's ears, and then, again, blackness.

When she woke for the second time it was in a bed that was not hers. A face – not the girl's – was looking down at her.

'Marcus!'

'Aye. Who else?' He bent forward and kissed her forehead next to the dressing that someone had put on it. 'Well, you made a proper job of that, didn't you?'

'Yes. I'm sorry.' Albilla tried to smile. 'Where am I?'

'Home. My home, that is. Senovara brought you here an hour ago. Dad's sent Trinnus into town for the doctor.'

'Senovara? That's the girl you . . .'

'Brocomaglos's daughter.' Marcus grinned. 'Aye. You want to see her? She's still here.'

'In a moment.' Albilla swallowed. 'Marcus, I'm sorry.'

'What about?'

'The accident. It was my fault completely. I was—'

'Not now. It'll keep.' He closed her mouth with a finger.

'But I . . .' The tears came again, and this time she could not stop them. 'She isn't hurt, is she? Your mare?'

'Lacta's fine. A sprain. I've put a poultice on it. And she's not my mare, she's yours.'

'No.' Albilla shook her head. 'I can't ride her. Not well enough. She's too good for me.'

'That's nonsense!'

'It isn't nonsense. I tried. I tried my best. Marcus, I'm sorry!'

Her eyelids felt suddenly heavy, too heavy for the effort of keeping them open.

She slept.

'Thank you for bringing her back.' Severinus looked across at the tall girl with the red hair and green eyes leading her pony from the paddock.

Senovara shrugged. 'It was nothing. Luck. And I'm glad to pay the debt.'

'What debt?'

'For Eisu. At the shop.'

'There was no debt.'

'Was there not?' The girl laughed. 'Then there was no repayment. My congratulations, Marcus Severinus. You have a fine' – she hesitated – '*fiancée*.'

They had been speaking Celtic, but she used the Latin word. Severinus grinned. 'Aye, well,' he said. 'My thanks in any case.'

'You're welcome.' Senovara mounted her pony and turned his head towards the gate and the road that led back to the Dun. Severinus watched her until she was out of sight.

15

Braniacum, the Place of the Crows, was well named. As Severinus walked with Clemens towards the headquarters building the sound of their cawing was all around him.

'Are they always this noisy?' he said.

Clemens returned the salute of the guard on duty and mounted the steps on to the verandah. 'The birds? Aye, these buggers never shut up. Give it a year or so and you won't notice.'

Severinus smiled. 'Is that so?'

'Let's just say it's yet another thing I won't miss about the place.' Clemens opened the outer office door. The young military clerk behind the desk rose as they entered, stifling a cough. 'Here we are. At ease, Lucius. How's the cold?'

'Coming along nicely, sir.'

'That's good. Bloody climate.' Clemens opened the second door and stepped aside. 'After you, Severinus.'

Severinus looked around. The inner office was small and sparsely furnished with a desk and three chairs. A window opened on to the parade ground at the building's front.

Clemens closed the door behind him and took his place behind the desk.

'Don't stand on ceremony,' he said. 'Have a seat. It'll be all yours from tomorrow, anyway, Lucius's cold and all.'

Severinus sat down on one of the other chairs. He felt a little in awe of Clemens. The outgoing commander wore his own uniform as if he had grown into it and he was as compactly solid as a marble block, with hard eyes that looked far older than his thirty years.

'The men seem happy enough,' he said.

'Oh, you'll have no trouble with the Foxes.' Clemens's face split in a grin that made him look ten years younger. 'Especially since the nearest settlement worth the name's half a day's ride away. On the plus side the hunting's better than fair if you don't get sick of boar meat, but as far as entertainment goes that's all. We're pretty well cut off here.'

'I don't mind,' Severinus said.

'Is that so, now?' Clemens laughed. 'Jupiter! Well, I said the same myself when I started. Give it six months and you'll be climbing the walls like the rest of us.'

'It can't be that bad.'

'Oh, it is. And if you're wise you'll hope it stays that way.'

'You mean the procurator's assessment?'

Clemens's smile disappeared. 'So you know about that?'

'Aye. Adaucius Montanus is a friend of my father's. I've known of it for months.'

The other man grunted and leaned back in his chair. 'Well, it saves us a bit of time, anyway. It was something I wanted to talk to you about before I left. Jupiter alone knows what game Catus is playing, but if he isn't careful his so-called assessment'll set our friends across the border by the ears good and proper, and that'd be bad news for all of us.'

'You've been given a date?'

'I've been given several these past two months. Montanus has been dragging his heels, and good luck to him. We've been expecting his men to pass through here any of a dozen times, but every time he's called off at the last minute. Thank the Mothers someone has a bit of sense. If Catus thought with his head rather than his backside he'd countermand the order altogether.'

'You think there'll be trouble?'

Clemens pulled at his ear. 'You know the Iceni yourself, by reputation at least. They're a touchy lot, proud as hell, and for all her better qualities Boudica's no exception. Her chief adviser has no time for us, either, and he's a smart beggar who knows what he's about. Yes, I think there'll be trouble. I'd be a fool to expect otherwise.'

'My father thinks Catus wants a revolt. So we can annexe the kingdom.'

'Does he so?' Clemens frowned, but he showed no surprise. 'Then Catus is an even bigger damned fool than I took him for, especially now Paullinus is in the west with half the army.'

'There's the Ninth at Dercovium.'

'Cerialis has his own problems. He's the Corieltauvi and the Brigantes to watch out for, and that shower's as slippery as they come, Cartimandua or no Cartimandua. In any case, the Ninth's scattered. We're spread too thin to play games, and that's the simple truth. If the Iceni rise we'll have our hands full.' Clemens's lips pursed. 'Or you will. I wish you luck.'

'You're joining your new command soon?'

'Before the month's out.' That brought another sudden grin; a young man's grin, with the pride showing through. Severinus understood how Clemens felt: a cavalryman's first Wing was always special. 'The Sabinians. Backing the Fourteenth in the west. The governor's—'

He was interrupted by a knock at the door. Severinus turned as a stocky grey-haired man stepped into the room.

Clemens looked up. 'Modianus. Just the man,' he said. 'Your second-in-command, Severinus. Juventius Modianus. He'll keep you right. He managed with me for five years, so he's had plenty of practice.'

The cohort's senior centurion closed the door behind him and drew himself up to attention. His teeth through the smile were brown and uneven.

'Welcome to Braniacum, sir,' he said to Severinus. 'A pleasure to meet you. I served with your father.'

'You were at Alodunum?' Severinus's eyes took in the impressive array of discs on the centurion's chest.

'Aye, sir. How is the commander?'

'Well enough. He told me to give the Foxes his regards.'

'I'll tell the lads. There's still a few of the old-timers left, and they'll be pleased.' Modianus turned to Clemens. 'I'm sorry to interrupt you, sir, but I thought I'd better report straight off. There's word of a Druid in the fenland, up Catuvernum way.'

'Sweet holy Mothers!' Clemens looked at Severinus. 'Catuvernum's not five miles from the Icenian royal Dun.' He turned back to Modianus. 'How long has he been there?'

'A month at least, maybe longer.'

'A *month*?' Clemens stared at him. 'Jupiter Almighty! Why the hell didn't we know sooner?'

Modianus's expression was wooden. 'You know the locals

yourself, sir. It's not the sort of thing they'd talk about. Not to strangers. The trader who brought the news only had it by accident. We were lucky he took the trouble to report in.'

'He's still here?'

'Aye. I've got him outside.' The brown eyes twinkled, although the centurion's expression did not change. 'Not his idea, and he's a bit upset, but I thought you'd like a word personal.'

'Good. Give us a moment, then bring him in.' Modianus brought his fist up in a crisp salute and left, closing the door carefully behind him. 'A Druid among the Iceni's bad news, Severinus. Very bad, especially now. I'm sorry to land you with the problem.'

Severinus shrugged. 'It can't be helped,' he said. 'We'd one ourselves a few months back.'

'Did you indeed? You caught him?'

'We tried. He got away. This may be the same man.'

'Not necessarily. With Paullinus on his way to Mona the beggars'll be going all out to stir up trouble at his back throughout the province.'

'You'll bring him in?'

'No.' Clemens shook his head. 'This isn't the Colony, or even the frontier. Icenia's a client-kingdom, even with Prasutagos dead. Oh, aye, we'd be within our rights; Druids are the army's concern. But it would cause a lot of bad feeling, and we can do without that at present.'

'So what can you do?'

'Me?' Clemens's mouth twisted. 'Nothing. As of tomorrow he's not my business. What *you* can do is send word to Boudica, maybe even go to the Dun yourself. Let the queen know you know he's there, and Rome's not happy about it. If you're lucky, that'll be action enough.' He paused. 'And the other thing you can do, Severinus, is be careful. Be very careful. Find the man and have him watched.'

'You think Boudica knows?'

'Oh, she knows, all right. Forget the helpless widow, that one's twice as sharp as her husband ever was, three times as tough and ten times the better ruler. In that sense Catus is right. We'd be safer without her.'

'Prasutagos left the kingdom to his daughters.'

'Aye. So he did. But it'll be five years before the elder girl's old enough to rule. Meanwhile Boudica's regent, and as a daughter of the old royal house she had the better claim to begin with. That was why Prasutagos married her. Boudica's no Cartimandua, Severinus, never forget that. She has no love for Rome, and as far as her own people are concerned she doesn't need our backing. Taken with ability, that's a dangerous combination.' There was another knock at the door. 'All right, Modianus, we're ready. Come in.'

'The trader, sir.' Modianus stood to one side to allow the man to pass. He was a southern Gaul, big and fleshy, and he did not look happy.

'Very well,' Clemens said. 'That's all, Centurion. Thank you.' Modianus saluted and left, closing the door behind him. 'I'm sorry, sir, I wasn't told your name.'

The Gallic trader stood glaring.

'Titus Carvilius,' he said stiffly. 'Commander, I have a schedule to meet. I've already given your centurion what little help I can in this matter, and I really feel that—'

'Yes, sir. I realise you're busy, and we're very grateful.' Clemens was smiling, but his voice was firm. 'This is my successor, Julius Severinus. He's just arrived and will be handling the situation, but because he's unfamiliar with local conditions I thought perhaps a first-hand account would be preferable to a subordinate's report. If you can spare the time, naturally.'

'Well, I suppose that's reasonable.' Carvilius's stiff expression relaxed as he sat down on the room's only other chair. 'Certainly a few minutes won't make much difference to me. And I'm always ready to place what knowledge I may possess at the disposal of those less experienced than myself.'

'Quite.' Clemens did not look at Severinus. 'You travel in wine?'

'Wine and oil. Not the best quality, naturally, but the Iceni aren't connoisseurs.' He patted his large stomach. 'I do well enough. Three trips a year, and a full order book each time. This is my sixth year.'

'You supply the royal Dun?'

'And the outlying aristocracy, yes. At least when they pay in coin. Salt pork and pickled fish are all very well in small amounts, but by the cartload they're hardly negotiable currency.'

'I see.' Clemens looked down at his desk for a moment, then raised his eyes again. 'Tell us about the Druid, sir, if you would.'

Carvilius shrugged. 'There's little to tell. I was at one of the outlying farmsteads negotiating a sale when I overheard two bondsmen discussing one of their fellows who had been cured of a persistent headache. They mentioned a Druid at Catuvernum.' Another shrug. 'That's all.'

'And the month?' Clemens said. Carvilius frowned. 'You told my centurion the man had been in the kingdom for a month, did you not?'

'Ah. That was later, and my own doing. I had it from old Veloriga, Comuxovalos's mother, over by Aballiacum. She's in her seventies and getting a bit' – the trader twirled his forefinger against his temple – 'you know. I simply asked in passing how long Icenia had been blessed with a holy one and she told me. Mind you, as I say, I wouldn't put much credence on anything Veloriga said. Some days she doesn't even recognise her own kin.'

'You heard nothing at the royal Dun itself?'

'No. Mind you, I'd gone there first, before I knew of the man's existence. I always do. Coriodurum is my largest market. The country districts are secondary, and I don't always bother with them.'

'And you have no other information?'

'None. That's all I know, Commander. I hope it's been of help.' Carvilius stood up. 'Druids are bad for trade, and I'm always happy to assist our army. You do a splendid job. Splendid.'

'I'm sure the governor will be gratified that you approve of his efforts.' Clemens stood also. 'My thanks, sir. I won't keep you any further. A safe journey to you.'

'Thank you.' The man nodded to Severinus and turned to go.

'So.' As the door closed behind him, Clemens smiled. 'We can sleep secure in our beds knowing that if the Iceni revolt the merchant community at least is on our side. But I don't like the smell of that Druid. I don't like the smell of him at all.'

*   *   *

Dumnocoveros cradled the nine pebbles in his cupped hands. Each was a perfect sphere, its surface smooth as milk, and they had taken him all day to find. He looked up. He had timed it well: the sun was setting below the trees which marked the slightly higher ground of the royal Dun an hour's journey to the west. The day-flying birds had already gone from the sky, but in the reed pool nearby two black-backed terns were still feeding, their beaks darting here and there, making tiny ripples in the water.

Carefully, deliberately, he shut them out from his mind. Then he did the same for the whispering of the reeds and the touch of the chill evening wind on his exposed skin. When he felt himself beginning to drift from his body, he stretched out his hands, still holding the pebbles, and opened his eyes.

The hands felt nothing; the eyes saw nothing. That was as it should be.

Ogmios, be my hands' cunning, he prayed. *Be the cunning of my eyes, Ogmios, and of the brain within my head. Ogmios, I am empty. I open myself to you.*

Time passed. Somewhere nearby a dog-otter whistled, but Dumnocoveros did not hear him.

The god came suddenly. Dumnocoveros felt the hollow of his skull swell up like a bladder with too much air and the plates of bone grated as they were forced apart from within. He screamed as his outstretched hands sprang open and the pebbles fell to the ground between his knees, taking the god and the pain with them like a birth.

The pebbles bounced and rolled, then settled.

Dumnocoveros opened his eyes and breathed deeply, letting the world flood back. The terns had gone, disturbed by his screams, and the cold air had turned the sweat on his face to a thin film of ice.

He stood up, careful not to disturb the pattern that the pebbles had made on the ground at his feet. Their message was clear and unambiguous, leaving no room for doubt.

Druid though he was, Dumnocoveros wept.

16

Two days later, along with Modianus and a half squadron of the Foxes' cavalry, Severinus rode to the royal Dun: sixteen men, the centurion had advised him, was the optimum number.

'Any more, sir,' Modianus had said, 'and you'll set the bastards' hackles up so high it'll take six months to calm them down. Any less and we'd be showing too much consideration, which'd make the whole ruddy exercise pointless. I'll pick the men myself so you get ones that look good in the saddle. They're very strong on a decent turnout, are the natives.'

Severinus had left him to make the arrangements. He was beginning to have a great respect for Modianus.

The road to Coriodurum was Roman-built. It ran straight as a spear across the fens, ignoring the land around it: a causeway of hammered earth laid on logs half sunk into the marshes. Round about in all directions Icenia stretched flat and green.

'Fine countryside, Centurion.' Severinus had enjoyed the ride. Either spring had come early or the dull grey weather of the past few days had lifted temporarily.

'Aye, it's not bad, sir.' Modianus grinned. 'Some of the best grain and grazing land in the province. Nice horses, too. Beautiful. You have to watch yourself, though.'

'How do you mean?'

The centurion pointed. 'See that stretch there? Between the two branches of the river?'

Severinus looked. The rough square of grass was a brighter green than the rest, with shimmering pools of water showing here and there on the surface.

'Try riding over that and you'd never reach the far end. I've seen it happen more than once. Some places, there's nothing a couple of inches below the grass but muddy water, and the first thing you know you're six foot down and still going.' Modianus spat with disgust. 'The land's two-faced as Janus, sir. That goes for the natives, too. I'd not forget that in a hurry, if I was you.'

The Dun lay on a low swell of dry ground deep in the marsh. Unlike Camulodunum it had few outlying ditches or ramparts: before the causeway had been built the natural maze of waterways, pools and marshes that ringed it had been defence enough, and now Rome kept the peace there was no need for them. The causeway ran straight to the gates.

They were shut.

'Bloody effing Jupiter!' Modianus muttered under his breath. 'Bastards!'

'This isn't usual?' Severinus brought Tanet up beside him.

The centurion shook his head. 'No, sir. But there's nothing to worry about. They know we're here, and why.' He raised his voice and, still speaking in Latin, he shouted, 'Marcus Julius Severinus, commanding the First Aquitanian Mounted Cohort for the Caesar Nero Claudius Drusus Germanicus, to talk with Boudica, wife of Prasutagos of the Iceni. Bloody open up, you buggers!'

The last words were spoken in an undertone. Severinus grinned into his helmet-strap.

The gates swung open.

'That's better,' Modianus murmured. 'You lead the way, sir. Go straight ahead and don't stop for anyone.'

There were guards inside. As he rode past them Severinus was painfully aware of their hostile eyes on his back.

'Centurion?' he said.

Modianus, a length behind, brought his horse up level.

'These men had spears and shields. Natives aren't allowed weapons; the queen must know that.'

'Aye. It's all right, though, sir. They're an honour guard.'

'A *what*?'

'For the queen. Governor Scapula let King Prasutagos hang on to them after Antedrigos was beat and he took over. There's barely a dozen of them, but it keeps the tribe happy. Like I say, the natives put a lot of store by appearances.'

'They're mean-looking beggars, whatever.' Severinus jabbed his heels into Tanet's flanks and the mare increased her speed.

He could see the palace ahead: a sprawl of wattle-and-daub buildings that stood out from the jumble of other huts more by size than construction. The acrid stink of goats and the smell from the pigsties and dungheaps within the rampart, mixed with the stench of human sewage, caught at his nostrils. 'Mothers alive!'

'You're lucky it's a cold day, sir.' Modianus was grinning. 'You should smell it in summer.'

Eyes were following them, blank, incurious, or frankly hostile. Severinus was reminded of the Trinovantian Dun, but here there were no signs of Rome at all. Prasutagos may have been an ally but it seemed that where he could he had kept Roman civilisation outside his borders.

The beaten earth track led straight to the palace. There were no gates, but two more armed guards stood by the ditched entrance to the compound. They leaned on their shields watching.

'You get used to it.' Modianus had not spared them a glance. He nodded towards the man obviously waiting for them at the doors of the palace itself. 'That's Ecenomolios. One of the local princes and the queen's chief adviser. Watch out for that bastard, sir. He doesn't like us at all.'

'Is that so, now?' Severinus took in the man's confident stance and his well-muscled arrogance. 'Just an adviser? He looks like he owns the place. The queen as well.'

'Aye, and if he doesn't it's not for want of trying. The queen's no fool. She'd think more than twice before she let that one into her bed.'

Severinus grunted. He saw what Modianus meant: Ecenomolios radiated hostility. If Boudica had any political sense at all she would choose a lover or a husband less obvious in his dislikes.

They dismounted, and Ecenomolios came forward. He was tall and broad, topping Severinus by a head and outweighing him by half as much again. The massive gold twists of a warrior's bracelet shone on his upper arm.

'The commander honours us.' He spoke in Celtic. 'His business must be pressing, to come so soon after his appointment.'

'Pressing indeed, Ecenomolios.' Severinus kept his tone equable, and his Celtic as formal as Ecenomolios's own. 'But not quite pressing enough to be given out at the door with dirty hands and a throat full of dust.'

Behind him he heard Modianus chuckle. Ecenomolios flushed. He made a sign and two bondsmen hurried inside, to reappear with a basin and towel and a cup of honey beer. Carefully, without looking at Ecenomolios, Severinus washed his hands, face and neck, dried them with the towel and drank the beer.

'I am overwhelmed,' he said gravely, handing Ecenomolios the empty cup. 'Your house's courtesy blinds me.'

The bondsmen's lips twitched, and Ecenomolios's colour deepened.

'The queen is waiting.' He turned. 'You'll follow me, please.'

'Stay with the troop, Modianus,' Severinus said.

'Aye, sir.' The centurion saluted.

Once over the threshold, Ecenomolios stepped to one side, allowing Severinus to pass. After the brightness of the open air the room was dark and stuffy, and the smoke from the torches around the walls and the log fire that burned in the hearth at its centre caught at Severinus's throat. He stopped and looked around him while his eyes adjusted to the dimness.

The reception hall was huge, with a beaten earth floor and plain undecorated walls. The roof far above his head – there was no ceiling – was supported by four massive wooden pillars, and the rafters were black and caked with soot. The queen was sitting on a raised formal dais beside the hearth. On either side of her were two girls, the elder no more than eleven, the younger seven or eight. Severinus had expected a tall, red-haired, big-breasted woman, but even seated Boudica looked small and ordinary. In the market at the Colony, he would have taken her for a Gaulish matron with her mind on the price of eggs.

Then he noticed her eyes.

Perhaps it was a trick of the flames, but they burned with a light of their own that no Gaulish matron's would have. Glancing sideways, he noticed that Ecenomolios, for all his swaggering outside, knuckled his brow and kept a respectful distance.

They were alone. Apart from the royal family on the dais, the hall was empty.

'Queen Boudica,' he said.

'You are welcome, Commander.' Boudica spoke a slow, careful

Latin, clear but heavily accented. Behind him, Severinus felt Ecenomolios shift. 'Ecenomolios. Leave us, please.'

That, too, was in Latin. Severinus did not turn, but he heard Ecenomolios go. Much of the tension went with him.

'I am happy to meet the queen of the Iceni.' Severinus spoke Celtic.

The queen smiled. Her mouth was broad, the teeth white and even. Twenty years ago, even ten, she would have been beautiful. Even now her strong face had a beauty of its own.

'You speak like a Gaul,' she said in Celtic.

'I was born among the Treveri. My father's Aquitanian, from Aquae Tarbellicae.'

'So.' The queen nodded. 'Then you're as much Celtic as Roman, despite your name. That's good. We have common ground.' She indicated the chair opposite her. 'Come and sit. Be comfortable.'

Severinus mounted the platform's steps and took the chair. 'You have fine daughters,' he said.

The girls were staring at him. The younger giggled, but the elder's mouth stiffened and her head came up like a blood mare's.

'Segoriga and Belisamovala.' Boudica's hands touched their shoulders. The younger girl laid her head against her mother's arm.

'Good names. Strong names.'

'Aye, they are. Names matter. Yours means, I think, the Grave One; mine the Victory-Winner. We, too, have strong names.' She smiled. 'Better than Cat, certainly. I have always distrusted cats, Julius Severinus. Are you a cat lover yourself?'

The choice of words, and the gentle, baiting tone, were deliberate; that was obvious. Severinus found himself wanting to smile in return, although he knew he could not. Whatever his private opinion of the procurator, he was here as the representative of Rome.

'Cats go their own way,' he said. 'They're no concern of mine.'

'Indeed? Then you're fortunate.' Boudica was not smiling now. 'For the moment, at least. But you know little about cats. A cat will make itself anyone's concern if it thinks that person can be useful. Myself, I don't trust cats. I never have.'

A log fell in the hearth, sending a cloud of sparks towards the rafters. Boudica ignored it.

'They have their uses,' Severinus said. 'They help to keep the mice down.'

The queen stiffened. 'We have no mice in Coriodurum. Or none that is a Roman cat's concern.'

'Perhaps not here. But certainly at Catuvernum.'

The silence lengthened. Finally Boudica turned to the elder girl.

'You see that Romans can be subtle too, Segoriga,' she said. 'Never forget that, little one.' The girl kissed her cheek, then shifted her gaze to Severinus. Her eyes were as hard as Boudica's own, but she did not speak. 'So.' Boudica turned back to Severinus. The friendly tone had vanished. 'You come about the Druid.'

'Aye.'

'He is doing no harm.'

'Druids are a banned sect. Harbouring one is against the law. Even in a client-kingdom.'

'Against Roman law, perhaps.'

'Is there any other?' Severinus knew the words sounded harsh and arrogant, but it was his job to say them.

'You Romans have never understood Druids. You have nothing like them yourselves, so you fear them and squeeze them into compartments of your own where they do not fit. That way they can be dismissed in simple terms.'

'Simple terms?'

'You claim they are a danger to the state. A political danger. Only that, no more. You see them through your eyes, not ours.'

'Are you saying that the Druids are not a danger to Rome?'

Boudica shook her head. 'No. Only that you've forced them to become so. But to us Druids have many faces. They stand between us and the gods. They watch the passage between this world and the other, and keep the balance. They are our scholars and healers, teachers and protectors. If you take them from us, then what do you offer us in their place? Cats?' She stood up. 'The audience is over, Commander. You have had a long ride from Braniacum. No doubt you will want to get back quickly.'

Severinus felt his face redden. He, too, stood, forcing down his anger.

'My thanks for your hospitality, Queen Boudica,' he said. 'We'll meet again, no doubt. Meanwhile, Rome would be obliged if you sent any Druids that you know of beyond your borders.'

'Aye.' Boudica had turned away. 'I'll consider it.'

Outside, Modianus was waiting. He took one look at Severinus's expression, then mounted without a word.

They rode back through the gates along the causeway towards Braniacum.

17

Tigirseno stopped for the hundredth time that day to catch his breath and rub his aching side. All around him, the mountains raised their cloud-capped heads like gods sitting in council. If he had not seen them for himself he would never have believed that they could be so high. He had come closer to the sun these past few days than he had ever imagined men could come, yet still, ahead and beyond, the mountains rose. This, surely, was the roof of the world. A land for gods.

Certainly it was no land for men, or for plainsmen at least. Tigirseno pulled his cloak tighter about his shoulders and tried to forget the cold and the wet and the cramping spasms of his empty belly. It had been four days since he had eaten, a hare brought down by a lucky spear-cast the day after he had crossed from Cornovian into Ordovican territory. Even then, before the mountains proper had begun, he had come close to starving: the Cornovii had little liking for strangers, especially those from within the province proper. They kept themselves to themselves, and they guarded their own hunting trails jealously. The Ordovices might be friendlier, but Tigirseno had done all his hunting in woods and marshes. Their mountains were a different world.

A confusing world, too. When he had left Camulodunum everything had seemed simple. He had known that to reach Mona he must travel west by north, and until he had crossed the Ordovican border it had been easy to keep the general line, especially for a hunter used to reading the sun and stars and the earth-signs. If he had gone slowly, or doubled back on himself, it had been for other reasons, not least a desire to avoid the patrols from the Wolves' camps which policed the main tracks.

But the mountains were a maze. They offered problems of their own that, used to the flat land around the Dun, he had not expected or imagined. A valley might lead in the direction he wanted to go, then turn almost back on itself or end in a tumble of rocks impossible to climb. Paths that began wide as roads broke up like spreading tree roots and lost themselves in the heather.

Then there was the mist.

Tigirseno was used to fogs in the marshes, but mountain fogs were terrifying. The clouds would sink without warning or roll down from the mountain's summit fast as a horse could run, leaving him in a moment isolated, blind and deaf. Tigirseno was no fool. The first time it had happened he had sat and waited for the fog to pass; but when it finally did half a day had been lost and the damp cold had soaked through his cloak and into his bones.

It had happened many times since then. Each time, he had wondered if it would ever clear, or if he would sit there until he froze.

He had seen no one. In the five days since the last patchy fields had faded into the distance at his back and he had begun to climb he had seen not one living soul.

He looked up. The sky ahead was dark with black clouds moving eastwards, trailing a grey mantle beneath them. He had been following a fold between two crests; hardly a valley, but it led roughly north. He could already see where it ended, and where – if he wanted to regain his line – he would have to climb the western crest and plan a fresh route. That would mean that the rainstorm would catch him on the open slope, without any hope of shelter.

The sun was already low in the sky. It was hardly worth going on, even allowing for the weather. He found a tumble of rocks and settled down behind them, squeezing himself into a narrow crevice and drawing his damp cloak round about him for the little warmth it would give.

Darkness fell. His stomach rumbled.

They would be eating the evening meal now, at home: a stew of mutton or pork thickened with spelt, along with hunks of warm barley bread and bowls of fresh curds, or the soft goat's-milk cheese that he had loved since he was a child, spread on oat bannocks hot from the fire . . .

His stomach growled again, and he hugged it in sudden anger. His family were welcome to the stew. If he had been eating it himself it would have choked him.

None the less, he could not get the scent of it out of his nostrils. Imaginary or not, it refused to go away . . .

Tigirseno sat up, his mouth filling with saliva as the smell of stewing meat grew stronger.

He was not imagining it. The smell was real.

He looked out from his shelter. The storm had passed without breaking and it was a clear night. Back the way he had come, but slightly to the south where the fold he had been following branched, a thin strand of smoke rose against the stars, then swung in his direction as the night breeze caught it.

Picking up his spear and moving quietly and carefully as if he were stalking a deer, Tigirseno moved towards the fire.

The man had his back to him. He was stirring a pot set on top of a stone at the edge of the flames. Beside him was a huge pack, big enough for a mule. He was no warrior, then, Tigirseno decided, only a merchant or a tinker.

Tigirseno stood.

'Peace to you,' he said loudly.

The man dropped the spoon and grabbed at the dagger stuck in the ground by his right knee, rolling as he did so to face the threat. Tigirseno stepped forward, reversing his spear, and waited just within the firelight. For a moment, the man stared at him. Then he set the dagger down slowly.

'Where the hell did you spring from, lad?' he said. His voice had laughter in it, and Tigirseno felt himself flushing.

'I was camped nearby,' he said. 'I sm—' He stopped himself just in time. 'I saw your fire.'

'You've none of your own?'

Tigirseno drew himself up at the gentle mockery of the tone. 'No,' he said. 'Only my cloak. That is enough for a warrior.'

'Aye. Aye, very likely.' The man found the spoon he had dropped, wiped it on his cloak and turned back to the stewpot, drawing his hand across his mouth. 'Sit you a while in any case. Unless you find the heat oppressive on such a close night.'

Tigirseno's hand tightened round the spear-shaft, but he

walked towards the fire and squatted within arm's length of the flames. The warmth began to seep back into his bones, driving out the chill.

'I thank you for your hospitality,' he said stiffly.

The smell and sight of the stew had been torturing him ever since he had come close enough for it to be obvious. Now, to his embarrassment, his stomach growled. The man smiled.

'You'll share my meal?' he said. 'Aesu's young wife is generous, and there's too much there for one man.' His left eyelid trembled on the edge of a wink. 'I'm talking of the stew, of course.'

'I would be honoured.' Surreptitiously, Tigirseno wiped the saliva from his lips with the back of his hand. 'A little would be welcome. Although I have eaten already today.'

'Aye.' The man was pulling another bowl from his pack. It clinked, as if it held more metalware than he needed for a simple meal of stew. 'Doinos. That's my name. Bound for Mediolanum.' He paused expectantly.

'Tigirseno.'

The eyebrows rose, but Doinos said nothing. He scooped stew into the bowl, tore a chunk of bread from the rough barley loaf at his side, and handed both to Tigirseno. Then he watched in silence as the boy ate.

The stew was delicious, the best Tigirseno had ever tasted: pheasant with wild garlic, in a thick gravy sweetened with honey beer. He wolfed it down and wiped the last scrap of bread round the inside of the bowl. Still without a word, Doinos took the bowl from him and refilled it, adding another lump of bread. Tigirseno finished that, too.

When he looked up, Doinos was leaning back against his pack. The pot was empty.

'I've eaten your supper.' Tigirseno had never felt so ashamed.

Doinos laughed. 'No harm, boy. A meal missed won't hurt me, and you needed it more than I did.' From the side of the pack he brought a skin of beer. 'This'll help it down. Although I'd be grateful if you left me a mouthful for myself. Travelling's thirsty work, especially with a pack on your back, and I'm not too fond of burn water.'

Tigirseno's face, he knew, was redder than the flames of the fire. 'Your courtesy overwhelms me,' he said.

'Ach, lad, no need for that. You're welcome.' Doinos poured the beer into two horn beakers and passed one over. 'Besides, I expect payment.'

'Payment?'

'Don't look at me like that, boy! I don't want money, and you can keep your cloak and spear! Just satisfy my curiosity, that's all. What's a Trinovantian chariot-ranker doing wandering lost in the Snowy Mountains?'

'How did you know I was chariot rank?'

Doinos laughed. 'Tigirseno's no commoner's name, although you gave me no father's to hang it on. And the day I can't recognise a Trinovantian accent, or any other among the tribes between Ituna and Vectis, I'll dedicate my soldering iron to Epona.' The eyelid twitched again. 'And I'm not ready to do that a while and a while yet, I can tell you!'

'I'm going to the Holy Island, to defend it against the Wolves.' Tigirseno tried to give depth to his voice. 'I took a vow.'

'So. So.' Doinos nodded. 'I thought perhaps that might be your reason.'

Tigirseno picked up the spear that he had laid aside to eat. 'I can use this well,' he said. 'I'm the best hunter on the Dun, and the best horseman. And I am a prince. The Ordovices will give me a sword.'

'Indeed.' Doinos opened his mouth to say something, then obviously thought better of it. 'Indeed,' he said again.

'Is it far? To Mona?'

Doinos hesitated. 'Far enough.'

'You say you're going to Mediolanum. That's in the same direction?'

'For part of the way, aye.'

'Then you can set me on the right road.'

'There're no roads in the Snowy Mountains, lad. Barring the ones the Wolves've made for their armies, and these you wouldn't want to travel. Besides, they're using them themselves at present, or building them as they go.'

Tigirseno stiffened. 'The attack has begun already?'

'Not on Mona itself, no, although that can't be long in coming.

The Wolves are fighting the passes to the south, driving north and west. You were lucky to miss them. And they say the Wolves' commander is sending ships around Ganganorum Promontory to meet him at the straits.'

'But the Ordovices and the Deceangli. They're resisting, surely?'

'As far as they can, aye.' Doinos frowned.

'The Wolves are beating them?'

The frown deepened. 'Lad, listen to me. I'm no warrior; I fix pots and pans and sell new ones. I don't know these things, and they don't concern me. I only say what I've heard.'

'Tell me!'

Doinos took a slow mouthful of beer before setting the beaker down on the grass.

'The last commander, Veranius, his name was. He smashed the Silures a year back, and they were the equals of the Ordovices. This Paullinus is just as good. Better, maybe. He knows the mountains, and he doesn't make mistakes. Aye, the Ordovices are being beaten. It'll take time, but they'll lose in the end.'

'And Mona? The Holy Island?'

'The Wolves will reach the straits in a month. Maybe more, maybe less, but they'll reach them. Whatever the Ordovices do.' Doinos shrugged. 'After that it's in the hands of the gods.'

The hands of the gods. Tigirseno rose and picked up his spear. 'I thank you for your hospitality,' he said.

Doinos did not move. 'Sit down, you young fool. There's nothing you can do. Certainly not at this time of night.'

'If you'll tell me which direction Mona lies . . .'

'Sit down, boy! You'd end up breaking your neck in a gully, and what help would that be?'

Tigirseno's fingers tightened on the spear, but Doinos had neither looked up nor raised his voice. Finally he sat, cheeks blazing.

'You'll show me the path in the morning?'

'Aye. If you insist.' Doinos hesitated, then looked at him directly. There was pain in his eyes. 'Take my advice, lad. You'll never get better. Forget Mona. Forget it now. It's finished.'

Tigirseno stared as if the man had slapped him. 'What?'

'You can't help. If the gods want Mona to fall then it'll fall, whether you're there or not.'

'I made a vow.' Tigirseno let the contempt in his voice show, wanting to wound. 'Although of course the vow of a warrior is something far beyond the understanding of a tinker.'

Doinos's expression did not change. 'Aye,' he said. 'That's true enough. I don't deny it.'

The tone shamed Tigirseno as anger would not have done. He dropped his eyes.

'I'm sorry,' he said. 'Truly. A guest who insults his host insults the gods. And after your kindness it was unforgivable. I take the words back. Still . . .' He made to get up.

Doinos laid a hand on his arm. His fingers gripped hard enough to bruise the flesh.

'Listen to me,' he said.

Tigirseno froze, looking down at the man's hand. Doinos's grip slackened. Now it was Doinos who looked ashamed.

'We see things sometimes,' he said. 'Our family. I saw something when you first came into the firelight. Don't go to Mona, boy. There'll be enough deaths there on the beach without yours.'

Tigirseno felt the hairs rise on his neck. He was too sensible to ignore the warning. The Trinovantes had their own seers.

So, he thought, and the thought was cold and clear as an ice-block. I'm marked for death.

Death was nothing. Less than nothing. The soul, which was himself, was immortal, and death could not touch it. The Druids said so, and Druids could not be wrong. He swallowed down his fear and felt it replaced by a great feeling of calm.

'An oath is an oath, 'I thank you for your warning, Doinos, but I'll go all the same, if you'll show me the way.'

Doinos sighed. 'Aye. Aye, well.' He turned away, so that Tigirseno could not see his face. 'You'll share my fire for tonight, at least?'

'If I may. I'd be honoured.'

He woke when the night was half spent to see Doinos sitting upright, still wrapped in his cloak, his eyes empty and blind, white in the starlight.

'Tigirseno?'

'I am listening.' Tigirseno spoke softly, but the hairs on his neck crawled.

'Beware the kite, boy! Beware the kite!'

Doinos lay down again beside the dying fire while Tigirseno stared into the darkness.

18

Aper handed Pollux's rein to the slave outside the provincial offices and walked up the steps past the flanking guards. He was worried; more worried, even, than he would admit to himself. Montanus's slave had arrived just after dawn, and it was not like Quintus Montanus to send a messenger directly to the villa, especially an unofficial one who could give no explanation for the meeting or a reason for its urgency. The procurator's representative was a bureaucrat to his fingertips, and friend or not he would stick to the proprieties.

The Iceni. It had to be the Iceni.

Irus, the little bald-headed Sicilian Greek who had been the agent's principal clerk since he had arrived in the Colony six years before, was busy at his desk with a notepad and abacus. He looked up and smiled as Aper came in.

'Commander,' he said. 'Good morning. Not a pleasant day outside, but the snow seems to be shifting at last.'

'Aye. Not before time, either. How are you, Irus?' Aper unfastened the fleece-lined cloak that Ursina had bought him for the Festival and draped it over a stool near the brazier. It had been a cold ride from the villa, with more than a touch of rain in the air, but the provincial offices were well heated and the room was as warm as an oven. 'Montanus is expecting me, I think.'

'Yes, sir. If you'll bear with me a moment I'll go and see if he's free.' The clerk made a final entry on his pad, then laid it aside, rose and walked down the corridor towards the agent's office.

Aper stretched out his hands to the brazier. Aye, it had to be the Iceni. Montanus had delayed as long as he could, but the king had been two full months dead and with Catus breathing down his neck he couldn't drag his heels indefinitely. Now the weather was showing signs of breaking up and the roads north were clearing, whether he liked it or not he would have to make a move. Aper hoped that that was the sum of his news, but he doubted it: the early summons with no information was ominous. Unless, of course, Montanus had had fresh orders from Rome . . .

Footsteps sounded behind him. He turned.

'You can go in now, Commander,' Irus said.

Quintus Adaucius Montanus was a small man in his late fifties with sparse grey hair like an unruly bird's nest. The childhood illness that had left him partially paralysed from the waist down had not touched his brain; cripple or not, Montanus had one of the sharpest minds in the province.

'Good morning, Titus,' he said as Aper closed the office door behind him. 'Have a seat. My thanks for coming so promptly. Ursina's well?'

'Aye.' Aper took the chair opposite. His worry deepened: there were lines round Montanus's mouth and eyes, and his face had the tired, pinched look that went with lack of sleep. 'She's fine.'

'Good. Good. And your son?'

'Marcus too, the last I heard. He's up at Braniacum, commanding the Foxes.'

'So he is. I'd forgotten.' Montanus lowered his eyes. He had picked up a message tablet in front of him and was turning it round slowly as if unsure what to do with it. Finally, he looked up. 'Titus, you must understand that we're not having this conversation. Most definitely we are not. And after the last time I don't even expect you to act on what I'm going to tell you. But someone should know and I'm afraid you've drawn the short straw.' Aper said nothing. 'This arrived for me by special messenger yesterday. Read it, if you will.'

He passed the letter over. It was from Catus: short, no more than a few lines. Aper read it and replaced the tablet on the desk.

'So,' he said. 'He's bypassed you.'

'Yes.' Montanus's voice was empty of expression. 'Well, I'd half expected it. Perhaps it would have been better if I'd been more' – he hesitated – '*zealous* in consulting the procurator's interests where Icenia was concerned, but there was always the hope that our masters in Rome would see a bit of sense and countermand his instructions. That, of course, has not happened.'

'Aye.' It had been a faint hope at best; Aper knew that already. 'Who's this Homullus?'

'One of Catus's toadies. And if it's trouble he's after then he couldn't have made a better choice.'

'You still think he wants to goad the Iceni into revolt?'

'It's the obvious explanation. Otherwise why choose Homullus.'

'He's that unsuitable?'

'Oh, Homullus is efficient enough on his own ground.' Montanus toyed with a pen. 'But up to now his only contact with the natives has been with southerners like Cogidubnus's Atrebates, and he has no knowledge of or sympathy with the less civilised tribes. On a personal level he's touchy, self-opinionated and completely devoid of subtlety and imagination. He will do what he's told, exactly what he's told, by the shortest route, whatever the consequences. He's also venal, given the opportunity, and you know what that means in a procurator's agent.'

Aper sat back. Holy Jupiter! Well, he'd been answered.

'In other words,' he said, 'he's totally the wrong man for the job.'

'Not at all.' Montanus was frowning. 'That's the whole point. Catus knows what he's about, Titus, you can be sure of that. He doesn't make mistakes. Yes, I think he wants trouble, and he's going to get his wish.'

'There's nothing you can do?'

'Not now. It's out of my hands. Catus is acting privately for the emperor, and he has the right to employ whatever agents he pleases. If he chooses to send a specially commissioned deputy direct from London then he's fully empowered to do so.'

'Can't you lodge a formal objection?'

'Who with? Not Catus himself, certainly. The emperor? The more of Icenia Nero can get his hands on the better he'll be pleased. And if I tried to stop Catus from giving him it he'd have my head on a plate.'

'The governor should know, at least. I'll write to him myself.'

Montanus's lips twisted. 'Save your ink. Paullinus has other fish to fry at present. And I doubt if he would interfere in any case. He's already made that abundantly clear. Like I said, this time there's nothing either of us can do.'

'So if it'll do no good, Quintus, then why tell me?'

Montanus looked away, towards the shuttered window that looked out over Residence Road towards the Annexe and the bulk of Claudius's temple.

'Because I'm a selfish coward. Because I want the one man left in this Colony with an ounce of brain between his ears to be in full possession of the facts. And finally, because I need to know that there is someone who believes as I do and who shares my knowledge and therefore my guilt. You understand?'

Aper's anger died. He nodded wordlessly.

'Good.' Montanus cleared his throat. Reaching forward, he picked up the message tablet and retied the lacings. His voice now was calm and matter-of-fact. 'If Catus gets his way and the Iceni rise then the province is heading towards a major bloodbath. The fact that most of the blood spilled will be native does not console me in the least.'

Aper collected Pollux, mounted and turned the horse's head towards the south gate. The wind was freshening, blowing in from the south and bringing with it a drift of rain. What patches of snow still remained banked against the north-facing walls of the provincial offices were rapidly turning to slush, and the eaves dripped water from the tiles. In a day or so, three at most, the road to Coriodurum would be open; the procurator's deputy might be on his way already.

As he wrapped his cloak around him and settled back into the saddle, Aper tried not to think of Marcus at Braniacum. *Most of the blood*, Montanus had said. Aye, well, they were all in the gods' hands. And, as the agent had said, there was nothing, now, to be done. They could only wait.

Aper touched his heels to Pollux's flanks and rode slowly back to the villa.

19

Severinus pressed the heels of his hands into his eye sockets and rubbed the stickiness out of them. Life at Braniacum wasn't quite what he'd expected of his first command. The pile of reports waiting to be read and signed seemed to grow daily, and the only action he'd seen so far had been a fist-fight between two troopers who had quarrelled over a dice game. He grinned sourly. Clemens's estimate had been generous. Less than a month and he was climbing the wall already.

He picked up the next wax tablet in the pile, undid the lacings and began to read. It was a letter from a civilian corn-chandler, in reply to his complaint ten days before about a consignment of mouldy grain. Severinus sighed, added an instruction to his quartermaster to look for a more reliable supplier, signed his name and reached for the next.

There was a knock on the door. He glanced up as the senior centurion came in and drew himself up to attention.

'Yes, Centurion?'

'We've visitors, sir.' Modianus's voice was expressionless, but a muscle at the side of his jaw moved.

'Visitors?'

'Aye, sir. The procurator's men. On their way to Coriodurum.'

'The assessment deputation?' Severinus laid the unopened tablet down. 'Mothers alive, we've had no warning!'

'There's a dozen of them plus escort.' The centurion was still standing rigid. 'The deputy would appreciate a word with you.'

'"Deputy"? Montanus himself?'

'No, sir.' Modianus cleared his throat and the muscle twitched again. 'It seems the deputation's come straight from London, sir, from Procurator Catus personal. Deputy's a man called Pompeius Homullus. Would you be free to see him, sir?'

'Yes, of course. Very well. Bring him in.' The centurion saluted and left.

Severinus felt numb. Sweet Jupiter in heaven! If the deputation had come direct from the procurator it meant that Catus had decided to take the matter into his own hands; and that was bad news. The worst.

Modianus reappeared with a man in a civilian's plain white mantle and travelling cloak.

'The procurator's agent, sir,' he said.

Severinus indicated a chair while Modianus closed the door behind him. The man was in his mid-forties with a pinched face, sour mouth and hard eyes. Severinus disliked him on sight. 'Have a seat, sir,' he said. 'Welcome to Braniacum.'

Homullus sat, carefully arranging the folds of his mantle as he did so. It showed no trace of dampness or mud splashes; he had either travelled by litter or changed for the interview. Severinus doubted if it had been the second: Catus's envoy did not look the type to take special pains over a meeting with a junior commander of auxiliaries.

'Julius Severinus,' he said. 'Sextus Pompeius Homullus, deputising for Procurator Decianus Catus. I'm delighted to meet you, Commander.' He brought out a roll of parchment and handed it over. 'My credentials.'

Severinus opened the letter and read it quickly. Apart from the simple accreditation it gave no other information.

'You're from London?'

The narrow lips parted just sufficiently to allow the sound out. 'I am.'

'I understood that the assessment was being carried out from the Colony by members of Adaucius Montanus's staff.' Severinus rolled the letter up and handed it back.

'That was the original intention, yes. However the procurator thought that under the circumstances a more direct representation was required. Between ourselves, he considers Montanus not to be, shall we say, wholly committed to the project. Able though that gentleman is in his way.' His hand strayed again to his mantle. Plain or not, it was best lambswool, probably – from the quality – bought in Burdigala or even sent out from Rome itself. The signet ring on his middle finger would have cost Severinus a month's pay. 'Procurator Catus's decision being rather a sudden one it was not possible, I'm afraid, to apprise you of the imminence of our arrival. You have my apologies.'

Severinus nodded without comment. 'You've had experience of the Iceni before?'

'No.' Homullus's lips pursed. 'Fortunately most of my dealings have been with the more civilised tribes south of the Thames. The Cantii and Atrebates particularly.'

'I see.' Severinus kept his expression and voice neutral. 'Then you may find the situation up here rather different, sir. Coriodurum isn't Calleva, and Boudica's no Cogidubnus.'

'Oh, I don't think that affects matters to any great degree.' Homullus smiled. 'Natives are natives, after all. I would prefer to be dealing with an amenable ruler like King Cogidubnus, naturally, but I'm prepared to put up with a little hardship in the course of duty.'

'That wasn't exactly what I meant.' Hardship was clearly a relative term in Homullus's vocabulary: Severinus was careful not to look again at the man's immaculately laundered mantle. 'The southern tribes have accepted Rome and Roman culture. The Iceni haven't.'

'So I have always understood, although I am of course glad to receive confirmation from someone as experienced as yourself.' The agent's tone missed sarcasm by a hair's breadth. Severinus felt himself flushing. 'But frankly, Commander, that is the Iceni's problem, not mine. My duty is quite clear, and I have enough to think about without bothering with petty tribal sensibilities. I'm sure Queen Boudica will appreciate that and extend me every assistance. She is, so I've been told, quite an intelligent woman.'

Severinus leaned back, trying to conceal his growing anger.

'She is, sir,' he said carefully. 'Very intelligent. She also rules according to British, not Roman, traditions. I think you might do well to bear both of these facts in mind. Especially the second.'

Homullus's smile disappeared. 'Rome is quite used to handling native rulers. She has been doing it for quite some time now and I don't believe she needs any instruction from you on how to improve her technique. I thank you, however, for the advice. Be assured it has been carefully noted.'

Their eyes met and locked. Severinus stood.

'Very well,' he said. 'Then I wish you every success in your task. I won't keep you from it any further.'

Homullus, too, was on his feet. 'Oh, I'm sure there will be no difficulty, Commander,' he said. 'We'll meet again, no doubt, although I hope under rather more congenial circumstances. Meanwhile may I take your best regards to the queen?'

'Certainly.'

'Good.' Homullus turned to go. 'I'll keep in touch, of course. With you as well as with Legate Cerialis. It's always reassuring to know the military arm are close at hand.' He smiled again, thinly. 'Should they be needed.'

Severinus walked with him out on to the verandah to where the procuratorial deputation and its military escort were waiting. Sure enough, there was an empty litter with four well-groomed slaves in matching tunics. Without looking back, Homullus got in and nodded to the litter-men. Severinus watched while they shouldered their poles and set off towards the camp gates.

Modianus was loitering in the parade ground, talking to one of the cohort's farriers, obviously waiting for Homullus to leave. Severinus beckoned him over.

'Sir?'

'A word or two, please, Modianus. In my office.'

They went back inside. Modianus closed the door behind him. Severinus sat down at his desk.

'There's going to be trouble shortly,' he said. 'Serious trouble.'

'Aye.' The centurion scratched his ear. 'I thought so from the gentleman's attitude when he first arrived. And that fancy chair of his won't help matters, either. The stuck-up beggar's going to go down with the locals like a mouthful of goat's piss.'

'That's one way of putting it, Centurion. Although perhaps not altogether in words I'd've chosen in respect of an imperial representative.'

'Sorry, sir.' Modianus straightened, his face bland. 'Your orders?'

Severinus hesitated. He might be in danger of overreacting, but it was better to be safe than sorry. And he felt instinctively that Clemens would have done the same. 'Tell the NCOs to tighten up. Keep the men on standby, alternate troops alternate days.

A word of warning to Cerialis at Dercovium wouldn't go amiss either, even if he probably does know about our friend already. Arrange a messenger and I'll draft a letter.'

'Aye, sir.' Modianus paused. 'That Druid, by the way. He's still at Catuvernum?'

'Last I heard.' Severinus had taken Clemens's advice and had the man watched by two of the cohort's native scouts.

'Then I'd pull him in fast if I was you, Commander. If there is trouble a loose Druid could make things worse. These buggers have a nose for an opportunity, and they get themselves listened to. A b— someone like Pompeius Homullus throwing his weight around in the kingdom would be a godsend.'

'Fine.' Severinus nodded. 'See to it yourself. But keep a low profile. And for Jupiter's sake make sure you get him.'

'We'll do that all right, sir, no problem. I'll go now and take half a squadron with me. That should do the job right enough.' He paused, his hand on the latch. 'Do you want him alive or dead?'

'Alive. If at all possible. But take no chances. None at all.'

'Aye, sir.'

Modianus saluted and left.

20

Pompeius Homullus looked about him with distaste through the open side curtains of the litter at the jumble of huts and muddy, stinking wasteland. The priggish young cohort commander had been right in one respect, at least: Coriodurum was no Calleva, and in comparison with the Atrebates the Iceni were animals.

Animals, too, who had been indulged by the local authorities to a degree he found incredible. The gate he had passed through had actually been guarded by men under arms, in flagrant breach of the law which forbade natives to carry them, and their greeting had been surly, perfunctory and completely lacking in the respect due to an imperial representative. He really ought to have had his escort flog them on the spot. When he saw the queen he might, still, insist on it.

Changes would be made, he promised himself, tight-lipped. Oh, yes, very definitely. Changes would certainly be made.

'That will be the royal palace over there, sir.' His interpreter, the Atrebatian Cabriabanus, was pointing a disdainful finger at the ditched enclosure straight ahead of them and the untidy sprawl of huts it contained, larger than those that surrounded it but no less barbaric.

Homullus grunted his acknowledgment. He had no real need of an interpreter: as a Gaul himself he spoke Celtic fluently. Nevertheless, a precedent must be set. And Catus had been most insistent. Homullus had been instructed to take a firm line with the natives, and he would obey his instructions to the letter.

As they drew closer and the stench grew worse, he held his hand over his nose. Jupiter, what a slum! The very pigs lived better in Calleva. And didn't they have *any* arrangement for the disposal of animal waste?

Two guards, again armed with illegal spears and shields, were lounging in front of the entrance to the largest hut. Slowly, they rose to their feet and walked towards the approaching litter. The litter-slaves halted.

Homullus nodded to Cabriabanus and sat waiting, his eyes fixed on a point above the guards' heads.

'Tell the queen,' Cabriabanus said to them in Celtic, 'that the imperial assessor Sextus Pompeius Homullus has arrived and wishes an immediate interview. He also requires suitable quarters to be placed at his disposal. These will be my concern and subject, of course, to my approval. See to it at once, please.'

The guards stared. Finally, without a word, one of them turned and disappeared inside. The other leaned on his shield and picked his nose.

Somewhere, a goat bleated.

Finally, the guard reappeared and motioned with his spear for the litter-slaves to set their burden down. Carefully, not looking at the man, Homullus climbed out, holding the hem of his mantle clear of the mud.

'Tell these bad-mannered louts,' he said in Latin to Cabriabanus, 'that on future occasions they will either treat the emperor's representative with proper respect or be flogged. Make sure that they understand completely and realise that they are to pass the information on to their fellows. There will be no further warnings.' He waited while Cabriabanus translated, watching the guards' faces. They stared back at him impassively, ignoring Cabriabanus himself. He could smell their sweat, even through the stink of the compound middens. One reached out and fingered the silk curtains of the litter.

Homullus closed his eyes. 'Animals!' he murmured. He turned to Cabriabanus. 'Come with me.'

They went inside.

The hut's interior was bare of both furniture and decoration. Homullus frowned. This he had not expected. The native aristocracy were like magpies; they filled their nests with bright, shining objects more noted for cost than artistic value, and Prasutagos had been no different from the rest. Yet there was no evidence of wealth here. None at all.

It was most disquieting. *Most* disquieting.

His eyes turned towards the hearth at the hut's centre. The

queen was sitting waiting for him in silence, on a raised platform equipped with two chairs. In front of it stood a third, little more than a stool. Homullus stepped closer and inclined his head slightly, noticing as he did so the gold bracelet on her right wrist. It would weigh, he estimated, not less than five pounds: hardly evidence of groaning coffers, but promising none the less. And indicative of what there should be.

'My greetings, Queen Boudica,' he said. 'Pompeius Homullus, representing the imperial agent Decianus Catus. 'You have been expecting me, I think.'

He had spoken in Latin. Cabriabanus translated. Boudica's eyes rested on him for a moment, then moved away.

'Indeed,' she said, also in Latin. 'But we will have no need of your tame jay, Pompeius Homullus. He may go.'

Homullus shrugged. 'Very well, madam,' he said. 'As your majesty pleases.' He turned to Cabriabanus. 'Wait for me outside.'

The Atrebatian gave the barest of nods, his contempt almost palpable. Homullus understood it, and sympathised: compared with Cogidubnus's palace, the Icenian queen's was a hovel. Between Boudica and Cogidubnus, no comparison was possible.

Boudica waited until the man had gone and gestured towards the third chair, the one beneath the dais.

'Sit,' she said.

Homullus mounted the steps to the platform and took the chair at her immediate side. She watched him but made no comment.

'My commission, madam.' He brought the scroll which Catus had given him from a fold in his mantle and handed it to her. She set it aside unopened, and Homullus felt himself flush. 'The emperor sends his regards and trusts that both you and his two wards are in good health.'

'My daughters are well enough,' Boudica said. 'As for me, you see for yourself.'

'I rejoice. The emperor will be glad.' Homullus paused. 'He is most anxious, also, that your mutual business be concluded as quickly as possible.'

'The Caesar Nero's anxieties are his own concern, Homullus. And as to what precisely his business is with the kingdom of the

Iceni I am at a loss to understand. We are the Caesar's allies, not his subjects.'

'The king your husband—'

'Is dead. I am queen here now, until my daughters come of age. Icenia is a loyal ally to the emperor and will remain so. But within our borders we are an independent kingdom. Beyond the Caesar's right to dictate our friends and enemies he has no place here except by invitation. Nor do his representatives. Do I make myself clear?'

'Abundantly.' Homullus kept his voice level. 'But I'm afraid, madam, you are mistaken. Icenia is not independent. Your husband Prasutagos was made king by the Caesar's then governor, and with his death the kingdom reverts to Rome. The emperor is quite willing to confirm present arrangements, but only if certain conditions are met. Your husband's will—'

'My husband's will has no validity.'

Homullus forced himself to smile. 'Oh, but it does. It was drawn up and witnessed in proper form and it is binding under Roman law. King Prasutagos appointed the emperor co-heir with his daughters. That is a matter of legal fact.'

'Your master Catus said that the arrangement was purely a formal one.' Boudica's eyes were hard, but the fingers of her left hand were twisting at the bracelet on her wrist. 'A means of safeguarding our daughters' inheritance. Is Catus a liar, then, Pompeius Homullus? A straw-man without honour?'

'No doubt Prasutagos misunderstood. In any event the procurator has fulfilled his part of the bargain. The Caesar Nero is willing to forgo his claim to the throne itself, even his right to appoint a nominee.'

'That is generous of him.' Boudica's voice was dry. 'In exchange for what?'

'Queen Boudica, let us have no games, please. You already know that your husband's will divides his property equally between your daughters and the emperor. Nero will be content with that arrangement.'

'His property?'

'Icenia, of course. What else would it be?'

The fingers froze on the bracelet. Boudica's eyes came up sharp as knives.

'You expect me to give up half my kingdom?'

Homullus smiled. 'Naturally. Speaking politically, the whole of it belongs to Rome already. In effect, however, you and your daughters would retain one half outright under the existing arrangement while the other becomes the private property of the emperor, administered for him and its revenues collected through the procurator and his agents. In this instance, myself. As to the king's private monies and movable possessions, including any realisable articles of furniture or bullion, wherever they might be at present' – he glanced round the empty hall, allowing his contempt to show – 'well, I'm not an unreasonable man, and nor is Catus. I'm sure we can come to an amicable arrangement.'

Boudica had not moved. She was still staring at him, her eyes chips of ice. Under their gaze Homullus shifted uneasily.

'There will be no arrangement,' she said. 'Amicable or otherwise.'

'I would strongly advise, madam, that you co-operate fully with myself and my staff over the coming months, until my assessment is complete and a fair division can be made. In your own interests and in the interests of your tribe. If not—'

'Pompeius Homullus, you will leave me, please. Go now.'

'Madam—'

The queen half rose. From her throat came a noise like a dog growling. Startled, Homullus stood up.

'I really do advise you—' he began.

'Leave me!'

Homullus swallowed. There was nothing to gain by staying, he told himself. In any case, he had done all he could for the present.

Ducking his head in a bow, he left. Quickly, and with what dignity he could manage.

21

Dumnocoveros crouched in the musty, sour-smelling darkness of the underground grain-pit. He knew that the Roman soldiers would not search the farm, not thoroughly enough to find him, and with the Little Man at the royal Dun and his agents quartering the countryside they would not press matters, either. Icenia was already as unsettled as a prodded wasps' nest, and it would take very little more for the wasps to swarm. If the soldiers did find him then it would be their misfortune, not his.

It would seem that the gods did not need a Druid's help to rouse the tribes. They had arranged for the Wolves to do it themselves.

From above came the sound of spades, and voices. Dumnocoveros stiffened, but the voices were Celtic, and when the straw matting was taken away the faces that appeared over the rim of the pit had British moustaches.

'You're all right, lord?'

'Aye. Pull me out, Tarvos.'

Strong hands gripped his wrists. The old man and his sons waited as he stood blinking in the sunshine and brushing the grain from his cloak.

'The Wolves have gone, then?'

'Aye, lord, they're away.' Tarvos spat into the dung that had covered his hiding place. 'I've sent young Britos after them to be sure, but they're headed towards Comux's place.' The man's long face, brown and wizened like a long-dried apple, split in a grin. 'Much good it'll do them. Comux carried a spear with me in the old king's day. He has no liking for Wolves, and his dogs aren't much for company, either.'

'That's so, lord,' his eldest son, a young man with the shoulders and brow of a bull, grunted. 'They took the seat out of my own trousers not two days since, and I've known the buggers from pups. They'll give the Wolves a welcome to remember, don't you worry.'

Dumnocoveros laughed: the reverence that the ordinary tribesfolk paid to Druids might be considerable, but it was not unqualified. When all was said and done they belonged to no one but themselves. That was something the Wolves had still to understand.

'Good,' he said. He turned to Tarvos: 'I'll sleep beneath your roof tonight, my friend, if I may.'

The old farmer raised his fist to his brow.

'My house will be honoured, holy one,' he said.

'I'm sorry, sir,' Modianus said. 'He must've been warned.'

'How the hell could he have been?' Severinus leaned back in his chair. 'He was being watched by two of our best scouts!'

'He gave them the slip the night before I left.' Modianus's face was wooden beneath his helmet. 'One of the bastards was asleep. The other was out catching eels.'

'He was *what*?' Severinus stared at him. 'Sweet holy Jupiter!'

'Aye. The centurion's expression had not changed. 'My feelings exactly.'

'You've no idea where he went?' Severinus was careful not to ask what Modianus had done to the scouts. Whatever it was, the fools had deserved it. 'Where he is now?'

'He wouldn't have gone far from the Dun, sir. We checked the area but it's like looking for a needle in a haystack. And the locals were touchy as hell.'

'Well, it can't be helped. He'll show himself eventually, and when he does we'll nail him.'

Modianus hesitated. 'I picked up a bit of news from Coriodurum while I was at it, sir. The procurator's agent isn't exactly making himself popular there.'

'Really?'

'Aye.' Modianus almost smiled. 'Mind you, things could be worse. The queen's co-operating, but he's riding her hard. He's got men out all over taking inventories. Land, grain in storage, livestock. And the horses. That's bad. Really bad. You know how the locals feel about their horse herds.'

Severinus nodded: horses were prized possessions among all the tribes, but to the Iceni they were sacred. For an Icenian tribesman, losing one of his horses would be worse than losing a child.

'There's another thing. Gutter talk, maybe, but someone should know about it. There's stories that Homullus's men are fooling with the local women. Young girls from respectable families. Wives, even, out in the country districts. It's causing a lot of bad feeling.'

Severinus stared at him in real shock. 'Where did you hear this?'

'Like I say, it's gutter talk, sir. Maybe there's nothing in it, but the word's going round all the same, and that's just as bad. The locals're careful over their women, and if someone doesn't tell the agent to keep his men in order pretty damn quick there'll be throats slit.'

The fool! The bloody, arrogant fool! From what Modianus said Homullus was treating the Iceni like a conquered people. Whether he was acting on Catus's instructions or not was immaterial. Establishing Roman authority was one thing; stirring up rebellion was another.

Severinus made his decision.

'Call Lucius in here. Now, please.'

Modianus looked at him, then turned without a word and crossed to the door. He reappeared a moment later with the clerk from the outer office.

'Take a letter, Lucius,' Severinus said. 'Two copies, immediate dispatch, both for personal delivery. One to Procurator Catus in London, the second to the governor.'

Modianus cleared his throat. 'You think that's wise, sir? Catus *and* the governor, direct?'

Severinus had his own doubts, but these could be kept for later. 'You said it yourself: someone should speak to Homullus before it's too late. He certainly won't take my advice, let alone my orders. I've no other option.'

'But if the procurator already knows—'

'Perhaps he doesn't. Even if he does, he should be aware of what the result could be. The same goes for Paullinus. And to answer your question, Modianus, no, I don't think it's wise.' He

grinned suddenly. 'If anything it's bloody stupid. But unfortunately it's also necessary. Whether it costs me my command
or not.'

'Aye, well, sir.' Modianus did not smile back. 'It might do, at
that. Still, it's your decision.' He turned to the orderly. 'You've
your orders, lad. One misspelling and I'll have your guts.'

Severinus did not sleep that night.

He had no regrets about sending the letters, or about present-
ing the facts as he saw them. A local commander, no matter
how junior, was obliged to report direct to the governor any
problem within his territory that might develop beyond his
ability to control. On the other hand, if Homullus was acting
under Catus's instructions with the governor's knowledge and
tacit approval then to complain formally about his methods
would be professional suicide. The thought that Homullus's
actions might be deliberate policy agreed on by the province's
two chief officials sickened him. If that was all it had to offer
the British then Senovara had been right in her assessment of
Roman law . . .

Senovara.

The thought of her brought Severinus up short. He shook his
head. He should be thinking that way about Albilla, not a British
girl he had seen only twice and might never see again. Yet he had
hardly thought of Albilla either, since he had left the Colony, let
alone written.

Jupiter, they were engaged!

It was almost dawn. The sky through the unshuttered window
of his sleeping quarters was beginning to show red. He got up
quickly and dressed; not in his commander's uniform but a plain
tunic from the chest against the wall. Then he went outside.

The fort was coming to life. As he went past the barrack blocks
on his way to the stables he could smell the porridge cooking in
the communal pots. Under the verandahs men were scraping the
stubble from each other's chins with bronze razors and polishing
armour for the morning's guard duty, or sitting around in groups
chatting or throwing dice. Although he was out of uniform they
stiffened into immobility as he went by.

Roman discipline, he thought. The best in the world. When

it comes to obeying orders no other nation can touch us. He wondered why the thought was sour.

We always belong to someone else, never to ourselves. That's the Roman way of things, the price of empire, of being and staying the best. The ones who always win in the end, even against all the odds. And we pay it gladly, without thinking.

It's what we are. We can't escape it. It's bone of our bone.

He brought Tanet out of her stall, saddled her himself and rode past the guard through the open gates. Then, before she had cleared the outer ditch and reached the causeway proper, he drove his heels savagely into her flanks, pushing her up to the gallop and holding her there. The causeway flew beneath her hooves and the morning air, cold with a trace of rain, buffeted him.

Five miles along the road to Coriodurum, he brought the mare to a halt and let her stand while the steam lifted from her sides, mixing its smell with the smell of his own sweat. Then he turned and rode back at an easy canter.

Modianus was standing by the gate as he came through. He held Tanet's bridle while Severinus dismounted.

'Better, Commander?' he said.

Severinus patted the mare's neck. 'You were waiting for me?'

'Aye, sir.' The centurion hesitated. 'A courier's just come in. From the governor.'

'How could . . . ?' Severinus stopped in time to save himself from sounding foolish; of course, the message could have nothing to do with Homullus. His own messenger would take days to arrive. 'He rode all night?'

'Not quite, sir. He started from Camboritum.'

'Did he indeed?' Severinus handed Tanet over to a trooper and led the way to his office. The staging post at Camboritum was only a few hours away to the north-west, but it would still mean a pre-dawn start.

Whatever the courier was carrying was important.

The man was waiting in the outer office, chatting to the duty orderly. He drew himself up to attention as they came in.

'You've come direct from the governor?' Severinus asked.

'Aye, sir.'

'How are things going?'

The man grinned. 'We're getting there, sir.'

Severinus nodded, satisfied. The ordinary squaddie might know nothing about strategy but he had a feel for how a campaign was progressing. If this courier was happy then Paullinus was doing well. 'So,' he said. 'What have you got for me?'

The man took a sealed message tablet from the pouch at his belt, handed it over and stood at attention. Severinus broke the seal, opened the tablet and read the first lines . . .

Mothers! The fool! The purblind fool!

He looked up. The courier was still waiting, his eyes politely blank.

'Was this the only message you had to deliver?' he said.

'No, sir. I'd one for the commander at Duroliponte and I'm to carry on from here to Caesaromagus.' The man shifted uncomfortably. 'Orders were to make the best speed I could, sir. Begging your pardon.'

Severinus closed the message tablet. He was trying, without much success, he thought, to keep the anger from his face and voice. 'Get a fresh horse and some breakfast. The reply'll be with my orderly.' He turned to Modianus. 'Centurion. A word in private, please.'

'Sir.'

He led the way into his office. Modianus followed and closed the door behind him. Severinus threw himself into his chair.

'We're ordered to join the governor for the push against Mona.'

Modianus stared. 'Beg pardon, sir?'

'You heard. The Foxes are ordered west.'

'What, the whole cohort, sir? All of it?'

'Aye. The whole cohort. I'm to leave a scratch garrison. 'As small as I consider commensurate with security and under competent command.' Presumably Duroliponte and Caesaromagus get the same. And that's just through the one courier. Paullinus is stripping the province.'

'There's still the Ninth at Dercovium, sir.' Modianus was pale with shock. 'The governor won't touch them.'

'They might've been enough three months ago, but if Homullus stirs up the Iceni they'll have their work cut out. And there's enough discontent among the other tribes already for trouble to spread. Jupiter Almighty, what a mess!'

'Aye.' Modianus nodded slowly, his face grave. 'So what do you do, sir?'

'There's nothing I can do. We're ordered out by Paullinus himself, "With all possible dispatch". That means as of yesterday.' He tossed the message tablet on the desk. 'I don't even have the time for a bloody query.'

'The governor won't know the situation, sir. He won't have your report for days yet. And if he's already worried about security . . .'

Severinus turned on him. 'Modianus,' he said, 'I'm just one very junior commander, and I've only held that exalted rank for about five minutes. How do you think an experienced general like Paullinus will react if I tell him I'm not taking my cohort anywhere and suggest to him that he let the commanders at Duroliponte and Caesaromagus plus whatever other auxiliary troops he's called up off the hook as well?' Modianus said nothing. 'Exactly. Blowing the whistle on Homullus is one thing. Disobeying a direct order from the commander-in-chief is another. I might as well slit my wrists now and be done with it.'

'The governor may change his mind. Countermand the order.'

'Aye. And pigs may fly.' Severinus blew out his cheeks. 'You'll forget this conversation, Centurion. It never happened.'

'Aye, sir.'

'Instructions. The cohort's to prepare for immediate departure, first century excepted. That's a fifth of our strength and as near the wind as I can go. You're to command.'

'Very good, sir.' Modianus's face was a frozen mask.

'One more thing. I want a signal station on the Coriodurum road, manned day and night. Beacon fire.'

'That's bad country for watch stations. Too flat, too many trees. We could put it at Derusentum. There's a scrap of higher ground there that might do at a pinch. Better than nothing, anyway.'

'Derusentum it is. Give it priority.' Severinus sat back. 'That's all. Give me a moment, then send Lucius in.'

'Sir.' Modianus saluted and left.

Severinus stared at the closed door for a long time. He felt sick.

He had had no choice. None. But he knew that, if the Iceni rose, a garrison of eighty men blocking their path was not going to make much difference, even with what advanced warning the signal station could give them. He might have just passed a death sentence.

Modianus knew it, too.

22

The Colony was a different world.

Senovara felt stifled as she rode through the gate. She had never been inside the Romans' town before. The place was all straight, hard lines with no space between, as if the ground on which it stood was an irrelevance. The buildings crowded together in weary ordered rows like moulting birds, each a copy of the last down to the identically placed shuttered windows. The smells, too, were different. Even those that ought to be familiar, like dung and woodsmoke, were muted and strange, drawing their character from their surroundings. And always there was noise; not the noise of the Dun but harder, more angular sounds: the rumbling of iron-bound cart-wheels on gravel and the impersonal buzz of too many people crowded into too little space.

Most of the faces that stared at her as she passed were alien, too: shuttered like the houses, the men's obscenely naked with their shaved upper lips and close-cropped hair, the women's flour-white with splashes of red at the cheeks and the eyelashes unnaturally black. Colourless, both, in dull cloaks and tunics or ridiculously swathed in mantles, the women veiled, creeping about as if apologising for existing.

How could people live like this?

Ahead of her was the new temple, an ungainly mass of stone without grace or beauty, already dominating the ruined land around it. She knew that the Romans worshipped their dead emperor as a god, but the *why* still escaped her. Gods were gods, people were people; the smallest child on the Dun knew the difference. And how could you trap a god, even a sham one, between four stone walls?

Insane; but then the whole Colony was insane.

'Are you looking for someone, lady?'

She glanced over her shoulder. The man was Trinovantian, although he wore a tunic instead of trousers. He was carrying a basket.

'Aye,' Senovara said. 'A Roman woman. Uricalus's daughter.'

'Uricalus?' The man set the basket down slowly and spat into the mud. 'Then you're properly astray. He lives by the market, the other end of town. Turn right at the east gate, ask for the biggest house and you've found him.'

'My thanks.' Senovara turned the pony's head. The man moved closer, and set a hand on the bridle.

'You're the chief's daughter?'

'Senovara. Aye.'

'Then tell your father that Inam Lugotorix's son presents his respects. Tell him his shoulder's sore carrying nails for Romans. Tell him he's not alone, either.'

The man released his grip and stepped back. Senovara dug her heels into the pony's flanks and galloped down the hard straight road towards the gate.

Inam had been right: the house was unmistakable, twice the size of her father's. On a bench in front of it a man sat shelling dried peas into a bowl. As she dismounted, Senovara tried to conceal her disgust: he was obviously a Celt, but his upper lip was naked pink, shaved clean of hair. He would be a slave, she thought, using even in her own mind the Latin word. Romans did nothing for themselves. They even bought someone to open the door to guests.

How could you *buy* another person?

The slave had seen her coming. She felt his eyes move over her, taking in the British cloak and mantle and dismissing the wearer.

He set the bowl down.

'Yes?' The word was Latin.

'This is Uricalus's house?' Senovara spoke in Celtic, knowing the man would understand her.

'Aye.'

'Then I've come to see his daughter Albilla.'

'Indeed? And what business would a Dunswoman have with Uricalus's daughter?' The man spoke the Celtic of Burdigala as if it burned his tongue.

Senovara's head went up. 'My business is my own,' she said.

'Is it so?' He picked up the bowl again. It was a cheap-looking thing of shiny red clay with stiff, lifeless figures moulded on to the surface. 'Then you can keep it for yourself, woman. But I can tell you the mistress isn't taking on servants at present.'

'I'm no servant.' Senovara felt the blood rush to her face. 'My name is Senovara. Daughter of Brocomaglos, chief of the Trinovantes.'

The man's thumbnail ripped a pea pod apart. The dried peas rattled against the baked clay like bones.

'Well, Senovara chief's daughter,' he said, 'you're still too early. Come back later when the mistress is awake.'

Senovara's temper snapped. 'Do you think, smooth-lip, that I've come all the way from the Dun to swap words in the open street with a half-man?'

The slave stared at her open-mouthed, his colour rising. Before he could move Senovara stepped forward and gripped the neck of his tunic. He grunted in surprise and the bowl slid from his knees to smash on the paving slabs at his feet. Shelled peas ran in all directions like frightened ants.

The shuttered window above them opened.

'Justus!'

Senovara looked up, relaxing her hold. She was breathing hard. 'Good morning, Albilla,' she said in Latin.

'Senovara! Oh, marvellous!'

'Like enough.' Senovara did not smile. 'Is this the way Romans greet their guests?'

'No! Of course not! I'm—' Albilla glanced behind her, then back. 'Wait! Please!'

She disappeared inside. Senovara wiped her hand on her mantle and turned away. The slave was sitting staring at her, his face now the colour of skimmed milk.

'My apologies, lady,' he said. 'I didn't understand.'

But Senovara was tying her pony to the hitching-post in the house wall.

The door was jerked open.

'Senovara, I'm sorry.' Albilla was still in her night tunic, with a cloak round her shoulders. She rounded on the slave. 'Justus, you will apologise.'

'He has done that already.' Senovara spoke in her slow, careful Latin. 'The matter's forgotten.'

'It most certainly is not. I'll have him whipped.'

Senovara's stomach went cold. 'That you will not. I've no wish to see a man shamed for something that is less than nothing.'

'But—'

'We whip dogs, Albilla, not men. Let that be an end of it.' She turned her back on Justus. 'How is your arm?'

Albilla smiled. 'Better. It doesn't hurt any more when I move it. Look.' She tried and the smile slipped. 'Well, almost better. Come inside! Please!'

Senovara followed her in.

It was the first time she had been to a Roman's house, except for Aper's villa, and then there had been other things to distract her. She felt its strangeness close around her: the painted walls, the cold polished stone floor hard beneath her feet, the niche with its bronze god. He had wings on his ankles and hat, but he was as stiff and dead and earthbound as the figures on the broken bowl. My little Ahteha could make a better clay man than that, she thought. The artist should be ashamed.

'Father's out already and Mother isn't up yet.' Albilla smiled at her. 'I'm sorry. They would have liked to thank you themselves.'

'For what?'

'For saving me, of course.'

Senovara laughed. 'It was only a broken arm and a bumped head. You said yourself you were better already.'

'Almost better.' Albilla opened one of the doors off the lobby corridor. 'We'll sit in here. Have you had breakfast? The slaves can bring you porridge and milk. Or bread and honey if you'd prefer.'

'I've eaten, thank you.' Senovara looked round the room. It was like the corridor outside, cold and formal. Dead. Even the air smelled dead. And the furniture and decoration were gauche and ugly. 'How is your fiancé?'

'Marcus?' Albilla frowned. 'I don't know. He hasn't written. Sit down, please.'

Senovara sat on one of the three couches. Albilla settled herself opposite, full length, leaning on her right elbow.

They stared at each other across the table, a vast, gaudy thing of polished wood and gilt. Albilla, Senovara thought, was quite pretty without the paint and powder that Roman women used to cover their faces. She could almost be a Celt . . .

But then of course she was.

'Your father's from Gaul, isn't he?' she said.

'Yes, from Burdigala. Mother, too.' Albilla laughed. 'So you see, Senovara, I'm not really a Roman. Very few people are. Especially here.'

'Yet you speak no Celtic?'

'Only a very little. But Father and Mother do, and my grandparents. We always spoke Latin at home, even in Burdigala. Father thinks it's more civilised. Her hand went to her mouth. 'Oh. I'm sorry.'

'No need. Gaul isn't Britain. And you've had the Romans there far longer than we have here. Perhaps in another fifty or a hundred years we, too, will be . . . civilised.'

'I hope not.'

'You hope *not*?'

'You haven't been to Gaul, have you?'

'No.'

'It's nice, but it's sad. Neither one thing nor the other. And they're so frightened of Rome.' Albilla's brow furrowed. 'No, not frightened. But they respect her too much. A Gaul would never have behaved as you did with Justus outside. He'd just have gone away.'

'Then he would have been a fool and a coward. I am neither.'

'Exactly. You see?'

Senovara nodded slowly. 'Aye, I see,' she said. 'I'm surprised, though, that you see it too. That is interesting.'

'How do you come to speak Latin?'

The question took Senovara off guard. 'My father thought we should learn it, my brother and me. I was taught by my uncle's wife. She's an Atrebatian, from Calleva.'

'You have a brother?'

'Aye. A younger brother, two years younger.'

'What's his name?'

'Tigirseno.'

'He lives with you? On the Dun?'

'No. Not at the moment. He's' – Senovara hesitated – 'away. And I've a very young sister, Ahteha. That's what you call a pet name?' Albilla nodded. 'She's really Branocovera.'

'Could I meet them some time perhaps?'

'Aye. Perhaps.' Senovara felt uncomfortable talking to a Roman woman about her family, especially about Tigirseno. He would be in the mountains now, fighting Roman men. If he was still alive. 'How is your mare?'

'Lacta?' Albilla scrambled to her feet. 'Oh, of course! The sprain! Would you like to see her? She's in the stables.'

'Gladly.' Senovara got up too, relieved. 'She's a good horse. One of Moricamulos's best.'

'A pity she doesn't have a rider to match.'

Senovara looked at her sideways. 'You apologise too much, Albilla,' she said.

'Do I? I'm s—' Albilla caught herself, and laughed. 'Yes. Perhaps I do.'

'It's not necessary. And it's unusual in a Roman.'

'But I'm not a Roman. Not a proper one. I told you.'

'Aye,' said Senovara. 'So you did.'

The groom Catti was mucking out. As they crossed the yard he straightened, a forkful of dirty straw poised above the barrow.

'This is Senovara, Catti,' Albilla said. 'She found me, remember? The day of the accident?'

'Aye.' Catti dumped the straw, leaned the fork against the stable wall and wiped his hands on his tunic. 'I'm honoured, lady,' he said in Celtic.

'She's come to see how Lacta is.'

'A . . . sprain, wasn't it?' Senovara spoke Latin, stumbling over the word.

'Aye, lady, but she's fine now. Better than fine. See.'

Catti led the way to the stall at the far end of the range. The mare was pulling hay from the rack. She turned easily as they came in and nuzzled Senovara's shoulder.

'She remembers you!' Albilla said.

'Oh, we're old friends.' Senovara's hand was on the mare's neck, smoothing it while the horse's lips nibbled at her shoulder brooch. 'My father has had horses from Moricamulos before, and I was at this one's foaling.' She bent to examine the leg, searching it for any sign of swelling. There was none, and the hoof-joint moved smoothly between her hands, with the mare showing no discomfort. 'That is good. What did you use on it, Catti?' she asked in Celtic. 'A comfrey poultice?'

The old man grinned. 'The lady is a horse-doctor,' he said, then changed to Celtic himself. 'Aye, madam. Witch-hazel first, to draw out the heat, then comfrey in a boiled mash. There's no weakness there now. You could gallop her to London and back and she'd take no harm.'

Senovara stood up and smoothed the hairs on Lacta's muzzle. Like the rest of her coat they were immaculate, shining like milk. 'You're fortunate, Albilla,' she said. 'Both in your horse and the man who cares for her. You're riding again now?'

Albilla shook her head. 'Not yet. I . . .' She hesitated. 'I've been out with Phoenix once or twice. Phoenix is the pony I had before. But no, not Lacta.'

'Your father, then?'

'Father's an even worse rider than I am. And he doesn't have the time.'

'So who exercises her?'

Catti avoided her eyes. 'I do,' he said. 'When I can. As much as I can.'

'This one is no town horse, Catti. Her soul needs grass and space to run.'

'Aye, I know, lady.' He shifted with embarrassment. 'Only the master . . .'

'Father doesn't approve of Catti riding her,' Albilla said quickly. 'He says Lacta cost him too much to risk an accident. And slaves can be clumsy.'

'*Esus!*' Senovara stared at her. 'What does the cost matter? She's a horse, not something to be locked away in case it's dropped and broken!'

'I know, but . . .'

'Knowing isn't enough!' Senovara would never have believed that even Romans could be so stupid. 'A horse must be ridden. Especially a horse like Lacta. If your father tells him that he's afraid of losing what he paid then Moricamulos will take her back gladly.'

'No!'

Even Catti blinked at the force behind the word, and the mare tossed her head and backed away. Senovara paused, feeling her own anger drain. 'Aye. So.' She nodded. 'That's good. Lacta is important after all. To you, not your father.'

Albilla swallowed. 'Will you take her? To look after, until Marcus comes back?'

'Me?'

'Why not?' Albilla tried a smile. 'It's the obvious answer. You're right, she needs to be ridden properly. I can't do it. Even when my arm's better I won't be able to do it. Catti isn't allowed to. And Father will agree. I promise you that.'

'Will he?'

The smile broadened, touching the eyes. 'Oh, yes. Persuading Father to do something he doesn't want to do is something I can manage.'

Senovara looked at the mare. Lacta had come forward again and was nuzzling the girl's shoulder. She decided that, Roman or not, she liked Albilla; she liked her very much.

'Will you take her, to keep for me?' Albilla was watching her. 'Please?'

'Aye. But when you're ready I will teach you to ride her properly. Then you can have her yourself.'

'That would be lovely. But I'm a poor student. I won't hold you to it.'

'Nevertheless, that is a promise.' Senovara's outstretched hand caressed the mare's neck.

23

Tigirseno lay flat among the bracken. Five spear-casts away, the Wolves had already passed the valley's mouth and were moving along its length; eighty of them, the scouts had said, although to Tigirseno they looked more. They were not spread out, as a normal war party would be, but in a column of fours, their shields held close. The early morning sunlight flickered on the metal facings as if on a snake's scales.

Tigirseno's mouth was dry. It would be his first battle.

Cautiously, he raised his head and looked round. The warriors to either side were burrowed into the undergrowth, their shields and spears beneath them. There were hundreds more scattered across the surrounding hill slopes, but these he could not see at all.

Vepocomes, half an arm's length away, dug him in the ribs.

'Keep down, you fool!'

Tigirseno swallowed and ducked his head. His bladder felt ready to burst, and he prayed to all the gods he knew that he would not disgrace himself. He glanced sideways at Vepocomes. The old warrior's eyes had shifted back to the Wolves. Tigirseno wondered if he, too, was nervous or if he was truly as calm as he looked.

The leading Wolf had stopped, his eyes scanning the tops of the surrounding hills. Tigirseno stiffened, counting his heartbeats. Finally the man moved forward, and his century followed.

Three spear-casts more and the last of the Wolves would be level, inside the ring of hidden warriors. Two spear-casts. One . . .

Far to Tigirseno's right the leader of the ambush rose with a yell, and the slopes on both sides of the valley were suddenly full of warriors. They poured downhill towards the Wolves, spears levelled, shields at their sides.

Tigirseno was running too, spear in hand, shield up, his heart hammering against his ribs. The ground flew beneath him, and he no longer felt afraid. He wanted only to kill.

Below, the rigid column shifted, breaking lengthwise into two with a clear space in the centre, forming a double line that faced both ways at once, the movement so smooth that it seemed that a single animal was transforming itself as a moth breaks from a chrysalis. Then in the space of a single breath the two lines rippled . . .

The first attacking wave broke as the javelins struck, their shouts changing to screams. Before they could recover, a second volley smashed into them and the charge faltered. Tigirseno heard a *thud!* close beside him. He turned to see Vepocomes stumble, vomiting blood, a javelin fixed in his throat.

His brain went numb and he stopped running. The warriors behind cursed as they pushed their way past, trampling Vepocomes's threshing body underfoot, but Tigirseno stood and watched the old man die. It was a strange thing, but he could hear the sea in his ears, even above the shouting and the screams. Someone, somewhere had lit a fire; he could feel the heat of it on his face and neck. When Vepocomes stopped twitching, he looked away towards the Wolves. Everything now was slow and clear and somehow unreal. The twin lines were tightening again, becoming a wall of shields; he could hear the rattle as the edges met, and see the glint of swords.

Yes, of course the Wolves would have swords; he should have thought of that. Still, it was interesting . . .

A warrior crashed into him from behind, driving the breath from his lungs and bringing him back to himself. The sea noise was suddenly gone from his ears, and with it the cold clarity.

The battle had become a waking nightmare. There were no battle-cries around him now, scarcely any sound at all, only a gasping, heaving half-silence. Tigirseno stood still, shivering, his spear and shield trailing in the grass. He knew, beyond any possible doubt, that he wanted to live, and the knowledge shamed him.

The Wolves' line shifted for the last time, breaking outwards and apart into eighty armed men who moved slowly and methodically forward and outward from the valley bottom on to the hill slopes, step by step, killing as they went. What warriors still remained on their feet broke and ran; and Tigirseno ran too.

The sun in the cloudless sky above his head had hardly moved.

24

Severinus looked back at the ordered lines drawn up on the fort's parade ground waiting for his signal: four-fifths of the cohort, four hundred men and most of the horses, the bulk of his command. He had sent a second messenger to Paullinus. It would do no good, he knew, but there was no helping that now.

'Good luck, sir.' Modianus at least sounded cheerful, whatever his private feelings. 'We'll take care of things here.'

'Let's hope you don't have to.' Severinus twitched Tanet's rein as the mare shifted beneath him. The bridle-links rattled. 'Or not for long at any rate. And make sure you keep that signal station manned.'

'I'll do that, sir.'

Severinus's eyes went to the empty stretch of road ahead. The Foxes would be moving at infantry speed. It would take him fifteen days to reach Deva, and a messenger changing horses at every posting station could reach Paullinus and be back before they had covered half the distance. Also there was still the chance that his first message had persuaded the governor to change his mind and new orders were already on their way.

Aye. And pigs might fly.

Modianus was waiting for his dismissal, his broad face blank. Severinus turned back to him.

'One last thing, Centurion. You report any change in the situation direct to Cerialis. That's clear?'

'Aye, sir.'

Modianus stepped back and saluted.

Tanet was fidgeting, anxious to be off. Severinus wheeled her round and raised his hand to the trumpeter.

The First Aquitanians set out for Deva.

*　　*　　*

Seated at his desk in the poorly lit, earth-floored room that passed for his office, Pompeius Homullus was glaring at the latest set of reports. On the evidence of the figures in front of him it would appear that in hard cash terms the dead king's personal assets were well below the official estimate. Homullus was no fool. After his interview with the queen he was well aware that the items detailed in the reports represented only a minute fraction of Prasutagos's estate. He, and through him Rome, was being swindled.

He tapped his front teeth with his pen.

There was a knock at the door, and his assistant, Oppius Verecundus, came in. Verecundus was a large man, and despite the chill in the room he was sweating.

'Sorry to disturb you, sir,' he said.

Wearily, Homullus laid the pen down.

'What is it this time, Verecundus?'

'The horse inventory, sir. You ordered it started this morning.'

'And?'

Verecundus swallowed. 'We can't do it, sir. The queen's denied us access to the royal stables.'

Homullus felt his face redden.

'She's done *what*?'

'The doors're barred, sir. She won't let us near them. I thought I'd better tell you at once.'

'Holy Jupiter!' This was too much: Homullus's temper broke. 'Doesn't the woman realise we've got better things to do than pander to her silly whims? Tell her from me to—'

'There's one more thing, sir.' Verecundus shifted nervously. 'There's . . . she's put spearmen on guard.'

Homullus stared at him. 'Spearmen? Did you say *spearmen*?'

'Yes, sir. I could've forced the issue but I thought I'd better inform you first.'

Homullus was on his feet now, and furious: this went beyond simple obstruction; it was out-and-out rebellion. 'You did right,' he said. 'Quite right. Where is she now?'

'In the throne-room.' Verecundus backed away. 'At least I think—'

'I'll see her myself.' Homullus reached for his cloak. 'Tell Saturius to fall his men in in the courtyard.'

Without waiting for a reply, he pushed past Verecundus and strode from the room. This went beyond everything. It was a direct challenge to Roman authority, and one to which he knew the emperor himself would not take kindly: the Icenian royal stables were the finest in the province, and the horses, at least, would bring in some sort of a profit.

Spearmen! Immortal bloody gods, spearmen!

The throne-room's dais had been removed on Homullus's instructions. Boudica was sitting on a plain chair in formal state with her daughters beside her. She looked up as he came in.

'Pompeius Homullus,' she said. 'You wanted to see me?'

Homullus forced himself to speak calmly. 'My staff tell me you have refused them permission to enter the royal stables, madam, and that you have placed armed guards to prevent them doing so. Would you care to explain why?'

Boudica turned to her elder daughter. 'Segoriga?'

The girl lifted her head. 'The horses are sacred.'

'That's nonsense!' Homullus snapped; he was still looking at the queen. 'They're property like any other, and will be treated as such.'

'You would take half, then?' Boudica said. 'According to the terms of the will?'

'The emperor is a horseman himself. He would appreciate it' – Homullus paused – '*appreciate* it, I say, if the other half of the stable were set against some other part of his claim. He would wish me, I am sure, to be generous.'

'In other words you would take all in exchange for nothing but the emperor's "appreciation".'

The younger girl, Belisamovara, sniggered. Homullus did not answer.

'And you ask why I set men at the stable doors.' Boudica had been speaking quietly. Now her voice hardened. 'Homullus, you never cease to amaze me. Ecenomolius warned me at the beginning, but I would not listen. I thought, foolishly, that if I co-operated with you I might keep your greed within bounds.' She drew herself up. 'You have proved me wrong, time and again, and this is one time too many. You are a thief, Homullus. Your master Catus is a thief. Your emperor is a thief. In Icenia we know how to deal with thieves.'

Homullus flushed. 'You insult Rome,' he said softly. 'Your husband made the will, which is subject to the strictures of Roman law. The emperor is as bound by it as you are.'

'That is good. Then we will keep our horses and be generous in our turn. Perhaps given his affinity for leeches the Caesar Nero would accept an extra bog or two.'

Both girls were grinning openly now. Homullus felt the blood rush to his face.

'Madam, I would be grateful if you and your daughters would remember that I am the emperor's representative. I expect and demand proper respect, both for him and to me; also that you comply immediately with any instructions I or a member of my staff may give you. Otherwise I cannot answer for the consequences.' He paused. 'I give you such instructions now. The guards on the stables will be removed. If not by you then by the troops under my command. Have I made myself clear?'

There was silence. The girls turned towards their mother.

Boudica stood up. Although not a tall woman, she topped Homullus by half a head. Involuntarily, he took a step back and glanced behind him. The hall was empty.

'You talk of respect?' Boudica hissed. '*You?*'

'Madam, be careful—'

'You plunder my kingdom.' She was close enough, now, to touch. 'You shame my folk. You take away my royalty and order me about in my own hall. You rape my women. All in the name of a half-man a thousand miles away who has stolen the world and is greedy for more. And you dare to demand *respect?*' Suddenly she drew her hand back and brought it forward in a stinging slap across his face. '*That* is all the respect you will get from me! Now or ever!'

Homullus's hand moved slowly upward to his cheek. Without a word, he turned and walked from the room.

Saturius, the centurion seconded to the commission from the governor's staff, was waiting in the courtyard as ordered with his small detachment of legionaries. He was bored. Coriodurum offered few amusements. Even active service would be better than being stuck out here in the middle of the marshes with nothing but goats for company. Native beer and lice-ridden native women were no compensation.

Why the governor hadn't simply ordered a few cohorts in right at the start Saturius didn't know. All this pussyfooting around was a waste of effort. And now, when the Monkeys had had the nerve to close the stables, instead of ordering him in direct to bounce the little buggers off the walls the procurator's agent had gone smarming to their queen.

Saturius was a soldier, and proud of it. Politicking made him sick.

The palace door opened and the agent emerged. Saturius barked a command to his men and drew himself up to attention. Then he saw Homullus's face, and the red mark across his cheek. His eyes widened.

For a long time the imperial agent did not speak. Then he turned back to the door and made a curt gesture with his hand.

'Bring the bitch out here,' he said. 'Flog her.'

25

Dumnocoveros jerked awake to the sound of screams. The barn around him was empty and innocent in the dawn light, but it was becoming insubstantial, dispersing like smoke as the vision took its place.

They were slaughtering them like pigs. The ground was already a muddy red paste and the blood-stench filled his nostrils. Retching, he stumbled to his feet and lurched outside, holding the vision at bay for as long as he could.

Solla, the farmer's wife, was standing by the door of the hut feeding the chickens from a bowl of bran mash and vegetable scraps. She dropped the bowl and ran towards him, but he hardly saw her. His eyes and ears were full of screaming mouths and gaping throats.

'Lord?' The girl's voice, small as a fly's buzz, seemed to come from a vast distance. He could see straight through her to the heaving mass of figures beyond. 'Father, are you ill?'

'No.' He pushed her away as gently as he could, forcing himself to answer: she was little more than a child, and would be frightened. 'No, Solla. Don't worry. I'll be all right soon.' He felt rather than heard her gasp as he clutched at the frame of the barn door and let the vision take him completely . . .

A pit. He was standing next to a pit, like the grain silo he had hidden in half a month before, although this one was much bigger, and empty; empty, at least, of grain. There were faces all around him, savage faces marked with lines of blue and white clay. As he watched, another man – heavily built and jowly – was pulled forward struggling, his arms tied behind his back. His eyes bulged in their sockets like a terrified bullock's, and spittle ran from the corners of his open mouth. A hand caught at his close-cropped hair, wrenching his head backwards, and another drew a knife across his throat, severing it from ear to ear. Blood jetted and the knife was jerked back hard, its edge grating on bone. There was a snap like a twig breaking, and the head came free. The body collapsed, rolling over the edge of the pit to sprawl among the corpses beneath while the head itself was left swinging from the killer's fist. The man laughed and tossed it to a woman standing to one side. She caught it neatly and spat full into the mouth before fixing the thing to a stake.

Dumnocoveros was suddenly aware of eyes on his back. He turned. Boudica was sitting with her daughters on a low dais watching the killing. Her face was impassive and her hair carefully braided, but she wore no cloak and her dress was in tatters, leaving her breasts exposed. The girls' dresses, too, were ripped and filthy. Unlike their mother's, their eyes burned with the steady, mad glare of a wild-cat's. There was blood on their hands.

So, Dumnocoveros thought. *It has begun.*

The crowd parted. Out of it stepped a warrior with huge moustaches and a massive arm-ring, dragging a much smaller man by the scruff of what had been a fine woollen tunic. Fresh blood dripped from a ragged wound in his scalp.

Dumnocoveros knew now why the vision had been sent, and what he must do. This would be the leader, Pompeius Homullus; little in name, little in soul, but a leader nevertheless. And a leader was never to be killed lightly: his death had power.

He waited.

The warrior had thrown the man face-down at Boudica's feet. Now he took the knife from his belt and gripped the Roman by the hair, jerking the man's chin clear of the ground and straddling him, bending to place the blade's edge across the windpipe.

Dumnocoveros moved into the vision. Stepping forward, he threw his cloak over the man's back. It lay there insubstantial as a wisp of mist.

'No, Boudica,' he said softly. 'Not this one. Not yet. Save him for the gods.'

Although the queen made no sign of having heard, she put out her hand to grip the warrior's arm.

'Wait, Ecenomolios,' she said. 'Not Homullus. Him we keep.'

Ecenomolios growled out a curse but straightened and slipped the knife back into his belt. He pulled the Roman upright and, with a shove of his knee, sent him sprawling at the feet of the nearest warrior.

'Take the bastard away, Corux,' he said. 'But be careful where you put your hands. He's shat himself.'

The warrior and those around him laughed. Homullus was hustled off, moaning, and another man in a soldier's tunic and breastplate was dragged towards the pit.

The Druid had seen enough. He gathered his spirit back into himself and willed the vision to fade.

After the shambles of the Dun, the farmyard seemed unreal, the grass too green and the smells of dung and woodsmoke too bland. He was still propped against the door of the barn, with Solla's face staring into his own. He doubted that more than half a dozen heartbeats had passed since he had pushed her away.

'Father?' she said.

Dumnocoveros took a breath and let it out slowly. He felt drained, his body an empty husk.

'Fetch your husband, Solla,' he said.

She ran towards the house, awkward as a colt, her skirts flying about her bare brown legs, while Dumnocoveros went back into the barn for his staff and satchel.

They came back together. The farmer – he had been out at a lambing until late the previous night and Dumnocoveros did not know his name – looked worried.

'You wanted me, lord?' he said, knuckling his brow. Beside him Solla stood silent.

Dumnocoveros closed his eyes momentarily, fighting off the last vestiges of dizziness. 'You have a war-spear hidden somewhere? A shield, perhaps?'

'Aye.' The man grinned. 'There's a chance I might find both these things, if I looked hard enough.'

'Good. Then look.'

The grin faded. 'Father?'

'The Wolves on the Dun are dead. The tribe is rising.'

Both stared at him open-mouthed, although neither asked him how he knew. Dumnocoveros would have been surprised if they had: you did not question a Druid.

Without another word, the man turned and ran towards the house.

Dumnocoveros was already shouldering his pack.

'You'll eat before you go, Father?' The girl's face was grave. 'A bannock and some fresh milk?'

Dumnocoveros shook his head; after the vision even bannocks and milk would have choked him. 'No, Solla,' he said. 'My thanks for the hospitality of your house.'

'The house was honoured.' She smiled. 'And the thanks are mine.'

She was still watching when he looked back at the turn in the track, slim as a birch tree, her belly showing no sign yet of the Wolf-child that his herbs would take away when the moon began to wane. He raised his hand in a final blessing, then turned his face towards Coriodurum.

Long before he reached it he could feel the anger all around him, in the air and in the ground, so strong that his head was thick with it and the hairs rose on his neck. The gates were guarded, but at the sight of his Druid's cloak the guards reversed their spears. Dumnocoveros walked past them in silence.

The Dun reeked of blood. The men and women he met were dyed with it, necks and arms and faces. They stared but kept a respectful distance, knuckling their brows as he went by.

The pit of his vision lay just within the entrance to the royal compound. It had been filled with dung, and the ground round about was trampled flat and stippled with red pools. Around the empty dais and along the front wall of the palace itself were the heads. Some of them the crows had already found, and the eye sockets were empty.

As he approached the palace door the warrior who had dragged Homullus through the crowd came out to meet him. His arms and hands, too, were stained with blood, and now he carried a sword.

'You're welcome, Father.' The man raised fist to forehead. 'Enter, please.'

Dumnocoveros nodded. 'Thank you. Join us, Ecenomolios.'

The warrior looked startled, but he said nothing. Where his

fist had rested, under the fringe of his back-pulled hair, was a fresh smear of red.

Boudica was sitting alone by the unlit hearth. She had changed her torn dress for one of flame-red wool. Her eyes, too, burned.

'You come too late for the feast, Druid,' she said.

'So I see.' Dumnocoveros smiled and took the chair opposite hers. 'Your guests seem to be giving a feast of their own outside.'

Ecenomolios, standing behind him, chuckled. 'Aye,' he said. 'They're generous in their deaths, if nothing else. But then they can afford to be. It costs them nothing.'

'You have the leader safe? The little man with the soiled tunic?'

He caught the sound of Ecenomolios's indrawn breath. Even Boudica stirred on her chair.

'We have,' she said.

'Good. He'll be needed.'

'Use him as and when you will.' Boudica turned to the servant behind her chair. 'Tammonios. Some food and wine for the holy one.'

The man nodded and left.

'You're in pain, daughter,' Dumnocoveros said; not a question but a statement. His physician's eye had noticed the stiffness in the movement and the tensing of the muscles around her mouth before she spoke.

'It's nothing of importance.' The queen's head went up.

'To be flogged is not nothing, Boudica. Either for the body or the soul. And you will need to be strong in both. You will let me see what the Wolves did to you, both you and your daughters.'

Boudica shrugged. 'It's not important,' she said again. 'The Wolves have already taken the sting away. As for Segoriga and Belisamovala I doubt if even a Druid's salves can heal a broken maidenhead.'

Dumnocoveros stared at her. 'They were raped?'

'You didn't know?' Boudica's mouth twisted. 'So, then, a Druid's knowledge has its limits. Aye, they were raped. What else would you expect of savages like the Romans?'

'Those responsible died slowly.' Ecenomolios's hand stroked the blade of his sword. 'Very slowly.'

'So.' Dumnocoveros nodded. 'Good. That is good. I'll see the girls none the less. There are certain potions that will make them forget . . .'

'No!' The queen's eyes blazed. 'There will be no forgetting! My daughters took their own revenge, as was their right. You will not deprive them of that memory with potions.'

'Very well.' Dumnocoveros put it aside. 'As you please. What now?'

'First we clear the Romans from our borders.' Ecenomolios had sat himself in the chair to the queen's right. His sword was still loose in his hand, and he laid it across his knees. 'After that, we count our friends. The Corieltauvi will join us, and the Trinovantes. The tribes of the west and north are already with us, or will be when they smell forts burning. We drive the Wolves back to Gaul where they belong. And if they will not go then we kill them where they stand.'

Boudica laid a hand on his arm.

'No, Ecenomolios,' she said. 'Those who flog women and rape children have given up the right to be treated as warriors. The Romans are vermin, and we will treat them as such. We kill them all, wherever and whoever they are; whether they run or not.' She turned to Dumnocoveros. 'You agree, Father?'

Dumnocoveros closed his eyes; foreknowledge was a terrible thing, but gods were gods. They looked after their own concerns, and mortals could not interfere.

'I agree.'

'That is good.' Ecenomolios smiled. His fingers caressed the blade of his sword. 'So, then. We kill.'

26

Albilla swallowed down her nervousness. She had never been inside a native shop before; like all wealthy Colonists she bought her presents from the stores on Cloak and Praetorian Streets where the shopkeepers were citizens and spoke good Latin. Beyond the south gate was foreign territory, as strange as another world. If her mother had known she intended to look here for Marcus's birthday present she would have been furious.

Albilla didn't care. If the present had been for anyone else the Colony shops would have done. But not for Marcus. And he had been here himself, the day he had met Senovara.

She tied Phoenix's rein to the hitching-post and went inside.

The room with its wooden counter looked reassuringly normal. Apart from the shopkeeper it was empty.

'You're Eisu?' she said. The man was staring at her, but she had expected that. 'I'm sorry. I've no Celtic. Can you speak Latin?'

'Aye, lady. A little.'

'I'm looking for a present. A birthday present. For a man. A ring, perhaps.'

Eisu bent down and brought a soft leather bag from under the counter. The contents scattered across the wooden surface and he gathered them together in a pile.

'Rings I have, lady.' They were silver, chased with swirling patterns as she had seen on Ursina's brooch.

'They're beautiful.' Albilla sorted through them, holding each one up to the light to see the design. Finally she picked one out. It was heavier than the rest, a twisting knot with a leaping horse carved into the bezel. 'How much is this one, please?'

Eisu smiled. 'The sir is a horseman?'

'Yes.'

'Then wait. Perhaps I have something better.' He disappeared through the curtained doorway behind the counter and came back holding a small round disc. 'Here.'

Albilla took the thing from him. It was a gold coin, the size of her thumbnail. On the uppermost face was a running horse made up of a few simple curves, so real it seemed to leap from the metal. As soon as she saw it she knew that it was perfect.

'Cuno.' Eisu pointed to the lettering beside the horse. 'Is king before Romans.'

'Cunobelinus,' Albilla said. 'Yes, I know.'

'And look here.' He took the coin from her and turned it over. 'Camu. Camulodunum. Is make on Dun.'

'But the letters are Roman.'

'"Letters"?'

Albilla pointed. 'Roman letters, British horse. Both together.'

'Ah.' Eisu smiled. 'Cunobelinus likes Romans so he makes coin half-half.' He held up his hands, the fingers interleaved and overlapping like the pattern on the rings. 'Half Roman, half British, both in one. You understand?'

'Yes, I understand.' Albilla laughed. 'It's perfect.'

'You want?'

'Very much.'

Eisu smiled. 'Good.'

'It's beautiful, Albilla.' Ursina held the coin up to the light. 'Very unusual. Yes, Marcus will like that. Are you giving him it as it is, or having it made into something?'

'I hadn't decided.' Albilla was glad Ursina liked the coin. Her own mother, she knew, would hate it: it was too crude, too unRoman. And, as Ursina said, too unusual: Bellicia gave presents that looked like presents, bought from proper shops. 'I thought about a ring, but that would spoil it somehow.'

'You could have it put on a chain, perhaps.' Ursina turned to Aper. 'Titus, what do you think?' She paused. '*Titus!*'

'Mmm?' Aper had been staring into the flames of the brazier. 'I'm sorry, Bear-cub. What were you saying?'

'Albilla was wondering whether to have Marcus's coin made into an amulet or a ring.'

'Ah.'

'Titus, dear, you're hopeless.' Ursina passed the coin back.

'There's plenty of time to decide, of course, Albilla. You'd want to give it to him yourself, and he won't be back until the autumn.'

'That long?' Albilla knew the question was stupid before she asked it, but the words had spoken themselves.

'He can't leave his command, lass,' Aper said gently. 'Especially now the Foxes've been ordered west. And even if the campaign's over quickly the new territories'll have to be garrisoned. You wanted a soldier, you've got him.'

'Titus!'

'Aye. Aye, I know, Bear-cub.' Aper massaged the socket of his missing eye. 'I'm sorry. Albilla, my apologies. I'm not fit company for anyone this afternoon. A touch of the bone-ache.'

'Ask Trinnus to rub you with goose-grease,' Ursina said.

'Mothers forfend! That beggar has hands like roof tiles!'

'Have you heard from Marcus at all?' Albilla asked, as casually as she could manage. The question had been her main reason for coming out to the villa, but she had felt too embarrassed to ask it.

'No.' Aper shook his head. 'Not since Braniacum. But that's no great wonder, lass. He'll still be on his way to Deva, and when he gets there he'll have better things to do than write letters he can't send back. When we've news we'll tell you, don't you worry.' He held out his hand. 'Meanwhile let's see this coin of yours.'

Albilla gave it to him. 'The shopkeeper said it was struck on the Dun.'

'Aye.' Aper turned the gold piece in his hand. 'There was a mint there before we came. Governor Plautius called the money in and had it melted down. There won't be many of these around now, you can be sure.'

'I liked the horse.'

Aper chuckled. 'He's a character, isn't he? Or maybe I should say "she". I've seen her before, cut in the chalk hills between Verulamium and Calleva.' He passed the coin back. 'Very nice. Very nice indeed. And speaking of mares I hear you've fostered out that new one of yours with Brocomaglos's daughter.'

'Senovara? That's right. Our groom Catti said Lacta needed

the exercise, and I still can't ride properly with this arm.' Albilla laughed. 'I can't ride properly at the best of times. Lacta's better where she is until Marcus gets back.'

'You made a fine choice, certainly. That one'll take care of her like she was a visiting princess.'

'She said she'd teach me to ride.'

'Did she, though? Then you're honoured, lass. And lucky.'

'If she doesn't break her neck for her,' Ursina said.

When Albilla had gone, Aper went through to his study, closed the door and lay down on the couch to think.

The scraps of news and rumour he had picked up on his visit to town that morning had been worrying. The gods alone knew what was really happening at Coriodurum, but if Montanus had been right about Homullus then it could be nothing good, and now Paullinus had withdrawn so many of the policing garrisons even the Colony was beginning to feel the effects. People with native servants complained of skimped work and surly behaviour. At the baths Firmus, the man in charge of the Temple workforce, had complained of a spate of accidents: carts whose axles broke from overloading, cement lost to water damage. When Aper had suggested that the 'accidents' had been nothing of the kind, Firmus had laughed.

'These beggars don't have the imagination for that sort of thing, Titus,' he had said. 'Take my word for it, there's nothing more sinister involved than clumsiness and sheer bloody lack of brains.'

Aper frowned, remembering the total absence of concern in the man's voice. And Firmus could have been speaking for almost every Roman in the Colony.

Mothers! he thought. Am I the only sane one left?

He got up and crossed to the bookshelf where his translation of Xenophon sat. Taking it from its battered leather case, he opened it at random and settled himself back down on the couch to read. As always, the old Greek's serene assurance of his own infallibility calmed him. By the third page he was feeling more in command again. Carefully – the roll was beginning to split in places now with age – he wound the book back on to its spindle and replaced it in its tube.

Perhaps it was already too late, but the attempt had to be made. He would go to Brocomaglos.

Aper had never known the Dun so deserted, or so silent, or so full of invisible eyes. The fields, normally busy at this time of year with last-minute ploughing and sowing, were empty. At one point a stone flew past his head, and he turned. The road behind him was bare, but his eye caught a flicker of movement beside one of the hurdles as if someone had ducked out of sight.

He rode on, his spine prickling.

As he passed through the compound gate Durnos, Brocomaglos's dog, leaped at him the length of his chain and stood barking; not a warning bark, but a furious, frustrated yapping that continued as he dismounted and tethered his horse.

The door was shut. Aper walked up to it and knocked. Then, when there was no answer, he beat on it with his fists.

Finally, it opened. Aper stepped back.

Brocomaglos stood four-square in the doorway, his hair unbraided and his face haggard.

'Aye?' he growled.

Aper pushed past him, shouldering the heavier man aside.

'We talk,' he said.

He had half expected the room beyond to reflect the chief's appearance but it was neat and clean as always. There was no sign of Matugena or the girls.

'The commander is wasting his time.' Brocomaglos had followed him inside. 'There's no need for talk.'

'You're wrong.' Deliberately, Aper sat down on one of the chairs by the hearth. 'There's every need. Otherwise our swords may speak for us.'

'And would that be a bad thing?' Brocomaglos had remained standing. Aper noticed that the man's right hand was slowly clenching and unclenching, as if the fingers were stiff with lack of use.

'Mothers, you fool!' he snapped. 'You ask me *that*?'

Brocomaglos flushed. 'Aye, I know,' he said. 'But sometimes there is no other choice.'

'There's always a choice!'

'For the wolf, perhaps. We've had this conversation before.'

'Have you had it, too, with Matugena and Senovara and young Ahteha? What did *they* say?' Brocomaglos did not answer. Aper took a deep breath. 'Brocomaglos, I am begging you for the good of your folk and mine to help me keep the peace.'

Brocomaglos glared at him.

'And do you think I would have it otherwise?' he growled.

'Then help me!'

The anger slowly left Brocomaglos's face. He sighed and turned away.

'It is not a question of help,' he said. 'I'm not like your Nero Caesar, my friend, to give an order and have it obeyed without question, nor would I wish to be. The Trinovantes are their own men, and they make their own paths. I will ask you something in my turn. Tell your people to pull down Claudius's temple and give us back our lands. Tell them to let us live by our own laws and customs, and when they have done it come back and ask again. Perhaps then my people will listen to both of us.' Aper said nothing. Brocomaglos nodded. 'Aye, well. I've said all I have to say. Go home, Julius Aper. Go as a friend.'

Slowly, Aper got to his feet. Without looking at Brocomaglos he crossed to the door and opened it. Then, remounting his horse, he rode home.

27

The forward base at Segontium dominated the coastal plain opposite Mona; a ditched, palisaded camp bigger than the Colony, with space enough for two full legions plus half as many auxiliaries. The land rose behind it, up and up, until it ended in a distant line of mountains halfway to the sky, with the winter snow still glistening white on their summits. The mountains stretched to the province's borders: a hundred miles eastward, more than twice that south to the Sabrina estuary, in an almost solid mass. It was no wonder, Severinus thought, looking at them, that Paullinus had been so doubtful of Rome's chances of a rapid conquest. If they kept to their mountains, the western tribes might hold out for years.

So long as they had Mona. Mona was the key, the granary of the west: an island of fields, protected by its strait and mountain barrier. Even warriors had to eat, and without Mona there would be no corn. If Mona fell then the rest would follow.

And Mona was about to fall. That was clear. The proof lay all around him.

Segontium – the Place of Power – deserved its name. Used as he was now to Braniacum, Severinus felt dwarfed by it, not only by its size but by its air of purpose. From the moment the Foxes had disembarked from the barges that had brought them up from Deva he had felt himself part of an intricate machine. Everything he saw as he walked up from the quayside and through the fortress's gates towards the headquarters building at its centre was geared to a single aim, and organised to the last detail. In a way, it reminded him of the interlocking pattern on the brooch he had bought for Ursina, with its perfect balance of line and space.

British and Roman. Two sides of a coin, perhaps; but perhaps the two sides were no different, after all.

*   *   *

The headquarters building was as busy and as noisy as the rest of the fortress. Finally, Severinus managed to push his way through to the duty centurion's desk.

The man looked up.

'Yes, sir?'

'Marcus Julius Severinus, commanding the First Aquitanians. I'm reporting in.'

'That's fine, sir.' The centurion consulted a plan. 'You're in the south-west corner, beyond the Sabinians.'

'The Sabinians? Commander Publius Clemens?'

'That's right, sir. He's a friend of yours?'

'My predecessor.'

'You're in luck, then.' The centurion made a tick on a roster and looked up again. 'Stable your horses with theirs, outside the back gate. Commander Clemens has the watering schedule.' He consulted a notebook. 'Oh, and you're to have a word with the general, sir. Straight away.'

Severinus's mouth went dry. 'I'm to do what?'

'He left instructions he was to be told as soon as you got in.' The man stood up. 'I think he's free, but I'll check with the adjutant.'

He disappeared through a door behind the desk. Severinus felt numb. A private interview with Paullinus, especially when the governor insisted on seeing him as soon as he arrived, spelled trouble.

The centurion reappeared. 'That's all right, sir,' he said. 'Just go on through.'

Severinus stepped past the man into a smaller room in which clerks were working. One of them got up and knocked at a second door, opened it and stood aside. Paullinus was sitting behind a desk piled high with reports. Severinus drew himself up to attention and saluted.

'Ah. Julius Severinus, isn't it?'

'Yes, sir.'

'I'll be with you in a moment.'

Severinus waited. Paullinus added a note to the bottom of the tablet, then laid it and his pen to one side.

'So,' he said. 'You had a good voyage down from Deva?'

'Good enough, sir.' Severinus kept his voice expressionless.

'Fine.' Paullinus's fingers tapped the desk. 'Commander, forgive me if I come straight to the point. I was more than a little concerned about your recent dealings with the emperor's representative at Coriodurum and the two rather – not to put too fine a point on it – alarmist reports I received from you subsequently. I thought that perhaps you might care to give me an explanation.'

'Certainly, sir.' Severinus felt the muscles of his face stiffen. 'I believed that Procurator's Agent Homullus was acting in a way likely to goad the Iceni into revolt.'

'So I gathered, young man.' Paullinus's voice was dry. 'But I'm asking you now for reasons, not opinions. Pompeius Homullus is a highly experienced civil servant. He is also, as I said, acting privately for the emperor within strict legal parameters well known to the Icenian queen, in the execution of a will signed by that lady's husband. Accordingly, if the Iceni feel put upon in any way then that is their problem, not ours. And certainly they have no option but to accept the situation or suffer the consequences. Do I make myself clear?'

'Yes, sir, of course. But . . .'

Paullinus's jaw set. 'Severinus, listen to me, please. You have by my reckoning something less than three months' experience as an officer in the imperial army, and that of a very limited nature. Just how much weight do you think that lends to any opinion you may hold on the niceties of provincial government?'

Severinus flushed. 'None whatsoever, sir.'

'Exactly. None whatsoever. So don't bloody well try to tell me my job!'

'That wasn't my intention, sir.' Severinus could feel the flush spread to his neck.

'So I should hope. Although that was the distinct impression your reports gave. Especially the second, which was, to say the least, ill-judged in the extreme.'

'I'm sorry, sir.'

'So you damn well should be!' The governor sat back. 'You have, I think, an excellent career ahead of you. You may even, given the modern trend to encourage provincials, find yourself commanding a legion eventually, if not here in Britain then elsewhere. Since any legionary commander may under certain circumstances find himself deputising for a provincial governor in his absence it is essential that he appreciate the importance of detachment. You understand me?'

'Yes, sir.'

Paullinus half smiled. 'Good. That's something, anyway. Then pin your silly ears back, boy, because some day what I'm taking the time and trouble to dun into your thick skull may help you. Now. A governor's duty is to use the resources at his disposal as efficiently as possible to keep his province secure and when instructed to do so to extend its borders beyond their current limits. You agree?'

'Yes, sir.' Under the other man's cold, steady gaze Severinus felt himself beginning to sweat.

'Fine. That, for your information' – Paullinus's eyes did not waver – 'is his prime and only duty, superseding all other considerations, not least the attitude or feelings of the provincials. That last may be an unpleasant fact, but fact it remains, and it is only by observing it strictly that we have an empire at all. Are you still with me?'

Severinus shifted. 'Yes, sir.'

'Congratulations. Now you will have noted that I used the phrase "as efficiently as possible". For my part, my resources, like any governor's, are limited. I have to balance and prioritise, and make my decision accordingly. That is no easy task. In the present instance I must take the longer view. Britain can never be secure until the mountain tribes on her borders are brought to heel and the Druid priesthood is destroyed. A constant threat calls for constant defence, which ties up valuable resources unacceptably. It is better to deal with it when the time is ripe once and for all, to one's utmost ability. Do I make myself clear?'

'Yes, sir.' Severinus swallowed.

'Second, and allied to this, a province must pay its own way. So far Britain has not done so, and accordingly, as you may or may not know, there is a lobby of opinion at Rome at the highest level which advises cutting our losses and dropping the place down an extremely deep hole.' Paullinus paused. 'No. I see you didn't know. That is part of the difference between a governor and the commander of a junior cohort.' Again the almost-smile. 'The reason we're not all on our way back across the Channel, Severinus, is that current intelligence indicates that the mountain regions which I am now in the process of subduing contain gold and silver deposits which brought under our control would tip the balance considerably. Conquest thus becomes not only a military but a fiscal priority.'

'I see that, sir.' Severinus kept his voice level. 'None the less, the eastern tribes—'

'Gods alive, boy!' Paullinus's hand slammed down on the desk. 'You haven't been listening to a word I've been saying, have you? Or are you an even bigger fool than I took you for? Don't talk to me about tribes! Even if the Iceni do decide to cause trouble, they've got a whole bloody legion camped on their doorstep! And as for the Trinovantes the Colony has enough veterans to wipe their noses for them twice over! That's why we put the beggars there to begin with!'

Severinus stiffened. 'Yes, sir. I'm sorry, sir.'

Paullinus drew a hand over his mouth. 'There's one more thing. I told you that the policy-makers at Rome have seriously considered abandoning Britain. Personally I think it would be a mistake. We have too much invested here to give the province up, and it has a great deal of potential. That is relevant. Your friend Homullus may be a little over-zealous in carrying out his duties but he is acting for the emperor. Anything that will persuade that . . .' He stopped and went on more carefully: 'Persuade Nero to retain Britain as a viable proposition must be encouraged, and the presence of an imperial estate here would go a long way towards doing it. Whatever the initial difficulties might be. Again, do you understand?'

Severinus did not trust himself to answer. He nodded.

'Good.' Paullinus's lips twisted. 'Note that I said "understand", not "approve". Neither your approval nor mine or that of any individual is relevant. Sometimes, my boy, a governor has to turn a blind eye to certain actions for the good of his province as a whole. That's not to say he approves of the actions themselves, only that other considerations must take precedence. That is another unpleasant fact.' He took a deep breath. 'Now have you followed what I have been saying, or would you prefer me to draw you a picture?'

'No, sir.'

'Very well. That, you will be relieved to know, is the end of the lecture. Remember it, please. In your own interests.'

'Yes, sir.'

'You may now go back to your cohort and see them settled in. Don't forget what I said: you show great promise, and once you gain a proper sense of perspective I'm sure you'll go far.' Paullinus picked up a report and reached for his pen. 'Dismissed, Commander. Oh, and welcome to Segontium.'

'Thank you, sir.' Severinus saluted and turned to leave.

His teeth did not unclench until he had reached the Foxes' lines.

'The man's insane!' Severinus hit his knee with his fist.

'Of course he's insane.' Publius Clemens leaned over from where he was sitting on the camp stool in the lee of the tent flap and poured army-issue wine into both their cups. 'All governors are. That's why they're governors.'

'Don't bloody joke. He actually wants that bastard Homullus to encourage a revolt so the emperor can have Icenia as his own private park!'

'Aye, well.' Clemens shrugged. 'Look at it his way, Marcus. The reasoning's fair enough as far as it goes. Nero can't see further than his own pocket, and if giving him Icenia to help finance a few more dinner parties is the price of keeping the rest of Britain then that's that. He's right about priorities, too. If we don't deal with the western tribes now we'll pay for it later.'

'If there is a later.'

'Marcus, we're talking days here. The army's ready. You and the Foxes are among the last to arrive, and the attack plans are already made. Once Paullinus has Mona the campaign's over. He isn't going to change things now, whatever happens. Not unless the whole east goes up. He's got too much to lose.'

'The attack's that soon?'

'It's that soon. We're expecting the final briefing any time now. You didn't see the barges when you docked? Normally they'd be sent back for supplies, but the governor's given orders for them to be kept.' He grinned. 'Us cavalry are all right, we can swim the horses over, but the squaddies'll have to be carried.'

Severinus's brain was buzzing. A quick campaign would change everything. Once Mona fell there would be no more need for Paullinus to keep a full army in the field; with the mountain tribes beaten and the Druids stamped out a single legion based here at Segontium would be garrison enough, and that would free the second Eagle and most of the auxiliaries, more than enough of a threat to nip any revolt in the bud. Perhaps the governor's balance would hold after all. Also there was the prospect of action; his first action, and in command of the Foxes.

Despite himself he felt the first prickle of excitement.

'How's old Modianus, by the way?' Clemens reached for the wine jug. 'He got you trained yet?'

'More or less.'

'Aye. He would have. Still, I'll bet the bugger's chewing nails at being left behind. Make sure you bring him back a crown for the Foxes' standard or he'll never forgive you.'

'If I can I will. If not maybe he'd settle for a Druid's staff.'

'Don't joke.' Clemens was suddenly serious. 'There'll be enough of those around when we go in, certainly. More than enough for my liking.'

'Jupiter!' Severinus grinned and set down his wine cup. 'You believe the Druids have special powers?'

'Maybe not, but the British do.' Clemens's tone had not lightened. 'Worse, so do most of our lads. The governor's right there as well; we have to smoke these bastards out now and kill them where the natives can see it done, or the province'll never be safe.' He held up the wine jug. 'Another cup? Then we can go over to the Thrushes' tents and I'll cut you in on a dice game.'

'Not for me.' Severinus rose. 'I've the guard to inspect. Goodnight, Publius.'

It was a clear night. As he walked back to the Foxes' tents, the constellation of Orion shone brightly in the south-west above the peaks of the Ordovican mountains.

28

It was time to go back.

With the thought came the movement. Dumnocoveros felt himself slip downwards, pulled by the golden thread that linked him to the body waiting beneath. As always the first touch of enveloping flesh brought with it revulsion and the temptation to go no further. It would have been easy to break the thread: a simple act of will would allow him to rise again, leaving his physical husk to stiffen and rot . . .

Sighing, Dumnocoveros put the thought aside. Death was a privilege, not a right, and the gods would have little welcome for a soul who chose personal gratification over duty. Like all those trained to walk in the star-country he had learned that lesson early, and although the price was high it allowed no bargaining.

The rejoining of soul and body was agonising. As feeling returned to muscles locked since sunset, he bit his lip until it bled. Then, slowly, he unhooked his right foot from where it lay across his left knee and straightened the leg. Carefully, gradually, as the pain lessened, he pushed himself upright. When he could walk again he stripped and washed in the pool at the grove's centre, then dressed himself in a new white woollen robe and braided his hair for the ceremony. The knife lay where he had set it the previous night, its blade now wet with dew. He tucked it into the cord of his robe.

It was full dawn; the sun's disc shone like a gold coin between the bars of the easternmost trees. Dumnocoveros turned to face it, stretching his arms wide, soaking up the god like a sponge, allowing him to fill the empty shell that he had made of himself. Beyond the trees, the men were already waiting to bring him to the Dun. They were painted for war and their hair was carefully braided. As he stepped from the circle of the grove they rose to their feet, fist to brow, eyes nervously averted. None spoke: to speak to a Druid at this time meant death, not of the body but the soul. Turning, they moved ahead. Dumnocoveros followed.

The host of the Iceni was waiting in front of the gates, filling the broad space and extending the length of the ramparts as far as he could see. It parted as he approached, the women and warriors on each side knuckling their foreheads as he passed.

Boudica stood with her daughters on a platform in the gate's shadow. Round her neck was the torc of a king and war-leader, and she was wrapped in a cloak of thick wool dyed scarlet. Like the girls beside her she held herself straight, her eyes fixed on a point beyond the host. Dumnocoveros's guard halted, and he climbed the steps alone.

The host was completely silent. Suddenly above Dumnocoveros's head a lark rose, pouring its song into the clouds. Dumnocoveros glanced upwards, then turned to face the folk.

The ceremony began.

There was no sound now. The world was empty, waiting for the gods to fill it.

He struggled as they brought him forward, a wild-eyed little man in a filthy tunic who threw himself from side to side between the warriors holding his arms. The steps were wide enough for three, and the guards mounted them without changing their grip. Dumnocoveros stepped back to allow the first to pass, drawing the knife from his sash as he did so.

The warriors stretched the man so that his back was to the Druid and his arms were spread stiffly to either side like wings.

They stood, waiting.

Dumnocoveros set the knife to his lips, then drove it its full length into Homullus's back a hand-span beneath the left shoulder-blade. Homullus screamed. At the same moment the guards released him. As he fell forward Dumnocoveros wrenched the blade free and blood jetted from the opened wound, spattering his robe and the robes of the queen and her daughters.

Still the crowd was silent.

Dumnocoveros watched the dying man at his feet, careful to miss nothing of the message that the gods were sending him. Finally, Homullus gave a convulsive heave, drawing his knees up to his stomach; his right forefinger jerked, then curled slowly into the palm of his hand as a thread of blood trickled from his sideways-turned mouth, forming a small pool beneath his left cheek.

The silence broke in a barking roar that changed to the long, rolling thunder of spears beaten on shields.

As the noise died Boudica stepped forward, drawing something from beneath her cloak. She raised her arms, turning until the whole of the host had seen the live hare that kicked between her palms. Then she threw it down into the clear space at the platform's base. The hare stumbled, righted itself and sprang away, running sunwise. The warriors in its path cheered and leaped aside to allow it free passage, shrieking with joy as it raced towards the south. The host rippled like a field of barley.

Boudica stretched out her right hand, palm up, then clenched it into a fist and brought it down.

'Follow the hare!' she shouted.

The war-host of the Iceni roared, and moved southwards.

Lucius Cudrenus, Trooper First Class of the Foxes' first century, dispatched to Coriodurum by Acting Commander Modianus, climbed down from his horse and pissed into the ditch by the side of the road. The royal Dun couldn't be far off; ten miles at most, an hour's ride. He'd timed it nicely: when he got there the Eagles would be cooking up their evening flatcakes and settling down to wine and dice. Cudrenus grinned and with his free hand fingered the three delicately weighted bone cubes in the pouch at his belt. He was looking forward to the dice game; the chance to skin a few Eagles of their pay didn't come often. The wine would be welcome, too: two hours since the Darusentum signal station, and his throat was as dry as a Vestal's purse.

He turned back to his horse. As he reached for her bridle the mare skittered, flicking her ears. Cudrenus frowned. Then he caught the sound himself. It came from up ahead: a deep drumming, low and insistent, just on the edge of hearing. He looked up and saw the riders . . .

There were fifty of them at least: warriors, and armed. The sun glinted on the tips of their spears.

Mothers! Cudrenus thought numbly. *Sweet effing Mothers!*

He gripped the saddle-horn and swung himself up on to the mare's back, hauling on the reins and digging his heels into her ribs, sending her galloping back the way he had come. He glanced over his shoulder. The riders were a scant quarter-mile behind and closing fast. The first of them had pulled ahead of the rest, crouching low against their horses' necks and pressing their spears tight against the animals' flanks. Cudrenus's left hand fumbled blindly at the strap that fastened his shield to the back of his saddle. Stupid! he cursed himself. An effing war party behind me and I leave my effing shield tied up! There was no hope of slowing, either. His fingers caught at the fastening and he pulled, feeling the small plate that held the strap tight shift sideways from its groove . . .

The shield spun away, clattering on to the road behind. Cudrenus swore, knowing that he was dead, that without a shield to cover his back it was only a matter of time before one of the natives' spears found him. He looked round. The leading riders were no more than two hundred yards off now, and his mare was already tiring. He couldn't outrun them. His only chance was to take to the open country.

Hauling sideways on the rein, he kneed the mare in the flank and sent her over the ditch.

She landed awkwardly, her left foreleg buckling. Cudrenus rolled free. He barely had time to stumble upright and draw his sword before the first spear took him in the throat and the second and third in the chest.

Ecenomolios dismounted and walked over to the dead Roman. Loosening the cavalry sabre from the man's grip, he used it to hack through the neck. Then he fixed the head to his saddle and swung himself up behind it.

'Well, well. Will you look at that, now?' Docilis said. 'Three whole sixes.'

Julianus Gratianus, nicknamed 'Tadpole', looked, and spat into the fire. Wordlessly he slid his last copper coin across towards the grinning Docilis. Masavo did the same with one of his, but he did it with better grace: Masavo had more coins left.

'Cleans you out, Tadpole, does it?' Docilis was adding the coins to the pile in front of him.

'Screw your effing grandmother,' Gratianus said sourly.

'No need to be like that, boy! It's only a game.'

Gratianus got up without a word and tucked his empty pouch into his belt. Masavo chuckled.

'Bad loser,' he said to Docilis. 'Ba-a-d loser.'

'It's clouding over.' Docilis was looking up at the sky. 'Rain tonight, maybe. Best cover up the beacon.' He jerked his thumb. 'Loser's job, Tadpole.'

Gratianus didn't argue. He sent another gob of spittle into the flames of the small cook-fire and began to climb the ladder that led to the platform. Masavo was already gathering up the dice for another throw.

'*Very* bad loser,' he said.

Docilis laughed.

Gratianus reached the platform that held the signal beacon, sixteen feet above ground level and eight higher than the palisade. Docilis had been right: the wind was freshening from the north, and it already had a touch of dampness. He pulled the hide covers across the dry brushwood and took the lighted torch from its socket. His hand was already on the ladder rail when he saw something move in the darkness below. He stiffened, watching.

The movement was not repeated.

'Hey, lads,' he said, pitching his voice as low as he dared.

'What is it, Tadpole?' Docilis's voice, cautious.

'Come up here a minute. Something's going on.'

'Screw it, you bugger. Just fix the effing beacon. We're not biting.'

'I'm serious.' The hairs were crawling on Gratianus's neck. 'We've got trouble.'

Out in the darkness a dog-fox barked, but Gratianus did not relax. Slowly, carefully, he reached out a hand and pulled the covers from the oiled wood.

The night erupted with yells. Figures swarmed over the parapet, figures with painted faces, clutching spears and knives.

'The beacon!' Docilis was shouting. 'Tadpole, light the effing beacon!'

His right hand shaking so much he needed the other to steady it, Gratianus thrust the torch towards the brushwood; just as a thrown spear from below took him beneath the jaw and smashed through the roof of his skull.

Below him, the others died, too.

29

Tigirseno crouched among the low grass of the dunes, his eyes on the mainland opposite where the Wolves' army had been gathering since dawn. Beneath him the strait lay calm and glittering in the sunlight, bright as a newly polished blade. From this distance the barges looked like roaches. He had tried to count the men as they boarded, but there had been too many.

He swallowed, trying to control his fear. It will be different this time, he told himself. This time I will fight.

The warrior beside him, Cartivel, nudged his shoulder.

'You all right, lad?'

'Why don't they come?' Tigirseno could hear the nervousness in his own voice, and it made him feel ashamed.

Cartivel's teeth flashed in a grin, white against the blue of his war paint. Old as he was – forty, at least – he was still a big man for an islander, broad as a door, with the scar of an old sword-cut on his forehead.

'They'll come soon enough,' he said. 'And when they do we'll make them wish they hadn't. The gods're with us today, boy. Look there.'

Tigirseno followed his pointing finger. Above one of the sand-banks a flock of gulls dipped and whirled, feeding on the small fish caught by the retreating tide.

'Trust the birds, lad,' Cartivel said. 'They know. These heavy boats can't come too far inshore, not laded like that. Their war-riors'll have to wade the last stretch, and the sand's treacherous. It'll gulp them down or hold them firm while we spear them.' Cartivel chuckled. 'It'll be as easy as catching fry. Besides, we can't lose, not with the Holy Ones here with us.'

Tigirseno looked towards the higher ground where the Druids stood. Their chanting had begun at dawn, rising and falling like the slow beat of the waves. When it had started the hairs on his neck had lifted and the saliva dried in his mouth. After the ceremonies and sacrifices of the past few days, the barrier between men and gods was thin as a nail-paring already. Now the Druids were breaching it altogether. When the Wolves came, the gods' anger would break over them and they would die, all of them, body and soul for ever.

Tigirseno knew this; he knew it absolutely. Even although the Romans were enemy, the thought terrified him.

There was a rustling in the grass behind him, and the sound of footsteps. He turned. Greca, Cartivel's daughter, was coming down the slope carrying a stoppered jug and a wicker basket. She was tall and dark, and she was the most perfect thing Tigirseno had ever seen.

Cartivel had turned too. He swore softly.

'What the hell are you doing here, girl?' he said. 'You should be safe in the hills at Mamucium.'

Greca set the basket down. 'My place is with my menfolk, Father,' she said. She did not look at Tigirseno, but he could feel her eyes.

'Is it, now?' Cartivel laughed and tousled her hair, black and glossy as a starling's wing. Greca said nothing. 'Aye, well. Your mother would have said the same, and you're her daughter right enough. But you go straight back. Now, you hear?'

Greca bent to uncover the basket. 'There's bread and cheese, and mead in the jug,' she said. 'I thought you'd prefer it to sheep's milk.'

'Greca, you will go! Now!'

She sighed. 'Very well, Father. Bring me back a wolf-pelt.'

'Aye. Two, if I can.'

They hugged, and Cartivel kissed her forehead. She half turned.

'Tigirseno . . .'

He looked directly at her for the first time, but whatever she had meant to say the words had stuck in her throat. Laying the jug against a tuft of grass so it did not spill, she walked away. The sun caught at her hair one last time and the dunes swallowed her.

Cartivel had picked up the jug and was pulling out the straw bung.

'She's a wild one,' he said. 'Just like her mother was, although her heart's in the right place. She was right about the mead, though. Before a battle's no time to be drinking milk.' He passed the jug over. 'Here, boy. You'll fight better with some of this inside you.'

Tigirseno drank. The mead was strong and thick, with the flavour of thyme. He set the jug down.

'Is she promised?' The words came of themselves, and even in his own ears they sounded harsh and arrogant.

Cartivel picked up the mead jug. He took a long swallow and wiped the back of his hand across his mouth. His eyes were on Tigirseno's, speculative.

'No,' he said. 'Or not that she's told me of, anyway.'

Tigirseno's mouth felt dry, despite the mead. He drew himself up straight and clenched his hands to stop them shaking.

'Then I ask you for her.'

Cartivel's eyes widened, and he whistled through his teeth. 'You choose a strange time to do your courting, boy, with half the Wolves in Britain snapping at our throats.'

'That's as may be.' Tigirseno reddened. 'Your answer?'

The big man laughed. 'Aye, take her if you want, lad,' he said. 'I doubt she'd pay me no heed if I said otherwise in any case. The vixen made her own mind up five minutes after she saw you.'

'Your hand on it?'

Cartivel laid aside his spear and stretched out his hand. They shook.

It was only then that Tigirseno remembered Doinos, and the kite; but the thing was done, and he would not have had it otherwise. After all, even seers could be mistaken . . .

From the dunes to the right, someone shouted. Tigirseno looked back across the strait.

The Wolves' barges had begun to move.

From where he waited with the Foxes two miles down the coast on the mainland side of the strait Severinus could hear the chanting only as a distant murmur.

'You understand what they're saying, sir?' His acting second, Valens, was an Iberian from Laminium, and he had no Celtic.

Severinus noticed that he was fingering a bluestone amulet on a cord round his neck.

'No.' He glanced round at the soldiers nearby. They were sitting quietly in huddles, and more than one had their fingers crossed in the sign against witchcraft. 'Forget it, Valens. It doesn't matter.'

'Aye, sir.' Valens went back to staring across the estuary to the empty shore beyond.

Severinus looked up at the sun. The attack had been timed for mid-morning to coincide with the period of slack water. His instructions were clear: when the signal came he was to swim the horses over with the unmounted part of his cohort clinging to their manes and bridles or using their shields as rafts. Once across and in command of the beach he was to form up and provide skirmishing support to the main army's flank.

That would be the easy part; waiting for the signal was far more difficult.

'You've fought the British before, Centurion?' he said.

Valens turned, his seamed face breaking into a grin. 'Aye, sir,' he said. 'Off and on.'

'Any advice for a first-timer?'

The grin broadened, and Severinus felt the man relax. 'You'll be all right, sir,' he said. 'Just remember the buggers've no style. They'll come at you screaming like bloody madmen but it's all show, they haven't the sword-sense. Even Rubrius there could manage the best of them without breaking sweat.' He raised his voice. 'Eh, Rubrius?'

A small, monkey-faced man with a cavalryman's bow legs looked up. 'Piss off, Centurion,' he said cheerfully.

Valens laughed and there were chuckles from other men in the group. The tension eased.

'The British're no problem, sir.' Valens had turned back to Severinus. Now he spoke more quietly. 'It's these Druid bastards that're worrying the lads. Give them swords to face and they'll get stuck in, but no one can keep his mind on the job with a pack of effing priests singing his balls off.'

'Druids're nothing, Centurion: we drove them out of Gaul and if they had any real power they would've used it long since. And

I'd back the Foxes against all the curses in Britain any day of the month.'

Valens grinned. 'Well, maybe you're right, sir. We'll see it through anyway, balls or not. Even so, I'll be glad when it's over.'

'Commander!' Rubrius was pointing.

Severinus turned. A thin column of smoke, broken in the middle, was rising from the direction of the fort. A cold finger touched his spine.

'Here we go, sir,' Valens said.

The barges turned south-west, moving along the coast towards the mouth of the strait, their oars beating in a fast, synchronised rhythm like the legs of a water-beetle. All around him Tigirseno could hear men cursing as they leaped to their feet, breaking cover and stumbling along the dunes to follow the barges' line. Tigirseno was cursing himself. The Wolves would find it easier to beach further down the coast where the sand-flats began in earnest, and there would be few warriors already in place to stop them: they were already past the centre point of the hidden army, and even the closest of the tribesmen would be hard pressed to reach the landing point in time.

'Belenos, the tricky bastards!' Cartivel swore. 'Run, boy! Don't wait for me, there'll be enough for both of us!'

Picking up his spear and long shield, Tigirseno ran. Beyond him the chanting of the Druids faltered and died away.

Severinus drew his sabre as Tanet breasted the shallows and her hooves found firm sand at the shore's edge. Paullinus's tactic of unravelling the British line had obviously succeeded, and there were no more than a hundred warriors scattered along its length in a ragged, broken chain. Out of the corner of his eye, he saw the arm of a man ahead and to his right go back. Almost without thinking, he brought his shield over Tanet's poll as he would have done in the Knot, catching the thrown spear full on the armoured boss. Then he urged Tanet forward, clear of the water, aiming her straight at two defenders who were running down the beach towards him. The first raised his spear as Tanet's chest caught him on the shoulder, spinning him round to fall beneath the hooves of the following rider. The second was armed with a sword. As he swung it back, Severinus brought his sabre down hard above the man's right ear. The man screamed and fell; and Severinus, trying not to think of the bloodied corpse he had left behind him, urged Tanet up on to the beach proper.

There were other spears, and other faces, but Severinus fought mechanically, and later he would have no memory of them. All around him now the cohort's mounted third were safely on shore, fanning out in a protective screen for the still-struggling infantry. With only isolated groups of the enemy to deal with, their movements were leisurely, made with a parade-ground neatness: short, brutal cuts to the neck and head, or punching thrusts delivered from the shoulder that left the opponent screaming in the sand with half his face gone. Within minutes the principal groupings had been hacked apart, stragglers were being ridden down and the sand-flats were strewn with bodies. By the time the infantry had come ashore the battle, such as it was, was over.

Valens brought his horse across to where Severinus was waiting.

'Amateurs,' he spat disgustedly. 'Bloody amateurs. We could've been riding in to a picnic for all the fight that lot put up.'

'Still worried about your Druids, Centurion?' Severinus was breathing hard. Beneath him, Tanet shifted.

'No, sir. The lads neither.' Valens grinned. 'Your orders?'

Severinus looked up at the dunes. 'Form the men up on the high ground, cavalry first. Then we move up the coast. Casualties?'

'Lost one. Youngster in Carus's century took a spear in the eye. Just cuts, otherwise.'

'Fine. Well done.'

The grin widened. 'You did well yourself, sir. I reckon you can call yourself a Fox now, good and proper.'

The battle had already been joined when Tigirseno reached it. The Wolves' barges were drawn up in the shallows beyond the mouth of the Afon River and their soldiers were streaming towards the shore like ants, in solid columns each behind its wolf-pelted leader holding his standard aloft. They had already smashed through the first screen of defenders, and the sandbanks were littered with corpses and a jetsam of spears and shields.

Tigirseno, his lungs bursting, felt the first hard sand beneath his feet and water splash against his calves. This time he felt no fear, only anger. He took a firm grip of his spear, bracing it for the thrust and shouting a war-cry that even his own ears could not hear above the din and the shouts of those around him. The tribesmen were massing now, flowing down from the dunes in their thousands, a screaming, solid wave that threatened to envelop the Wolves like a thrown cloak.

From one of the barges, a trumpet blared. The columns halted, then spread from rear to front until they formed a double line of shields that matched the wave in length and curved beyond it. The trumpet sounded again, and the Wolves came on, more slowly this time, foot by foot.

The human wave struck, taking Tigirseno with it.

And suddenly, for Tigirseno, there was no ordered line of Wolves but a wall of shields and grim helmeted faces that became one shield and one face. He screamed at the face and thrust at the gap between shield-top and helmet-strap. The shield lifted, catching the spear-point within its rim, and then was thrust forward, brushing his own shield aside as easily as a leaf. The metal boss smashed into his unprotected ribs like a punch from an iron fist, and he screamed again, in pain this time, as the ribs snapped like dry twigs. He hardly felt the sword as it darted round the shield's right edge, in and out; and after the sword he felt nothing at all.

Gaius Milvius, the Kite, legionary first class of the third cohort, Fourteenth Legion, stepped over the body of the young warrior and brought his shield back into line; just as – although he did not see them – the first of the cavalry which had crossed further up the strait fell on the shattered British from the rear and cut what remained of them to pieces.

30

The road to the Dun, and the farmland on either side, was deserted. There were no carts and no people, nothing at all; even the animals had gone.

Aper's sense of unease increased as he approached the gates. He knew he was acting stupidly, but he had no choice: the first of the refugees had arrived in the Colony the day before, carrying with them news of the revolt and of the approaching Iceni; small-time traders, packmen who had worked the villages near the Icenian border. Gauls and Spaniards mostly, foreigners certainly. There had been no natives among them, no Trinovantes. And if the Trinovantes were thinking of joining the revolt then only Brocomaglos could stop them.

He could see the gateway now ahead of him. It was blocked across its width with hurdles and piles of drying gorse. Aper slowed his horse to a walk. His eye caught a flicker of movement on the rampart to one side, and the glint of metal. Twenty feet from the barrier he stopped.

'I've come to see your chief,' he said. There was no need to raise his voice. The silence might be total, but he was not alone: the feeling of eyes was like ants on his skin.

He waited for an answer, but there was none. Carefully, he lifted himself in the saddle.

The spear came without warning, straight at his face. Aper wrenched his horse's head round, feeling the wind of it on his cheek as it flew past and buried itself in the ground behind him. Digging his heels into Pollux's side and crouching low, he rode for safety, expecting every moment to feel the bite of iron in his back.

But there were no more spears; only, as he reined in to catch his breath, the silent Dun behind him and a blackbird singing on a hawthorn branch.

*   *   *

The council-room was unheated, and chilly. Through the open windows high in the wall opposite where he sat came the sounds of the market-place. Aper's eye ran over the councilmen. They were grouped into two parties, veterans and merchants. The ex-army men, Hasta, Bassus, Columella and Radix, stood together in a knot by the door, grey-stubbled and hard-faced. All of them had fought in the last Icenian revolt, Hasta and Columella as centurions, Radix as a First Spear, Bassus, the only cavalryman, as decurion with his own Thracians. At least they would understand the situation; whether they would appreciate its gravity was another matter.

The merchant group was more numerous: smooth, prosperous-looking men with well-shaven cheeks and well-laundered mantles. He ticked off the names in his mind: Uricalus and Vegisonius, who between them owned or controlled the biggest slice of the Colony's retail businesses. Fidus, the banker from Rome, smelling of barber's talc and money: a big fish, by his own reckoning, in a small pool. Agrippa, the only Spaniard, younger than the rest, whose family owned half the tanneries and shoe factories in Corduba and had sent him to open up a market in the new province. Natulis, whose cargo boats ran between the port and the Rhine mouth. Finally Carillus, the Sicilian horse-dealer and the outsider of the group, who grew his hair to hide a clipped ear and even in summer wore long-sleeved tunics to cover the brand on his arm. Carillus, he knew, would take no part in the discussion. As an ex-slave he was beneath the others' social notice. He stood apart while the rest chatted together in low voices.

Uricalus laid a hand on Vegisonius's shoulder and went over to the portable altar in the centre of the room.

'If you'll be seated, gentlemen,' he said, 'then we'll make a start.'

'Load of damn nonsense,' Natulis, the oldest of the merchants, grunted as he lowered himself on to one of the benches. 'All for the sake of a pack of riff-raff. Holy Augustus, I've a business to run.'

There was a general murmur of agreement. Uricalus scattered incense on to the coals of the altar's small burner and settled himself on the chairman's bench.

'We're now in session, Commander,' he said, his voice and expression neutral. 'You asked for this meeting at extremely short notice, and we all have pressing business elsewhere. Perhaps you'd care to explain your reasons.'

Aper looked at the bored faces around the room. He was already finding it difficult to hold on to his temper: only the veterans were giving him their full attention. Vegisonius was still in conversation with Agrippa. Fidus, the Roman banker, had a wax tablet on his knee and was making notes in the margin.

'I would have thought they were obvious,' he said. 'With the Iceni less than four days' march from here the Colony's ruling body might like to consider defensive measures.' He paused. 'And as for taking up your valuable time, gentlemen, if you expect me to apologise for that then you're even bigger fools than I thought you were.'

The room was suddenly silent. Radix, sitting with the other army men to Aper's left, whistled softly between his teeth.

Uricalus puffed himself up and cleared his throat. 'I really don't think, Commander—' he began.

'Aye, I know,' Aper said. The cavalryman Bassus snorted, and Uricalus glared at him. 'None of you do. Or not with your heads anyway.'

Uricalus's face froze. 'Commander Aper,' he said. 'If your sole purpose in coming here is to insult us then I will adjourn this meeting forthwith.'

'Very well.' Aper sat back; at least they were listening now. 'But let's get one thing clear.' His eye moved to Natulis. 'The Iceni are not riff-raff. And this, the Mothers help us, is no damned nonsense. If you can get that through your heads now, *gentlemen*, then perhaps we'll all live into old age.'

Fidus put down his pen.

'Commander, I'm sorry, but really!' he said in his cultivated Roman drawl. 'Aren't you being just a little alarmist? There've been problems with natives before. The Iceni may be causing a bit of a stir at present but they have nothing in their favour but numbers, and those are probably exaggerated. Native unrest is the army's concern, and they're quite capable of dealing with it without our help. I suggest we let them get on with it.'

'I agree.' Agrippa was twisting the heavy gold ring on his

middle finger. 'We're civilians, Commander. Businessmen. It has nothing to do with us.'

'Perhaps you'd like to explain that to Queen Boudica,' Aper said.

'Oh, for the gods' sakes, man!' Fidus snapped.

'Perspective,' Vegisonius grunted. He was examining his fingernails. 'That's what we need. No point running around like headless chickens just because a few hooligans start kicking over the traces. Cerialis'll sort them out fast enough, don't you worry.'

Aper turned on him. 'The Ninth's doing a full-time garrisoning job. It's spread thin enough already.'

'Come, now, Commander.' Fidus looked down his straight Roman nose. The Coritani have given no trouble for years. They pose almost as little threat as our Trinovantes.' He smiled. 'Or would you include them, too, in your list?'

'Aye, I would.'

'Oh, now really!'

'When was the last time you were up on the Dun, Fidus?'

The banker's smile broadened. 'My dear fellow,' he said, 'why on earth should I go there? Place is full of bloody natives.'

Aper waited until the laughter had stopped. Then he said quietly, 'Then I suggest you don't start now. I tried it myself this morning and got a spear for my trouble.'

Shocked faces, including Fidus's own, stared back at him. The room was totally silent. Then the storm broke.

'But that's—' Uricalus began.

'Jupiter's holy mother!' Bassus was on his feet. 'One of the monkeys threw at you, sir?'

Aper had not moved. 'Aye. And now I've finally got your full attention perhaps we can discuss what to do about it.'

Bassus glanced at the other soldiers. 'Give us an hour, Commander. We'll get some lads together and teach the bastards a lesson they won't forget.'

'Too right,' Hasta growled.

'Don't be a fool, man!' Aper snapped. 'Leave well alone! Either you'd find your head on a pole or you'd bring the whole tribe down on us. Probably both. Now sit down and act sensibly.'

'Perhaps we should all start acting sensibly.' Fidus straightened a fold in his mantle. 'Aper, I appreciate what you're saying, but there are hotheads on the Dun as much as anywhere else. One spear doesn't make for a rebellion, certainly not where the Trinovantes are concerned.'

'The Dun was closed off. There's a barricade across the road, and Brocomaglos has brought all his folk inside the ramparts. Doesn't that tell you something?'

'Frankly no, except that Bassus is correct. We cannot ignore an attack on one of our most distinguished citizens. About that, at least, something should be done.'

'Bloody right it should!' Bassus had sat down, but he was still scowling.

'Fine.' Angry as he was, Aper kept his voice level. 'Then go ahead, Decurion. Only don't forget that the Iceni'll be knocking at our door in a matter of days and that there're several thousand Trinovantian warriors up on the Dun who already hate our guts. I suggest you bear these facts in mind.'

'Commander.' Fidus leaned back. 'Your argument might be valid if the Colony were defenceless, but we have two thousand veterans here. That, together with the auxiliary cohort stationed at the port, is almost half a full legion. Trinovantes or not, it would be sheer suicide for the Iceni to attack us even if they were considering it.' He glanced at Bassus. 'I'm right, am I not?'

'Aye.' Bassus turned to Aper. 'I'm sorry, sir. I can't back you on this. From all accounts not one in four of them's armed with anything better than a knife, and they've brought their women and kids with them. You know what that means. Numbers is nothing. They're not an army, they're an effing rabble. Our lads could take them without breaking sweat, even without General Cerialis's help.'

'I agree.' Radix, the First Spear, bunched his huge fist on his chair arm. 'The Iceni're no problem, sir. You've fought them yourself; they're brave enough but they've no discipline. And like Bassus says, with the women and kids along they're a rabble, not an army. Cerialis'll go through them like a spade through a rotten beetroot. As for the monkeys on the Dun they'd fall down if we so much as fart.'

There were several chuckles. The Spaniard Agrippa coughed and put his hand to his mouth.

'Radix!' Uricalus snapped. 'This is a council chamber, not a wineshop!'

'Man's got a point, though.' Natulis was scowling. 'If you ask my opinion, Uricalus, we're wasting our time here. Fidus summed the thing up right at the start. The Iceni're the army's concern. Let Cerialis deal with the them. Once they're beat the Trinovantes'll come to heel soon enough. They're fence-sitters, they always have been.'

'Hear hear.' Agrippa was nodding. 'Come on, Uricalus, call the meeting closed and let's all go home.'

Uricalus placed his hands palm down on the table. 'Is that the general feeling?' He paused. 'Very well. Commander? With your permission?'

Aper stared round the ring of closed, hostile faces. Aye, well, he thought numbly, I've done my best. It's out of my hands now.

'Perhaps I can propose a small compromise,' Fidus said. 'That we ask London for supporting troops.' He smiled. 'I'm sure Procurator Catus would be sympathetic, and it's the least that gentleman can do in the circumstances.'

'Jupiter, Fidus!' Vegisonius had already got up. 'Why should we bother Catus? We've got men enough already, and Cerialis'll settle the beggars' hash long before they get here.'

Natulis hitched irritably at his mantle. 'Oh, let Fidus have his way, Vegisonius,' he said. 'It might make the bastards up the hill think twice before they throw any more spears.' He got to his feet. 'Now I don't know what your immediate plans are, gentlemen, but I've a shipment due in this afternoon.'

'A moment, Natulis,' Uricalus said. 'The motion stands. Your votes, please.' He looked round the room. There was a perfunctory raising of hands. 'That's agreed, then. I'll put the request to the procurator on your behalf. The meeting is adjourned.'

Aper stood up. He had never felt so angry, or so helpless.

'Thank you, gentlemen,' he said quietly. 'For your time and your indulgence. And the Mothers rot you all.'

He left without waiting for a reply.

31

Petilius Cerialis rose in the saddle and massaged his aching buttocks. The day and a half's journey from Dercovium had rubbed more than his temper raw. He'd cut it fine, too bloody fine, that was becoming more obvious by the hour; still, the beggars couldn't be far away, and once his scouts had them in sight it would be all over bar the shouting. He eased himself back down on to the cushioned leather and glanced over his shoulder at the column of infantry, stretching from the cavalry's rear halfway to the bridge and posting station at Duroliponte three miles behind him. Three thousand men; all he could spare without stripping the outlying garrisons but still more than half his Eagle. More than a match for the rabble ahead. His jaw tightened against the strap of his helmet. They would pay, by the sweet gods they would! And after the battle . . . well, victories got a man noticed. He might even claim to have saved the province; Jupiter knew that might be true enough with Paullinus off in Mona. The governor was a fair man by his lights. He wouldn't grudge Cerialis his due, and he'd have laurels enough. Then, after his tour of duty expired, it would be back to Rome, a consulship and eventually a province of his own. Not Britain, though. Never Britain.

Life was full of opportunities. The trick was to grasp them.

He leaned back gingerly against the saddle-horns.

'Scout coming, sir.' His aide pointed. Cerialis's eyes followed the man's finger.

He was riding hard; a single horseman in an earth-stained jerkin and leathers, galloping across the open ground between the road and the trees a hundred yards to the left.

Cerialis reined in as the man pulled up and saluted.

'We've got them, sir,' he said. 'About ten miles off to the south-east.'

'Numbers?' Cerialis felt the first stirrings of excitement.

'Can't say exactly, sir. They're spread out.' The scout's horse fidgeted, and he pulled it in hard. 'Foraging, most likely. But I'd reckon eighty, a hundred thousand.'

'Sweet Jupiter!' The aide, a smart young tribune, had edged his horse up on the man's other side. 'That's practically the whole bloody tribe!'

'All the better, Gaius, lad.' Cerialis had taken off his helmet and was wiping the sweat from his face and neck. It was almost noon, and the April sun was hot enough for midsummer. 'It'll save us trouble later.' His lips tightened. 'Ten miles, you say?'

'Yes, sir,' the scout said. 'Moving south. But you're level with the last of them now, and they're going slow.'

'Terrain?'

'The woods clear further on, sir. Five miles down the road there's a big stretch of open country to the east. I reckon if you press on hard and cut across where the road starts to bend you'll catch them nicely. But we haven't checked that way yet. Perhaps it'd be safer to wait until—'

'We're in a hurry, man. We don't have time to waste on technicalities.'

'Yes, sir.' The scout frowned. 'But that's a lot of ground not to know about, and being as to how you're in marching order—'

Cerialis flushed. 'Mars's holy balls, soldier, are you trying to tell me my bloody job?'

'No, sir.' The man stiffened in the saddle. 'Of course not. But—'

'They're a pack of goatherds from the sticks, man, not Hannibal and his bloody elephants! Dismissed!' As the scout brought his fist up in the salute and rode off he turned to his aide. 'Tribune. Orders to infantry commanders. Double the pace, column to stay tight. Cavalry to move forward at a canter.' He smiled suddenly: the tribune's father was a prominent senator, and a drinking partner of the emperor's: an acquaintance to cultivate. 'You're a hunting man, Gaius, I believe?'

'Yes, sir.'

'Good.' Cerialis knotted the kerchief round his neck and replaced his helmet. 'Then you'll enjoy this.'

*   *   *

Ecenomolios parted the screen of bracken as gently as he would have done to watch a deer drink at a pool. The Romans were coming sweet as a partridge to a snare: half one of their precious Eagles, the Corieltauvian messenger had said, and three hundred horse. He could see the leader clearly, a big man armoured and crested like a gilded bird. That would be Cerialis, the legate: full of himself as a dog with two tails, the Corieltauvian had told him, and as ready to bite. Behind him was the legion's Eagle. Ecenomolios knew enough of Roman custom to understand its value; the loss of an Eagle would mean more to Rome than the loss of a battle. Also, it would prove to the tribes that the Wolves could be beaten.

Ecenomolios smiled to himself as his fingers closed round the hilt of his sword, stroking the worn leather. The sword had been his father's, and his father's father's, and when he set his ear to its blade he could hear it whispering of the heads it had taken.

'Today you will take more heads,' he told it softly. 'Better: today you will take an Eagle.'

He looked back at the column. Its solid line was dividing, the cavalry moving ahead and opening a space between itself and the infantry. Ecenomolios's smile widened. A divided army was a weakened army. The Corieltauvian could have added stupidity to the legate's failings.

He waited until the last of the cavalry had long disappeared over the rise and, far to the right, the tail-end of the infantry column had passed what would be the edge of his hidden right wing. Cerialis, now, would be a good mile off, and the cavalry with him. Ecenomolios rose to his feet with a yell.

A heartbeat later, the woods on either side of the road erupted and twenty thousand Icenian warriors poured across the clear stretch of ground between the forest and the now isolated legion, swamping it.

The sound of bugles and the deeper, harsher braying of the British war-horns wrenched Cerialis round in his saddle. For a moment the sheer impossibility of the attack numbed him.

'Jupiter!' he whispered. 'Sweet holy Jupiter!'

It needed all his training to stave off the freezing panic and bring his mind back to cool rationality. His tactics were clear.

The hundred yards' stretch between ditch and trees had been stripped of vegetation for just such an eventuality, and it would have allowed the infantry precious time to adopt what defensive measures they could. Also, it would give the cavalry the space they needed to regroup, sweep up the wings and attack the enemy's unguarded flank and rear.

If they were unguarded . . .

With the thought, the panic flooded back.

The cavalry. Three hundred horse. Three hundred bloody horse, half the legion's strength, that's all we have! If the beggars've attacked in force with cavalry support of their own we won't need just tactics, we'll need a miracle . . .

He shook his head to clear it. He had no option. Back there his legion was dying already.

'Bugler!' he snapped. 'Cavalry to the wings, wide order! Stay with me!'

He set his horse at the ditch as the man blew the first notes. The sudden thunder of hooves was deafening. Obedient to the signal, the cavalry were moving, peeling away from the road on either side. They wheeled in a long curve and halted with parade-ground exactness, two lines deep, a spear's length between horses, poised and waiting for the next command.

Thank the gods at least for army discipline, Cerialis thought, calmer now. If the infantry had held the defensive line of the ditch they might win through yet.

The aquilifer had followed with the Eagle. He sat his horse waiting, the bugler beside him, his dour, competent face impassive beneath the snarling wolf-mask that covered his helmet. That was something else to be grateful for. Cerialis felt the cold sweat break out down his spine at the thought of the legion's Eagle in enemy hands. To lose an Eagle was the ultimate disgrace, the one unforgivable crime. He had acted, he knew, with incredible – culpable – stupidity, but the Eagle at least was safe. It must remain so at all costs. Without its Eagle the legion was dead.

So, militarily and politically, was its legate.

'Stay close, Centurion!' he said to the aquilifer. 'Bugler! Sound the advance!'

The line of cavalry swept back up the road towards the beleaguered legion.

*   *   *

Cerialis halted as he crested the rise. The marching column had vanished. In its place was a heaving mass of painted warriors that spread out along the line of the road and halfway to the flanking trees almost as far as he could see.

Thousands. There must be thousands, tens of thousands. Sweet holy Jupiter!

Three cohort standards were still aloft, but even as he watched one of them dipped and fell. He felt sick. There was nothing he could do. Nothing.

The legion was already gone.

His fist tightened on the reins and came down hard on his horse's neck. The animal started and shifted sideways, its ears laid back.

'Sir?'

Cerialis looked round, his mind a blank. The young tribune, Gaius Opimius, had reined in behind him.

'Do we attack, sir?' The tribune's horse – a patrician's stallion, small-headed and fine-boned – was twitching with excitement after its interrupted gallop. The same could be said of Opimius himself. He was bright-eyed and the knuckles of his hand were white on the hilt of his sabre.

'What with?' As Cerialis watched, the two remaining standards disappeared. 'Don't be a fool, Tribune.'

'But, sir, we can't just—'

'Use your eyes, boy! There's no point. We might cut our way through but there'd be no one to rescue and no way back.'

Opimius's jaw tightened with an audible snap as discipline took over. He jerked back on his horse's rein. A speck of foam from the bit splashed his thigh. 'Very well,' he said. 'Then what do we do exactly, sir? Run?'

'Gods alive!' Cerialis's face had flushed, but he kept his voice calm. 'Tribune, you may be allowed the luxury of heroism, but I am not, and I won't throw lives away unnecessarily. Do you understand me?'

'Yes, sir. Perfectly.' Opimius's face was wooden. He saluted smartly, pulled his horse's head round and trotted back towards the waiting lines.

Cerialis frowned. He didn't blame Opimius: the fault was his, and no doubt he would answer for it. Well, it was done. All he could do now was save what was left of his command and send a message to Paullinus.

To Paullinus, and to the Colony. The Colony would have to take its own chances now, and he did not rate them highly.

'Opimius!' he snapped. 'Here, please!' The tribune came forward again, his lips still set in a hard line. 'Take ten men. You're to ride to the Colony. Tell them what's happened and that they must look to their own defence. Then London. Give Procurator Catus my compliments and ask him to send as many troops north as he can. Also to raise levies from King Cogidubnus's Regni.' He was clutching at straws and he knew it: Catus had only two auxiliary cohorts, and he would not leave London undefended. And when the troops came – if they came – it would only be to find the Colony a gutted shell. Still, the effort had to be made. And at least the emperor's crony Opimius Nerva would have a better chance of seeing his only son and heir again.

'Sir, I'd prefer to—' Opimius began.

'Do as you're bloody told!' Cerialis wheeled his horse away. 'Bugler!' The man rode up, his face devoid of expression. That was to be expected, too, Cerialis thought grimly: it was all a general who had just lost his army deserved. 'Sound Form Wedge! Cavalry to the Eagle!'

It was, he knew, the only hope left. The Iceni were still busy with the last of the infantry, and up to now their arrival had gone unnoticed. His eyes scanned the battlefield. The line of the road led through its centre, and it was blocked by a solid-packed mass of bodies, living and dead. To go that way would be suicide. To the north-east the press was thinner. A determined charge at the gallop in wedge formation might force a passage before the natives could rally and swamp them by sheer numbers. Once through, the road was clear back to Dercovium.

Might be clear. If there was no second Icenian army or worse still a fresh force of Corieltauvi, moving south. And if the Corieltauvi had risen behind him then there might no longer be a Dercovium to return to . . .

So many ifs. He didn't know! He just did not know!

They had been seen: the bugler's signal to the cavalry had been answered by the hoarse booming of the native war-horns and the

Icenian army was shifting like corn-heads in a gale. From the roar that carried even above the noise of the battle Cerialis knew that unless he moved now it would be too late.

'Aquilifer!'

The man took up position at his right knee, the pole of the Eagle standard set firm in its sheath against his horse's flank. Cerialis lifted his hand and with a silent prayer to whatever god would bother listening to him now brought it down in a chopping slash.

Ecenomolios was leaning on his shield, his grin stiff under its mask of paint and blood. His father's sword was dyed red, and he could feel it purr like a contented cat. He stroked it absently. All around, as far as he could see, dead Wolves lay piled in heaps. Several of the warriors were already stripping them of their arms or hacking heads from necks to fasten to their shields.

Camulos, that had been a fight! One that the storytellers would remember for a hundred years. A thousand.

The sound of a Roman bugle and the answering boom of his own war-horns brought him back to himself. He turned. The Wolves' cavalry were streaming up from the south in a solid body, the Eagle at their head.

The Eagle . . .

Ecenomolios straightened, his weariness forgotten. Yelling to his guard to follow, he plunged into the press, forcing his way through the mass of warriors that lay between him and the battle's edge. He knew long before he reached it that he was too late. As he watched, the wedge-shaped body of horse cut through the army's thin flank and swept on towards the safety of the open country beyond.

He stood staring after them for a long time. Then he shrugged and turned away. He was a realist; he might have lost the Eagle, but the Wolves had lost an army. And there was nothing, now, between his warriors and the Colony.

Ecenomolios pulled up a handful of grass and began to clean the blood from his sword.

32

In the yard of Adaucius Montanus's house, Albilla was watching Ursina unpack the contents of the coach.

'Father says there's no real danger,' she said.

'Oh, I'm sure he's right.' Ursina was pulling at the chest in which she had packed the family plate. 'Titus always looks on the black side.' The chest shifted. 'Trinnus, take this to Montanus for me, please.'

Albilla moved aside to let the coachman through. 'But you're still leaving the villa.'

'It's best to be safe.' Ursina dusted her hands on her cloak. 'And we are very isolated out there. I've told Titus time and time again in the past, but you know him; he never listens.'

'You'd've been welcome to stay with us. We've plenty of room.'

'And have Titus sharing a roof with your father? No, thank you, dear. He's difficult enough at the best of times.'

'I don't think Father would've minded.' Albilla gave a pale smile. 'And Mother would be delighted.'

'I'm sure she would,' Ursina said drily.

Albilla laughed. 'She isn't that bad, is she?'

'Of course not.' Ursina pulled a double armful of book-cylinders from the coach. 'Albilla, I'm grateful for your offer of help today, but I assumed you meant the practical variety. Here. Carry some of these.'

'Actually, I'd thought more in terms of supervising.' Albilla was still grinning.

'Disillusionment is a terrible thing in the young.'

Albilla's grin widened. She liked Ursina. Her own mother would never have said something like that with such a straight face. And Bellicia would certainly not demean herself by carrying books.

'What about the slaves? Can't they do it?'

'These are Titus's babies.' Ursina was resting her chin on the top of her own half of the pile. 'He won't even let Trinnus touch them. Now stop complaining, or we'll never be finished.'

The front gate opened on to a verandah surrounding the garden. Montanus's house was small only by Albilla's standards, and since the death of his wife two years before he had occupied it alone. Apart from the kitchen, the south wing was self-contained, and there was a small room for Aper to use as a study. They carried the books inside and laid them carefully on the couch.

There was a knock at the door, and Adaucius Montanus came in, shuffling between his sticks.

'Trinnus brought me your box, Ursina,' he said. 'I had him put it in the strongroom. You have everything you need otherwise?'

'Yes, thank you, Quintus.' Ursina straightened. 'We're very grateful.'

'Nonsense. I appreciate the company.' He shifted painfully. 'Titus not back yet?'

'No, but he had business over at the residence. I expect he's been delayed. He shouldn't be long.'

'Then we'll wait dinner a while yet. You'll join us, Albilla?'

'If you don't mind. That'd be lovely.' Albilla looked sideways at Ursina. 'Business about the revolt?'

'So I'd imagine.' Ursina was putting the books into a small book-chest.

'Father says it'll be over in a day or so.' Albilla moved to help her. 'Petilius Cerialis is bringing the Ninth down from Dercovium. And the procurator's sending troops from London.'

'He's a good man, Cerialis.' Montanus smiled at her. 'I shouldn't worry, Albilla. Your father's probably right.' He turned to Ursina. 'I've given orders to bring in extra braziers. This part of the house can be cold in the evenings.'

'You're spoiling us.'

'Not at all.' Montanus paused. 'Have you heard anything from Marcus, by the way?'

'One letter since Mona.' Ursina closed the lid of the book-chest. 'Marcus is no writer. And the military life seems to suit him.'

'Does it, indeed?' Montanus looked at Albilla. 'I'm surprised.' His eyes twinkled. 'When's the wedding?'

'As soon as the campaign's over.' Albilla felt her cheeks flush. Her fingers strayed to the pendant at her throat: the gold coin that she had bought for Marcus's birthday. 'The fighting's finished, of course, but the governor wants to—'

She broke off as the door opened and Aper came in.

'Ah, Titus,' Montanus said. 'You're back. Dinner'll be in about half an hour, if that's all right.'

'Fine.' Aper took off his cloak and, turning round so his back was to them, hung it carefully on one of the wall-pegs. 'Thank you.'

'Titus, what's wrong?' Ursina said quietly.

Albilla glanced at her, then at Montanus. They had both gone very still.

'A messenger's come from Cerialis.' Aper's hand brushed at the cloak, straightening its folds. 'His senior tribune. The Ninth's been ambushed this side of Duroliponte and the infantry massacred.'

Albilla felt her knees begin to shake and she sat down heavily on the reading couch.

'Sweet Jupiter!' Montanus whispered.

'All of them?' Ursina looked, suddenly, old. 'The whole legion?'

Aper turned round. His face, like his voice, was empty of expression. 'Aye, Bear-cub. All he brought with him, anyway. Three thousand out of the five. They were in marching column without cavalry support, and the Iceni took them by surprise. By the time Cerialis got back there was nothing he could do. He's taken the cavalry back to Dercovium.'

'Then we're on our own,' Albilla said. To her own ears her voice seemed to come from very far away. 'There's no army coming after all.' She giggled.

'Albilla, stop it!' Ursina snapped.

'So, Titus.' Montanus, too, had sat down, on the stool beside the desk. 'What do we do now?'

'What we can. There are still the veterans, plus the auxiliaries attached to the port. And Catus's two hundred infantry arrived this morning.'

'*Two hundred?*' Montanus stared at him. 'Gods, man, is that all he sent? He has two full cohorts!'

'Catus has London to protect. And London's merchants.' Albilla could detect no bitterness in Aper's voice, only a weary resignation. 'He has his own priorities.'

'Yes. Well, that's true enough.' Montanus was frowning. 'I suppose we're lucky to get that many. If the damned council had had its way—' He stopped, with a glance at Albilla. 'Well. Never mind that now. It can't be helped.'

Albilla shook her head. She felt lost. 'What about the governor? He'll send us troops when he gets the news, surely?'

The two men looked at each other without speaking.

'It'll take a messenger six days to reach Mona, dear,' Ursina said gently. 'And more than twice that again for the legions to get here, even if they set out at once. I'm sorry, but that's too long. Paullinus can't help us. Or not soon.'

'Then we're dead.' Albilla put her knuckles to her teeth, trying to choke back the scream building up inside her. 'We're all dead.'

'Nonsense, girl,' Aper grunted. 'All it means is that we have to hold out until he gets here. They're only natives, after all.'

'That's not what you told my father!'

'Listen to me, Albilla!' Aper's hands reached out to grip her shoulders. 'We're not helpless. We've two thousand veterans in the Colony and more than half a regular infantry cohort. Aye, the rebels outnumber us but their fighting strength isn't a quarter of their size. Better, they've been lucky, and because of that they'll be over-confident. We can beat them, and we will.'

Albilla took a deep breath. 'I'm sorry,' she said. It's just—' A sob caught at her throat. 'Don't mind me. Of course we'll win. We have to, don't we?'

Aper's grip relaxed. He glanced at his wife, who nodded, her lips set. 'Aye, of course we do,' he said. 'Now go with Ursina. Quintus and I have to talk.'

'It's hopeless, isn't it?' Montanus said calmly when the women had left.

'Aye.' Aper went over to the desk and poured two cups of wine from the jug that sat there. 'From what young Opimius said Boudica must have at least twenty thousand men to our three, probably a lot more. And after what happened to the Ninth she'll have all the arms she needs. We've no walls and no time to build them. And even if we did the Colony's too big to defend.'

Montanus took his cup and sipped. 'So,' he said.

'So.'

'How long have we got?'

'The gods know.' Aper lowered himself on to the couch and set the cup down untasted on the table beside him. 'They can't be any more than twenty miles off. On the other hand young Opimius says they're moving slowly. If we're lucky they'll leave us alone for the present and concentrate on looting. They know we're here and how many we are, but on the other hand they know we'll fight. That might hold them off for a while.' He frowned. 'Three days? Five? That's assuming the Trinovantes don't get us first.'

Montanus set his cup down. 'Jupiter in heaven!'

'Aye. As of today the whole tribe's up, border to border, not just the Dunsmen. Opimius said he was lucky to get through.'

Montanus shrugged. 'Well, I don't altogether blame them, I suppose. We deserve it.'

'Don't be so bloody reasonable, man! The time for that's past!'

'Yes, I suppose it is.' Montanus sat silent, staring at nothing. 'So. We add the Trinovantes. What's the plan?'

'You're asking me?'

'You're our ranking veteran. You commanded a wing and you have thirty years' military experience under your belt. Yes, I'm asking you, Titus. Of course I am.'

'Aye. Well.' Aper's lips twisted. 'I can only say what I said to Albilla: when Paullinus gets Cerialis's message – if he gets it – he'll bring the army back from Mona. It's up to us to hold the Colony until he comes.'

'You think we can?'

'No. Do you?'

Montanus stood up and moved painfully to the window.

'No,' he said quietly, looking out over the city.

'Then we're agreed on that, at least.' Aper cleared his throat.

'Now. Weapons first. The veterans and the auxiliaries are provided for, but I've got Bassus organising teams to collect all the scrap iron for melting he can find. Old armour, too. We're going to need all the men we can get under arms, military and civilian, and we can't send them out naked.'

Montanus half turned and gave a barking laugh. 'I never thought I'd see Gaius Vegisonius wearing a tin mantle! Have you told him?'

'Aye.' Aper didn't smile. 'And the others on the council. The business with Cerialis hit them hard, Quintus. They'll give no trouble now.'

'What about the rest? The other Colonists?'

'Uricalus is spreading the word. As of tomorrow we abandon everything west of Cloak Street and south of Residence Road and move to the Annexe. There're enough building materials there to cobble together some sort of rampart. And if need be we can make a stand on the higher ground round the temple.'

Montanus was still looking out of the window.

'As of tomorrow?' he said.

'As far as a general evacuation's concerned, aye. Work on the rampart's already started and it'll go on all night. I left Radix in charge with as many of the veterans as he can muster. There's no reason to bring the women and children over, not yet. Tomorrow'll be soon enough.'

Montanus was silent for a long time. Then he said, 'I suppose there's no way of getting them away altogether? We've four hundred regular troops. They wouldn't make much difference to us but they'd make some sort of escort at least.'

'Jupiter, man, do you think I haven't thought of that? No, not with the Trinovantes in revolt. It's too risky now.'

'Indeed.' Montanus sighed. 'Titus, come over here a moment, would you?'

Aper felt his spine go cold. He got up quickly and joined the other man at the window.

Where the traders' huts straggled along the line of the Estuary Road towards the Dun, he could see a heavy pall of smoke lifting, spreading west across the sky in the early evening breeze.

'I'm afraid,' Montanus said gently, 'that tomorrow may be too late.'

33

When Aper and Montanus came outside Ursina and Albilla were standing by the coach with Trinnus and the household's slaves, staring at the sky.

'It's the Trinovantes, isn't it, Titus?' Ursina said.

'Aye.'

Albilla glanced at them but said nothing.

'Isn't there anything to be done?'

He laid an arm round her shoulders. 'No, Bear-cub, not now. We can only get ourselves to the Annexe as quick as we can and hope others have the sense to do the same.'

Ursina sighed and leaned against him. 'Well,' she said.

'Well indeed, Bear-cub. Well it is.' Aper gave her another squeeze, then let her go and turned to Montanus. 'Your folk'll need weapons, Quintus. Whatever you have: kitchen knives, cleavers, spits, anything. It's half a mile to the east gate. We should have time enough, but I'll take no chances.'

'I'll see to it. Or Rufus and Canio will.' Montanus cleared his throat. 'I won't be coming with you, Titus.'

Aper stared at him. 'You're not serious?'

'Perfectly serious.'

'For Jupiter's sake, man!'

'Quintus, we can take the coach.' Ursina said.

'It has nothing to do with my lameness. Or not in the way you mean.'

'Then why?'

'Because I'm tired, Ursina. And because, frankly, I prefer to die at home than go traipsing all the way over to the Annexe to do it.' Montanus smiled. 'Don't worry, I'll arrange things comfortably and painlessly. So no arguments, please, and no discussion.'

Aper looked at him, then at Ursina. She nodded, once.

'Very well, Quintus,' he said finally. 'I'm sorry. The gods be with you.'

'And with you, Titus.' Montanus beckoned to the two gawping male slaves. 'Come on, Rufus. Canio.' He led them into the house.

Albilla had been watching the exchange in disbelief.

'You're letting him kill himself?' she said.

Aper was fetching his cavalry sabre and belt from the coach.

'Aye,' he said.

'But you can't!'

'It's Montanus's decision, Albilla. And his right.'

'But . . .' Albilla covered her face with her hands for a moment, then took them away. 'Yes,' she said. 'Yes, I'm sorry.'

'Good girl.' Aper slipped the belt over his head and shoulder and settled the sabre in place. 'Trinnus, you have your knife?'

'Aye, sir.'

'Where's Sulicena, Bear-cub?'

'I sent her for some blankets.' Ursina looked round just as the old woman, her arms full, appeared in the doorway. 'Here she is now.'

'Fine. Then as soon as Quintus's lads come back we'll go. Albilla, get—'

'No.' The girl was shaking her head. 'I can't come either. Not without Mother.'

Aper stared at her.

Ursina laid a hand on his arm. 'Albilla,' she said, 'Bellicia knows where you are, and she'll have seen the smoke herself. She'll be gone already. Don't be silly, dear.'

'I'm not being silly. Mother won't . . . she wouldn't just leave everything and go. She'll believe me. Please!'

'Your father will bring her, surely.'

'Father isn't there. He went out before I left this morning. He had business at the port.' Albilla was crying now. 'Ursina, I must! *Please!*'

Ursina looked at Aper. 'Titus?'

'It's too dangerous,' he said. 'And there's no time. Albilla, you must see that.'

Trinnus cleared his throat. 'I'll go with her, sir. We're safe enough yet. It won't take long, and if they haven't left we'll have Uricalus's lads with us afterwards.'

Aper took a deep breath. 'Very well,' he said. 'But be quick.'
Albilla hugged him.

Albilla and Trinnus set off through the crowd-choked streets in
the direction of the market. The Colony was in chaos. They
passed several carts that had been abandoned fully laden, the
oxen standing white-eyed and shaking while the human river
flowed around them. What Albilla noticed most was the silence.
There was no talking, no shouting, no sound of human voices at
all. Not even the children cried.

South of Market Square, the crowds began to thin. They were
on Main Street now, beyond the Praetorian Street junction,
almost home. Most of the shops were tightly shuttered, but
some lay open and gutted, their goods strewn across the road.
Trinnus kept his knife ready, but even the looters had gone.

They turned into Uricalus's street. It, too, was empty. The
house itself was locked and the windows barred.

'They've gone already, miss,' Trinnus said. 'We'd best be . . .'

Albilla saw him freeze. She spun round, following his eyes. For
a split second, she wondered what was wrong; what the reason
had been for the look of surprise and terror on Trinnus's face.
The men were only natives, after all . . .

Then she remembered, and ran, Trinnus beside her.

The spear caught him with a sound like a butcher's cleaver
hitting a carcass. He grunted and fell sprawling in a tangle of legs
and arms. Albilla stopped and stared down at him in disbelief.
He lay on his face, twitching, the spear-shaft ludicrously erect
like a pole below his shoulder, the bloodied head standing out
a hand's-breadth beneath his chest.

She screamed.

Behind her, she heard the sound of running feet. Hands caught
at her and pulled her round, lifting her. The world was suddenly
a sea of grinning faces, painted blue and red above the long
moustaches. She smelled sour curds and stale honey beer.

She screamed again. The hands were gripping her, crushing
her ribs. Another hand, coming out of nowhere, smashed across
her face. Inside her mouth, something broke and she tasted
blood.

'Please,' she said. 'Please . . .'

Someone laughed and spoke. The hands shifted, to her arms, her legs, gripping and tugging. She felt herself pulled backwards and forwards at the one time. The world lurched sickeningly, out of control, and the sea of faces vanished. The sky stretched above her like a blue blanket.

The man's voice spoke again. Other voices answered.

'Please,' she said. 'Please, I'm sorry, I don't understand. I don't speak . . .'

Something hard and sharp thrust itself between her thighs. The pain was unbelievable. She screamed, and kept on screaming, thrashing from side to side, helpless in the hands' grip as the pain drove deeper and swelled to blot out the world.

Then, with a sudden white-hot wrench, it was gone, and there was only the friendly, welcoming darkness.

Something was glinting at the dead woman's throat. Inam reached down and yanked the pendant free, breaking the chain and sending the head thudding into the gravel of the roadway. He held the thing up to the light: a gold coin, with a running horse and letters that he could not read.

He slipped the coin under his belt and, spitting into the upturned, death-blind face, pulled his spear free from between her legs.

Then, leaving her corpse where it lay, he followed the others.

34

Senovara let the white mare pick her way between the stands of broom and birch which edged the higher ground overlooking the estuary. The marshes stretched beneath her, a patchwork of green and black and silver, completely still but for the gently shifting reeds. Here and there she could see the dark shapes of feeding ducks and moorhens. Directly below her, a pair of herons stood motionless as statues, their beaks poised above the water.

Eight miles to the north, she knew, people would be dying. Earlier that morning she had watched the warriors set out for the Colony, their faces painted and their spears newly sharpened and gleaming. She had seen the fires, too, in the distance and smelled the smoke: not the clean smell of cooking fires but the sour reek of burning wattle and roof-thatch. Perhaps she had been a fool to go out at all, and before he had left to join the hosting of the tribe the day before her father had forbidden it, but she had felt stifled waiting for news with the other women. Here, at least, the air was fresh, and it had no death-smell.

Lacta had found a path; no more than a thread of crushed grass that wound through the undergrowth. Senovara touched the mare's flanks with her bare knees and urged her into a trot. The path widened, leading towards a thicket of seedling beech and hawthorn. Beyond it she glimpsed the slope of a tiled roof. She reined in; then, hesitantly, she sent Lacta forward.

She recognised the villa at once. The path ended at an open gate in the garden wall. Beyond the gate, a horse was tethered to the trunk of an apple tree. It turned its head and snorted.

Senovara dismounted and led Lacta through the gate. The two horses nuzzled each other while she tethered the mare to an overhanging branch. The man stood half a dozen paces off, watching her. His face was painted, and he was holding a sword.

'Father?' she said.

'You should not be here, girl.' Brocomaglos did not move.

'No.' She walked over to him and stood, waiting.

He made a clearing gesture with his hand and looked away. 'I used to come here once. Before they landed, when I was a boy. There was a beavers' lodge in the stream over by the three willow trees. It's gone now. Beavers won't build near people.'

Senovara said nothing.

'There's a fireplace in this wall. Look.' He pointed with his sword. 'The hot air's carried under the house's floor to warm it.' His lips twisted. 'No smoke, no flames even. Just heat that you can't see. Clever. Too clever, like them. We would never think of that, Senovara. We would wrap warm on a winter's night and watch the flames. Their roads, too. Hard-packed gravel, not mud, and cambered so the water runs off at the sides into ditches. Clever. And what do they use them for? To move armies.'

'Father . . .'

Brocomaglos was not listening. He looked, she thought, lost. She had never seen her father look lost before.

'Father,' she said, 'why did you come?'

He shrugged. 'To burn it. I thought it needed burning. Only I can't do it. People I knew lived here. The Romans may be enemies, they may have to die for what they've done to us and what they might do yet, but I can't hate them for being different. Do you understand me, girl?'

Senovara nodded. 'Aye,' she said.

'That's good. Because I don't understand myself.' He grinned suddenly, and the lost look vanished. 'Ach, well, we'll let someone else do the dirty work. Here, at least. You'd best get home. Your mother'll be worried.'

He walked over to the horses.

'You're coming too?' she said.

'No.' He unfastened the stallion's halter, gripped its mane and mounted. 'No, lass. Keep you safe.'

Wheeling the stallion, he set his heels to its flanks.

'And you, Father,' she said; but he was already gone through the gate.

Senovara mounted Lacta and rode back to the Dun. She knew,

as if someone had whispered it to her, that she would never see
him again.

35

Aper looked about him with satisfaction.

The transformation of the Annexe from building site to fort was well under way. On either side of a gap left for access facing the junction of North Cloak Street and Ditch Street stretched a solid line of upturned carts reinforced by masonry blocks and heavy wooden beams, with every twenty paces a raised fighting platform wide enough for four men and protected by a breastwork screen of tanned ox-hides. It was far from perfect, he could see that: the carts, wedged though they were from behind, could be pulled forward to leave gaps in the wall and there was no fronting ditch. Still, as a barrier it might hold long enough for an attack to be broken.

'Will it pass, Titus?'

He turned. Ursina was watching him closely.

'Aye, Bear-cub, it'll pass. If we're for the death mask then at least we'll go down fighting.'

She reached up and kissed his cheek.

A broad-shouldered man in a centurion's uniform was making his way towards them.

'There's Radix coming now,' Ursina said. 'Don't hurry, Titus. We'll be by the temple steps when you finish.'

'Fine.' Aper kissed her and turned to the veteran. 'Everything going well, Radix?'

'Aye, we're getting there, Commander.' The First Spear in charge of the construction saluted and grinned. 'When they come they'll have their work cut out getting past that little lot.'

Aper looked across to the right; the barrier continued along the south side, facing the residence and the new provincial offices, but there it stopped. 'What about the north and east?'

'I thought we'd concentrate on the town side first, sir. But there's still lads out scavenging for stuff with what carts we have left. Give us an hour or two and we'll finish the square.'

'If you can take it you can have it.'

'We'll manage. And if not, well, it comes to us all, doesn't it?'

Aper grunted. 'Javelins?'

'Bassus's had the armourers working flat out all day. He reckons we've ten to a man already, at least. That's military personnel only, Commander, if you're agreed. These townies couldn't hit a cow broadside on at ten yards.' Radix pulled at his ear. 'I'd give a year's pay for a cohort of archers, mind, or even a hundred slingers. Speaking of which, sir, we've a few good bowmen.' He turned round and nodded towards the temple. 'If we put them up on the roof there they'd do a tidy bit of damage on their own account.'

'Fine. Two more suggestions. Hurdles outside the barrier where the ditch should be, as many as you can find. Bring them in from the fields. And put a man on the roof now. One with a good pair of eyes.'

Radix grinned. 'Already done, sir. Don't you worry. Whenever the bastards come they won't catch us napping. I'll see to the hurdles, though.'

An hour later the city was blazing in earnest. A thick blanket of smoke moved slowly from west to east across the Annexe, turning the setting sun red and bringing with it the stench of burning buildings. Specks of soot, carried on the evening breeze, fell as a constant rain, covering everything in a greasy black film.

Aper walked through the makeshift fort. It was a hive of desperate activity. Along the wide strip of ground left clear around its edge a constant stream of carts moved, loaded with lengths of planking, furniture, empty oil jars: anything that would serve as an obstacle. At intervals gangs were working on the fighting platforms, lashing the scaffolding poles together with rope. The civilians – some fifteen thousand, Aper estimated – had grouped themselves around the temple podium: women and children mostly, crammed together in tight huddles that filled the limited space completely. They sat in almost total silence.

The faces that turned to Aper as he made his way between the groups were pinched and drawn, and what talking there was was in whispers. Some of the women had lit fires and were stirring cooking-pots balanced on stones above the flames.

At least there's no panic, he thought. Thank the gods for that. The Colony – or its core – was army. Army wives and children did not panic easily. Walking through the crowd, he felt a sudden surge of pride, and of anger at the sheer waste.

He could see Ursina now, and Sulicena, sitting by the temple steps with Bellicia; but the people round about them were strangers.

Aper's mouth was dry as he quickened his pace, pushing through the crowd. Ursina looked up as he came closer, but Bellicia's eyes were fixed and staring at nothing.

'Where's Albilla?' he said.

'I haven't seen her, Titus.' Ursina's voice was low and controlled. 'Nor Trinnus. Bellicia was here already.'

A cold knot had formed itself in Aper's stomach. They should have come by now; the last of the Colonists had passed the barrier long since and the gaps were closed. Uricalus was missing, too, but that he had half expected. His mouth tightened. There was nothing he could do; nothing anyone could do.

'Aye, well,' he said.

Ursina reached out and touched his wrist. 'Liberius has been looking for you,' she said. Liberius commanded the London troops. 'He's inside, I think.' Then, when he hesitated: 'Go on. I'll look after Bellicia.'

He nodded and went up the temple steps. He had never felt so old.

The temple was vast, empty and echoing. And bitterly cold, despite the torches; the chill that seeped from the stonework cut through the warmth of Aper's cloak and made him shiver. Straw mattresses had been laid down one of its sides, and at the door end, where the light was better, a round-shouldered man with thick eyebrows and the olive skin of an Asiatic Greek was talking earnestly to a slave carrying an armful of salves and bandages.

'Cadmus, is Liberius here?' Aper said.

The Colony's chief medical officer looked round, frowning at the interruption.

'In the priest's robing-room.'

He turned back to the slave.

Aper walked towards the temple's far end where the statue of the emperor-god stared back at him across the cold incense braziers. The robing-room was behind it; small, hardly more than a cupboard, and scarcely big enough for the four men who occupied it, sitting knee to knee around a folding table. They looked up as he came in.

'Commander.' Liberius was a man in his fifties with strong patrician features. 'Good, you're here. I was worried.'

'Aye.' Aper put his own worries and griefs aside and pulled up the camp stool that Castor, the officer in charge of the port garrison, had unfolded for him. 'I thought I'd better have a look round the defences first. Good evening, Bassus. Fidus.'

Bassus nodded. Fidus did not: the Roman banker, his urbane polish gone, sat slumped, half leaning on his forearms.

'And your conclusions?' Liberius asked.

They were all watching him closely, Fidus with an almost hungry desperation.

'We might hold the first attack. Maybe the second, if we're lucky. After that, no.'

The obvious tension in the room seemed to ease. Bassus and Castor grunted with what sounded almost like satisfaction. Fidus simply stared straight ahead.

'Yes,' Liberius said, glancing at him. 'That was exactly our view of the situation, Commander. That being so the question is what to do once the wall is breached. I'm thinking numbers, of course. We've fifteen thousand civilians outside. When the enemy break through with the best will in the world we can't protect them, not with the men we've got. Certainly not for long.'

Aper nodded. 'No,' he said. 'No, that's true.' Beside him Fidus shifted and opened his mouth to say something, but stayed silent. 'All we can do is bring as many here inside the temple as we can and have them bar the doors.'

'Indeed. The temple will hold – what?' Liberius looked at Castor. 'Twelve hundred?'

Castor grunted. 'Fifteen, at a squeeze.'

'Let's call it fifteen, then.' Liberius closed his eyes briefly. 'By all means, fifteen. Yes. I agree, Commander. Bassus?'

The decurion nodded. 'Aye, me too, sir,' he said. 'It's all we can do. The place is solid stone and the doors are metal. Once they're closed and barred they'll be safe enough. For the time being, anyway.'

'Good.' Liberius turned to Fidus. 'Fidus, you can organise that?' There was no answer. '*Fidus!*'

The banker's head jerked up and round.

'Fidus, I asked if you could organise the temple side of things.'

'What about the rest?' Fidus's cheeks were shaking. 'The other thirteen and a half thousand? Where do they go? And do the lucky ones select themselves, Liberius, or do you expect me to play god for them as you're doing now?'

'Gently, Fidus, gently,' Aper murmured. 'None of us wants to play god.'

Fidus looked at him, then dropped his eyes.

'No,' he said. His voice was barely a whisper. 'No. I'm sorry, gentlemen. Don't worry, I'll see to it.'

Moving like a sleepwalker, he stood up and left the room. The others watched him go.

'Now,' Aper said. 'What forces do we have exactly?'

'Regular troops,' Castor said, 'my own lads, that's a cohort. With yours, Liberius, say seven hundred altogether. Veterans another eighteen hundred.'

'Nearer the two thousand,' Bassus put in. 'Five hundred of them're cavalry, but I doubt if we've horses for half that number. Say two hundred mounted and equipped.' He grinned. 'The rest of the buggers'll have to fight on their feet for once.'

'Male civilians and slaves, approximately another four thousand.' Castor rubbed his eyes. 'Not all those'll be armed with anything better than a knife, but we've a few bowmen and slingers.'

'Put those on the roof,' Aper said. 'Radix's idea. Decurion, your cavalry. Two hundred mounted, you said.'

'Aye, sir.'

'We'll keep them in reserve. As for the rest, when the barrier goes we fall back towards the temple steps.' Taking the knife from his belt, Aper drew an oblong in the wood of the table, then three lines in front of it, covering the sides. 'Non-combatants at the back, armed civilians in the centre, veterans and regulars forming a screen in front and on the wings. We hold the temple frontage at all costs for as long as possible. The podium's high enough at the sides and back to secure our rear, and what there are left of us can use it to make a final stand.' His lips twisted and he set the knife down. 'After which any further arrangements are a matter of personal preference. That's the plan, such as it is. Comments?' There was silence. 'You agree, then, gentlemen?'

Bassus grinned sourly.

'Aye,' he said. 'I reckon that'll do us nicely, sir. And if nothing else we'll take a few of the bastards with us.'

'We'll do that at least, Decurion.' Aper stood up. 'That we will certainly do. Meeting adjourned.'

36

The first attack came from the south as the daylight faded. The Trinovantian war-host flowed across Ditch Street and Residency Road towards the barricade. As it reached the outlying barrier of hurdles its momentum checked and faltered.

A single trumpet blared.

The javelins struck out from the fighting platforms and upturned carts in a solid wave, tumbling body after body on to the growing heaps until the dead formed a third wall breast-high and three paces deep. For the space of twenty heartbeats the attack held as fresh warriors poured in to take the place of the fallen. Then, as javelin followed javelin and the piled dead began to outnumber the living, it slowed, wavered and finally broke apart, the screams now pain, not anger as those behind clambered over the corpses of those in front and died in their turn.

The war-horns on the flanks and rear sounded. The milling crowd of painted warriors shifted, broke and scattered. The world was suddenly still. Here and there, among the smashed remains of the attacking force, a figure raised itself to crawl over the heaped corpses towards the line of the road.

'That's learned the buggers!' Radix was exultant. 'They'll think twice before they try that again!' He turned to Aper. 'Permission to send a company out, sir, to recover javelins.'

'Aye. Go ahead, Centurion.' Aper was pleased, too: the attack had been easier to beat off than he had expected. 'Tell Bassus to give you cavalry cover.'

'Right you are, sir.' Radix saluted and went off whistling.

The mood within the Annexe had lightened. As Aper walked back to the temple steps more than one veteran held up a hand to him in the Victory salute. There was even, by Claudius's altar, a knot of children playing. He could still smell the sour, charred odour of burning buildings, but it was overlaid now by the homelier scents of porridge, flatcakes and bacon fat.

Well, he thought, so we aren't dead yet after all. Perhaps the gods'll be kind. His lips twisted.

Sulicena had cooked a chicken, spitting it on a shaft of hazel over a fire of wood chips. The grease dropped hissing into the flames. Aper settled down with a sigh on the blanket next to Ursina. She kissed his cheek without a word and handed him a cup of wine. Setting his back to the temple step, he looked up at the sky. It was a fine evening with a moon halfway to the full. The wind had shifted to the north, and now the smoke from the burning town had dispersed the stars shone down bright and unclouded. He wondered if Marcus, too, was watching them.

At least they wouldn't have to fight in the dark.

'Where's Bellicia, Bear-cub?' he said.

'Safe inside.'

Aper nodded and sipped his wine.

'You think they'll come back tonight?' Ursina poured wine for herself and Sulicena.

'Maybe.' The fingers of his left hand brushed her neck. 'Tomorrow, certainly.'

'So.' Ursina was not looking at him. 'Titus, Sulicena and I have been talking.' The old woman looked up, then turned back to her cooking. 'When they come, if they break through, promise me you'll . . . see to both of us yourself.'

Aper set the cup down and placed a finger over her lips. She moved away.

'I'd rather it was you, and then. Promise me, please.'

Aper said nothing.

'Titus.' Her voice hardened. 'Have I your word or not?'

He looked at her for a long time. Then he nodded, once, his throat tight.

'Aye, lass,' he said, kissing her. 'Of course. You have my word.'

He was woken just after midnight by a shout from the temple roof. The lookout man was pointing, not to the south but to the north-west, across the fields that bordered the river. Aper could hear a low rumble like distant thunder.

Ursina was awake too. She watched him as he slipped the sword-belt over his head and arm.

'They're coming?' she said.

'Aye.' He adjusted the sheath at his side. 'Rouse Sulicena.'

All around them people were stirring, but quietly as if noise would bring the enemy all the faster. The moonlit Annexe was full of flitting, silent shadows and the muted rustle and clink of weapons being readied as the barricade was manned and the troops formed up round the standards. Aper mounted the steps with Ursina and Sulicena behind him. Radix was already standing at the podium's edge staring out towards the river. He glanced round briefly but said nothing.

Aper looked.

The moonlit fields that bordered the river's banks were a moving sea of people, a dark wave that spread westwards as far as his eye could reach in a long curve that took in half the length of the Colony beyond. Here and there tiny sparks of light bobbed like fireflies, accentuating the blackness that surrounded them and giving it depth. As he watched, the dots of light drew nearer and the low rumble swelled, breaking into separate, distinct sounds: the braying of war-horns, isolated shouts and the beating of spear-shafts on shields.

The Iceni had arived.

He was aware of Ursina standing at his shoulder. He turned.

'Take Sulicena, Bear-cub,' he said gently. 'Wait for me by the temple doors.'

She reached up and kissed his cheek, then left without a word.

'I'll be getting down to the barricade now, sir,' Radix said. His eyes had never left the advancing war-host. 'You'll need a signaller.'

'Aye.' Aper drew his sabre. 'Good luck, Centurion. Give the lads my best.'

Radix saluted and moved off towards the temple steps.

The attack was sudden, savage and total, pouring towards the barricades and swamping them at the first rush as completely as if they had been a child's wall of sand. What defenders remained alive scattered, running for the sheltering lines of the main body of troops drawn up in a three-quarter circle around the temple, their wings curving round to touch the mid-point of the podium walls. Aper, standing with the signaller on the podium's topmost step, watched the dark tide stream across the broken line of carts and spread like spilled ink to cover the stretch of ground beyond the shield line where the bulk of the Colony's civilian population had gathered. As the killing and the screams began he clenched his jaw until he could feel the teeth almost crack under the strain, knowing that in a few minutes they would all be dead and that there was nothing, nothing in the world, he could do to stop the butchery.

Thirteen thousand people! Merciful Jupiter, thirteen thousand!

He forced the thought and the screams from his mind and shifted his attention to the silent lines of veterans and auxiliaries waiting beneath him. The tide flowed on towards the temple, dark no longer but a sea of yelling warriors with painted faces and bodies.

Eighty yards. Seventy . . .

Aper's head went up.

'First volley, Bugler,' he said.

The signaller blew a single note. The lines shifted, and the first wave of javelins smashed into the howling mass. Men fell screaming, clutching the iron shafts that had sprouted suddenly between their ribs.

Forty yards. Thirty . . .

'Second volley.'

Again the wave of javelins struck. It was like throwing handfuls of gravel into a torrent. The first ranks were down in a kicking tangle of bodies, but there were thousands more behind them. The gaps that the javelins had opened up closed in moments. And the rush had not checked.

Twenty yards. Ten . . .

'Draw swords.'

The two lines met with a crash of shield on shield. Here and there, a head sank down to be replaced by another. Most of the heads wore Roman helmets. The line shivered, and buckled inwards; held the space of a breath, then slowly began to give ground.

'Signal to cavalry,' Aper said. The bugler blew three rising notes.

The circle broke, leaving a gap on either side of the podium's lateral base. From where they had been waiting behind the sheltering wings, Bassus's two squadrons of horse burst through the defensive screen and struck the ragged edges of the close-packed mass of warriors like a hammer-blow, smashing them aside. They galloped in a tight arc across the open ground, then, wheeling, drove hard against the Icenian flanks, hacking their way towards the centre.

Aper held his breath, praying to every god he knew.

Slowly, like slack water caught in a contrary current, the mass below him began to waver as the panic at its edges spread inwards. With the forward pressure reduced, the infantry line, or what remained of it, gathered itself and re-formed.

The cavalry attack faltered and died. Buried deep in the Icenian ranks, and unable to move, the horsemen were struggling to keep their seats. One by one they were sucked down into the press until the last bobbing head had vanished. Aper watched for a moment, then set his jaw and turned to the bugler.

'Sound lock shields,' he said.

At the signal the line, barely longer now than the podium's width, moved quickly backwards, forming a tight crescent around the temple steps and opening a clear space between itself and the Iceni. There was a rustling clatter as the edges of the metal-rimmed shields overlapped.

'Archers.'

The bugle sounded again.

From the roof above and the podium walls to the sides, arrows and slingers' bolts swept the exposed Icenian battle-front, scything into the close-packed ranks and turning them into a screaming chaos of dead and dying. The warriors at the front of the press threw themselves forward at the shield wall; but this time the wall did not break.

Nor, though, did it advance. And the line was too thin now to leave its wings unguarded. Aper knew it; and so did the Iceni.

They drew back. For the space of a dozen heartbeats, Roman and Briton faced each other in silence across an empty no-man's land half a spear-cast wide. Then, from the Icenian rear, a single war-horn blared.

With a spreading roar, the huge host moved forward.

Aper watched the human tide surge towards the temple's base. There was nothing more to be done, no more reserves to call on. This time it would be man against man, and when the line broke it would stay broken.

He felt neither fear nor anger, only a great sadness.

Gods, what a waste! he thought. *What a god-awful waste!*

'Bugler?' he said quietly.

'Aye, sir?' The man was granite-faced, expressionless: a Spaniard like himself, he would guess from the accent, but from the south, near the Baetican border.

Aper shook his head. 'No orders, lad. Not now. Off you go.'

The bugler saluted. Then, setting his bugle down carefully against the pillar, he drew his sword and went down the steps.

There was not much time left, but it would be enough, barely. Aper walked over to where Ursina and Sulicena stood waiting by the temple doors and hugged them. The old woman was crying, but she held herself erect as his sword took her in the chest. Ursina did not flinch either; he had not expected her to. He made sure both women were dead and checked that the doors were securely barred from within. Those inside could hold out for another day, perhaps more, depending on how long the men on the roof could keep the Britons at bay. Even although their arrows and slingshot were exhausted, there would still be plenty of tiles to throw.

After that . . .

After that. Aye, well; there was no point dwelling on it. As Radix had said, it comes to us all.

He went down the steps to join the battle.

Two hundred yards to the south, outside the still-intact barricade, Brocomaglos lay where he had fallen in the first attack, stretched across a hurdle with a javelin in his throat.

37

Severinus was in a vast dimly lit room with stone walls and a high ceiling. In front of him a grandmother whose jaws were no more than gums was hugging a teenage girl. On one side of her a young mother was suckling a baby, and on the other a dark-skinned woman with a squint clutched a wide-eyed toddler. He could feel their fear, as close and stifling as the air in the room itself.

He looked round. The room was filled with people. There were hundreds of them, packed together shoulder to shoulder: girls, mothers, elderly matrons . . .

Jupiter, they're all women! he thought. Women and children!

From the ceiling directly above him came a bumping, scraping noise as if workmen were busy on the roof. As he listened, the noise changed to the dull thud of axes. The toddler whimpered, burying his face in his mother's shoulder, and the old woman broke into a keening moan, rocking back and forward on her thin buttocks. All at once a hole opened in one of the ceiling panels. A shaft of sunlight lanced down, bringing with it a shower of debris. As Severinus watched, horrified, a roof tile fell lazily through the thirty feet that separated ceiling and floor and struck the middle-aged woman sitting directly beneath, smashing her skull to a pulp.

The hole widened, letting in more sunlight, and the shower of debris increased. Other gaps were opening. Severinus tried to get up but found he could only move his head. Turning round as far as he could, he found himself staring into the eyes of a massive bronze statue. A cold finger touched his spine. Jupiter! he thought. This is the Colony! I'm in the temple!

What was happening? What the hell was happening?

Light was pouring in now through the shattered roof and people were screaming in panic, clambering over each other to reach the comparative safety of the walls. The rain of single tiles and roof-boards had given way to huge wooden beams that crushed whole bodies beneath them.

Mothers! Why don't they get out? Severinus thought, close to panic himself. There must be a door, surely!

Around the edges of the holes figures were moving, black against the light. He caught snatches of raised voices and laughter. The rain of debris changed to brushwood and dry branches, wattle screens, scaffolding poles, broken hurdles, cement hods and smashed boarding. Wood; always wood, falling in heaps and load upon load, until it reached a quarter of the way up the walls. The temple floor-space was a chaos of timber among which women and children struggled and screamed.

Then the torches came.

Sweet gods! They're burning us alive!

The torches arced down like meteors. Their flames caught on the dry brushwood, and the air was suddenly filled with choking, lung-hurting smoke and the sickening smell of charred flesh. The screams rose until they blanked out every other sound in the world.

Whatever it was that held him would not let him go. He struggled to break free, fighting the panic that welled up inside him. The flames washed over him in an agonising wave. He felt his hair blaze and turn to ash. He screamed . . .

He was sitting bolt upright, his blanket wrapped tightly around his arms.

'Mothers!' he whispered, appalled. 'Dear holy Mothers!'

That had been a nightmare. Easily the worst he had ever had since he was a child.

If it was a nightmare. Some of the people he had recognised: the toothless grandmother sold pots and pans in the market with the girl helping her, and the woman who had been hit by the tile was Fidus the banker's wife. It had been so real! He could still smell the burning flesh and hair . . .

The memory caught at his stomach. Retching, he got to his feet and stumbled towards the tent's entrance. He lifted the flap and stood for a long time in the cool of the pre-dawn breeze. The camp was beginning to stir. The cook-fires were already lit, and he could smell flat-cakes kneaded with bacon fat. The men of his cohort were taking turns to shave each other in front of their tents, polishing their armour ready for the morning parade or lounging by the fires tossing dice. All normal, all familiar. He stood until the last vestiges of the nightmare had drained away, then went back inside and washed the sweat from his face and neck with water from the basin his orderly had left the night before.

The tent was suddenly stifling. For a moment the panic returned, and he knew he had to get out. From the folding table next to the bed he picked up a fresh tunic, a towel and his oil-flask and scraper. He left the tent, walking through the camp to the river at its western edge.

The river was hardly more than a stream, but where it curved the engineers had dammed it to form a pool fifteen yards wide and five feet deep. The pool would be busy later in the day, in the afternoon when most of the officers and men were off duty, but now it was empty. Severinus stripped off his sweat-sodden tunic and dived in, keeping his head down and letting the force of the dive propel him the width of the pool. Then he turned on to his back and allowed himself to drift.

To be caught like that, like rats in a trap, and burned to death . . .

Jupiter, what was wrong with him? It was only a dream!

From the direction of the camp's centre, a bugle sounded four notes, repeated. He struggled to his feet. The signal meant Officers to General. Briefing meetings were held every day at mid-morning. A summons now made no sense. Unless . . .

The hairs on his neck rose. Quickly, he waded ashore.

He was almost the last to arrive, and the headquarters tent was already full. Paullinus and his staff, including the tribune Agricola, were grouped behind the folding map table at its centre. Around them, filling the tent to its walls, were the rest of the army's officers.

Clemens was just inside the door. Severinus edged in beside him.

'What's going on, Publius?'

Clemens shook his head and put a finger to his lips.

Paullinus cleared his throat and looked around him. 'Good morning.' His voice was devoid of expression. 'My apologies for disturbing your breakfast, but I'm afraid this will not keep.' He waited until the last murmurs had died down and he had their full attention. 'Some time ago I received word of unrest among the Iceni. I instructed Legate Cerialis to monitor the situation and in the event of trouble to take whatever action he thought necessary. It now appears that following the tribe's rebellion and Cerialis's attempted intervention the Ninth has been ambushed and rendered militarily ineffective.' He paused. No one spoke. 'As a result, gentlemen, I am afraid that the kingdom of Icenia is no longer under our control.'

Severinus could feel the sense of numbing shock spread among the assembled officers. The silence was total. Finally one of the auxiliary cohort commanders raised his hand.

Paullinus turned. 'Yes, Quirinius.'

'You've mentioned the Iceni only, sir.' The man's voice was as carefully neutral as the governor's had been. 'What about the other eastern tribes? The Trinovantes and the Catuvellauni?'

Paullinus frowned. 'The legate's messenger could give me no definite information on that score. My own hope is that they have remained neutral, but naturally I cannot take that for granted. The ambush took place beyond the Icenian borders, some twenty or thirty miles from the Colony and within Trinovantian territory. We must therefore assume for practical purposes that the loyalty of that tribe, at least, is now in doubt.'

'And the Colony itself, sir?' That was Quirinius again, although from the surrounding silence Severinus knew the question was in everyone's mind. 'If the Trinovantes're up and the Ninth's gone then—'

'The Ninth is not "gone", Commander. At worst Cerialis has lost five cohorts out of the ten, and as I understand it his cavalry is intact. Furthermore, the Colony has considerable resources of its own. The situation may be serious, but we must not overdramatise.' Paullinus paused. 'Even so, I take your point. The Ninth can no longer be regarded as viable. Accordingly as of now we must make other arrangements. The purpose of this meeting is to acquaint you of what these are.'

Severinus felt the tension around him sharpen. Obviously Paullinus felt it too. He straightened.

'Your orders, gentlemen. The campaign is suspended forthwith. The Fourteenth will prepare for instant departure, minus its attached cavalry which will transship for Deva under my personal command, after which it will proceed in advance of the infantry. The relevant commanders are instructed to wait behind after this meeting. Is that clear?' There were nods. Severinus glanced at Clemens; his lips were pursed. 'We cannot go further than that at present until we have more information, at which time plans will be drawn up accordingly. Your questions, please.'

A hand was raised; one of the senior centurions.

'You're not bringing the Second over from Isca, then, General?'

Paullinus's brows came down. 'No, Longinus, I am not. You know the situation there yourself. With the former legate's death last month and in the absence of the senior tribune' – he glanced at Agricola – 'Dumnonia is unsettled enough at present. Camp Prefect Postumus is an experienced officer, but he's new in post and he has his hands full. The Dumnonii are well aware of these facts, and intelligent enough to take advantage of them. To move the Second from Isca at the moment would be counter-productive at best and at worst foolhardy. Next?'

The centurion cleared his throat. 'But what about London, sir? If the rebels push south then—'

'Centurion.' Paullinus's tone was sharp. 'I say again, we're in danger of overreacting here. Postumus has been instructed to hold himself and his legion in readiness, and he will naturally move if and when ordered. However until I have fuller information I will not jeopardise the province's overall security for what may yet well prove to be a very localised disturbance. That is my job, and I intend to perform it to the best of my ability. Is that understood?'

'Yes, sir. Only . . .'

'Gods, man!' Paullinus flushed. 'These are natives! A rabble, not an army! The Colony has troops already, as does London, and if need be King Cogidubnus can provide local auxiliary support from the Regni. One legion and an interrupted campaign is all I'll allow our friend Boudica for the moment.' He paused. 'Now, are there any more questions?' The room was silent. 'Very well.

Gentlemen, you're dismissed. Relevant commanders, as I said, excepted.'

As they filed out, Severinus thought of his dream. There was a knot of coldness in his stomach that would not shift.

Whatever Paullinus said, he knew that the Colony was already dead.

38

Paullinus fastened the leather flap of his sleeping-tent behind him, walked over to the folding table beside the bed and poured a cup of wine, forcing his hands to hold both the cup and the flask steady. The wine was strong, and almost neat. He drank the cupful straight down.

Jupiter on high. What a mess! What an unholy mess!

Keeping the massive concern from his face during the officers' meeting had taken all his self-control. Ever since the messenger had arrived, he had been able to think of nothing but his own and Cerialis's monumental stupidity: Cerialis's for walking into an ambush that the greenest junior auxiliary commander would have foreseen; his own for undervaluing the strength of the native unrest.

His bunched fist hit the table. *They'll pay! By the gods they'll pay!*

Catus would pay, too. If the procurator hadn't been so god-cursed greedy none of this would have happened . . .

He stopped himself, frowning. It was useless to blame the emperor or his advisers, even privately. Useless, and very, very dangerous. As it was, his own career was finished, or at best in serious jeopardy. He reached for the wine flask, then willed his hand to stop. Instead, he sat down on the folding stool and considered the situation. The auxiliary commander, Quirinius, had been right. If the Trinovantes and Catuvellauni had risen then the Colony was finished, probably already destroyed. It might hold out for a few days, but not long enough for reinforcements to arrive. And six days ago the Iceni had been only thirty miles away . . .

He closed his eyes and tried desperately to put aside the thought of all the people who might already have died.

Fool!

From the parade ground beyond the tent door came the shouts of command as the guard was changed. The familiar sound steadied him. Fool or not, he was doing his best now. The Fourteenth would reach Verulamium in fourteen days; the cavalry, with the time saved by transshipping to Deva, in less than six. There were still some auxiliary garrisons en route which could be pressed into service. Perhaps, after all, it was as he had said at the meeting and the insurrection was only local.

Perhaps. He rubbed his eyes, squeezing the tiredness from them. He had too few men, and there were too many factors, to insure against every possibility. A legion withdrawn from Mona would leave the remaining forces seriously weakened. If resistance had not been crushed as completely as he thought, if the Ordovices or the Deceangli managed to put together a second army, if the remaining Druids managed to stir up the western Brigantian tribes despite Queen Cartimandua . . .

If. There were always ifs. The Fourteenth should be enough . . . But if it wasn't?

The fear flooded back, and Paullinus fought for control.

Fear and indecision are the destroyers. A general must not give way to them, or even acknowledge them in his own mind . . .

Should I have ordered the Second from Isca?

No, he answered himself, calmer now. I was right there, hard though the decision was. The risk's too great. We already hold the south-west by the skin of our teeth, and to bring the Second east would be to court disaster. That is a fact, and you can only base your actions on facts. How you handle this thing depends on how serious you find the situation is, and whether it can be remedied . . .

Whether it can be remedied . . .

Paullinus forced the thought from his mind. What was done was done, and the future would take care of itself.

Meanwhile he had a debt to pay.

Rinsing his face in the water basin, he undid the tent flap. The guard outside snapped to attention.

'Find out where the Foxes are billeted. I want to see that young commander of theirs straight away. In my office, please.'

The guard saluted and left.

*   *   *

Severinus stared at the governor over the folding table.

'I'm to go with the cavalry?' he said.

'If you wish.' Paullinus's face was expressionless, and his voice as measured and controlled as it always was. 'It's not an order. The choice is yours.'

'Could I ask why, sir?'

'Consider it a staff appointment. And, if you will,' – Paullinus's lips tightened – 'an apology. At our last interview I dismissed your opinions regarding the Iceni as ill-informed and callow. Events have proved that that was a mistake, and I believe in admitting my mistakes.'

Severinus swallowed. Staff appointments went either to senators' sons or to high-flyers like Agricola. He was neither.

'Thank you, sir,' he said.

'Oh, it's no reward, young man.' Paullinus gave him a cold smile. 'You'd be safer and far more comfortable sticking with the Foxes. And beyond Pennocrucium I don't know what to expect.'

Severinus remembered Pennocrucium from the outward journey: a quiet auxiliary fort fifty miles south-east of Deva on the Corieltauvian border.

'You think the Corieltauvi may be in revolt as well, sir?'

Paullinus's brows went down. 'Don't be a bigger fool than you can help, Commander. And don't jump to unwarranted conclusions. There's enough of that nonsense around at present without your adding to it. I mean exactly what I say: beyond Pennocrucium I have no information whatsoever concerning tribal movements or loyalties, either those relating to the Corieltauvi or anyone else barring the Iceni.' He sat back in his chair. 'My main hope, however, is that reports have been exaggerated, that our only business is with Boudica, and that a sudden swoop now with the cavalry will catch her unprepared, or at least hold her until the army arrives. Do I make myself clear?'

'Yes, sir.' Severinus tried to keep his voice level. 'Forgive me, General, but does that also apply to the Colony?'

Paullinus looked down at his hands, then up again. 'I gave my views on that subject at this morning's meeting,' he said. 'At which, I think, you were present. I can be no more informative now.'

'Yes, sir.' Severinus stiffened. 'I'm sorry. We'll be leaving when, sir?'

'First thing tomorrow morning.' Paullinus got up; Severinus, already standing, straightened to attention. 'You'll report at dawn to Tribune Agricola. Dismissed.'

Severinus saluted, and left.

39

The barges, stripped for speed and only half laden, made the journey to Deva in a day and a night. From there they rode hard and fast down the legionaries' road that drew a line from shoulder to hip south-eastward across the province.

Beyond Manduessedum the countryside changed from pasture-land to open fields already green with wheat and barley. Severinus remembered this stretch, the north-western cor-ner of Catuvellaunia, from the outward journey. The natives' solid-wheeled ox-carts had been a common enough sight on the trackways that spread on either side of the road, but now there were none; no people, no carts, no oxen. Nothing. The land lay empty and silent, a desert where nothing moved.

A hostile desert, or one that had been hostile. At Tripontium, the three wooden bridges which gave the place its name were intact but the posting-station was a blackened ruin, its thatched roof collapsed and sagging and the paddock beside it empty.

There had been an altar, Severinus remembered, by the side of the road a few yards from the door. The retired soldier who had looked after the station had been a Gaul from Nemausus, and he had done the carving himself. The god was a small, square-shouldered, ugly figure who glared wide-eyed from the stone with both hands raised.

'There's no inscription,' Severinus had said. 'Who is he?'

The man had shrugged.

'You can call him what you like, sir. Me, I call him Luos, but he's Lugh, Logi, Mercury, Hermes, any of a dozen others. I'd a Thracian by once called him Sabazius, and that was fine by me. Him, too, I'd reckon. The old boy doesn't mind, he knows himself who he is. So long as he gets his cup of wine he doesn't care. And he's honest; give him his wine and he'll keep you safe.'

Severinus had poured the wine. Now, as he passed, he looked

for the altar. It had been pulled down into a patch of nettles and the god's face had been hacked away, leaving only the rough torso and the arms. For some reason the sight sickened him. He turned Tanet's head back towards the road.

Eighty miles to the south-east lay Verulamium.

They reached it in the late morning of the fourth day, knowing by now what to expect. The town was a burned-out shell reeking of sour smoke and rotting flesh.

As they passed through the gate, a flock of crows lifted and circled. The young senatorial tribune to Severinus's left reined in, staring at what had been a line of shops by the side of the road. They were timber-built, and they had been burned; all except for one wall which was intact to three-quarters of its height. Hanging from this, fixed in position by the nails through his hands and feet and the spear through his chest, was what had once been a man. Both his eyes and half his face were gone.

The tribune leaned over in the saddle and vomited on to the gravel road.

Paullinus, riding a dozen paces in front, half turned. 'Dammit, Titus!' he snapped. 'Keep position!'

The young man, grey-faced and tight-lipped, wiped his mouth with his kerchief. He dug his heels into his horse's flanks and moved forward.

The crucified man was not the only body. They lay scattered on all sides like broken dolls, heaped together or lying where they had fallen. Most were headless; anonymous lumps of cloth from which the limbs stuck out grotesquely. The road was littered with them; Tanet, like the other horses, was picking her way carefully between the bundles, shivering, her ears flat against her poll.

They rode in silence towards the town centre. Ahead and above and all around them, flocks of crows rose heavily into the air and then settled again. Over to Severinus's left, something moved: a fox or a dog, scavenging.

There were no other signs of life.

The market square was a butcher's yard, buzzing with flies and smelling of rotten meat. At its centre, stacked with hideous neatness, lay a pile of human heads. Around the edges, among the half-burned chaos of gutted shops and public buildings, were more bodies, this time mostly women, perched incongruously on the stakes that impaled them. Severinus found himself counting, his eyes moving along the line that stretched the square's perimeter.

The young tribune beside him was shaking his head slowly from side to side, his eyes blank.

'Savages. They're nothing but bloody savages.' His eyes were hard and glistening. 'I hope we kill them all.'

Severinus said nothing.

40

London lay twenty-three miles beyond: an ordered sprawl of red-roofed houses reaching back from the river, guarded by its two forts on the higher ground. In the fifteen years since its founding it had spread along the line of the two parallel roads either side of the new bridge and northwards beyond the wharfs.

'We'll go there first, Gnaeus.' Paullinus nodded towards the nearer of the forts, where the command centre would be. 'Stable the horses, get the men settled. And after—'

'After, General?' Agricola glanced at him. The tribune's face, Paullinus noticed, had new lines in it. He no longer looked young.

'After, I talk to the procurator.'

'He's gone, sir,' the auxiliary commander said.

Paullinus set his helmet down on the desk.

'He is *what*?' he said softly.

'Procurator Catus commandeered a galley four days ago.' Saturius Pudens was a tough, square-built Lusitanian. He was obviously furious and, equally obviously, trying hard not to show it. 'He'll be in Itius now, or further. He left an assistant in charge, Oppius Lupianus. You'll find him at the provincial offices.'

'And you didn't try to stop him?' Pudens stared back in silence, and Paullinus turned away. 'No, Commander, of course you didn't. My apologies; I'm tired and it was a stupid question. Did he give a reason?'

'None, sir.' Pudens's lips formed a thin line. The third finger of his right hand was missing; he had commanded a cohort, Paullinus remembered, under Plautus at the Conquest.

'I see.' There was no more to be said; Catus's reasons were clear enough, and both men knew it. Well, Paullinus thought, let the emperor deal with the bastard himself, if he ever catches him. He pulled up a stool and sat down, easing his stiffened leg muscles. 'You've had reports from the north?'

The other man relaxed. 'No, sir. Not officially, not since Legate Cerialis's message. We know from refugees that the situation's bad, but—'

'Verulamium's gone.' Paullinus was blunt. 'The Catuvellauni are in revolt. About the Trinovantes and the Colony I don't know. Or the Iceni.'

Pudens nodded, his face impassive. 'Well, I can tell you about the Iceni, at least, sir, but it's stale news. Opimius – he's the one who brought the message, the Ninth's senior tribune – said they were moving this way. Slowly, but they'd've reached the Colony six days ago. And the Trinovantes are in revolt as well. Opimius was lucky to get through.'

'Opimius is here?'

'Yes, sir. You want to talk to him?'

'Later. Did he give you an estimate of the Icenian numbers?'

'He wasn't sure, sir. Certainly in excess of eighty thousand. But that was—'

'Eighty *thousand*?'

'That was including non-combatants, sir. However, his guess was twenty thousand warriors at the very least.'

'Merciful Jupiter!' Paullinus leaned back and closed his eyes. Twenty thousand! And that wasn't counting the Trinovantes or the Catuvellauni. Let alone the Corieltauvi. Even moving slowly, the rebels could not be far away. 'How many troops do you have here, Commander?'

Pudens paused. 'The two cohorts, sir. Less two hundred Procurator Catus sent north.'

'You think they can hold the town?'

'No, Governor. Of course not.'

'"*Of course not,*"' Paullinus grunted. 'I agree. Of course I agree. So. What do we do now?'

'With respect, sir,' Pudens said carefully, 'that isn't my decision.'

'True.' Paullinus's lips twisted.' Breaking bad news is a governor's prerogative.' He was silent for a long time, weighing the course of action he had already decided on, knowing that, now, it was the only one possible. 'Your orders, Commander.'

'First: The city is to be abandoned forthwith. You will instruct the council and the leading merchants to meet me at the procurator's offices an hour before sunset, when I will explain my reasons personally. Not discuss, explain. Second: tomorrow by midday at the latest you and your men will escort the civilian population, or such as wish to go, to the crossing at Pontes where you will remain while they continue to Calleva and the protection of King Cogidubnus. The forts and the town are to be stripped as far as is possible of all supplies and equipment that may be of use to the enemy, but personal civilian baggage is to be kept to a minimum. Use your own discretion, and employ reasonable force to ensure that your instructions are obeyed. Third: two separate couriers are to be sent to the Fourteenth Legion at present advancing towards London. I will word that order myself.' He paused. 'Fourth, you will send another courier to Isca ordering the acting commander Poenius Postumus in my name to proceed in full force to Calleva with all possible speed. Have the order prepared for my signature. Repeat, please.'

Pudens did so.

'Good. Last, I want some maps, and your best local scout.'

Oppius Lupianus stared at Paullinus with an expression as close to disbelief and disgust as a first-level administrative assistant could safely risk when interviewing a provincial governor.

'You're abandoning the city?' he said.

'That is correct.'

'Governor I'm not sure that you appreciate how much we have invested here. London is no backwoods settlement to be abandoned because it suits short-term military policy. It's the province's major port, and it holds a position unique in Britain. We have been careful to nurture that aspect, and the fact that we've managed to attract considerable private investment from as far afield as Rome itself shows how successful we've been. Now you're asking me to throw all that away because of a gang of poxy *natives*?'

Paullinus leaned forward, trying to control his personal dislike for the man, and his anger.

'I am not "asking" you to do anything, Lupianus,' he said quietly. 'As the province's governor, I am telling you that as from tomorrow I cannot guarantee the city's safety. If you or any other civilian choose to stay behind and wait for the Iceni to arrive then you're quite at liberty to do so, inadvisable as that may be.'

'What about our own troops? And the force you brought yourself? Surely—'

'Saturius Pudens has seven hundred men. I have a further six hundred. At current estimation the fighting force of the rebels is some twenty times our total. Those odds do not, either in my view or in Commander Pudens's, augur well for a successful defensive operation. In simple non-technical terms the result would be a massacre. Moreover, a massacre without point.'

'The emperor is not going to like it.'

'The emperor can bloody well . . .' Paullinus stopped himself as he saw the corner of Lupianus's mouth lift and went on more carefully. 'The emperor will understand that I have no choice in the matter.'

'I see. I may, of course, lodge a formal objection?'

'You may. Consider it done.'

'Thank you. But I was thinking more on the lines of with my superiors in Rome.' Lupianus laid down the pen he was holding. 'So, Governor. If you do not intend to protect us might I ask what your plans actually are?'

'As far as your citizens are concerned, I've ordered Pudens to escort them the length of Pontes. From there they can go to Calleva where King Cogidubnus will, no doubt, be happy to take them under his care. I doubt if the rebels will risk invading Atrebatan territory. Not at present, anyway. I'm sure Boudica will have enough to occupy her here for the time being.'

'So I would imagine.' Lupianus's voice was glacial. 'In effect you are abandoning us in order to buy yourself time.'

'If by "us" you mean the city, not its population, who I hope will have more sense than to stay behind, then yes. And your military acumen, Lupianus, does you credit.' The agent flushed. 'As to the army, I can tell you that the Second are ordered from Isca and will rendezvous with the Fourteenth at Calleva. Thereafter—'

'You're falling back on Calleva?' Lupianus stared at him, all pretence of politeness gone.

'No. Not quite. The final rendezvous point will be closer to Pontes, which Commander Pudens has been ordered to hold.'

'But that's—' Lupianus caught himself. 'Governor, you're still abandoning everything north of the Thames. Would you mind explaining why?'

Paullinus finally let his own anger show. 'Because the rebels will take it anyway. Have taken most of it already. Because I need my forces concentrated on friendly ground with the river between them and the enemy and my supply lines assured. Because, as I said, the Iceni will at least think twice before they cross either at Pontes or here at London Bridge into territory held by a powerful and unfriendly tribe. Because, lastly, Oppius Lupianus, if I'm to save what I can of your unique bloody position from your gang of poxy natives it's my only option. Now do I make myself clear or would you like to suggest an alternative strategy of your own devising?'

Lupianus dropped his eyes. 'My apologies, Governor,' he said. 'I didn't mean to—'

'Accepted,' Paullinus snapped. 'Now, I've arranged a meeting here in two hours' time with the city authorities and the principal merchants. I will naturally expect your full support and co-operation. Do I have them?'

There was a pause. Finally Lupianus said stiffly, 'You have them, Governor. Subject to my report, as I told you.'

Paullinus stood up. 'Fine. Then that's all I require.'

Severinus looked back towards the city. The road was a mass of people and carts moving slowly westwards, flanked by marching infantry. Behind them spirals of cook-fire smoke still rose, and he could see several figures perched on the rooftops watching the column pass beyond the city bounds. Not everyone had chosen to go to Calleva. At least two thousand had stayed behind.

People had stayed behind at Verulamium, too. He tried not to think of that. Or of the Colony.

'They're fools.' Gnaeus Agricola, sitting his own horse at his side, was looking back too. There was no anger in the tribune's voice: the words were simply an observation made after careful assessment. 'You always get them, especially among civilians. Ostriches. You know about ostriches, I suppose?'

'I've heard of them, aye.' Severinus patted Tanet's neck and she tossed her head, eager to be away. 'Big stubborn birds with fixed ideas and a nasty kick.'

Agricola ignored the tone; or perhaps he did not notice it. 'Show an ostrich danger and his immediate reaction is to stick his head in the bloody sand. No logic, no intelligence.' He shrugged and turned away. 'Well, there's no arguing with pig-headedness. Let's just be grateful we were born with a bit of sense.'

He rode off to join the governor, waiting at the head of the cavalry column. Slowly, Severinus followed.

Paullinus gave the order, and the troop set out towards Calleva.

41

London died quickly and brutally. Scant hours after the first British warriors reached the north bank of the Thames it was no longer a city but a shambles, its streets littered with corpses. Along the line of the wharves on either side of the bridge, the huge granaries which had stored the grain of Catuvellaunia and Trinovantia for transshipment to Gaul and the Rhine legions were a mass of flame. The bridge, too, was alight, its timbers blazing above the thick oak piles, the central stretch, wide enough for two carts to pass, already fallen in a hissing cloud of sparks and steam. Along the length and breadth of the sloping ground between river and road, the private warehouses sprawled gutted, roofs sagging above their gaping walls, their contents scattered for the taking: jars of wine and oil, bales of cloth and carded wool, red-glazed pots wrapped carefully in straw and now a mass of broken shards trodden underfoot, olives and honey and pickled fish, shoes and sandals, hoes and mattocks, smoked bears' paws, peacocks' brains and nightingales' tongues in aspic. All the empire's plenty. And all around in every direction, even on the Thames itself where the barges and galleys had lain moored to their anchor-stones in mid-stream or waited for cargoes at the quayside, the city burned and stank.

Ecenomolios leaned on his sword, scowling at the smoke that rose from what had been the procurator's offices to mingle with the dark cloud spreading slowly westwards.

Fools! Bloody, bloody fools!

He turned back to face the queen, sitting her pony proud as Cunobelinos himself, surrounded by the other chiefs and sub-chiefs. Round her throat glinted the massive gold torc of the Icenian royal line, and the sight of it swelled Ecenomolios's fury. The torc had been King Subidastos's before the Romans had given it to their creature Prasutagos. Subidastos would have understood; he had been a warrior. Whereas the military sense of this stupid bitch and the men who passed for her advisers would have shamed a palace washerwoman.

'Ecenomolios, the decision is made,' Boudica repeated.

'Then unmake it,' he said. 'Prove yourself a warrior. Finish what we've started. London is nothing.'

'London is revenge.' Boudica's eyes flashed. 'You wanted revenge yourself. And now you call it *nothing*?'

Ecenomolios's head went up. 'Madam, listen to me! We must destroy Paullinus. If we move westwards and cross the Thames now we can take him before his armies gather and have both. Believe me, you must do this!'

Boudica had stiffened. 'You do not, Ecenomolios, say *must* to me. Your place is to advise. You are my war leader, not my husband.'

Ecenomolios flushed: stupid Boudica might be in some ways, but she was no fool. And he knew that unless he could persuade her they were lost.

'Very well, then,' he said. 'Let me speak as a war leader, and perhaps the queen of the Iceni will listen.' He pointed to the pile of severed heads that lay heaped at the market square's centre. 'How many of those wore helmets? Did they carry swords or tally-sticks?'

The chiefs around Boudica shifted angrily. A few fingered their sword-hilts.

'A dead Wolf is a dead Wolf,' one of them, a Catuvellaunian with a chief's thick golden bracelet round his arm, grunted.

Ecenomolios turned on him. 'Vosenos, where are your wits? Gone with stolen wine? If we're to beat the Romans we need the heads of their warriors, not their shopkeepers. Which is more important to the Catuvellauni, victory or plunder? Are they warriors or thieves?'

The Catuvellaunian's hand went to his sword.

'Vosenos!' Boudica's voice cut like a whip. The man relaxed, glaring.

'Perhaps, Ecenomolios, you should distinguish between the terms more carefully before you throw them in our faces.' Cabriabanos, also Catuvellaunian, spoke softly, but he held his own sword unsheathed. 'A thief takes what is not his own, a warrior kills the man who steals it. That we have done. That the Iceni have also done, and the Trinovantes. This land and everything in it was ours, and now we have it back the thing is finished. Any Roman within these bounds is an enemy, but those beyond are no concern of the Catuvellauni. Let them stay or go, whichever they please.'

'And if we had let the Wolves we killed on the road to Camulodunum stay or go? Which is safer, Cabriabanos, a wolf left alive to bite again or a dead one?'

'Have you no ears, you fool?' Toutomatos, the old Eastern Iceni sub-chief with the red battle-scar on his left cheek, growled. 'They were in Trinovantian territory. The Trinovantes are friends and allies. These Wolves are in Atrebatia, and the Atrebates are neither. Do you think Cogidubnus will sit paring his nails at Calleva while we cross his borders?'

'Cogidubnus is the Romans' dog. Why should we care what he thinks, or does?'

'Because dog or not he can call on the spears of five tribes!' Toutomatos snapped. 'Cogidubnus may be the Romans' dog, but he's a cautious one content to stay and growl behind his own ditch. He'll bite quick enough if we cross it. Cabriabanos is right. We have what is ours. If the Wolves want what they stole back then let them come to us and try to take it.'

There were murmurs of agreement. Ecenomolios looked round, but his eyes met only closed faces.

'Am I the only one with sense, then?' he said.

No one spoke.

'The decision stands.' Boudica jerked the rein of her pony. 'Icenia is free, and Catuvellaunia and Trinovantia. That is enough; the rest is not our concern. If the Romans come, Ecenomolios, then we will fight them, but not unless.'

Ecenomolios thrust his sword into its scabbard and walked off without a word.

Dumnocoveros had been standing behind the queen, but he had said nothing: military matters were not a Druid's business unless he chose to make them so, and Dumnocoveros did not. Could not. He closed his eyes against the pain of his own knowledge.

Perhaps I'm wrong, he thought. Perhaps I misinterpreted the gods' message. Ogmios, Lugos, prove me wrong!

He doubted if they would. The dream last night had been unambiguous.

He had been standing at the mouth of a stretch of bare ground that reached back into raised woodland like the fish-traps that the Iceni used in their marsh-pools; narrow at the neck, spreading out beyond until it formed a broad, curving bulge. Behind him was a river, deep and slow-flowing, fringed with willow and alder, and the noonday sun beat on his bare neck.

He was waiting.

The man came through the trees from the higher ground far in front and to his right, where, had this been a fish-trap, the bait would hang. He was dressed as he had been before for hunting, but this time he wore no war paint. His spear was reversed and his hair flowed loose over his shoulders, unbound for mourning. The three jewels shone brightly in his belt.

'Lord.' Dumnocoveros raised his forearms, crossing them at the wrist.

The hunter stopped. 'So, Druid,' he said. 'We are here.'

'Where is "here", lord?'

'You don't know?' The man smiled, but the smile did not touch his eyes. 'This is the end of all roads. Look.' He pointed to the high ground of the valley's belly. 'Beyond here is nothing. No path. Only death.'

'Death is itself a path, lord.'

The young man laughed. 'Aye, that's true,' he said. 'Call it a beginning, then. That would be equally true. We must all climb the hill, at one time or another.'

'You, too, lord? Even you?'

'Even me. Even, finally, the Wolves. Change rules us all.'

'Change for the better?'

'Change.' The hunter's voice was flat. 'It has been a good hunting, Druid, but it will end here. Nothing you can say or do will alter that. And it will not be wasted, I promise.'

'There is no other way?'

'You said yourself: death is only another path. Paths need to be trodden if they are to form and become roads. A road creates its own way.'

'Roads need direction, lord. Otherwise what is their purpose?'

'They are their own purpose. A road implies a destination. That destination may not exist at first, but it will; it must, eventually, because the road is already there. Do you understand me, Dumnocoveros?'

'No, lord.'

'Then at least trust me.' The young man raised his hand, the jewels in his belt flashing. 'Enough. Remember, when you stand here again, that it was a good hunting.'

Dumnocoveros had bowed, and turned, and walked away. The river beyond the valley's neck was blood-red, the trees that fringed it stripped of leaves. It had been the last thing that he had seen before he woke.

'I trust you, lord,' he said, now, as he watched Ecenomolios go down to the river between the burning buildings of what had been the Roman city.

42

Ten days later, fifteen miles from Pontes along the native track that led to the ford at Marcoritum, Paullinus sat his horse and for the hundredth time turned his strategy for the coming battle over in his mind.

It would work. Possibly. If Boudica took the bait. If the Iceni had not moved since the last report. If the ground he had chosen was as the scouts had described it, and where they had described it. If . . .

If, if, if. There were always too many ifs. He tried to put them aside, and Poenius Postumus, the acting commander of the Second, with them. The Second should have arrived from Isca days ago, on the heels of the Fourteenth which had reached Calleva ahead of time. It had not. There had been no message, no news, and without the extra legion, with only the Fourteenth and Cogidubnus's auxiliaries, he was still seriously under strength. Should he have waited another day? Two days? But with supplies running short . . .

Damn Postumus!

Fear destroys, he told himself firmly. You've troops enough, your plan will work, the rebels will be beaten and the province will be saved. All this will happen.

A tiny movement in the air ahead of him caught his eye. Above the open stretch of rough grassland by the river's edge, oblivious of the marching column beyond, a sparrowhawk hung motionless, its wings beating to keep the still body aloft.

'Scout, General,' Aulus Pasidienus, the Fourteenth's legate, murmured.

Paullinus looked away from the bird. The man was coming in from the east: an Atrebatian, one of the auxiliaries Cogidubnus had sent from Calleva. He brought his shaggy pony to a halt and put fist to brow in the British salute.

'Ford is empty.' The scout's Latin was thick as curdled milk and almost unintelligible. 'Thames is empty. No nothing but burn, five miles, ten from ford.' He grinned. 'Sod all. Understand "sod all", General?'

Paullinus nodded, keeping both the smile and the relief from his face, 'How far to Marcoritum?'

'Two mile. Less.'

'The Iceni?'

The man pointed to the north-east. 'Big camp after London, five miles, eight. No move or small-small. But you come, they come fast, so I think. Also scouts, north bank, good horse.'

'Then we'd better hurry.' Paullinus turned to the signaller beside him. 'Double pace, Bugler.'

As he spoke, the hawk fell, folding its wings and dropping to earth like a stone. Almost immediately it rose again and flew away westwards.

The scout, too, had seen it. He grunted with satisfaction.

'Good.'

'What?' Paullinus frowned.

The man pointed. 'Good sign, General. Lucky.'

'Jupiter, man! It's only a bird!'

'Good all the same.' The scout saluted and galloped off.

They crossed the ford. Just out of sight, two miles downstream, London lay silent beneath its shroud of ash.

The valley was a pear-shaped defile fronted by a shallow stream, south-facing, surrounded on three sides by high ground thick with oaks and birch scrub and swelling inwards from its narrow neck to almost a mile in width at its base. It was perfect, all that Paullinus had hoped for. With the legion occupying the lower reaches and the auxiliary cavalry, slingers and archers guarding their flanks he could cut any attacking force to ribbons.

And that's what I will do, he promised himself savagely, remembering Verulamium. By the sweet gods I will!

Beside him Pasidienus had taken off his helmet and was looking around him with a satisfaction that matched his own.

'A fine choice of ground, General. My congratulations.'

'It'll do. It'll do very nicely.' Paullinus looked back at the late-afternoon sun, half hidden now by the thickly wooded slopes to the right and behind. For the first time he felt his worry lift and confidence return. 'We camp at the far end. Send plenty of scouts out. We don't want the beggars to catch us napping like they did Cerialis.'

'Yes, sir.' The legate saluted, then turned to snap orders at the signaller.

With the first notes of the bugle, smoothly, efficiently, the marching column spread outwards across the base of the valley, breaking into its cohorts and centuries. Paullinus knew that within an hour what was now flat, anonymous grassland would be transformed into a chequerboard of tents and roads. The thought, as always, awed him. This was Rome at her best; why in a hundred years even a frontier province like Britain would be civilised.

But first she had to be tamed. And when the rebels came, as they would have to come, that was something they would learn for themselves.

By the gods they would!

Severinus fondled Tanet's ears as he watched the slow-moving wave crest the skyline to the east, flowing across the open country in a broad sweep a mile wide like water from a flooded river. The Iceni were too far away yet for detail, but he could already hear them: a low murmur like the rumble of distant thunder broken by shouts and the braying of war-horns.

'Jupiter, will you look at that, now?' The decurion commanding the cavalry troop waiting in the trees around him was staring in awe. 'How many of the bastards do you reckon, sir?'

'The general said eighty thousand.' Severinus tried to ignore the cold knot of fear in his belly. 'I wouldn't know. I've never seen anything like it.'

'Me neither.' The decurion leaned over and spat to one side. 'Eighty thousand, eh? It'll be a scrap and a half, then.' Over to their left, one of the other horses snorted and shifted sideways, pushing its rider's leg against a branch of gorse. The man cursed and the decurion turned in his saddle to glare at him. 'Lucius, you gormless bugger! Tighten your rein or I'll have your guts!' The other men chuckled, and the trooper reddened. The decurion turned back to Severinus. 'Look at that, sir. Wagons.

They've brought the wives and kids along. Just like the effing circus, eh?'

Severinus could see the rear of the rebel army now. Behind the main body came a straggle of ox-carts, dozens, hundreds, moving sluggishly across the tussocky grassland. As he watched, the carts stopped, forming a huge ragged crescent.

'Senators' seats.' The decurion grinned. 'There's natives for you, sir. Effing crazy, the lot of them.'

The army proper, too, had stopped, a hundred yards below where they sat screened by the trees and five hundred from where the Fourteenth waited in three lines a spear-cast inside the valley's neck. It had no formal order. In the narrowing space between river and forest the extended wings had shrunk inwards towards the centre to form a compacted mass a third of a mile wide and the same in depth. The noise now was deafening, an ear-hurting roar of shouting men and booming war-horns. As Severinus watched, a single horseman galloped out of the press. Twenty yards from the Roman shield wall he swerved, raised himself and threw his spear, not into the helmeted heads but above them towards the Eagle standard to the rear. It fell short, but the standard dipped as the aquilifer's horse shifted beneath him.

A cheer rose from the British ranks as the man rode slowly back.

'Cheeky bugger,' the decurion muttered. 'Smart bit of riding, though.'

The front line of the Icenian army was fragmenting as more warriors broke away and repeated the first man's dash. The shouting and the war-horns now were interspersed with jeers and cat-calls, but the Fourteenth did not move or respond. Even when one of the thrown spears found a target the gap was simply quietly closed.

'Drives them wild, that.' The decurion cleared his throat and sent another gob of spittle into the gorse. 'They can't stand being ignored, the British. Pack of effing posers.'

Severinus had been looking for the queen. Boudica was standing in a chariot on a patch of higher ground to the south-east, a sword in her hand, head up and back straight, her eyes fixed on the Roman line. There was no trace of the matronly woman he had seen at Coriodunum. Even at this distance he could see that like the warriors and the captains round her she was painted for war, her hair stiffened with lime and a royal torc at her throat. He found himself, illogically, thinking of Senovara.

Boudica raised her sword, then brought it down. The host roared, rippled and surged forward.

'Here they come, sir,' the decurion murmured. He half turned. 'Steady, lads.'

The shouting and the braying of war-horns had swelled until it was a single solid wall of noise. Now the whole formless mass threw itself towards the waiting legion, its front no more than a few hundred yards wide, squeezed between the river and the narrow gap at the valley's mouth. From beside the Eagle, in the centre behind the third rank where Paullinus stood with his staff, a signal trumpet blew a single note.

'That's not for us, boys.' The decurion's voice was matter-of-fact, hardly louder than would carry over the shouts below. He had drawn his sabre but he held it loosely. 'Stay where you are and give the ironbellies a chance. You'll have your fun shortly.'

In answer to the trumpet, from the high ground on either side of the attackers came a shower of arrows and slingshot. At the same moment the legionaries' front rank threw the first of their two javelins, so closely timed that they formed a single wave that arced through the air and struck together along the length of the enemy's front. The British line was suddenly a screaming, bloody shambles, its centre a chaos of bodies jammed shoulder to shoulder with no space to move. Before it could recover, the second volley of javelins slammed into what was already no longer an army but a mass of heaving, trapped flesh.

The Roman lines shifted as the first rank parted and the second stepped through the gaps. A heartbeat behind the second volley of javelins came a third, then a fourth. The trumpet sounded again. The line of shields moved forward with an audible hiss as five thousand swords cleared their scabbards.

The decurion glanced at Severinus.

'Sir?'

'Aye.' Severinus nodded, his mouth dry, and set his heels to Tanet's flanks.

All around him the cavalry were sweeping down through the trees at the valley's edges.

Ecenomolios watched the advancing Wolves crest the piles of dead and dying warriors that blocked the valley's mouth. He glanced down at his sword-arm and the javelin that trailed from it, He felt no pain, only anger, and an immense frustration that his fingers would no longer obey him and grasp the hilt of the sword that lay at his feet. Stooping, he shrugged the shield from his left arm and picked up the sword. The leather bindings of its hilt were greasy to the touch and its contours, reversed now, were unfamiliar beneath his palm. As he gripped it he felt rather than heard the beat of hooves behind him.

He turned, just as the Wolf's sabre drove down across his neck, shearing through his spine, and the world dissolved in a red wash of pain.

On the other side of the valley the Druid Dumnocoveros died, too, his collarbone split by the thrust of a legionary's sword. Above him a lark rose, singing.

The corpse lay on its back at the edge of the trees; unmarked save for the single tell-tale wound in the chest left by the thrust of a legionary's sword. Beside it something lay glittering, spilled from the open pouch at the man's waist. Severinus bent down and picked the thing up. It was a native coin on a chain, gold, with a running horse on one side and an ear of barley on the other. The chain was broken, the links snapped.

Without thinking, he tucked it under his belt.

43

'I'm sorry, boy.' Junius Natalis, the Ninth's Commander of Cavalry and the officer currently in charge of reconstruction at the Colony, set the urn down carefully on the desk in front of him.

Severinus reached out a hand and touched the lid. It seemed incredible that all that was left of his father was contained in this small clay box.

'No need, sir,' he said. 'I knew he was dead.'

'He died well, if that's a consolation. They all did.' Natalis was army to the bone: a big brawny north Italian, florid-faced, but with a haunted look about the eyes that was common to everyone he had met these past few hours. The reason for the look was not difficult to guess. Severinus had seen both Verulamium and London, and they had been bad enough. When Natalis and his detachment had arrived from Dercovium the Colony had been dead for almost a month. It had taken them five days just to collect and burn the corpses, or what the wolves and birds had left of them.

His mother's had been among them. Her ashes, now, would be in the common grave beyond the west gate, along with Sulicena's and Trinnus's. And Albilla's. Thinking of Albilla, Severinus felt a sudden stab of guilt. He had scarcely thought about her at all. Certainly her death affected him far less than his parents', or even Sulicena's.

That can't be right, he thought. Jupiter, we were engaged!

'You'll want to bury it in the cemetery,' Natalis was saying. 'I'll detail a couple of men.'

'No, sir.' Severinus shook his head. 'I'll take it to our villa. My mother's name can go on the stone, and they can have their offerings together.'

'As you please. You've been there already?'

'Not yet, sir. I've only just got back from Braniacum.' Severinus forced down the vision of what he had found there, when Paullinus had sent him with the Foxes' cavalry reinforced by a squadron of the Sabinians. 'It's out by the estuary.'

'It may not be there any more. Most of the villas were burned along with the port and everything else.' Natalis pushed his fingers through his greying hair. 'Holy gods, it'll take us years to rebuild. Years.' He paused. 'I hear London was bad.'

'Aye.' At least his father had died cleanly. There had been nothing clean about London; it had been like Verulamium, a blood-soaked shambles. 'Aye. It was.'

Natalis grunted. 'A crying shame that bastard Catus got away. He's a lot to answer for. Did you see the new procurator?'

'Classicianus? No, he was expected but he hadn't arrived when I left. You know him, sir?'

'I know of him. A Gaul from Trèves, as much Celt as Roman. More. An interesting appointment, politically. And he's no friend to the governor.' For the first time Natalis's expression lost its severity. 'We'll see sparks fly shortly.'

'Paullinus certainly didn't seem too pleased.'

The cavalry commander pursed his lips.

'No, he wouldn't be.' he said. 'He and Classicianus've crossed swords before. Where natives are concerned our new procurator's for the soft approach, and the governor can be' – Natalis hesitated – 'well, let's say uncompromising. Especially now. Understandable, of course; the rebellion's finished him. Three cities destroyed, the gods know how much in trade goods and private property, the best part of a legion lost. Britain's a bloody shambles. And this punitive campaign isn't helping.'

'You don't approve.'

Natalis shrugged. 'I'm a soldier. I've lost friends in the massacres, good friends, and no soldier can see half his legion wiped out without hating the bastards who did it, let alone after he's given the job of clearing up the butcher's shop they left behind them. But as Jupiter's my witness if Britain's to have a future in the empire it has to end here, and it seems Paullinus can't see past revenge. No, the Mothers forgive me, Severinus, I don't approve.'

Severinus looked down at the urn. 'My father would've agreed with you.'

'Aye.' Natalis nodded slowly. 'I only met Julius Aper the once, years ago. He was a good soldier, a good Roman, and a good man. He'll be missed.' He stood up. 'Now. You'll want to get on, and I'm afraid I have things to see to myself. I'm pleased to have met you.' He held out his hand and Severinus shook it. 'If you need any help call in at the Dun. We've manned the fort up there and the centurion in charge'll be happy to let you have a squaddie or two.'

Severinus stared at him in surprise. 'You still expect trouble from the natives?'

'Oh, there're no natives there, boy. They've gone, what there was left of them, shipped to Itius and sold for slaves.' Natalis was frowning. 'I told you, the governor isn't one to do things by halves. We've had our instructions: the tribe's to be stamped out. Completely, one way or another, even the name. You'll find precious few Trinovantes here now, living or dead.'

The Colony was a ghost of itself. Only the streets remained, and even they were piled with debris, so choked in places that Severinus had to make wide detours round the heaps of rubble and charred timbers. Here and there, where the wind had carried the flames away from them, some buildings were still standing, but they served only to emphasise the scale of the destruction. The market square was a gutted shell where soldiers stripped to the waist were loading carts with half-burned beams and sections of wattle-and-daub walling, their kerchiefs wrapped across their mouths and noses against the lime-plaster dust that hung over everything.

Then there were the bodies; still and always, even after all this time, there were bodies. As he rode Tanet along what had been Praetorian Street a pair of legionaries stopped what they were doing to pull something from beneath a collapsed wall and bundle it into a blanket. It looked small, like a child, but then perhaps that had been all there was left.

Finally he reached the south gate and the open country beyond. Digging his heels into Tanet's flanks, he brought her to the gallop and sent her along the coast road, allowing the wind blowing up from the marshes to clean him.

At first sight the villa looked completely untouched. The

main block stood solid and familiar; it was only when he had dismounted and was leading the mare towards the stables round the side that he noticed the great black scar that had ripped through the east wing and the sag of the walls and roof.

Well, it was still better than he had hoped. The foundations could be reused. At least, unlike most, he still had a home to go back to.

Inside the stable, something moved. A cold finger touched Severinus's spine. Quietly, carefully, he let go of Tanet's rein. Setting the urn he was carrying on the ground, he drew his sword.

The thing was a horse; a white horse, smaller than Tanet but bigger than a pony. It stood in one of the stalls, a tether fastening it to the ring in the wall.

'Lacta?' Severinus said.

The mare turned her head, pulling at the tether as she blew through her nostrils. Severinus stepped forward, hand outstretched, palm down. Warm lips nuzzled at his wrist. He looked around him, noticing the fresh straw on the floor, the water in the trough, and the half-filled manger. Patting the milk-white neck, he went back into the sunlight.

'I saw you ride up the path.' The words were Celtic. Severinus turned, his sword raised. 'She's been well cared for.'

The woman was standing among the birch trees that fringed the stable's outer wall.

'Aye. So I see.' Severinus put the sword back into its sheath. He had forgotten how bright her hair was, and how she drew herself up and stared straight at the person she was talking to. 'My thanks.'

'No thanks. I gave my word I'd keep her for you.' Senovara turned to go.

'Wait!' Her head swung round, as Lacta's had. 'You've been living here?'

'No.' Her voice was as level as her gaze. 'I am no thief, Julius Severinus, to take what does not belong to me. Lacta is different. She belongs here.'

'I was told the Dun was empty.'

'Aye, it is.'

'Your family?'

Her chin came up. 'My father and mother are dead. My sister
. . .' She paused, her eyes hard. 'My sister died too.'

'I'm sorry.'

'Would you prefer them slaves?' The words slashed like a
whip.

Severinus waited. 'No,' he said at last, gently. 'I would not.
But I'm still sorry they are dead.'

Senovara nodded. He saw her throat move, but there was no
softness either in her face or her tone. She pointed to the urn
that still lay on the ground between them. 'Your father?'

'Aye. My mother's dead as well. Her ashes are not here.' He
forced himself to say the next words. 'Nor are Albilla's.'

Senovara turned her head towards the trees. She was silent
for a long time. Then she turned back to face him.

'I am sorry too,' she said, more softly this time. 'They were
good people. It was a waste. It was all a waste, a stupid, stupid
waste.' She hesitated, then indicated the urn. 'You came here to
bury it?'

'Aye.'

'Then I will stay a little longer.'

Severinus had brought a spade with him. He dug a deep square
hole beneath one of the apple trees, lowered the urn into
it and replaced the earth. Then he said a silent prayer for
all his dead and poured out the wine he had taken from
Tanet's saddlebag. It was thin stuff, army issue, but they would
understand.

Senovara had been watching him without speaking.

'Your father was a fine man,' she said. 'He'll be reborn a
warrior.'

Severinus put the stopper back in the flask. There would be
a stone here before the autumn covered the place with leaves
but for the present there was no more he could do. He felt as
empty as the wine bottle.

'Aye,' he said. 'Maybe.'

'You don't believe it?'

He shook his head without looking at her. 'We believe that
when a man is gone he's gone, Senovara. Or at least I do.'

'That is nonsense. Souls don't die. How can they? Where

would the new people come from? Bodies die, but never souls. He will be back when he has rested.'

'Perhaps you're right.' Severinus was too tired to argue. He picked up the spade and walked towards the villa, pitching the empty wine flask into the midden beside it. 'Have you eaten?'

'Aye.' The stiffness had come back to her face and voice. 'This morning.'

She was lying; Severinus knew that. Now he saw her from close up her features were thin and pinched, and he could see the bones of her arms through the skin.

'Then eat again,' he said. 'I've plenty of flour in the saddlebags and some army bacon. And another flask of wine.'

Her eyes flicked away.

'I'm not hungry.'

Severinus paused. 'You've brought me a gift, Senovara. If this had been your house and you were the host, what would you think of the guest who refused to sit at your table?'

'Very little.' For the first time, her mouth twisted in the ghost of a smile. 'And less because the offer was so politely made. My thanks, Julius Severinus.'

'There's no need of thanks,' he said.

They went inside.

44

The Colony was beginning to come alive again. In the five months since reoccupation the debris had been cleared and the ground surface levelled for building. Most of what Severinus could see as he walked Tanet down Ditch Street towards the residence area was still wasteland, but the first of the time-served veterans and their families had already arrived and there were enough houses to establish the line of the road. Here and there, knots of women sat gossiping in the autumn sunshine while their children played around them. Many wore pinned British dresses and their hair was braided. Severinus thought of Senovara, waiting back at the villa, and the child she was carrying.

On the higher ground to the east, reroofed but with its walls still stained black from the burning, Claudius's temple stood surrounded by its new web of scaffolding. From it came the sounds of hammering. He shivered, remembering his dream, and nudged Tanet into a trot. It would have been better to have destroyed the place altogether, levelled it to the ground and built elsewhere or not at all. The temple and the Annexe around it held too many ghosts, British and Roman.

The whole province held too many ghosts.

Jupiter, what a waste! he thought savagely. What a god-awful, bloody, senseless waste! A hundred and fifty thousand people dead and half the province devastated, all for nothing. And thanks to Paullinus the stupidity still went on. He had seen enough of it these past few months to last him a lifetime: the slave gangs, the gutted farmsteads, the fields stripped of their grain or burned to the stubble and the ragged skeletons who moved across them picking up what little the troops had left behind. What Paullinus was doing with Rome's blessing was as barbaric in its way as what the Iceni had left of London and Verulamium.

In the cleared ground behind Residence Road the first of the rebuilt government offices was already in use. Severinus dismounted in front of the porch and handed Tanet's rein to the waiting legionary.

'Marcus Julius Severinus,' he said. 'To see the procurator.'

As he passed through the open doorway Severinus realised that the neatness had been deceptive. Inside, the building was still incomplete, with the raw stone and timber joists showing. A bridge of wooden planks stretched across the half-laid floor of the entrance hall; men with bowls of fresh plaster were at work on the walls and he could hear the sound of carpenters' hammers overhead.

A secretary sat behind a makeshift desk. He looked up and smiled.

'Julius Severinus?'

Severinus nodded.

The man stood. 'Follow me, please.' He led the way along a short corridor, opened a second door and stepped back. 'Commander Severinus, sir.'

The office was finished and furnished, but it still smelled of new-sawn wood and lime wash. Not an unpleasant smell, Severinus thought as he took off his helmet and saluted the man behind the desk. There were worse.

'Ah, Commander, you've arrived.' Julius Classicianus was a big man, late middle-aged but still muscular. He indicated the room's only other chair. 'Sit down, please. My apologies for the mess, and the informality. We're still at sixes and sevens as you can appreciate, but you have to work somewhere.'

'Thank you, sir.' Severinus put his helmet on the floor. He was feeling ill at ease and puzzled. He had no idea why he had been ordered all the way from Braniacum for this interview. As procurator Classicianus had no military authority and so, technically, no right to summon him at all. 'And most places are a bit of a mess at present, aren't they?' He tried to keep the bitterness from his voice.

Classicianus gave him a sharp look.

'Yes, that's true,' he said. 'We've little to be proud of between us, have we, we and the British?'

Severinus was taken aback; he had not expected the procurator to agree, or even recognise the sarcasm. 'No, sir,' he said finally. 'I don't think we have.'

'Mmm.' Classicianus's long, heavily jowled face was impassive. 'Well, let's leave that aside for the moment. I need some information from you, Commander, if you'll be so good. I understand that you were attached to the – to Suetonius Paullinus's staff throughout the recent troubles?'

Severinus felt the muscles of his jaw tighten. 'Yes, sir. That's correct.'

'But that that is no longer the case?'

'No.'

'Would you care to explain why?'

'It was a temporary appointment, sir, and the emergency's over. I was returned to my normal duties.'

Classicianus pulled at his earlobe. 'This . . . return to normal duties. It was at Paullinus's order, naturally.'

'Not altogether, sir.'

'Indeed?' Classicianus's eyes had widened, although Severinus had the impression the information had come as no real surprise. 'You requested it?'

'I . . . yes, sir.'

'Would you mind giving me your reasons?' Classicianus paused. 'Commander, you're an intelligent man. You must be aware, as I am, that an appointment to the governor's staff is a career opportunity not to be thrown away lightly, especially – forgive me – by such a junior officer as yourself. I really must insist on an answer.'

Severinus kept his voice neutral. 'I'm sorry, sir. The reasons were personal. I simply felt that I could no longer continue as a member of the governor's immediate staff.'

'I see.' Classicianus half raised his hand to his ear, then stopped and lowered it to the desk. 'Yes. Well. We'll leave that aside, too, if we may. Second. I understand that you have contracted a . . . liaison with a British woman.'

Severinus flushed. 'We're married, sir, if that's what you mean. Two months ago.'

'Roman law, Commander, does not recognise marriage between a citizen and a non-citizen. You're aware of that?'

'Naturally, but—'

'Also that possession of a native wife, especially the daughter of an active rebel, will prejudice your future army career?'

Severinus felt the anger rise to his face. 'With respect, sir,' he said, 'I don't see what concern any of this is of yours.'

Classicianus held up a hand. 'Don't get on your high horse, young man. As I said, I'm interested only in information. I'm merely checking the facts as I know them at present, although I do admit that personally I find them a little puzzling. So. Let's recap, shall we? You give up a staff posting of your own free will and compound this sin by a spurious marriage – spurious in our terms – to a native woman of doubtful loyalty. These are both unusual actions, to say the least.' Severinus said nothing. 'Your family, I understand, died in the massacre.'

'Yes, sir.'

'And this had no bearing on your behaviour? You didn't feel, perhaps, that—'

'Procurator.' Severinus stood up. 'I'm sorry, but I think we should terminate this interview now.'

'Sit down, Julius Severinus.' Classicianus had not raised his voice, but the order was unmistakable. 'Please. It's certainly not my intention to insult you. If I seem to be doing so, then forgive me. These questions are necessary, and they serve a purpose.'

Severinus sat. 'Then could I ask you, sir,' he said, 'before we go any further, to tell me what that purpose is?'

'Not yet, no. Or not wholly.' Classicianus hesitated. 'Commander, I have been in Britain for what still seems to me a very short time, and I'm still feeling my way. Very much so. One of my tasks, not the least of them, is to talk to people and gather their views on the province's past, present and future. Please look on this interview in that light. I am no soldier, nor would I wish to be one; however, I do represent the emperor and from him I have received specific instructions' – he paused – '*very* specific instructions, to form an assessment. I would appreciate any help that anyone can give me.' He smiled. 'Even help from a very junior officer who seems to have all the wits and tact of a rhino.'

Severinus did not smile back. 'Very well, sir.'

'Good. Then tell me your opinion – your honest opinion, please – of our policy so far.'

Severinus took a deep breath. 'I think it's been short-sighted, sir. There would've been no revolt at all if we'd been less greedy and made some attempt, at least, to take local sensibilities into account. Now the revolt is over and Boudica is dead, I think the authorities are confusing punishment with revenge. The result may be a peaceful province, but it's peaceful only because the natives are either dead in battle or too starved to resist; in which case we're storing up trouble for the future. When that trouble breaks we'll have only ourselves to blame, and next time may be just as bad, or even worse.' There was silence. 'My apologies, Procurator. You asked for my honest opinion.'

'Yes, I did. And I agree.'

'You agree?' Severinus stared at him.

'Totally.' The procurator was not smiling now. 'Moreover, so does the emperor.'

'But—'

'Commander, please listen very carefully. I asked for your opinion and now I'll give you mine. We're not all fools by any means. This revolt has come very close to losing Rome a province. We have just witnessed seventeen years of work undone in two short months followed by a further five months of calculated, systematic barbarity which will ensure that we are hated for at least another generation.' Classicianus leaned forward 'Mothers alive, man, this isn't the bloody Republic! We want a province, not a desert! Of course I agree! What man of sense wouldn't?'

'Paullinus, for one.'

'I stipulated a man of sense. Suetonius Paullinus has many excellent qualities, but they do not include sense. Besides, as of five days ago he is no longer governor.'

Severinus blinked. 'I'm sorry, sir?'

'Paullinus has been recalled. The new governor will arrive, all being well, early in the new year. Who he will be I'm not sure as yet, but he will not have his predecessor's taste for blood. There has been enough of that spilled these last few months, Severinus. It's up to us, now, to see that it isn't wasted. In the meantime, as caretaker I am doing what I can, which includes putting together an administrative staff – a *sympathetic* staff – of my own.' He smiled. 'Hence this interview.'

'You're offering me an administrative post?' Severinus's head was still spinning.

'In my capacity as emperor's representative and interim acting head of province, yes.'

'Doing what, sir?'

'You would work directly for me as a procuratorial agent, with the responsibilities and duties that that would imply, but my principal concern – and the emperor's – is to undo the effects of the crass stupidities that caused this unholy mess. That are still causing it.'

'You think that's possible?'

'I used the word "sympathetic", Commander, and I used it advisedly. A sympathetic approach is essential. Perhaps, given time and reasonable goodwill on both sides we might at least make a start, but we need the right people to do it.' Classicianus paused. 'Well?'

'I'm no administrator, sir,' Severinus said carefully. 'My family's army, both sides, regular army, not political. I appreciate the honour, but—'

'Commander,' Classicianus interrupted. 'There I'm afraid for the reasons we discussed at the beginning of this interview you've burned your bridges already. At least as far as promotion is concerned. The decision is yours, naturally, but personally I think you'd be a fool to refuse. Also, I'd be failing in my duty to the emperor and to my own conscience if I did not try very hard indeed to persuade you. Britain is unique. We stand at the beginning here. If I can build a working relationship now with the tribes then the province will become a worthy part of the empire. That will take time, patience and – I repeat the word – sympathy, and I cannot do it without help. Intelligent help. There are enough Catuses and Paullinuses ready and waiting to use their methods even in this comparatively enlightened age, and the emperor, as you know, judges by results. Quite simply he is willing to indulge me, but I have to prove myself. It will be no easy task.' Severinus said nothing. 'Commander, you're a horseman, or so I'm told, as am I. Would you train a horse by beating it into submission?'

'No, sir. Of course not.'

'Quite. I told you; I want a province, not a desert.' Classicianus stood up. 'I won't ask you for an answer immediately. That would not be fair, and I will demand total commitment. Think it over, please. Only not for too long. I start back for London in two days. Give me your decision by then.'

45

In the villa's dining-room the table was set for the Samhain meal. The servant Ertola had left the shutters unbarred, and the draught from the open window behind them caught at the lamp-flames, making the shadows dance across the walls and ceiling. Senovara lay watching the patterns they made, knowing that there was more to them, tonight, than was due to fire and darkness. Samhain Eve was a time outside time when the barrier between the worlds was lowered and the dead returned to mix with the living. They would all be here: her father, Matugena, little Ahteha, perhaps Tigirseno, although the mountains were far away and even a ghost could get lost . . .

Senovara touched her stomach where the child, hers and Marcus's, was growing. Don't blame me too much, she thought. He will belong to all of us.

The lamps flickered. Romans, she knew, did not believe in ghosts, or not as the British did: that not all brought harm with them when they drifted in from the dark to sit with their kin. And the Romans did not celebrate Samhain. Senovara wondered if despite that Aper and Ursina were also here tonight, and if they were what they thought of a British woman living where they had lived, married to their son and carrying his child.

The thought made her uneasy. Samhain was a time for self-examination, and Senovara was still not sure herself why she had agreed to the marriage, any more than Marcus – so he said – had known why he had suggested it. It had not been a love match on either side, yet from the beginning there had been no doubt in either of their minds that it was right. It had seemed somehow natural, as if everything had been settled long before and tacitly accepted by both. Love, if it ever came, would be an extra.

She looked up into the shadows. 'Be welcome,' she murmured in Celtic, knowing that if Marcus's parents were here they would understand the words and accept them in the spirit they were offered; as even, perhaps, Albilla would if she was with them.

Albilla. She felt guilty, most of all, about Albilla . . .

Ertola, small and plump, brown-skinned and freckled like a thrush, put her head round the door.

'That's the master,' she said. 'I'll serve the dinner.'

'Thank you, Ertola.' Senovara sat up and straightened her dress. Her fingers brushed against the coin-pendant Marcus had given her, the British horse with its Roman letters. There had been a travelling goldsmith in the Colony half a month back, one of the signs of returning normality, and she had had him fix the broken chain. The man had been skilful, and it was almost as good as new.

Marcus came in. He had taken off his uniform, but his tunic and shaved upper lip still made him look foreign, alien. She thought of her father, with his braided hair, his trousers and his long moustaches, then, consciously, put the thought aside. He bent to kiss her cheek, brushing it with his lips, then lay down on the couch facing her. She saw his eyes go to the bowl of wine and plate of honey cakes with the nine lamps set around them, but he made no comment.

'You talked to the procurator?' she said.

'He offered me a post on his staff. I said I'd think about it.' His face wore the distant, too-mature expression that it often did, even when they made love. 'I did, all the way back.'

'And?' Senovara was still watching him carefully.

'I can't accept. It would mean leaving the army, and I can't do that; not now, not ever. I'll give Classicianus my decision tomorrow.'

The flames of the nine lamps dipped as if someone had blown across them, and the shadows swooped and plunged. Senovara looked up: she was lying next to them, and she had felt no draught from the window. Aye, they're here right enough, listening, she thought. All three of them.

Suddenly she knew beyond doubt what they wanted.

'What is he like, this Classicianus?' she said.

'A good man. He'll be good for the province, British and Romans alike. And Paullinus has been replaced. Thank the gods for that, at least.'

The door opened and Ertola brought in the meal, a mutton stew thickened in the British style with barley and spelt and a dish of kale with bacon fat. As Senovara reached for the serving spoon she was aware of a high, soft whisper at the edge of hearing, like a bat's voice.

Wait you, she thought. Let me do this in my own way.

'Yet you're turning him down because of the army?' she said.

'I have to. The men from the big Roman families can chop and change between army and administration, but for someone like me the choice would be final. Classicianus knows that; it's why he wants a firm commitment.'

'And you won't give him one?' Senovara felt her temper begin to rise.

Severinus sat up. 'We've been army for generations Senovara,' he said. 'Regular army. I'll not be the one to change that.'

'Aye. Well and good. So Classicianus chooses someone else, one of Catus's staff, or someone he's brought with him from Rome. Some little man from one of your big Roman families who's less concerned with whether he's fit for the job. What then?'

'Classicianus wouldn't do that.'

'No? And why would he not? It would be easier, in the end.'

'Maybe. But he isn't the sort to take the easy way out.'

'And you are?'

'Jupiter!' Severinus's hand slammed down on the table, and his eyes locked with hers. There was a long silence. Even the shadows were still.

'Answer the question, Marcus Julius Severinus,' Senovara said quietly.

'Very well.' He had dropped his gaze. 'The answer's no. Or I hope that I am not. Would you have married me if I were?'

'No.' Slowly, so he would not see her do it, Senovara released the breath she had been holding. 'No, I would not.'

'So, then.' He was still not looking at her directly. 'Is that what you think I would be doing? Taking the easy way?'

Carefully, as if she were reaching for an animal that might turn and bite her hand, she picked up the casserole and spooned the thick stew on to the plates. 'It's what you think you would be doing, Marcus. That makes all the difference.'

He stared at her for a long time. Then, slowly, he nodded.

'Aye, I suppose it does. Perhaps, then, I may think again.'

After they had eaten Senovara sat watching the Samhain lamps, her hands folded across her stomach. The flames burned straight and bright, and the shadows around her were at rest. She, too, felt contented: both his dead and hers, Roman and British, had had their cakes and their wine, and tomorrow they would be gone beyond the River to wherever ghosts went, leaving the future for the living to take care of as best they could, as they had always done.

That was the purpose of ghosts, whatever language they spoke and whatever they had believed in life; not to act, but to remind and point the way forward, however difficult it was and whatever changes it involved.

The future might not be easy, she knew, but then it never had been.

AUTHOR'S NOTE

The book is set in AD59/60, sixteen years after the Claudian conquest. Although it can (I hope!) be enjoyed by a reader with little or no previous background knowledge, the following notes may be of interest.

The Colony/Camulodunum

Later writers, including Tacitus himself, use the name Camulodunum to include both Roman colony and British settlement; understandably so, since following the revolt the latter – as such – ceased to exist as a separate entity. Contemporary Colonists and natives, however, would have made a clear distinction. Camulodunum ('the Fort of the War-god Camulos') was the original tribal capital, occupying an area of some ten square miles bounded for the most part by the Colne and Roman River valleys; what I have called the Dun being a sprawl of farmsteads to the south-east, centred around the modern Gosbecks Farm.

In contrast, the Colony (Colonia in Latin: the additional adjective Victricensis 'of the Victors' is perhaps later) was purely Roman. It originated with the decommissioning of the post-Conquest legionary fortress to the south of the Colne and its adaptation to civilian use. In common with other *coloniae* throughout the empire, it was not strictly a town per se but a military settlement of time-served veterans placed in occupied territory. As part of their discharge settlement, the ex-soldiers would receive tracts of land outwith the colony itself, and these would naturally be requisitioned from the tribe in whose territory the colony was sited: in this case, the Trinovantes. Hence, partly, the friction.

For those interested in Roman Colchester and its development, I would highly recommend Philip Crummy's book, *City of Victory* (Colchester Archaeological Trust, 1997).

Paullinus's movements and the final battle

Unfortunately, Tacitus makes no mention of Paullinus's movements following his abandoning of London, nor – apart from a physical description of the site – does he say where the final battle was fought. Current theory has him return the way he came, up Watling Street (the name is not Roman) towards the advancing Fourteenth Legion, and places the battle-site somewhere in the Midlands, possibly near Mancetter. To the novelist – who must, of necessity, deal with motive, albeit ascribed motive – this poses very serious problems: to have Paullinus choose to retrace his steps through territory that he already knows is hostile, slowed down by a large body of civilian refugees, would be to ask far too much of him as a character. Accordingly I returned to the earlier theory (see Spence, *Boadicea: Warrior Queen*) that he withdrew south of the Thames which – for the reasons I have him give Lupianus – makes good sense. This would place the site of the battle some one and a quarter miles south-west of (Roman) London between the Pentonville rise and the ford over the Fleet known in historical times as Battle Bridge; in terms of the modern city, just in front of King's Cross station.

Place names

Where possible, these are authentic; however, in some cases – notably in the case of the Ninth's fortress at Longthorpe near Peterborough – the original name has not survived and I have had to invent. In compensation, I have tried to make the Celtic name fit, as I have done with other invented names; thus Dercovium = 'the Seeing Place' (i.e. one with extensive views over the surrounding country). The Icenian tribal centre at Venta Icenorum (Caistor St Edmund, on the outskirts of Norwich) postdates the time of the revolt, and the capital I describe has not yet (as far as I know) been identified; perhaps it lay in the Breckland area north of Thetford. The name I have given it, Coriodurum, means 'the Fort of the Hosting' ('durum' implying flatter ground than the more usual 'dunum'). Braniacum ('the Place of Crows') is a complete invention.

Julius Agricola

The famous later governor, responsible for the push up into

what is now Scotland, did indeed serve as a senatorial tribune in Britain at the time of the revolt, and was on the governor's staff. Senatorial tribunes, although very young men in their early twenties, were – technically, at least – second in command of a legion, and the post was regarded as an apprenticeship for later legate status. Although what legion Agricola was attached to is not known, I have suggested the Second, based at Isca (Exeter) since, during the revolt, it was commanded by the quartermaster (*praefectus castrorum*), who would be third in command. Poenius Postumus is historical; having failed to carry out Paullinus's orders to bring the legion up in support, he later committed suicide.

One other major historical figure involved in the revolt was Titus, son of the later Emperor Vespasian and emperor in his turn; he, too, was a senatorial tribune. I have introduced him (but without formal identification) in the chapter dealing with Verulamium.

Julius Classicianus died in office, and his tombstone has been found in London. Paullinus's successor was Publius Petronius Turpilianus, a relative of the Petronius who appears in *Nero*.

My thanks again to Roy Pinkerton; to Ann Buchanan; to Derek and Kathleen McMillan for making their holiday detour; to Jim Green of the Holyhead coastguard; to Dianne Hobbes of the Ixworth library; to the staff of Carnoustie library; and to the Moug family, Terry, Elli and Richard, for their help with horses. Any mistakes – historical or otherwise – remain my own.

DAVID WISHART

SEJANUS

Well, young man, I'm dead and burned at last, or you wouldn't be reading this. Let me say first that I have no regrets, either about being dead or for having removed so many of my collateral relatives before their proper hours. I acted for the good of Rome.

Which brings me to the point of this letter. Aelius Sejanus. We talked a little about him the last time we met. Again the fact that you are reading this shows that the time for talk is past. The man is a malignant growth, a danger to Rome, and he must be removed. No; I dislike metaphorical euphemisms. Sejanus must be killed.

Empress Livia's extraordinary instruction from beyond the grave comes as something of a relief to Marcus Corvinus: life as a voluntary exile is too dull for the amiable Roman, and the chance to engage in more amateur sleuthing is irresistible – despite the obvious dangers ...

David Wishart is a Classics scholar and after working abroad in Kuwait, Greece and Saudi Arabia as a freelance teacher of English, he now lives with his family in Carnoustie, Scotland. His earlier Roman novels, I, VIRGIL, OVID, NERO and GERMANICUS, are available from Sceptre Books.

HODDER AND STOUGHTON PAPERBACKS

DAVID WISHART

GERMANICUS

The last thing Marcus Corvinus wants is to be involved once more with Empress Livia's diabolical machinations – she's as trustworthy as a snake with a migraine. But Livia has a way of asking favours that is impossible to refuse, and besides, Corvinus has been missing the little tingle at the nape of the neck that accompanies his amateur detective work ...

Once more employing his extensive knowledge of Roman history and culture to impressive effect, David Wishart presents us with a lively and engaging sleuth and a challenging historical puzzle.

Praise for David Wishart

'a Roman thriller ... [which] weaves into the plot a painless guide to fun, food and fear in the empire of Tiberius'
New Statesman & Society

'There's lots of action and a nice plot, full of suspense to keep you going'
Sunday Telegraph

'Witty, engrossing and ribald ... it misses nothing in its evocation of a bygone time and place'
Independent on Sunday

HODDER AND STOUGHTON PAPERBACKS

DAVID WISHART

THE LYDIAN BAKER

What starts out as a simple act of brokering for his stepfather lands Marcus in customary hot water. For the legendary Baker Statue, gifted to the Delphic oracle by Croesus of Lydia in the sixth century BC, is a treasure many would kill to possess – and is reputed to bring agonising death to those who touch it ...

'*innate humour and pace carry one through to the tragi-comic climax*'
Irish Times

'*enjoyable ... an ingenious solution to this ancient mystery*'
Sunday Telegraph

'*Like Chandler's Marlow, Corvinus wisecracks his way through a weary world of murder and intrigue until he hunts down the truth. A taut thriller in which ancient Rome springs to life.*'
The Times

HODDER AND STOUGHTON PAPERBACKS